Square Peg

by

Vivienne

Tuffnell

"As kingfishers catch fire, so dragonflies draw flame."–

Gerard Manley Hopkins

Copyright © Vivienne Tuffnell 2014

Cover Design © D.J. Bowman–Smith

http://djbowmansmith.com/

For Dr George Bebawi,

my dear friend and mentor

With thanks & love.

Square Peg

Chapter 1

Chloe leaned on the gravestone behind her, and sighed as she watched the other mourners pick their way across the damp grass back to the path. She didn't want anyone to see her stumble as the heels of the red boots sank into the soft turf. A flamboyant gesture like the boots only worked if you didn't then trip up or fall over, and she wasn't convinced she could manage the uneven, slippery grass without doing either at least once.

The October sun was weak and the wind was getting up, whipping her skirts around her, making the fabric snap like the sails of a ship. Despite her Gran's instructions to the contrary, there were a lot of flowers next to the open grave; but you can't stop people making conventional gestures, after all.

"Flowers are for the living," Gran had said, in her usual acerbic manner.

"Sorry, Gran," Chloe said, and pulled the little bunch of herbs bound with blue and red ribbon from her bag. "Not a flower in this lot, so you can't argue with that."

She put the little nosegay amid the other more florid tributes and staggered across the pockmarked grass, relieved to find herself on the firm surface of the churchyard path and hurried after the others, hoping that if anyone had noticed her pausing at the grave it would be assumed it was simply for that last quiet moment alone with

Gran, rather than because she didn't want to look an idiot in heels too high they made her stumble.

There was to be a gathering at the local pub. Not a wake, because, after all, they weren't Irish and only the Irish have wakes or so Gran had declared in that wide sweeping way she often used when she wasn't actually sure of her facts, daring anyone to disagree. Chloe had realised in the last few years that the old lady had actually been longing for someone to contradict her, and give her the exercise of a good argument.

The buzz of conversation in the pub hushed when Chloe walked in, all bright colours and wild hair, like a parrot amid ravens; but it soon started again, barely pausing, as Chloe reached the bar.

"What'll it be?" asked the landlord, who had known Chloe all her life.

"Orange juice; I've got to drive later," Chloe said, even though what she really craved was a double brandy.

"Coming up," said the landlord, with forced cheerfulness. "You know, Chloe, a lot of people around here are going to miss your grandmother."

"I know," Chloe said. "Inconsiderate old bag. What did she have to go and die for?"

There was a brief startled pause where she could feel the man struggling with what she'd just said, then he laughed in a half–shocked, half–amused way.

"That's just the sort of thing she'd have said," he said. "She wasn't one to pull her punches. She did say to me once that the beer that day tasted like a rat had died in it; mind you, she was right, it did taste funny, but no one else had said anything, so I'd just assumed it was OK."

"She always spoke her mind," agreed Chloe. "Not everyone likes it like that."

"Ah, but you always knew where you were with her. There aren't many like that," he said, and his eyes flickered to the figure of the local MP, Gran's occasional friend and more often her enemy.

Chloe smiled.

"I'd better mingle, at least for a while," she said, and clattered across the stone floor to where the great and the good were apparently conversing amiably about her late grandmother.

After about two minutes she felt sick, and made her excuses and went outside to where three or four weather-beaten picnic tables had acquired a handful of hardier souls unable or unwilling to go into the pub. At least two of them were currently barred, one permanently, but Chloe was impressed that they were here. They didn't speak to her at first, just watched her warily, as she picked a table and sat down, wishing she had a coat on. She'd been fooled that morning by the bright sunshine, and was regretting it now.

The oldest man among them came over to her after a moment.

"I'm sorry your Gran's gone," he said. "We're going to miss her. But then so will you."

Chloe shrugged, feeling her throat choke up with emotion she had not let herself feel.

"I will," she said, in a faint voice unlike her normal one. "I wanted to thank you all for coming. I know she would have appreciated it."

"Nah, she'd have been wondering if she'd locked the back door properly," he said.

Chloe laughed.

"That too," she said. "I'm off; I'll maybe see you around?"

"Maybe," he said, but as she got up, he caught her arm gently. "She was one in a million; I really meant it when I said we'll miss her. Not like that lot in there. They won't miss her whatever they say."

"I know," Chloe said. "That's why I'm out here. Take care."

She hurried out of the pub garden, trying to get warm by moving as fast as she could in these silly boots. Her grandmother's house wasn't very far away, but her feet were killing her by the time she got there. She'd left her driving shoes there, so comfort wasn't far away, if such a thing existed any more.

The house had that blank look that places take on when they are unoccupied, the windows reflecting the houses opposite. Chloe stood at the foot of the steps, looking up, waiting for the twitch of the curtain, a cat's tail waving on a window ledge, and that elusive feeling of being expected. Nothing. She climbed the steps to the front door and put her key in the lock and turned it, still waiting for sounds inside. Inside the hall she shut the door and leaned on it, kicking off her boots with relief, fighting the urge to call out, "Gran, I'm home," knowing there would be no acerbic reply this time.

The hall felt very still, and smelt of furniture polish and the faintest trace of herbs. She stood very still, listening to the silence, listening to the memories. She'd never once felt quite like this, at once happy and sad almost in equal measures, and she didn't quite know what to do with it. She padded through to the front room, where she had left her driving shoes, and sat down to put them on. It was a very elegantly shaped room, harmoniously coloured and furnished, but so full of her Gran's eccentric and eclectic tastes that it seemed impossible she would never walk in here again, and sit cross legged on the sofa, long bones creaking now she was old, or pull out one of the books and read aloud a passage to her uncomprehending granddaughter, or drink brandy with one of her more disreputable friends. Gran is gone, she said to herself, she's gone and I'm glad. Glad she went so easily, never slipping into the mental fog she'd dreaded, or the outright physical infirmity or pain. She'd just slipped away almost casually, three days after telling Chloe she was dying, leaving everything so well organised that Chloe knew she must have known for months if not longer.

"You're still an inconsiderate old bag," Chloe said to the room, and smiled, knowing how much her Gran would have relished that sort of insult.

Home then, such as it was, and leave all this for another day. She was tired, and really wanted just to go home and go to bed, and have a bloody good cry where no one would notice, and then start again tomorrow in a world where there was no Gran. It wasn't a long drive, and Clifford would be home waiting for her, as well as the cats, and she could curl up on the bed and let it all out.

She locked the door on her old home with a sense of strange finality, and got into her car, putting the silly boots on the passenger seat, and drove home as the first few specks of rain hit the windscreen. It was raining properly when she got home; icy needles of October rain that stung her face as she hurried up the path and let herself in to the house. The little house was very bare; almost devoid of furnishings, and they virtually lived in the kitchen or the bedroom. Clifford was attempting to feed the cats when she came in, but it was surprisingly hard to do with two large cats weaving round feet, jumping up onto the work surfaces, trying to take the fork out of his hand, and generally making a nuisance of themselves.

"How was it?" he asked.

"Horrible, like all funerals. She'd have hated it, of course, but then I could hardly do all the things she'd asked for. I was pretty sure she was only joking about having "Bat out of hell" played as the coffin left the church, but I couldn't face explaining it to the vicar. I wish you'd come. But she did say she didn't want you there, so I could do at least one thing she'd wanted. Anyway, a lot of the travellers turned up, which was brave of them, so it was a weird gathering all round, and I got away as soon as I could."

Chloe stooped and picked up the bigger of the two cats, a black and white monster called Chainsaw, who was being the most trouble about the food. He immediately began his trademark loud purr and settled into her arms.

"I don't really know why she didn't want me to be there," Clifford said. "I thought she liked me."

"Oh, she did like you," Chloe said. "I think that's why she didn't want you there."

What Gran had actually said was,

"I don't think it would be good for a baby vicar to see such monumental hypocrisy quite so early in his training. He'll get disillusioned soon enough; I'd rather he finished his training first though. You should only rock the boat when you know where the life-rafts are."

"Anyway, even the few touches she'd asked for shocked people enough. It was bad enough there were no hymns and no eulogy, but you should have seen the deputy mayor's face when they played that Paul Simon song, Gone at Last. He looked like he was expecting her to be standing at the back of the church grinning at her last joke. Various people read poetry they thought she'd have liked; a few of them got it right too, which did surprise me. I'm hungry; did you have any thoughts about dinner, or shall I go to the Indian?"

"Yeah, good idea. Toast your Gran with curry sauce; that seems appropriate somehow. I got a bottle of brandy in too. The menu's in the knife drawer."

Clifford put the two bowls of cat food down, but after a few mouthfuls both cats just stalked off in disgust.

"Why don't they eat? They were making such a fuss a minute ago," Clifford said.

"For Chainsaw, if it doesn't have a tail and whiskers, it's not really food at all. Well, not when we're looking anyway. He'll eat when he's hungry. And when they get let out again, no mouse is safe. I hope you like mouse on your cornflakes; that was Chainsaw's favourite trick. He'd wait till Gran sat down to eat and then bound in and drop whatever he'd just caught onto her plate."

Chloe grinned, remembering the time Chainsaw had honoured the mayor in such a way, by dropping the decapitated mouse into his teacup.

"Revolting animal," Clifford said fondly.

"Typical cat. Well, typical of the cats that Gran had, anyway, over the years. I don't know of many quite like hers, though. OK, I fancy something really hot, and lots of poppadums. I feel a need to break things."

As a valedictory dinner, it was somehow very comforting, especially since Chloe had been cold nearly all day, and the curry finally managed to warm her up. They sat in the bare living room, the ancient sagging sofa pulled up close to the fire, where the cats had become a living hearthrug. The hiss of the gas fire was a comforting sound, reminding Chloe both of winter evenings at home with her Gran, and also of student days, curled up next to the fire the gas turned down as low as it would go on a cold night, wrapped up in a blanket and feeling safe and warm against the night. Rain spattered on the windows and the gurgle of a busy drainpipe made them both feel glad to be indoors. The cats seemed oblivious to everything but the heat of the fire. Chloe pulled the rug off the back of the sofa and wrapped it around her shoulders, as Clifford opened the brandy and poured two hefty measures into mismatched glasses.

"Well," she said. "Here's to you, Gran, wherever you've gone."

She held the glass up to the light, and clinked it with Clifford's, and then drank the whole lot in one go, spluttering a little as the brandy burned her throat.

"I won't smash the glass in the fireplace," she said. "But it does feel as if I should, though. It was the end of an era, you know, not just for me, but for lots of people, half of them I didn't even know. It was so strange seeing that coffin. I couldn't quite see how that had anything to do with Gran."

"What poem did you read for her? I know you weren't quite sure this morning which one was best?"

"I nearly didn't read anything; I got up to read and felt so choked up I wasn't sure I'd make a sound. I chose that one about the kingfisher; you know, the one by Hopkins. It was her favourite; it seemed to sum up all she ever said about being ourselves."

"You look a bit like a kingfisher in that dress," Clifford said, stroking the silk of her skirt.

"I though I looked more like a parrot, actually," she replied. "Bloody boots were a mistake though; I was all right on a nice even surface, but once we got onto the grass in the churchyard, I was wobbling like a drunk. Gran would have laughed at that; I had trouble not giggling every time I thought I was going to fall over."

She picked up the last of the poppadums, and broke it in half, passing the larger half to her husband.

"The body of cracker, broken for you," she said solemnly, and then shrieked as Clifford tickled her mercilessly.

"Don't let anyone here catch you saying stuff like that," he said, a minute later. "I have a feeling no one will find it funny at all."

"Bloody killjoys, then," Chloe said, gathering up the crumbs of the crushed poppadums. "Some people don't seem to have a sense of humour at all; I don't know how they live without one. I know I'd go mad if I took everything that seriously."

"We're all different," Clifford said cautiously. "It'd be a very boring world if we were all the same."

"That isn't what I meant, at all," Chloe said. "I just find it very hard to understand people who take everything so seriously, that they can't laugh at themselves at times."

"Yeah, but you grew up with your Gran, and she never took herself seriously at all," he pointed out.

"No, I know that. But with her it was all a process of misdirection. She'd shock people into laughing at her, and they never quite twigged to the fact that they usually ended up doing what she wanted without realising it. I know she was a clever woman, but what she was cleverest at was upsetting the status quo. That's not an easy act to follow, you know."

Chloe gazed pensively at the blue flames in the gas fire, listening to that faint hiss and thinking of her own life, so changed now in the last month, and not just by the death of her grandmother.

"I'm so tired," she said softly, and leaned against Clifford. He felt very solid and real and warm. "Let's go to bed," she said, and stretched out her legs, disturbing the cats. Sylvester clawed at her feet, but half-heartedly, and quickly curled back up next to his brother.

Chloe lay awake longer than she'd thought she would, staring into the darkness and listening to her husband's sleeping breath.

There were too many images in her mind, phrases and words that circled around like leaves caught in a gust of wind, and each time they seemed to settle, another breath of air would whip them up and whirl them around her head. Getting slowly drowsy, she followed the leaves as they flew around, watching them spin and dip and fall in a strange woven mass of chaos that always seemed to be on the brink on forming a recognisable pattern, like the way trapped flies seem to be weaving an unseen web of lines that might just be something recognisable if you could just manage to visualise the invisible. She slipped into sleep without realising it.

*

The ground felt moist and cool, crumbly loam that stuck to her fingertips just a little and fell away as she dug, the small stones hurting her fingers, breaking the nails and making them bleed. She could smell the scent of rain, that cool green smell in the air, and the wind was rising as the first few drops touched her upturned face. When she looked down again, an eye was looking up at her from the scraped back earth. She jumped slightly, but didn't recoil as much as she would have expected. She plunged her fingers into the mud again and scraped away at the soil around the eye till the soft dirty fur of a toy rabbit began to show pinkish red amid the rich brown earth. The rabbit lay there, uncovered swiftly now by her burrowing fingertips, till she could pull it out entirely. It seemed to have been recently buried; the fur was dirty but not damp.

The hole seemed to gape far wider than her small fingers could have dug, a great deep crevasse that became wider and deeper the longer she looked at it. At the bottom of this pit she could see the edges of more things buried in the dirt; building blocks made of brightly coloured wood, soft toys, their fur clogged and filthy with earth, the leg of a doll, the rest of it buried. She stood up at the edge of the massive pit that yawned as wide as a volcano's crater, as deep as pain itself, and felt herself become dizzy and weak. She began to sway as unaccustomed vertigo took hold of her nerves and bones and muscles; however she tried to stop it, she felt herself begin to topple forward in that dreadful slow motion that just makes everything so much worse. She felt a scream raise itself from deep within her silent being, as she began to plummet into the pit, arms and legs flailing hopelessly as she tried to catch herself as she fell.

Chloe sat up in bed, gasping for air like a surfacing swimmer, her body slick with cold sweat and her heart pounding and lurching. The room was as dark and still as when she'd fallen asleep; Clifford was still sleeping quietly next to her, one arm flung out across the covers. She swung her legs out of bed, horrified to find they were trembling and felt as if she would crumple the moment she put her weight on them. She dragged on her dressing gown, and crept out of the room, avoiding all the boxes and crates that still littered the room.

Downstairs, the cats were asleep in their box by the boiler; Chainsaw raised a sleepy head, only one eye open, then tucked himself back down under his brother's tail, and ignored her. She put the light on, and then filled the kettle. The kitchen was cool but not cold, but she felt so chilled, so shaky, that all she wanted was a hot drink and something to anchor herself in this world, not the one of dreams where things changed the longer you looked at them.

Dropping a teabag in a mug, Chloe waited for the kettle to boil, longing to turn some music on to drown out the memory of her own screams as she fell. She was only surprised she had not woken up screaming out loud.

"It was just a bad dream," she said out loud to herself, trying to reassure herself, but the words sounded hollow in her own voice; it took the robust voice of her Gran to sound authoritative in such moments as this.

I'm not a child, she told herself sternly, I don't need Gran, and even if I did, she's not here. I wouldn't have rung her at, well, what time is it anyway, four thirty in the morning, even when she was alive, just because I'd had a nightmare. And it was a bloody silly nightmare anyway; it wouldn't even sound scary to anyone else. If I told Clifford about it, he'd not understand why it was so terribly disturbing.

The kettle brought itself quietly to the boil and Chloe made tea, and took it through to the living room. She lit the fire, putting it on low as much for the sound as for the warmth, and curled up on the sofa, pulling the rug round her and cupping her mug in both hands. Next door, she could hear a baby crying plaintively; she shuddered unconsciously and sipped the tea, barely tasting it, just enjoying the warmth as it slipped down. The memory of the dream slipped away as she felt the strange between times feelings of being up when nearly everyone else in the area was sleeping. It was like being between worlds almost, a secret feeling of being apart from the rest of humanity, apart from the few whose lives mainly happen at night, the shift-workers, the lorry drivers, the mothers of small babies, and the chronic insomniacs.

She put the empty mug down next to the sofa, and rested her head on one of the cushions, gritty with broken poppadums and smelling faintly of ghee and curry. The baby had stopped crying and the house seemed silent; a feeling of waiting, a pause in history, a moment before the plunge. Chloe slipped back to sleep.

Chapter 2

It was still light when Chloe got home from work; not something she usually managed, especially as the nights were drawing in as October drew on. But today, she reached home seething with rage at the unfairness of a life that could deal her two body blows in such a short time.

Clifford wasn't in; the cats were asleep on the bed and barely looked up as she came in to change out of her work clothes. If he wasn't home, she knew he'd be over at the college, either in a lecture or in the library. She had a limited number of places to search for him, and yet she still hesitated. She'd never yet gone into the college alone, and while she was unconcerned by walking onto a new building site and all that it sometimes entailed, this was different. She pulled on her running clothes, and left the house to look for her husband.

The main college building was Georgian, but that only housed the studies of the more senior members of staff; the rest of the college was nineteen-seventies public lavatory style of architecture as Gran had remarked rudely when she'd first seen it.

"Low budget shouldn't mean no soul," she'd said, and Chloe agreed, both then and now.

She felt desperately nervous, almost as if she were trespassing, as she tapped the code into the little pad by the door, praying that it hadn't been changed in the last week or so. It hadn't; in fact it was rarely changed at all, security not really being more than a purely theoretical concern. She'd been shown round at the introductory weekend, but she wasn't sure she remembered quite where everything was. It wasn't a big place, but it did have rooms tucked away where you wouldn't expect them to be. She found her way to the common room; it was quiet at this time in the afternoon. To her relief, Clifford was sitting alone with a cup of coffee and a newspaper.

"You're home early," he said, when he saw her.

"I know," she said. "Truly shitty day, I'm afraid. They've decided to make me redundant. Downsizing. Latest in, first one out. I've got a month's notice. I can't believe it. I gave up a better job for that one, just so's we could be nearer this place. Where's the fairness in that?"

Clifford said nothing, simply went across and held her. She was twanging with tension, every muscle rigid and hard with rage.

"And this soon after Gran, well, that's just ridiculous," she said. "Someone up there has a sick sense of humour, if there is anyone up there at all. Crap. Look, I'm going to go for a run, otherwise I'm going to deck the first person who speaks to me. I haven't got a clue about supper, and frankly I don't care at the moment."

"There's two suppers going spare tonight here; it's chapel night. Do you want me to sign us both up? It'd save cooking," Clifford said.

"I'll eat, but I don't know about chapel. I'm not so keen on the big boss at the moment. I'll probably just start shouting at Him. Yes, go on, sign us up for supper; I'll see you, what time?"

"Six, I think, for supper. OK, go and have that run, I'll see you later, love."

Chloe headed out of the building. It seemed deserted at this time of day; she had a feeling Clifford had only been in the common room because it was less lonely as well as significantly warmer than their sparse living room. There was little going on that afternoon to keep anyone there who had other more interesting things to do. At the college gates Chloe bent and touched her toes, stretching her calf muscles as a token warm up, and then began to run, starting off far too fast to have a hope of keeping it up for very long. Her sheer rage at the unfairness of life rapidly converted to more useful adrenaline, and she found her initial pace was actually more comfortable than she would have thought. The rhythm of running took over her angry brain, lulling her steadily into acceptance as she listening to her blood pounding, felt the energy surging through her body and slipped into a nearly mindless state of pure physicality.

When she got home about an hour later, wet with sweat, her lungs aching and her legs cramping, she felt immeasurably better. The house was still empty, apart from the cats, so she headed for the shower, and enjoyed getting clean even more than she'd enjoyed getting sweaty.

Downstairs at ten to six, she drank a pint of water and then shivered, as she ran back upstairs to dress, wishing she'd asked Clifford to come home so they could go in together. She'd never thought of it being difficult to just get on with being here; perhaps that was simply because she'd never intended to be here at all. She'd never thought she'd actually be involved at all.

"That's just being naïve," Gran had said. "You're involved whether you accept it or not, simply by being here. Your choice, no one else's. It's up to you how you live with it."

"Thanks Gran," Chloe said out loud to the chaotic bedroom, as she tried to find some clean clothes. It wasn't easy to find anything when everything was still in boxes and suitcases and they didn't own a single wardrobe.

I do now, she thought. I've just got to organise getting Gran's furniture over here.

But that meant going through her grandmother's house; that was not something she wanted to have to do. But she would have to do it; there was already someone wanting to rent the house, so she'd have to clear it really soon.

She watched a single tear run down her face as she put on mascara; and she gritted her teeth and no more fell. Her hair was turning into ringlets as it dried, turning into a fluffy cloud of dark red that would soon become a wild halo of curls. It was infuriating hair that fought hairbrushes and ate combs; even when twisted back into a tight bun for work, some of it always escaped and formed tendrils around her face. She tied it back now, with a scarf that would slip off within an hour, and left the house at a run, arriving in the college dining room as the principal finished saying Grace.

"Fuck it; late again," she said in a whisper to Clifford as she slipped into the chair next to him, and then realised that the rest of the table had heard. I'm not saying sorry, she thought furiously, and glared at her plate, fighting the urge to glare at the others. It's not their fault I'm having a horrible time lately. When she looked up as someone was pouring water into the glasses, she noticed there were two small children seated at the table half way along; not next to her, certainly, but close enough to have heard her swearing. Crap, why me? she thought, and passed her plate as requested to be served with cottage pie.

The noise in the dining room was intense; there were a lot of children present, which she'd not thought about before, only vaguely recalling that the college was said to be very friendly to families. So what am I doing here, she asked herself, picking at the mashed potato, her appetite vanishing as her awareness of her surroundings increased. The voices of small children seemed appallingly shrill; the crying of babies jarring on her like chalk squeaking on a blackboard. It took a while before she could begin to filter it out like white noise in the background.

"It's Chloe, isn't it?" said the woman opposite her, who was spooning cottage pie into the messy maw of a toddler. "I'm Nicky; we spoke at the introductory week-end."

"Did we? Sorry, I don't remember anything. It was all a bit of a haze, I'm afraid," Chloe said, cautiously.

"Oh, it was rather a scrum at the start of the new year, but you soon get used to it. We haven't seen you in college since then, have we?"

Chloe wasn't quite sure who she meant, then realised that Nicky was using the word "we" to mean a collective whole, the college as an entity, and she shivered. Where there is an "us" there is always a "them".

"No, I've not been in; I've been run off my feet with one thing and another," Chloe said.

There was a brief silence of incomprehension, as if Nicky couldn't imagine anything more important than being in the college, doing whatever it was she did here.

"Oh, right," she said, after a moment. "You work, don't you?"

I did till today, Chloe thought, but had not intention of saying anything about being laid off.

"Yes, I work," Chloe said, putting unnecessary emphasis on the word work.

"What is it you do?" Nicky asked, but not really as if she actually wanted to know, rather because it was what she knew she should ask.

"Civil engineering," Chloe said abruptly, feeling the anger rising again. "What do you do?"

Nicky looked at her blankly, as if Chloe was unimaginably stupid.

"I'm a full-time mother," she said after a moment to allow Chloe to catch up with the game.

Chloe glanced at the children on either side of Nicky, a baby of eleven months or so, a toddler of two-and-a-half; both little faces were smeared with food, there was a gobbet of mash on Nicky's sleeve, and the younger child was beginning to grizzle. Chloe felt a grin rising to her face.

"Oh, how nice for you," she said, and began fighting off a desire to giggle uncontrollably.

"What's so funny?" Nicky demanded.

"Nothing, nothing," Chloe said. "I just thought I was glad I have my life, and not yours."

Chloe saw the look in Nicky's eyes, and thought unrepentantly, oops.

"What's wrong with my life then?" Nicky said, in a cold hard voice unlike her earlier voice that had been almost syrupy.

"Nothing, nothing at all. It just wouldn't suit me, that's all," Chloe said, hoping to sound diplomatic.

"Are you not planning to have children, then?"

"Good God, not yet," Chloe exclaimed, a bit shocked. "It's not something I'm in a hurry about, let's just say that."

"Why on earth not?" Nicky asked, crossly.

At that moment, the baby chose to spit out a huge mouthful of semi-masticated cottage pie; it landed on the table with a revolting wet splat. Chloe began giggling.

"I don't really think I need to explain," she said, after a moment, and grinned at Nicky, thinking she would see the funny side of it.

There was a resounding, horrible silence as they looked at each other in horror. Then Nicky wiped up the table with a tissue from her bag , and sniffed hard as if fighting back tears.

"I think you must be a very unnatural sort of woman," Nicky said in a shaking voice, and picked up the baby and walked out of the dining room in such a jerky uncontrolled manner that Chloe realised she must be crying.

"Oh shit," said Chloe, apologetically. "I didn't mean to upset her."

The man who must be Nicky's husband from his proximity to the remaining child glared at Chloe.

"I think we'd all appreciate it if you moderated your language, Chloe," he said. "There are children present, you know."

"They'll hear worse when they start school," Chloe said, unrepentant. "But, yeah, OK, if it makes you happy, I'll use euphemisms while the rug rats are about. I'm sorry I upset her, but I don't know why what I said upset her so much. It's my life; I can decide whether or when I want children without asking anyone's permission. I don't see what it's got to do with her at all."

The uncomfortable silence around the table was rapidly broken by Nicky's older child crying for his mother; seldom had Chloe had cause to be grateful to a small child. Nicky's husband picked the child up and left the room. The rest of the table were still silent.

"What? What have I done?" Chloe said, mystified.

"Nicky had a miscarriage a week back," one of the other women said, quietly.

"Well, how the hell was I supposed to know that?" Chloe said. "Anyway, she's got two already; it's not like they didn't have any."

"That's a pretty insensitive thing to say," said the woman.

"Sorry but shit, sorry, stuff happens. You just got to live with it. I don't see any of you tiptoeing round me in case I've got sad stuff tucked away that the slightest comment might upset me about. You can't live like that."

Chloe had gone very red; she was angry with herself, but actually unrepentant, and meant what she said.

"Well, do you? Have sad stuff that we should know about?"

"Yes, of course I have. Everyone does. But why should you know about it anyway? What is it to you? What possible interest could my life be to anyone else?" Chloe demanded.

"This is a Christian community; we care about each other," the woman said quietly.

"Do you? How nice for you all," Chloe said, and stuck her fork resolutely in the cold pile of cottage pie on her plate. "Well, I hope dessert is a bit better than this. I had nicer school dinners. Oh, great, now someone's going to tell me that the cook's just found out his wife's been abducted by aliens and that's why the food's such crud."

Clifford was the only one to laugh. Chloe shook her head, dislodging the scarf still more.

"Well, what do you lot do around here for fun?" she asked, hopelessly. "Everyone needs to have a good laugh now and then. Or do you just hang round singing choruses and having prayer meetings?"

"We all have very full and rewarding lives," remarked the woman who had told her about Nicky's miscarriage. "I'm not quite sure what you mean."

Chloe rolled her eyes expressively.

"Obviously," she said. "OK, just forget I ever said anything. I'll be wall-paper from now on."

Dessert was considerably better, a rather excellent apple pie with ice cream. Nicky and her husband returned a few moments later, their children cleaner but not quieter.

"Er, sorry," said Chloe, after Nicky had sat down. "I didn't mean to upset you; I've had a terrible week and I'm not at my best. So can we call it quits and take it as read that I'm an idiot?"

Nicky just shrugged.

Oh, lovely, Chloe thought. I grovel and this is what I get for trying to be nice and do the Christian thing and apologise. Well, that's as far as I'm going.

She stuck her spoon in the pastry and concentrated on eating, and kept her head down and avoided any further conversation. After the table was cleared, she went downstairs to the ladies loo and in the privacy of the cubicle, she leaned against the smooth wall, and shed a few angry tears. What did I do wrong, she asked herself. I'm fine normally with strangers, what on earth went wrong tonight? Praising God and science for waterproof mascara, she went to wash her hands, and tried to decide whether she would attend the service in chapel or not. Maybe it'll give me a handle on how these people tick, she thought, I've got to live here for three years, I need some way of understanding when I'm stepping on a landmine.

There was an astoundingly large number of small children being escorted downstairs to the common room where the crèche was being held; it reminded Chloe of wildlife films where the migrating wildebeest hurtle into river crossings regardless of hidden predators. She waited till the flood became a trickle and she could go up the stairs without colliding with small people.

The college chapel didn't have either sufficient style or sufficient antiquity to give it any sense of the numinous, and effectively it was just a big room with lots of chairs and a few ecclesiastical fittings.

Clifford had saved her a chair at the back near the door; bless the boy, he knew how difficult she was finding this and had anticipated her need for an easy escape route.

"Sodding awful dinner," he whispered in her ear, making sure she was the only one to hear.

Chloe laughed out loud, enjoying both his solidarity and the crudity of his remark.

"Yeah but the apple pie was nice," she said, and sat down next to him, and bowed her head uncertainly, trying to find in that sudden moment of quiet the whole reason why they were here in the first place. In the darkness of her own head, she walked briefly round the place she called faith and found it was still where she'd left it, and then returned to the chapel by opening her eyes.

People were pouring in, students, wives, husbands, staff and a few older children too insulted by the prospect of activity clubs or crèche to tolerate being palmed off on someone else again. The music group were assembling, picking up and tuning instruments, and Chloe felt hopelessly uncomfortable again as someone started playing the piano, picking out a tune she remembered from university days hanging round on the fringes of chaplaincy and Christian Union.

Chloe observed the service without outward emotion, but didn't join in, beyond standing and sitting at appropriate moments. It seemed unbearably false, somehow; a pastiche of modern Christian worship, all jazzy and dressed up to seem contemporary and relevant. The music was bright and fast-paced, the singing actually rather lovely, all harmonies and well-trained voices, the music almost professional in standard. But when she looked at the words in her hymn-book, they were empty; they were full of sound and fury and signified nothing; resounding biblical-sounding lyrics that said nothing to her about the realities of faith. Faith was the moment in a draughty church at smoke-fall, or on a hilltop or at three in the morning when you've cried yourself dry, that moment when you know beyond reasonable doubt and explainable logic that you are not alone; not this jolly, glory stuff that made no sense, but sounded so good.

She caught Clifford's eye, and mouthed silently to him, I'm going home, and slipped quietly out of the door and down the stairs. She could hear the noise of the service behind her, and from the common room the subdued babble of the children in the crèche drifted through the door; there was a baby crying furiously, hardly seeming to draw breath between shrieks.

Outside, Chloe drew in a deep breath of chill night air and let it go in great wreaths of white vapour. She stood for a moment at the door, trying to get herself together, to try to understand herself.

"Forget that," she said aloud, forgetting that no one was listening now and ready to demand that she adjust her language. But anyone who heard her would have known exactly what she really meant to say.

Chapter 3

Chloe sat on the floor of her grandmother's bedroom, drinking black tea and putting off the moment she would have to start the inevitable process of sorting through the house. She'd already seen the representative from the removals firm, and set a date for moving her grandmother's effects to her own house at college; but the actual process of going through the old lady's belongings was still untouched. The room still felt as if she'd just walk back in at any moment; the bed had been stripped, of course, but the brilliantly coloured bedspread that covered the naked mattress was one of her favourites, and her old paisley dressing gown was still hung on the back of the door. It seemed an intrusion into the privacy of the dead to begin this methodical sorting. Oh well, better start, she though bitterly.

She lifted the lamp off the old trunk that had served as a bedside table for as long as she could remember; it was probably full of junk, as at a glance there seemed to be no junk anywhere in the house. For a long life, there was surprisingly little of the usual detritus.

"Rolling stones and all that," Gran had said.

She'd gathered a lot of amazing things, but no real junk; none of the pencil stubs, pieces of string, chipped cups and broken necklaces that fill the drawers and cupboards of most people at eighty or more.

"Comes of living out of suitcases most of the time," she'd remarked.

She'd posted home all sorts of things, over her wandering years, to Chloe's father, who had lived in this house once, long ago. But when she had returned herself, when Chloe's mother had died, she had returned with the trunk and two suitcases, and an exotic scent that Chloe would always remember. She knew now it was the scent of vetivert and patchouli, impregnated in her clothes, a hint of curry and sandalwood and saffron; but when Chloe first met her grandmother, she was two years old and the old lady had smelled like something out of a storybook, like no one else's grandmother could ever smell.

When she lifted the lid of the trunk, the scent came flooding out, slightly musty and old, but still familiar. There was a piece of silk at the top of the contents of the trunk, coarsely woven and brightly coloured, a brilliantly vivid sunshine gold. On the silk lay an envelope, with her own name written on it in her Grandmother's swirling flamboyant handwriting. The ink was very dark, unfaded by time, so Chloe knew it was a recently written letter, and she shivered suddenly. Both the scent of the trunk and the sight of her grandmother's handwriting made tears rise to her eyes. Scrubbing at her eyes, Chloe ripped open the envelope, and began to read.

"Dear Chloe," her Gran had written. "If you are reading this now then I am certainly dead, so stop crying please, and pay attention."

Chloe snorted with laughter.

"I've known for some time this was coming; I've been lucky all my life, and I've hardly had a day's illness, so I suppose it's only fair that the first real illness I get should be fatal. But at least I've had time to prepare for it. If you've started clearing the house, then you'll have realised I did a lot of sorting myself when I found out. No one should have to clear up after another person's mess; so there's very little mess, as such. Or at least I hope so. I'm not sure quite when I'm going to go; I hope it's fast. I've never coped well with pain, so I'm hoping I can manage what I've heard of many times in my travels, to just leave my body when I know it's time. The trick is to know when it's time. There's a bit in the book of Ecclesiastes, where it speaks of a golden bowl being broken and a silver thread being cut; I think the knack is to cut the thread oneself before the bowl is broken. Anyway, that's not important. I'm dead now, however it happened, and you're still alive. There are things I should have talked to you about and somehow never got round to it. The talk we had today was simply about my funeral, and yes, I was joking about Bat out of Hell; there's no point making a gesture using a song I've never liked anyway. I am hoping I may manage to talk to you in the weeks to come, but this letter is meant as insurance in case I don't get the opportunity or if I see the time to leave before I speak to you. If I have already spoken to you, then just put this down as me finally losing my marbles and repeating myself. You know how much I have always feared losing my reason; I trust that even at the end I was at least moderately coherent."

Chloe snorted again; her Grandmother had been quoting T.S. Eliot's Four Quartets five minutes before she had simply left her body behind. As exits go, it was a pretty coherent one.

"I have some regrets that I need to tell you about. The first is that I came back when your father asked me to. Not because of you, Chloe. I count it a great privilege that I had the chance to be with you as you grew up. No, it's simply that effectively I forced your father out by my lack of sympathy and understanding. I called him a coward and a weakling, and a lot of other things I shouldn't even have thought. If I had stayed away, he would have brought you and Cathy up fine; you'd still have a Dad and a sister. However, when his letter reached me, I let myself be influenced by guilt, and I came back because he'd never asked anything of me before. Well, not as an adult anyway, and I gave in because at the beginning and the end of it all, he was my only son and I did love him. He did come back and visit, after he left, but it got less and less often, and then he stopped altogether. I have kept his last few letters, along with the ones Cathy sent after she left. They are in this trunk, so that should you wish to you have a starting point from which you may be able to trace them both. I would advise you to do so; I did without family for much of my life and I know what the lack of it does to one. I would have you live a very different life to the one I chose; but then given your choice of husband, I think you will anyway. He's a nice boy, and I think you'll both be very happy together, whatever the rest of the world throws at you. I voiced my concerns to you once and I won't repeat myself now.

"If you have been paying attention to details, as I hope I brought you up to do, you will have noticed that the surname on my birth certificate is the same as the one on my death certificate. If I allowed people to think I was a widow, it was purely out of laziness and a need for privacy that I've never quite managed to shake off. I never married. The only man I would have married was your grandfather, and I was stupid about that and allowed my father to influence me. However, he regretted it when it became plain that I had become pregnant, and had no way of tracking down my would-be husband, since I didn't even know his full name. Since then, when I have been asked, I have let it be thought that I was a widow. Bringing up an illegitimate baby back then was a hell of a lot tougher than you can ever imagine. Fortunately, having the title of doctor gives a certain spurious respectability, and I never once had to lie and call myself Mrs Anything. People make assumptions; that can occasionally be useful.

"This brings me to something else that I ought to have talked to you about a long time ago. I think I have regretted so much being influenced by what my family thought of me, what anyone thought of me, that I set out to try and teach you to always and only be yourself. Retrospectively, I think I've done too good a job of that. You see, I was past thirty before I began to simply be myself, when I'd learned what it cost me to be anybody else. You have been trying simply to be yourself your whole life, and while that was what I wanted for you, maybe I should have taught you the gentle art of compromise. Trouble is I never mastered that one myself. Perhaps if I just tell you about it; you're a clever girl, maybe you'll figure it out yourself. I never did. Being fierce and outspoken and true to yourself, you end up with a few true friends but a lot of enemies who wear friendly faces. I found people coped far better with me as I got older; somehow it's far less threatening when it's a harmless old lady who tells the Emperor he's naked."

Harmless old lady, yeah, right, Chloe thought blackly. Harmless my arse.

"I've tried to live my life with this maxim: what I do IS me, for that I came. Only the truest, clearest of souls can live with that, and I've met more of those than you'd imagine and I found them wearing bodies that you wouldn't expect. It's not easy to do, either, because there's always the temptation to let people mould you into what they would rather you were, so that they will like and accept you. That's the biggest fear of all, you know, that we are all alone; that's why we do so many of the things we do. Out of fear of being alone.

"I think you know that we are never truly alone; even in the dark night of the soul, even when we've been there so long we think we've become nocturnal, even there we are never truly alone. Sometimes, on my travels, I have feared it so much, that we are truly alone; but whatever faith I have has always rescued me from those fears. It's not the sort of faith you will find at the college; I can put so little of it into words. I'd probably be accused of some weird form of Gnosticism. Still it's got me through a lifetime, of sorts. I'm getting tired now, so I know I haven't got much time, so I will try and say what I need to.

"Live your life so that you can say when you come to the point I am at now, I was true to myself and my God, I hurt as few people as I could, I did as much good as I could, and I can be at peace with my own soul. Remember: what I do is me; for that I came. You are a good woman and I am proud of you; nothing would have pleased me more than you did. But be gentle with yourself too, and then it'll be easier to be gentle with others. That was always my failing; I could never be gentle with those who needed it. I think especially of Cathy and your father. I came close to being cruel to them, and I hope one day they may forgive me. I can make no excuses for that.

"I won't say good luck, but I will wish you a good journey. I feel sure that we will meet again in some way; but no harps! No clouds and white nighties, either.

"After the kingfisher's wing has answered light to light, and is silent, the light is still at the still point of the turning world. Farewell, granddaughter."

That was it; no more words on the pages, sprawling drunkenly as her grandmother had become more and more tired as she had written. Chloe rummaged in the trunk; it was full of the most extraordinary things, as well as packets of letters written in fading ink, but nothing else like that letter which would haunt her for days.

She sat back on her heels, still holding the letter, trying to think, trying to understand. The letter had been written three days before her grandmother had died, on the day she had told her she was dying, and discussed funeral arrangements as calmly as she might have discussed the weekly shopping. If there had been so much more that she had wanted to say to Chloe, then why had she not been able to say it? Why had it had to be written down like this, why could she not have just come out and told her? And how much more had she lacked the strength to write? We do not know the ones we love, she thought, and rubbed her eyes again. She put the letter back into the trunk, clicked it shut and then awkwardly carried it downstairs and out to her car. This was one thing she could not risk losing in the inevitable confusion of removals; she would sift through the contents later in the quiet of her own home and in her own time.

It was an appallingly long day; even though her grandmother had been sorting and preparing for months, there were the things that she could not have done, like kitchen cupboards and the contents of the pantry, her wardrobe and chest of drawers, the things we cannot do ourselves, until we know the exact moment of our departure, and few can know that. For most of us, there is always the hope that tomorrow will come, and we will need clean underwear, and that extra pot of jam, and that new bottle of washing up liquid. Gran had been no different, really; she had not ordered more coal for the winter, certainly, but the daily mundane needs she had seen to in the same way she always would have done. Chloe went through everything carefully so that the removals men would simply be able to pack things into boxes. The wardrobe was the hardest to look at. It was so full of her grandmother's personality; every garment so typical of her that it almost hurt to look at them empty and shapeless. It seemed terrible to have to discard them. Some things she would keep and wear herself; they had been similar in build, and the old lady's taste had been eccentric and ageless.

When she drove home, with a boot full of memories, all she wanted was to sleep. Clifford came out to the car to meet her. She had refused to allow him to accompany her that day, feeling that it would be quicker and less painful if she did it alone, though she had wondered whether she was right as the day had gone on.

"I've brought some things back today, stuff I couldn't leave to the removals," she said, going round and opening the boot. "Can you give me a hand with it?"

"That's what I'm here for," he said amiably, peering into the boot, and pulling out the trunk. "What's in this, then?"

"The White Knight's recipe, I think. There's a letter I'd like you to read, later. I'm not sure about the other stuff, where it comes from. I think it's all the bits and pieces she collected on her travels, the sort of stuff she wouldn't have put out on display for whatever reason. Though I'm not sure why, because even what I had a look at didn't seem shocking at all, not compared to some of the things she had."

Chloe pulled out a lumpy object wrapped in her jumper, and carried it into the house as Clifford brought in the trunk. She sat down of the sofa and disentangled the object from the garment; Clifford remembered the statue, a battered wooden carving of the Buddha, which had emitted a lovely scent when the afternoon sun had slanted across the living room and warmed the wood where it stood by the hearth.

"You smell all smoky," Clifford commented as he put the trunk down next to the sofa.

"I broke a whole load of by-laws, and had a bonfire in the back garden," Chloe explained. "Some things were too old to give to charity shops and somehow I seemed wrong just to bin them like so much rubbish even if they were. So I burned them; Gran's old dressing gown, the one she wore in the winter, was full of holes, and so threadbare I'd thought about getting her a new one this Christmas. Oh, and her underwear. That lot went up nicely, oodles of smoke. I burned a lot of old newspapers and old dishcloths, stuff like that. She'd got rid of most of that sort of thing, but you know how it is, there's always something you forget about. The house felt so strange without her. I felt sick really, her not being there just didn't feel right."

She rubbed her eyes again, smudging what was left of her make-up.

"Can you bring in the other stuff in the boot? It's not a lot really, mostly clothes. I need a bath and a cup of tea," she said, stretching.

While he went out to the car, she filled the kettle and then went upstairs to start running a bath. When Clifford came upstairs a while later with a big mug of tea, Chloe was asleep in the bath, her chin bearded with bath foam. He looked down at her, with some pity as well as love, and touched her forehead gently.

"Tea," he said as she opened her eyes.

"I wasn't asleep," she said.

"Yes you were. You were snoring bubbles."

"Yeah right."

Chloe flicked foam at him, and reached for her tea.

Chapter 4

The removals lorry blocked the whole close, so there was no hope of doing this quietly and unobtrusively; Chloe could already feel the eyes of her neighbours peering out from windows around the area, and she heard the sound of a door opening in the house next door to her own.

"Shit," she said under her breath but didn't turn round, just continued to watch the lorry inching as close to her house as it reasonably could. By the time it stopped, she was relieved to see that there was room for cars to pass. She had become so absorbed that she hadn't quite registered that the woman from next door had come and stood next to her.

"I thought you'd already moved in," she said, making Chloe jump. "I'm Felicity, by the way."

"I'm Chloe," said Chloe and was annoyed by Felicity's reply.

"Yes," she said. "I know. So how come you're moving in twice?"

Chloe considered telling her to get lost and mind her own business, but it did seem an understandable sort of inquiry.

"This is my grandmother's stuff; she died recently," she explained. "We didn't have enough of our own to fill a transit van; we got married in the summer, so we'd not really set up home before."

"She left you everything, then," Felicity said, craning her neck to peer into the lorry as the driver opened the main doors. "That was handy."

"I'd rather have my grandmother than her furniture," Chloe said as mildly as she could manage, but it still sounded rather sharp.

"Sorry, that wasn't what I meant," said Felicity. "I mean, I'm sorry for your loss. But I suppose she was quite old?"

Chloe could tell fishing when she heard it.

"Inevitably," she agreed. "Grandparents usually are. At least they are by the time they're grandparents; they don't start out that way."

Felicity looked at Chloe for signs of mockery and saw none; like almost everyone else she'd heard about that encounter with Nicky at college supper, and was as puzzled by Chloe as all of them.

"Sorry, can't stop to chat, got to get on with unloading this van," Chloe said, and moved away from Felicity as fast as she could.

Felicity had been about to offer her help, but changed her mind though she did stand and linger for a few minutes to watch, as the furniture was unloaded. Chloe, aware of her scrutiny was relieved that the smaller items from her grandmother's house were safely hidden in layers of paper and bubble-wrap and entombed in packing boxes. Some of the exotica were not really the kinds of things she felt instinctively anyone here would understand or approve of; one of the erotic statues Gran had sent back from India had actually been banished to a back bedroom that had been largely unused. Some things were, she'd admitted, genuinely unfair on innocent callers. Chloe had a feeling that one might end up in the loft till she had a house that had a guest bedroom bigger than the one they had here. In fact, an awful lot was going to have to go up in the loft. She'd put some of the furniture into storage, the larger pieces she had measured and realised that they would fit nowhere in this small house. One wardrobe she'd been obliged to leave in the old house, as it would not fit down the stairs, whatever the removals men tried. She'd also discovered that her grandmother had been steadily selling off various things; some of the antiques she'd picked up over the years for the proverbial song, she'd sold off at an enormous profit. She'd told Chloe about this the day she died, explaining that the money would be more useful than the antiques themselves.

"There's only so much you'll be able to fit in that shoebox that place has the nerve to call a house," she'd said. "And storage costs money, so only keep what you really want. Oh, for goodness sake don't cry, girl. Did you think it'd all go on a big bonfire like a Viking send off?"

It took days to get the house sorted into any sort of order, especially since Chloe was still working her notice and could only get down to unpacking and rearranging furniture in the evenings. It was often past midnight when she stopped. The eventual effect was that of Gran's old house shrunken into a much smaller space; but at least the cats seemed happier with all their old favourite snoozing places back again. The loft was groaning with the weight of the boxes they'd stowed away up there; most of the china and glassware, as well as a lot of the books, had been surplus to current requirements as well as storage space in the small kitchen. However, it felt much more like a home than before; it had felt as if they were almost camping in the house, their few belongings looking lost in the little house.

"It's nice to have a sofa that doesn't sag in the middle or try to eat me when I get up," Clifford said, the first evening after Chloe felt they had finished really moving in.

Chloe nodded sleepily and snuggled into him, leaning her head against his chest and listening to his breathing through the heavy sweater. She felt very strange now the old house had been emptied of everything she had ever known, and most of it brought here to this small building, now hopelessly cramped with furniture too large for it. The old house was due to be let out to some Americans who had taken it for a three year lease, to be renewed as and when they knew how long they wanted to stay. She had decided that she ought not to sell the house. Keeping it meant that in some dim future when Clifford retired, they would have a home of their own. It was easy to forget the future, especially when the present was so complicated. She'd been applying for new jobs, but so far had not been lucky, though she had one interview coming up. But she had this cold hard core of fear somewhere deep in her stomach, a fear that she would not get another job, or quickly enough to stop this strange panic that rose inside her late at night and early in the morning, an insistent litany that asked in a loud whisper, "What are you going to do? What are you going to do?" and she couldn't answer it except by trying to blank it out and pretend she couldn't hear it. But it rose up at the edges of sleep, where she couldn't entirely control it, and at those odd moments of the day when she paused in her stride to hear it slip its insidious message across. It left a sour taste in her mind.

That weekend, Clifford had a church placement to go to; the ordinands were sent to various churches in the area to observe different styles of worship and preaching, and after more training were allowed to preach and take services as part of their training. Clifford was still at the observing stage, and Chloe had no intention on following him around to these placements, like some sort of accessory, and had no particular plans of her own for church attendance. It was a huge pleasure to be able to stay in bed, and have Clifford bring her tea in bed before he left that morning. The house was chilly and she turned over to go back to sleep pulling the duvet up to her chin as she curled up in the warm patch her own body had created.

She'd been drifting in and out of sleep for more than an hour when the doorbell rang. She jumped out of bed, dragging on the sweatshirt and jogging trousers she had worn the previous evening, and ran down the stairs. It must be something important if someone was ringing the bell at, well, what was it, half past nine on a Sunday morning. No civilized person would do that if it weren't important.

When she got to the door, the bell was ringing again.

"All right all right, is my roof on fire or something?" she demanded, yanking open the door, expecting to see maybe a fire crew or a policeman.

It was Felicity.

Chloe stopped dead; this was not was she had expected.

"Is there a problem?" she asked, as politely as she could, given her surprise.

"You're not up, then," Felicity said, glancing at Chloe's crumpled, slob-out clothes, her hair standing out around her head in a halo of unbrushed curls, and her bare face.

"Er, no, I was asleep," Chloe said.

"Oh, I am sorry, I didn't know you were ill," Felicity said, turning to go.

"No, I'm not ill, I was just having a lie in, like ninety percent of Britain. What's the matter, why were you ringing my doorbell? Is there something wrong?"

Felicity was looking at her strangely.

"No, there's nothing wrong," she said, carefully. "I just thought that when I saw Clifford going out in the car alone to his placement, I thought you would like a lift to church?"

Chloe stared at her, uncomprehending.

"Sorry," she said. "Am I missing something here? I wasn't aware church attendance was suddenly compulsory."

"I just thought you'd want to go," Felicity said. "The church we go to is very alive and active; there's a great kids club and crèche, and the teaching is very sound. I thought that if you haven't already found it, you might like a lift, since Clifford has the car today."

Chloe felt an unaccustomed surge of fury, and bit back the expletives that went with it.

"I've had a horrible week," she said. "So I was taking the chance of a bit of extra kip and a chance to chill out a bit. Frankly, church was way down on my list of priorities this weekend, and since you haven't noticed, a crèche and a kids club are not really much as incentives for the childless, and as for sound teaching, I generally prefer things to be unsound, as it tends to be more fun. If you ever feel like doing someone what you think is a favour again, I would suggest you actually ask them in advance whether it is a favour at all or simply a bloody nuisance."

She shut the door against Felicity and leaned against it, feeling the waves of anger cover her with sick heat, and then she began to shake. Outside, she heard Felicity say, "Well, really!" in a hurt but self-righteous voice.

Go away, Chloe thought, or I'm going to start shouting.

She bolted the door, as much for psychological protection as from any thought that the other woman might dare to try the door again, and marched through to the kitchen, and filled the kettle.

I don't believe that just happened, she thought, I don't believe it at all.

She made herself coffee and went through to the living room and lit the gas fire, and wished she could pick up the phone and call her grandmother. She had never suffered fools at all, let alone gladly, and Chloe had the same reaction to arrant stupidity, especially when it impinged on her own life. But her letter had spoken of a need to learn the art of compromise, and had left her to try and work out what she had meant by that. Perhaps it meant not blowing up at people who interfered. Well, if that's what it meant, she was buggered. There was no way she was going to be able to cope with people like Felicity if she couldn't say what she meant; that sort would walk all over you if you let them.

After a minute, she began drinking the coffee; her hands had stopped shaking at least enough to hold the mug without slopping coffee everywhere. Chainsaw wandered sleepily into the room, saw the fire and curled up abruptly in front of it.

"Cats; the world's original heat-seeking missile," Chloe said to the cat, leaning over to stroke the dense fur and start Chainsaw purring. The combined sound of purring and the hissing of the gas fire was one of the most soothing to Chloe and after a few minutes, even before she'd finished her drink, the whole incident had faded away. But that traitorous small voice whispered above the quiet sounds of cat and fire, what are you going to do, what are you going to do?

"I don't know," Chloe said aloud to the room, barely aware she had spoken at all. "What can I do?"

Sunday was ruined; that gloriously lazy mood she'd woken with had been broken by the doorbell. She couldn't go back to bed, not really; she was far too wide-awake now. She ran a hot bath, tipping in exotic bath oil that smelled like the wooden statue of the Buddha, and lay in the water trying to ease those barely-felt kinks in her mind. Each time she tried to identify what was wrong, it seemed to slip away, like oily soap from wet fingers. In the end, she gave up and went downstairs in her dressing gown to start cooking some lunch. There's nothing quite like boiling pasta for putting things into perspective, she thought, as the kitchen filled with steam. Now all I have to worry about is whether I have any tomato purée left.

Chapter 5

Clifford moodily knocked the snooker balls around the table; he was too strung up to go home now the day's lectures were over. Chloe was out today at a job interview, and wouldn't be home till later than usual. So he was playing aimlessly, with no thought beyond killing time. He was relieved for a moment when one of the students from his fellowship group came over and offered him a proper game; it was obvious quite quickly that Mike was a much better player and was likely to wipe the floor with him.

"I hear your wife has been upsetting a lot of people," Mike said.

Clifford miscued; swore silently and then said,

"I don't think two counts as a lot of people," he said cautiously.

"That's what the talk is; Chinese whispers I'm sure," Mike said.

"No, she did upset Nicky what's her name and Felicity from next door to us, but I think that's all, so far," Clifford said. "I think you should know it isn't like her at all to be quite so abrasive; I mean, she's pretty plain-spoken, but she's usually a lot less volatile."

"Oh yes?" Mike said.

"She's had a really bad few weeks," said Clifford. "Her Gran has just died; they were very close. She was brought up by her Gran; we even chose this college so she could be near enough to visit often, and then about a week into term, she tells Chloe she's got cancer and it's terminal. Just to cap it all, she got made redundant the day after the funeral."

Clifford watched as Mike made one shot after another, successfully potting balls with apparently minimum attention.

"I'll put the word out, if you like," Mike offered. "There's been people complaining that she shouldn't be allowed to get away with being rude to people."

"Two people. I'm not aware she's upset anyone else," said Clifford.

"Fair enough; doesn't bother me what she says to anyone. I thought that little spat at the dinner table was quite funny myself. The couples with kids can be unbearably smug about it, as if it's some sort of passport to everything," Mike said, and Clifford remembered Mike's wife looking tearful the other day when a new baby had been brought into college to be admired and cooed over. Some people were not childless out of choice.

"I thought it was funny myself," Clifford said. "I don't think Chloe has ever had much to do with kids and babies, and nor have I come to that, but I do think if we ever do have kids, she'll still manage to avoid looking like something the cat dragged in, however many times she's been woken at night."

"She is pretty eye-catching," Mike admitted. "She doesn't exactly seem vicar's wife material, though."

"No; I don't suppose she does. Though when we met, I wasn't exactly planning all this ordination thing anyway; it sort of crept up on me," Clifford explained. "She was always on the fringes of the Christian groups at University, so I knew her a bit but not well. She avoided getting tied down to anything, any one church or group, but one night at a party in our final year, I heard her say

50

something that made me stop and look at her again. The party was at that winding down stage where people are drinking coffee and trying to get sober enough to get home; you know the kind of thing. Lots of drunken people sitting around setting the world to rights. It must have been about half past four in the morning. Someone had been talking about the impossibility of proving or disproving the existence of God; and then Chloe got up off the floor and said, "I don't need to prove whether or not God exists, because I know." Then I saw her differently; I mean, I'd always half fancied her anyway, but I'd kept my distance because I'd always told myself I didn't want to be involved with a non-Christian, and the way she hovered at the edges of things, and never quite got drawn in, I'd thought she was one of the people who just sort of toy with faith and never take it very seriously. When she said that, I knew she was for real."

"And the rest, as they say, is history," Mike put in, grinning.

"I guess so. She's never felt she needed to formalise her faith, or conform to one particular form of worship; and she can't really see why anyone else can. We've had a lot of fun since then just going wherever to see what other churches do; I've always come back to the Anglican Church, but that's where I've been most comfortable. My uncle is a priest, and it was he who first suggested I might have a calling."

Clifford looked at the virtually empty table, and grinned at Mike.

"You're good at this," he said.

"Sign of a misspent youth," Mike admitted. "I briefly considered turning professional. So didn't your director for ordinands ask about Chloe when you went for selection?"

"Well, yes, but all he really wanted to know was whether she was happy for me to go ahead with it. And she told him that she was. Well, that's not true. What she actually said was, "It would be wrong to stand in the way of what God wants and that's for the selection panel to decide, not you and not Clifford and certainly not me." I think he was impressed with that; he never asked anything much about how she felt about what life might be like once I am ordained. She's never wanted to have much to do with it, really. I suppose it's the way her Gran brought her up."

"Didn't she have much time for the church?"

"Not as such, no. She was such a fierce old girl, she made Chloe look meek by comparison, but she was great fun, and she had a strange rather mystical faith herself. She'd travelled enormously, seen extraordinary things and I think she found ordinary Anglican churches rather tame and bland by comparison. So she took Chloe to all sorts of places when she was a kid, everything from Nigerian Pentecostal to High Anglican Mass, as well as other faiths. Chloe did choose to be confirmed an Anglican though; and she does go to church sometimes, just not every week."

"I don't think Felicity stopped to think before she called for her," Mike said. "I don't think many of them think anyway, but Felicity and Robert are so caught up with the church they're involved in, they can't either of them see it won't suit everyone."

"I can't imagine it'd suit Chloe," Clifford said.

"Nor can I," Mike said. "Look, I'll tell Jo that Chloe's been having a tough time lately, and she'll make sure everyone knows, so people will be a bit more understanding, but between you and me, I think your wife's fine. If she could pull her punches a bit, things would be easier for her."

Clifford grinned, thinking of the letter, and her Gran suggesting learning the gentle art of compromise.

"I'll tell her that," he said. "I think I'll concede defeat now; there's no way I can catch up with you now. Do you want some coffee?"

"Not the instant stuff they have here. Tell you what, come over to mine, and I'll break out the hard stuff. You won't sleep for a week; Jo got this Italian stuff that's black as hell and almost pure caffeine."

They both giggled, like schoolboys, at the thought of coffee as a hard drug.

"Yeah, great. I've got an essay to do tonight anyway, and Chloe's out on an interview so she won't be back till later. I could do with a break from this place. Funny, we've only been here weeks and it feels like this is all I can remember," Clifford said thoughtfully as they stacked the snooker cues in the corner and collected their coats.

"I know what you mean," Mike said. "It took us about a month to feel this was all we'd ever known. It does become sort of all encompassing, more so when you live in the grounds. The people who live further out don't seem to get as swamped; well, the ones without kiddies, anyway. I suppose the lure of free childcare a couple of times a week, as well as that crèche and playgroup, must be too tempting. It does seem strange that people who are so kid-focussed are so keen to get rid of them so often."

"I think they call it socialisation," Clifford said. "I've eavesdropped a few conversations in the common room. It's supposed to be good for kids to mix a lot with other kids. At least with the college playgroup, they can rest assured they won't be exposed to bad language."

"No, they leave that for the dinner table," Mike said, laughing. "She does call a spade a spade, doesn't she?"

"No, she calls it a bloody shovel," Clifford said, and grinned. "She only does it when she's really stressed; that was a pretty untimely comment."

"Yeah, but it was funny seeing the faces round the table. No one was quite sure they'd heard correctly."

"She was whispering, well, trying to," Clifford said. "I don't know quite what the problem was; the kids will soon hear worse at school. I know it wasn't tactful with the kids there, but it's only words."

They got to Mike's little house quickly; it was getting cold now and neither of them wanted to be outside for long. There weren't a great many houses in the grounds; many of the students lived further away, but a significant number of couples and families chose to live in the small houses belonging to the college. There were rooms for the single students too, rather like university halls of residence, which meant that the families often befriended those single students, often overseas students a long way from home.

Chloe had expressed the thought that they only did it to find free babysitters, and in some cases that was probably quite true. The whole feel of the residential area of college was that of a small village, almost like something out of Brave New World, full of very clever people trying to get on with other very clever people with often opposing views. It certainly felt like something out of fiction at times; if you listened in to the kind of conversations going on over garden fences in the warmer months, it would have seemed very strange indeed.

Mike's house seemed as cramped as Clifford's own; obviously they had moved from a larger house, and were determined to cram it all in somewhere. Clifford shuddered to think what some of the houses might be like with two or three small children and the accompanying clobber as well as the usual furniture.

"Only this year to go, and then we'll be out of this rabbit hutch," Mike said, filling the kettle.

Clifford felt suddenly rather sad; his first sort-of friend here, and he would be leaving at the end of the summer term.

"I bet that'll feel good," he said.

"Yeah, brilliant. It's been OK, but not what we'd hoped at all. I think we had unrealistic ideas of what it would be like. Jo's found it quite tough, though. All those babies; it hasn't been so bad for me, but the population explosion here seems to have upset her quite badly at times. It's silly; we're still young, and there's plenty of time, but even when I hear the sounds of all those kids at chapel crèche, even I get a bit broody and resentful. And incidentally, pass on to Chloe not to feel too bad about Nicky; Jo told me that every time Nicky's period is a week late, she calls it a miscarriage. She should try having a real one, for a change."

The kettle turned itself off abruptly, filling the brief uncomfortable silence that fell between the two men.

"Still, nothing we can do about it, is there," Mike said brightly after a moment. "It'll happen or it won't. I mean, the doctor said there's no good reason why it keeps happening."

He opened a cupboard and pulled out a large cafetière and a jar of very dark ground coffee, and set about making coffee, which was certainly strong enough to keep both of them up past midnight.

Clifford set off home, an hour later, having enjoyed both the coffee and the company, feeling much more positive and relaxed. It felt like he was less alone than he had been. Chloe got home about an hour and a half later, still hyped from her interview.

"How did it go?" Clifford asked.

"All right, but not brilliant. I'll be surprised if I got it, though," Chloe said, hanging up her coat. "The other candidates were all a bit older, and that bit more experienced, so unless they want me as the token woman on the team, I think that one's a non-starter. Still, it's all good experience, I suppose, at interviews. Can I smell dinner?"

"You can. Tuna lasagne and baked potatoes," Clifford said.
Chloe kissed him.

"You'll make someone a wonderful wife one day," she said. "Have I got time for a shower, or will it be ruined?"

"No, ten minutes won't be a problem," he said, and followed her upstairs, and sat on the side of the bath while she showered.

"I was talking to Mike, today, you know, the nice chap from the fellowship group," he said, after a moment.

"Oh yes?" Chloe said, sticking her face around the shower curtain. "That sounds ominous."

"No, not at all. He was very amused by your gaffe the other week," Clifford said.

"Nice to know someone was."

"It's just that I think maybe you ought to try and patch things up a bit with people. I know you didn't mean to upset anyone, and they were pretty stupid about things. We've got to live here and it'd be a lot easier if we were on decent terms with our neighbours. It's not like you to be so aggressive; you know you're not like that."

The water ran for a moment before Chloe put her head round again.

"So what do you think I should do? Apologise?" she said, but she didn't sound cross. Obviously the interview had somehow cheered her up a bit in some indefinable way.

"Well, yes, but don't grovel. You could leave them a note or something. If you said about your Gran dying, I think that'd count for a lot; might even make them feel a bit guilty. It isn't good to have that sort of resentment going on."

Chloe pulled back into the shower again.

"OK," she said, her voice muted by the flowing water. "I suppose you're right. I don't like the thought of saying I'm sorry, when partly I'm not sorry for what I said. But I am sorry I upset anyone. I don't mind apologising for that."

"Oh, and Mike said something else you might find interesting."

"What?"

"Well, he said that Nicky calls every late period a miscarriage, so this may well not have been at all."

Chloe put her head round again, her hair full of bubbles.

"Thank God for that," she said. "Silly cow; she obviously needs more attention. Pity she can't think of a less pathetic way of getting it."

She ducked back into the water and Clifford could hear her vigorously sluicing away the shampoo. Then the water was turned off, and she held out her hand for him to pass her a towel.

"God, that feels so much better," she said, wrapping her hair in the towel.

"Yes, but I've told you before, I'm not God," Clifford said, passing her another towel as she got out of the shower.

"I keep forgetting, oh my lord and master," she said, wrapping herself in the big soft towel. "But that does feel so much better. I was sweating blood while I was waiting for my turn."

Clifford lifted her blouse off the floor and inspected it carefully for suspicious stains.

"Nothing on this," he said.

"Metaphorically speaking, you moron," she said, and slipped past him to their bedroom to dress.

Over dinner, Clifford thought how tired she looked; she didn't seem to be sleeping properly, and he'd found her downstairs on the sofa a number of times when he'd got up in the mornings. She'd said she'd got up for a drink and hadn't wanted to disturb him by coming back to bed chilled.

She also seemed very pale; her skin seemed stretched a little too tight across her cheekbones. Her hair was drying into those mad ringlets he liked so much; she wore her hair tightly plaited or pinned up to work, and it always looked like an escaped animal when she let it down again at home.

"Good dinner," she said, her mouth full. "I'm starving."

"Did you not have lunch?"

"Did, but threw up later. Nerves. Can't stand interviews. Always seems to be about selling yourself. I mean, why should they choose one person over another except that one somehow promises more? We all have much the same qualifications, and experience or none of us would even be short-listed. So why choose one person and not another? I don't know."

"It's about a face fitting, I think."

"My face isn't going to fit anywhere; not today anyway. I know when I've got somewhere and when it's all been a rehearsal," she said, sawing open a second baked potato and putting half on her plate and half on Clifford's.

"I'm sorry," he said.

"No worries, mate," she said. "Every dog will have her day. Just wasn't mine today."

"I wouldn't call you a dog," he said. "You're something much more exotic than that."

"That's comforting. Let me guess. A wolverine? A serval? An ocelot?"

"No to all of them. Actually, I've no idea. But you are a bit on an animal, sometimes."

Chloe nearly choked on her mouthful and when she'd stopped laughing, she said seriously,

"I'll apologise to Felicity and Nicky for savaging them like some sort of rottweiler; but I don't want to. But I can't not do it. It's me that loses out, really. I don't know how my grandmother coped sometimes; maybe she just had very forgiving friends, or she really didn't care if she'd upset people. But I can't cope with the kind of animosity she sometimes used to get, and I'd rather the people here didn't hate me, if I can stop that from happening. I thought about it today, driving to work and then to the interview; I need friends. Gran was my best friend all the time I was growing up, but she's gone now and I can't get her back. So it's about time I started trying to make friends."

She ducked her head down and concentrated on eating, but Clifford knew now quite how badly her Grandmother's death had affected her. Such a vivid personality, such a huge spirit; her death had left a huge hole in Chloe, one he couldn't fill entirely himself, even if he tried. He shivered.

"I'll put the heating on; there's probably going to be a frost tonight," he said.

"Good," Chloe said, her mouth full again. "Sitting around with wet hair in a cold house isn't exactly my best way to relax and unwind after a difficult day."

"I can think of a few better ways," Clifford said.

"So can I, but can I finish dinner first?"

Chapter 6

Chloe sat in the blue dawn light and tried to read back what she had written; she should really turn the light on, but that would disturb Clifford who was still asleep beside her. She'd dashed off the two notes of apology late last night with the intention of sleeping on it and then checking them in the morning to see whether she'd said anything accidentally that might seem inflammatory, but this morning she was having her doubts about everything. Should she have gone out and bought cards, probably with teddy bears on holding up placards saying "Sorry", or would a quick note on her usual letter paper be sufficient? Should she nip down to the garage and buy some flowers as well? Oh stuff it, the letters would do. It wasn't as if she'd done anything truly worthy of a full-fledged grovel, like spilling red wine on a white shirt. This was a simple apology, not a grovel. She didn't care whether they liked her or not, that wasn't the issue. It was simply a matter of smoothing things over so that people wouldn't keep talking about the whole stupid thing. So why was she reading and rereading these wretched notes to check whether she'd managed to write in an unconscious time bomb?

She left the notes on her dressing table and went through to the bathroom to shower and get ready for work. By the time she was dressed, it would be time to bring Clifford his morning tea, and then he could decide whether she was actually shooting herself in the foot with these letters.

"No, they're fine," he said when she asked. "They were fine last night too, so don't worry. You've said all you need to; anything else will seem like you're trying too hard."

"I was thinking of putting something with them, I don't know, flowers or chocolate or something. I've got two little bars of Thornton's stuff tucked away for emergencies. What do you think?" she asked anxiously.

"Just as long as they're not kiddie chocs, I think that'd be a nice touch," he said.

"No, they're those Viennese things. What difference would it make if it was children's chocolate?"

"Well, they wouldn't feel bad about keeping them for themselves if it's something a bit sophisticated. It'd seem more of a gift if it was obvious it's meant for them and not the brats."

"God, I'll never get the hang of people," Chloe said, slumping onto the bed despondently.

"I've told you before, don't call me God," Clifford said, rolling her over and pinning her down to kiss.

"There's only one sort of God like you and I think the Romans used to have statues of him in the vegetable garden to frighten off pests," Chloe said, struggling free.

"Thanks a million!"

"Nah, don't take offence you moron. He was called Priapus, and I think it's his statue we hauled up to the loft. You know, the one with the great big–"

The kiss ended in a tangle of duvet and left Chloe half an hour late for work.

"What can they do you anyway?" Clifford asked as she rushed to straighten her hair. "Sack you?"

"Yes, but I'm still in need of a good reference and being late is still a black mark and I don't need any of them," she said, ramming pins into her tightly twisted hair. "Ah, stuff it, it ain't working." She pulled the pins out and fluffed up her hair. "They'll all think I've gone demob-happy, but what the hell? At least they'll all know what I really look like before I leave, instead of this weird version of Miss Jean Brodie."

"I'm not sure which will make those guys more uncomfortable, the real you or the fantasy dominatrix version."

"Give over, I'm not kinky. Now, I will have to go, so don't even come near me again or I might just decide to swipe a sickie today."

Chloe left the house feeling a good deal more positive and actually enjoyed that day more than she expected, even the comments about how different she looked with her hair down, especially how it looked with a safety helmet rammed down on top. She was actually going to miss this company, well, some of the people anyway, even if they had made her redundant at such an inopportune moment. When she got home that evening, there was a note from Clifford waiting for her on the kettle, saying he was round at Mike's and Mike had asked them to come over for supper that evening, nothing fancy just whatever was in the freezer, and did she mind?

"What the hell, why not?" she said to Chainsaw who was snoozing on the windowsill. "It'll save cooking."

She scooped up her two letters and the chocolate and left them on the doorsteps of Felicity and Nicky, ringing the doorbell briefly before hurrying away. She'd got far enough away into the gloom of the evening when the doors opened for neither woman to see her, and when she got to Mike and Jo's house, she realised she was shaking slightly. Part of her had been terrified of seeing either woman face to face, and she now realised she was scared of going to supper with people she'd scarcely exchanged two words with.

"Bugger this," she said to herself. "I've never been scared of anything before, and I don't intend to start now."

She rang the bell, hearing it inside the house, and after a moment the door was opened to her. To her enormous relief, it was Clifford.

"Thank God it's you," she said. "I wasn't sure I was in the right place. Your handwriting is very iffy and sometimes your numbers are smudgy."

"Oh shut up and come in out of the cold," Clifford said, pulling her inside and into his arms. "What did the boys at work think of the hair then?"

"Not certain, but I think they liked it. Not that it matters, anyway. I'm not sure I liked being seen as a sort of bimbo. Anyway, you'd better introduce me to your friends, since you're acting as butler for them."

Clifford led the way into the kitchen, though the lay-out of the house was identical to their own. Jo was standing at the fridge looking inside it with the air of an explorer on unfamiliar territory;

she glanced up as Chloe came in and then grinned with apparent relief.

"Is there anything I can do?" Clifford asked.

Jo handed him two cans of beer.

"Yes, take one of these for Mike and one for yourself and stay out of my way while I think what to cook," she said. "You want one, Chloe?"

She held out a can to Chloe and when Chloe nodded, she lobbed it across to her, very deft and sure of her aim.

"Careful when you open it; it'll fizz after that," she said and turned back to the fridge.

Chloe studied her carefully while she could stare without being obvious. Jo was much shorter than she was, with very shiny dark hair cut in a conventional bob. Chloe guessed she was a few years older than herself, and had an air on no-nonsense about her that Chloe found reassuring after all the flannel of other college wives. After a moment, Chloe decided to venture an opinion.

"I've got you down as a nurse," she said. "Am I right?"

"Nearly right; I'm a mid-wife, but damn good guess. Is it because I'm bossy?" Jo asked.

"Well, sort of. My Gran always said "assertive", rather than bossy. You also have something of the medical about you, but you don't seem quite as arrogant as doctors sometimes are," Chloe said, and then instinctively put her hands over her mouth as she realised her gaffe.

"Not quite as arrogant, mmm. Good way of putting it," Jo said. "You don't mess around, do you? Straight for the jugular. Sure you're not a barrister or something like that? No, you're a bit young for that."

She was looking at Chloe with a very straight face; then her mouth twitched at the corners and Chloe knew she was safe.

"I know what you mean about arrogant doctors, though," Jo went on. "I could slap some of them; you know, three minutes in a white coat and they think they're God."

"My Gran was a doctor; she was always saying arrogance was her greatest failing," Chloe said.

"Was it?"

"No, not really. I think most of that had been knocked out of her during her travels; some of her stories, well, she wasn't afraid of admitting when she'd made a god-awful hash of something."

"Clifford told Mike she died quite recently; you must miss her," Jo said, shutting the fridge door.

Chloe felt her eyes fill up with bitter tears, and bit them back as fast as she could, but still a few escaped, and dripped down her shirt.

"Sorry," she said. "Bit raw still; just ignore me."

Jo put her hands on her hips and glared at Chloe.

"No, I won't just ignore you," she said. "Come here, you silly thing."

She held Chloe very briefly in a tight hug and Chloe felt a surge of relief as Jo's sympathy flowed round her like a warm amber cloak. It felt like Gran, without the spikiness.

"There, now," Jo said briskly. "I could murder my husband, you know; we've got bugger all in the fridge and he expects me to do miracles with a slab of cheese, a few onions and bog-standard pasta."

"Look, you've given me beer and sympathy, I couldn't ask for more," Chloe said, rubbing her eyes. "Anyway, that sounds like the beginnings of macaroni cheese, which is as good as it gets on a weekday night, so let's get started. That's if you don't have any objections to sharing a kitchen. Some people do. That's fine. If you prefer, I'll just sit here with my beer and shout encouragement from the sidelines."

"No, you can chop some onions; it looks like your mascara is waterproof. Knives are in that drawer over there; chopping board over there," Jo said. "I'm not protective about my kitchen; my mother is, but I'm not and never have been. Oh, the onions are in the salad drawer in the fridge."

Chloe collected knife and board, and then went to the fridge. On the door, held in place by some magnets was a hand drawn calendar; it started with the first day of this term and ended on the last day of the summer term. The days that had already passed were marked off in emphatic strokes of red pen. She saw Jo looking at her, with raised eyebrows.

"It's my countdown," she explained. "Each time I cross off a day, it's one day closer to escape. It's just a small psychological thing. This is our last year here, and I'm going stir-crazy. Mike's got a curacy ready and waiting for him; we've just got to get through this year and then we're gone, free."

"Has it been that bad?" Chloe asked.

"No, not like that. Just a horrible disappointment really," Jo said. "I just want to get back to something like a normal life, if such a thing exists any more."

Chloe found the onions and started chopping them carefully, feeling her eyes prickling with acrid tears. Jo put a heavy frying pan on the stove and poured olive oil into it.

"Why was it a disappointment?" Chloe asked presently.

"Maybe I expected too much of it; I don't know. Perhaps it was because we'd sort of decided we'd start our family here; and then month after month, nothing. Or when there was something, it didn't stick around. Maybe we just had such high expectations of people too. I think we thought it'd be, well, a real community where people sort of get on and really support each other. And it isn't. Well, it hasn't been for us, anyway. Maybe if I'd had a baby it might have been different; the families seem to have it a bit better, or maybe that's just wishful thinking."

Jo filled a large pan with water and turned the heat up under it.

"I mean, they're always round each other's houses, swapping children. I'm often not sure which child belongs to whom. And every time I see a new baby here, I sort of grind my teeth. It's daft, because I don't feel like that at work, where there are new babies every day. Here it's somehow personal."

She went to the fridge and got a beer for herself.

"I think it's because at work I see the whole process of labour which does tend to reduce all women to the same level. Here, when they come in with a new baby, it's as if it's been dropped off by the stork, all clean and pink and none of the evidence of the grunt factor of labour. When I've delivered a baby for a woman, there's no way she ever tries to pretend it was easy. Oh, I'm not putting it very well, but it's as if they try to pretend that the baby just arrived direct from God on a special cloud. Maybe I'm just being over sensitive. Anyway, I can hardly wait to get out of here; Mike's started humming the theme tune from The Great Escape, but for me it feels more like Porridge. Josephine Alicia Fletcher, you have been found guilty of wanting to do what God wants and have been sentenced to two years imprisonment for your presumption. You are a hardened criminal and regard imprisonment as an occupational hazard... You get the drift."

Chloe snorted with laughter.

"I shouldn't really be so negative, especially as you're at the start of your time. What did you get, three years?"

"Three years, no time off for good behaviour," Chloe said. "Which is just as well, considering. I just hope they can't add any time on for bad behaviour, or we'll die here of old age just on the strength of how I've already upset people."

"Don't sweat it if it's Nicky," Jo said. "She's over-sensitive anyway. And I'll tell you something else that'll make you laugh. They've been trying for a new baby for a few months now, ever since she stopped breastfeeding. But she's so focussed on it it's got ridiculous; apparently she's got one of those ovulation kits, and whenever she's ovulating, she phones him on his mobile. Well, it went off in a lecture the other day, and he said he had a family crisis and had to go. Mike was going past their house when he got back, at a run. The bedroom curtains were yanked shut the second he got in. But the funniest bit is he was back in the lecture less than twenty minutes later. I nearly wet myself over that one. If you're trying for a baby it should at least be fun."

"I doubt she knows the meaning of the word," Chloe said, gloomily.

"Yeah, but I bet you do," Jo said, tipping pasta into the hot water. "Another beer?"

"Now you're talking."

They carried on cooking; Chloe felt strangely as if she'd known Jo for years, rather than minutes.

"I don't seem to be able to get on with people here," she said, after a few minutes where she concentrated on browning onions.

"You seem to be getting on with me," Jo said.

"Yeah but you seem human. I just seem to get nervous and say quite the wrong thing, and then there's this horrible silence," Chloe said.

"You mean like at dinner the other night? I was on the table next to yours, so I heard most of it. What you don't realise is the impression you seem to making on everyone even before you speak."

"What do you mean?"

"Well, and I don't mean to embarrass you, but you are very noticeable. Your hair is amazing for starters; totally pre-Raphaelite," Jo said.

"Pre-Raphaelite on acid, you mean," Chloe said, which was what her boss had said that morning.

Jo chortled.

"Yeah. And you're very alive and vibrant, and everybody looks at you. You don't have bags under your eyes and baby sick on your collar; you've got make-up on and a bit of perfume, and you look like you're ready for action. Can't you see how that makes some of the wives feel? Especially when their husbands are looking at you. It's just good old-fashioned jealousy that sours it for you," she explained.

"Jealous? Of me? Hell's bells, that's absurd!" Chloe said, horrified.

"That's a lot of it, I reckon. Of course, the F-word won't have helped. That just adds anarchy into the equation; if you can say that, what else might you do? They're scared witless of someone like you; you're not bound by the same conventions they've done a bondage job on themselves with. What puzzles me is how you've got here at all; our director of ordinands was dead funny about wives who didn't play the right games."

"Clifford's chap didn't seem very interested in me at all, to be honest. He seemed to think if I was OK with Clifford going for ordination, the rest would be fine," Chloe said. "I've not spent much time with Christians, to be honest. While we were at university, I hung around the edges of the Christian Union and the Anglican Chaplaincy, but I never got really involved. I don't really know why I spent any time with them; it wasn't even as if they had the best parties. But there was something there, I guess. It was in our final year that Clifford and I really connected. I'd sort of known him, the way you do with people you share a social circle with, but after one party he just suddenly offered to walk me home. Well, it was about four in the morning, so I thought, yeah, why not? The rest, as they say, is history."

"Sometimes people do things that make you see them differently," Jo said.

"That's just it. I hadn't really seen him at all, not really. Once I really saw him, really saw him, it was like, wow, how did I miss that? Everything looked utterly different by the time we got back to my bed-sit," Chloe said, remembering how strange she'd felt that what she'd thought an impossible fiction had happened to her, had happened so hard and so fast she was practically breathless with it.

"So we got engaged," she said.

"What, that night?"

"Well, it was morning by then, virtually. But yes, right then, we decided. I know how daft it sounds but it was the clearest thing I'd ever seen, ever known. It couldn't have been clearer if it had been written across the sky in letters ten feet high. We weren't totally mad, because that was, what, four years ago, and we got married in the summer, so there was plenty of time for minds to be changed and all that sort of thing."

"How romantic!" Jo said, sounding faintly envious. "We were in the same sixth form, started going out just before A levels, got married about three years later. Mike hardly has a romantic or impulsive bone in his body, but that's fine. I don't enjoy surprises, not that sort anyway. I like things steady and sensible."

"So did I. I thought my grandmother would go ballistic with me, but she didn't. She just said something about following my heart and then went off into the garden and started weeding one of the borders. I was a bit shocked at her lack of reaction. I'd thought I'd known her."

"She sounds like a real character," Jo remarked.

"She was an old cow sometimes; opinionated, stubborn tough old dragon who broke just about all the rules at some time in her life. I only found out the other day that my father was illegitimate."

"She sounds amazing," Jo said.

Chloe felt her eyes mist over with tears that had nothing to do with onions.

"She was; I miss her so much," she said, cross with herself for getting upset again.

"Not an easy role model to live up to though, I guess," Jo suggested.

"Christ, no. When I was a kid, I sometimes used to wish she had been one of those little white haired grannies who knitted hats and made chocolate cake and were harmless and inoffensive. She didn't take any crap, not from teachers, not from anyone. She had this weird friendship with our local MP who used to visit Gran regularly; Gran usually reduced her to tears of either laughter or frustration. I was never quite sure why she kept coming back, because Gran was never pleasant to her. I think in the end it was the one place she could go where she'd always hear the truth, no matter how unpleasant or unpalatable. There were always people visiting Gran for one reason or another, really strange people sometimes. She had a lot of friends among the travelling community and you know how they are about outsiders," Chloe said and sighed.

"What happened to your parents, then?" Jo asked.

"My mother walked out in front of a car when I was about two," Chloe said. "Dad tried to cope for a while, and then he wrote to my Gran asking her to come back. She'd headed off into the blue when my parents married; she just used to get a job in a hospital somewhere exotic and deprived and stay there as long as she felt like it. Then she'd send back a crate of stuff she'd accumulated and a new address would follow a few months later, often halfway across the world from where she'd been before. She criss-crossed the world like that. I'm pretty sure she was somewhere in India when my father's letter reached her, because the day she got to our house was the first time I met her, and I remembered all the scents she seemed to carry with her. As I got older I identified them all, curry and saffron and sandalwood and things like that. She never travelled again, not beyond Europe anyway. She got a job with the local GP practice, even though she was close to retirement age. She and Dad didn't get on though, and he left about a year later."

Chloe shut her eyes, thinking of the slamming doors and the raised voices and her own small self huddled under the bedclothes, uncomprehending.

"That's sad," Jo said neutrally. "Did you not see him again?"

"I must have done, I suppose, but I don't remember. My sister left about a year later; I haven't seen her either since then. But apparently they used to write to Gran; she left me a packet of their letters to look at so I can maybe track them both down. I don't know whether I will or not. I guess if I've done without them this long, I don't really need them at all." Chloe rubbed her eyes again.

"I would," Jo said. "Because when you had your grandmother, maybe you didn't need them. But she's gone now, so I think maybe you do need them now. Anyway, that's my pennyworth, take it or leave it. Now, are you any good at cheese sauce?"

"As long as you grate the cheese for me; I always end up grating my knuckles as well," Chloe said.

"Ah well, extra protein," Jo said, grinning. "Yeah, I'll grate for you. My sauce always ends up lumpy."

"Do you have any mustard powder?" Chloe asked, looking at the lump of mild cheddar. "It really adds a bit of bite to a bland cheese."

"Never thought of that," Jo said.

"One of my Gran's little tips," Chloe said, smiling at the memory. "I had the most highly-spiced childhood you can imagine. My school friends were scared of coming home for tea with me in case Gran did them curry. She never did, not till I was in my teens and my friends would really love it. They were all a bit scared of her, but that didn't make any difference to her, or to them for that matter. There's more than one kind of spice to life after all."

"I bet your house is a real treasure house of her mementos," Jo said.

"I've put the more exotic ones in the loft; even I can't look Priapus in the eye sober," Chloe said. "Look, you'll have to come over to ours for a rematch soon."

"I'd like that," Jo said, watching Chloe make the cheese sauce. "It's a pity you didn't arrive when we did; we'd have had a bit more fun last year."

Chloe thought about this.

"Nah," she said. "You'd have been sick of me by now if we had been here last year as well. But I could really do with help now. I don't seem to know how to stay out of the bad books and I don't really want to spend three years in the naughty corner."

"No worries," Jo said. "Mind you, I'm not the best example myself. But at least I've had a year to make my own mistakes."

"Such as?" Chloe asked curiously.

"Well, for starters, not realising that the prayer notice board outside chapel is actually a gossip hotline. I naively assumed it was what it's supposed to be and on a particularly awful day when I'd delivered a still-born child, I put up the names of the family on the board, so that people could pray for them. Three hours later I was caught up in this god-awful row about whether it was OK to pray for the dead. I mean the theology was lost on me, but the whole thing had gone round all the wives in college practically, back to the husbands and even the staff, and then came bouncing back on me for posting the request in the first place. Daft really as all I'd asked was for people to pray for the family; I didn't even go into the whole thing about praying for the soul of the dead child, I sort of took it as read I suppose," Jo explained taking a swig of her beer. "The other big mistake was getting at all friendly with Nicky. I got that one really wrong. She was crying after chapel one night after

76

the introductory weekend, so being a softie, I went over to see what was wrong. I've been trying to ditch her ever since."

"What was wrong, anyway?"

"Not a lot, actually. She makes a lot of capital about anything; looking for attention, I think. But being nice to her meant I still get her coming round here with the kids at least twice a week and short of telling her to sod off, I can't do anything about it."

"Why don't you just do that anyway?"

"I don't have your courage, Chloe. The fallout from that would be worse than sitting through half an hour of coffee and chat," Jo said.

"Yeah, but those half hours add up. I mean, you don't have to be rude, just firm. Say you're a bit busy, even if you aren't. If you don't want her there, you shouldn't have to put up with it," Chloe said.

Jo looked rather sad.

"I feel sorry for her, that's the bottom line," she said. "It's not just a question of her simply being an attention seeker. She's in real need of help of some sort. Let's face it, most of us wives who come here feel at first as if we've had both our arms ripped off. I mean, where we were before, we were the premier church couple; we did everything together, we were important. OK, big fishes in a small pond if you like, but we were both valued for what we did, for who we were. Here, it isn't even a case of playing second fiddle to our husbands; we're not even in the orchestra. That's why Nicky behaves as she does; she's had just about everything that was important to her taken away by moving here, so all she's left with is the kids. So it isn't surprising she's a pain in the bum. And she isn't the only one. Change the face and you've got half the wives here, in one way or another. Even me, though I get to go out to work and stay the same in some way."

"You're not like Nicky," Chloe said slowly.

"Oh, I am. I'm not as annoying or as stupid, but essentially I am the same. And so are you, whether you like it or not. You've come here because of your husband, not for yourself, and that means in that one particular way you are the same as Nicky."

Chloe digested this silently, feeling it churn and turn her stomach.

"No way, no how," she said after a moment. "OK, I came here for Clifford, but nothing else. I'm not here to join in this communal love-in, or play any of their games, or have babies or prayer groups that probably don't pray, and turn myself into the perfect clergy wife. I'll shoot myself rather than that. I'm me; that's all, nothing else. I came here because I love my husband. I didn't bank on anything else."

"None of us did," Jo said softly. "It took me by surprise, you know. It sits over there, the college, with all of us running round like a load of worker ants, and the same thing happens to all of us. Look, I don't like it either, but we all have to make of this what we can. I just plan to get through as best I can, and not get sucked in. I'm sure you're the same."

Chloe felt her face redden with the effort of not getting angry.

"Sauce is about ready," she said. "Look, I hear what you're saying. But why should any of us put up with it? Why can't we just ignore it, take no notice of it? That's what I've been doing."

"Up till now, yes. But none of us can be alone, not for long. You know, no man is an island, all that crap? It's true. You look around us here; this is our peer group. All of us have this one thing in common that no one else in our old churches can ever share; like being an army wife or something. It's another life and no one warned me what it might be like; there's a good reason. Except for other clergy wives, no one knows how different it is."

"What about clergy husbands?"

"So far, it doesn't seem to be an issue. Well, that's to say I've not yet had an in depth conversation with the husband of one of the women ordinands. But it is different for them; usually they have careers of their own by this sort of age. For us women, this is usually the age we start our families, and whatever that car sticker on Nicky's car says about mothering being a profession, it isn't. It's an interlude. That pasta looks ready to drain; shall I do that?"

Jo hauled the pan off the stove and drained the pasta into the sink, the kitchen filling up with steam as she did so.

"I don't know why they didn't put an extractor fan into this place; we really need one," she said, pushing open the window to let the steam out.

She glanced at Chloe.

"You look upset," she said. "Sorry; this is far too heavy a subject."

"No, it isn't. And yes, I am upset. But not with you; with myself. My Gran said I was being naïve to assume Clifford's vocation wouldn't affect me in anything other than geography; I think she was right. But I don't want to just lie down under this; I don't see why we can't change it, alter it onto something less appalling. There's a poem about St Margaret Clitheroe; she was pressed to death, you know. Stretched out with a door placed on her and then rocks piled on top till she had the life squashed out of her. There's a bit I like:

"Fawning fawning crocodiles
Days and days came round about
 With tears to put her candle out;
They wound their winch of wicked smiles
 To take her;"

That's what it feels like to me; surrounded with people who are always saying give in, knuckle under, fit it. I say no! Not that. I'll be me and nothing else."

Chloe felt the tears creeping from under her eyelids, full of bitter anger at incomprehensible injustice.

Jo stared at her, then tipped the sauce into the pan with the drained pasta.

"You do feel strongly," she said neutrally, and scraped the whole mass of pasta into a baking dish and put it in the oven. "Half an hour should do for that. Look, I'm not suggesting that you should ever be anything but yourself, but it may be more comfortable to acquire a certain patina of compromise."

Chloe shrugged.

"Do you not think it can be changed then?" she said.

"No; not by one woman alone anyway. You've got all the Nickys and Felicitys to fight against, and contrary to how it may appear, they're bloody tough and devoted to maintaining the status quo, more so as they've sacrificed themselves for it. There's nothing more savage that that. We'll be gone in seven months or so; I can't help much in that time, and then you'll be on your own again," Jo said. "Maybe your best bet is just to ignore it as much as possible, and get on with your own life?"

"Maybe," Chloe said cautiously, and then thought, or maybe I'll just try guerilla warfare instead. She had a sudden mental image of herself in camouflage gear, her face blacked out, creeping through the college grounds carrying a bag of subversive poetry, and she grinned.

"What's so funny?" Jo asked.

"Nothing," Chloe said, and finished her beer.

Chapter 7

Winter closed around Chloe like a cloak of dark cloth, cutting her off from the outside world in a way she would never have guessed possible. The first few days after her contract expired Chloe slept late, relishing the opportunity previously denied her of waking without an alarm to wake her, but after those few days were through, she found herself waking at six or earlier, wide awake and unable to slip back to sleep. As the weather became colder and wetter, she found herself stuck at home when she would previously have been out and busy regardless of the weather. She also found herself gazing out of the living room window at the college buildings, as if waiting for an animal to make a move.

She spent time job-hunting both on-line and through the papers, but while she was short listed and even called up for interview, the ultimate goal was elusive. She began to panic, thinking of this gap on her employment record and all that such an abyss might end up saying to potential employers, and she ground her teeth and made herself do something, anything rather than dwell on that.

As the year wheeled round to Christmas and the college term ended, she mentally ticked it off, much the way Jo had been counting off days on her calendar. One term done, eight more to go. Put that way it didn't sound so bad; one ninth completed. But it felt terrible, to have Christmas without her grandmother. One evening, as she returned home from her run, she saw the twinkling of fairy lights through open curtains in the houses she passed, and found herself blinking back tears of hopeless nostalgia.

The house was warm when she got in, her face chilled from the night but her blood hot from running, and while she showered, she washed away the traces of tears but the pain of memory remained, sweet and sore, in the centre of her chest.

Clifford came into the bathroom while she was drying herself.

"Good run?" he asked.

"Same as usual, maybe a bit faster. Don't know," she said. "I'll have to go morning as well, if I don't get work soon. All I seem to do is hang around snacking or baking more stuff to snack on. I'd turn into a blimp if I were a housewife for real."

"What do you want to do for Christmas?" he asked.

It wasn't unexpected, not really. She'd overheard him on the phone to his family, countering their requests for his attendance at the family home for Christmas, putting off a decision as long as he could, but she'd known he would ask her eventually.

"I don't know," she said slowly. "I know your family want us to come for Christmas, but I'm not sure that's what I want. But I'll go if it's what you want."

"I don't, not really," he said. "I don't think it's a good idea. You know what you and my mum are like; that on top of the usual stupidity of Christmas is just explosive. Tell you what, we could go for Christmas day itself and come home here that night. I think you could put up with Mum for one day, couldn't you?"

Chloe looked up from rubbing body lotion into her legs.

"Yes, I suppose so," she said, reluctantly. "Anyway, in future years, it isn't going to be an issue, is it? I mean, you're going to be working Christmas day from then on, so they can't ever expect you to be there for Christmas. So I suppose we should give your family these last few, shouldn't we?"

"You make it sound like a death sentence," he said, amused, and Chloe laughed, but rather mirthlessly.

"No, more of a life sentence," she said. "No, it isn't a problem, actually. Christmas is hopelessly over-rated, and I'd rather your mother cremated the turkey rather than doing it myself."

"I'll ring her, then and let her know," he said. "She's been on my case for weeks trying to get me to decide. You know, I would have loved to have gone to your Gran's for Christmas this year. It always seemed so exotic when I visited other years at that time."

Chloe smiled, remembering the smell of spices and baking and the colours and the mad round of visitors and the music always playing somewhere in the house.

"Yeah," she said. "Everything but the camels."

"She did know how to have a good party," he said, and saw the tears behind Chloe's smile.

"Well, that particular party is well and truly over," Chloe said, picking up her dressing gown. "Shame, but there you go. Nothing lasts forever, not even turkey and Christmas cake. Tell you what, first Christmas we have after this place, we'll do it properly."

"What, even camels?"

"Like I said, everything but the camels. All the spices and cake and booze and music and candles. But this year, we'll go to your family and enjoy that instead. At the very least I won't have to cook. And your mum's OK as long as I don't get drunk."

"She finds you the biggest puzzle since the Rubik's cube," Clifford said. "She couldn't cope with your Gran either, but at least she could be seen as a charmingly eccentric old lady."

"OK, go and ring her and say we'll come. I'll drive and then there's no chance of me getting silly with drink and upsetting them all again," Chloe said, knotting the belt of the dressing gown. "I'll go and get dressed and then we can have some supper."

As she dressed, she could hear him talking to his mother on the phone, and she bit down again on her memories as they welled up to drown her. She could almost hear the babble of voices at her Gran's house, most evenings in the week before Christmas, people talking, singing, laughing, filling the house with sound and life and the chink of glasses. She shook herself and stuck her feet into slippers. What's gone is gone and can't come back, she told herself fiercely.

*

They drove home tired and subdued, so late on Christmas night that it was virtually Boxing Day. Chloe was pensive but smug; she had behaved impeccably, had avoided all confrontation, all controversy, actually all conversation but the most meaningless and banal. She also felt horribly cheated, and probably one of the few people not actually derelict who was actually hungry. Clifford's family had a fear of anything exotic, so the cooking had been good but bland to the point Chloe had found it virtually inedible. She'd seen the rack of herbs and spices in Nadine's pantry; the contents of all the jars were a variety of shades of grey, even the paprika had faded to a shade of rusty grey. She'd wanted to ask, well why have them at all if you don't use them but she knew the answer already: every kitchen should have a spice rack, it's part of the décor. So as a result of a dinner where the most exotic item was cranberry sauce, from Harrod's, Chloe was aware of a rumble in the pit of her stomach and a craving for something fiery that would make her throat tingle.

When they got home, Chloe found a can of mulligatawny soup that had come from Gran's pantry, and they had that for a supper so late it should have been breakfast, dipping olive bread into the hot orangey mess, and then ate slices of Chloe's own Christmas cake, full of cinnamon and allspice.

"Is it worth going to bed at all?" Chloe said, mopping up cake crumbs with a slice of Wensleydale cheese.

The sky was still dark blue and the dawn, as such, was hours away; still the feeling of morning surrounded then.

"I think I'm jet-lagged," Clifford said, yawning. "I'm knackered, but I'm wide-awake. Shall we go for a walk?"

"Yes. Tell you what; shall we ring on all the doorbells as we leave the grounds? I've been so bloody good today, sorry, yesterday, that I feel like being absolutely wicked just to redress the balance," Chloe said, wiping her fingers on her handkerchief.

"No, let's just walk. No point in ruining someone else's day," Clifford said, and got up. "You hated it, didn't you? I can tell when you're trying to be nice and polite, but I know you had a horrible day."

Chloe sighed. She'd never failed to be surprised how different he was from the rest of his family, how wide his horizons were by comparison, how open his mind was and how hard he had to try to get on with them.

"Yes," she said finally. "It was like life without the colour switched on. Maybe I've been spoiled by life with Gran, but I didn't enjoy it at all. Give me glorious Technicolor every time."

He ruffled her hair fondly; in the artificial light it seemed blood red rather than its usual hot copper colour.

"Still, it's over now," he said. "No need to do it again for another three hundred and sixty four days."

"Get your boots on, and we'll go and see the dawn," Chloe said, pulling herself to her feet.

Dawn was a damp listless business; there was no one moment when they could have said that the sun peeped over the horizon, because the sun remained anonymous behind clouds so thick with rain that it was Clifford's watch that told them it was really morning. Returning to the house, Chloe saw the tiny green points pushing through grass and wet soil, barely above ground yet so full of promise that even this grey morning seemed like a midwinter spring.

January was a muddled mix of sodden mornings and freezing nights, and a growing irritation with the lives that circled around hers. What the other wives did and said should not have mattered to her, should not have even been of the slightest interest to her, but in the cold damp days she found herself becoming alarmingly obsessed with them. She caught herself standing at the living room window watching them come and go, pushing buggies and leading toddlers along, or driving past with edgy care, and it was all she could do to stop her lip curling with contempt.

"God lighten your dark heart, Margaret Clitheroe," she said to herself, making herself move away from the window and focus on something else.

But within an hour she had drifted back to the window.

Why do I hate them so much when I don't even know them, when they're just getting on with their lives and not really bothering me, she asked herself over and over again, each time she caught that contemptuous curl of her lip twitching the corner of her mouth. But she knew the answer, even if she wouldn't say it, knew it each time their glance flashed her way, seeing her figure in the window, or on the path or in the garden; the way they looked her up and down, the gaze lingering on her lower abdomen, then flashing back to her face and silent question marks showing in the eyes, and then that funny little smile. They think they're better than me; that they're the special ones, that I'm nothing and nobody without them, without their little groups and cliques.

Chloe watched the tiny green points just as obsessively, sometimes checking twice a day to see if they had grown any more, taking a hand fork to clear away the fine green shoots of self-sown grass from around the emerging bulbs. The first snowdrop to show its white face made her ecstatically happy, sitting on the front path smiling insanely for this one precocious flower that had dared the frost and stormy winds to bloom alone. More snowdrops, waxy white and fragile, bloomed in defiance of the weather, fine pearls in the dusk shining against the night and the cold. Crocuses followed, flames of purple and gold and cream, not as brave as the snowdrops but valiant still in the damp days of February when Chloe stepped into the car to drive to yet another interview. She caught a whiff of sweet wet earth, that green smell that is a precursor to spring, and the cold that is still to come is somehow not as overwhelming as before Christmas.

"Things have turned," she said aloud, and turned the key in the ignition.

She was far too early, having allowed enough time for traffic jams and delays that didn't happen, so she parked the car and went off in search of a coffee shop rather than the coffee offered her by the PA who she'd reported in to when she had parked. She didn't want to be observed when she was this nervous. The company headquarters were only a short distance away from the main shopping area of the city, so she walked briskly away, her city map in hand.

She didn't get far.

She stopped to glance at her map, and then forgot entirely about coffee. On the other side of the busy road a young man had cannoned into a smartly dressed woman, knocking her off balance long enough to snatch away her handbag, and then shoved her over as he hurtled away. Two seconds later, two men, big men at that, tried to bar his escape, and he swung round and flung himself across the road to get away from their attempts to grab and stop him.

Chloe watched as the day went into slow motion as the thief dodged traffic frantically, and as he tried to cross the lane nearest her, ran out of luck. She watched as a red car going too fast to stop, tried to stop. She watched as it ploughed straight into the thief, flinging him up like so many old clothes stuffed with straw, flinging him up in the air and away, spinning in reluctant flight and landing hard and rolling over and over and over till he lay at her feet. Then time started again.

He was very young, not twenty even, she reckoned. Around them horns blared; someone was screaming. The thief moaned and opened his eyes; hazel eyes, nearly green but not quite. There was blood on his face, slipping from his nose and mouth in sluggish trails. Chloe knelt down on the wet pavement.

"Don't try to move," she said. "Someone will call an ambulance."

He reached out a hand towards her, and she took it, grubby and cold as it was.

"It's so cold," he said.

Chloe wrenched off her jacket and put it over him.

"It's always cold in February," she said. "Next time you get run over, try to choose August."

He tried to laugh, but ended up coughing. It sounded horrible; she wasn't sure whether this was from the accident or whether he had a cough anyway.

Chloe was aware of the crowd gathering around them.

"Has someone called an ambulance?" she asked, without looking round.

Someone answered yes.

"Good; did you hear that? There's help coming, so just hang on in there," Chloe said to the thief.

He squeezed her hand weakly.

"It's so cold," he said again. "I can't feel my legs."

"It's the shock," Chloe said. "They're still there, believe me. Your jeans will never be quite the same, though."

She couldn't look at the twisted legs; she made herself focus on his face instead. He was very pale now, skin paper white against the red of his own blood.

"It's dark too," he said.

"Typical winter day, the sun's too lazy to get up," she said, but she knew that wasn't what he meant.

She sat with him, trying to keep him talking, keep him conscious, making him laugh even, waiting for the sound of sirens. A dull drizzle started, the rain feeling like fine needles in the cold air, and Chloe felt colder and colder as she sat on the wet concrete holding the hand of a bag-snatcher.

As she heard the first wails of a siren, he seemed to be drifting away from her.

"It's getting dark," he said.

It was ten o'clock in the morning, and while the mass of rain clouds meant it was dull, nightfall was a long way off.

"Hang on, the ambulance is coming," Chloe said. "Don't go to sleep; just think of all those nurses."

He smiled at her; a child's wide trusting smile at odds with what his life must have been. Then his eyes seemed to fill with light as if the sun had suddenly emerged from behind the smothering of rain-clouds and was reflected in his peat-coloured eyes.

Chloe heard the ambulance pulling up behind her and knew it was too late, feeling the life go from the grubby hand she held, and seeing the light fade from those eyes that didn't close.

*

When Chloe got home that afternoon, Clifford was home, taking a break from his studies, sitting with his feet up on the coffee table, Chainsaw asleep on his lap. He looked up when she walked in, then got up abruptly when he saw the blood stains on her clothes and her white face.

"What happened?" he asked, taking her into his arms. "Are you all right?"

"It's not my blood," she said, shrugging off the jacket. "I think this suit's ruined, though. There was a traffic accident; I had to hold the hand of the victim, largely because he landed at my feet when the car hit him. Talk about being in the wrong place at the wrong time."

"Was he all right?"

Chloe shook her head.

"He died just as the ambulance got to him; I've never seen anything like it, it was so strange," she said, still seeing that smile and the light of an invisible sun reflected in dying eyes. "I could murder a cup of tea, though."

Clifford went through to the kitchen to put the kettle on, and Chloe followed him.

"How was the interview?" he asked.

"Dire; I was late for a start, and I was in a real mess, so I think that one's a non-starter," she said, opening the biscuit tin and cramming two chocolate creams into her mouth. She hadn't eaten all day and she was feeling wobbly with low blood sugar and delayed shock.

"Didn't you tell them what had happened?"

"Well, obviously, but I don't think it meant very much. I mean, the kid who died was just a bag-snatcher. Beyond the immediate shock, I don't think anyone would understand why I was upset," Chloe said, remembering, her face scarlet with shame, how she had burst into tears during the interview. Well, that was that one buggered. They'd never employ a woman who didn't manage to keep her emotions under control.

Clifford made tea, tipping a slug of brandy into Chloe's without asking. She just looked at him silently, her mind still seeing those eyes.

"There's a dance at college for Valentine's Day," he said after a while. "Do you fancy going? Mike and Jo are going and they wanted to see if we'd join them. It might be fun; you like a good barn dance."

Chloe squinted up at him from the hearthrug where she was huddled next to the fire trying to get warm. She was feeling very odd; the brandy was going straight to her head and she was trembling continuously.

"Why not? Might as well do something; I guess it might be fun for an hour or two," she said recklessly. "Got to live a little; never know when you're going to die."

Clifford looked at her, worried.

"Don't worry," she said. "Couple of hours and I'll be fine again. It was just rather awful, as days go. Not the sort of thing you expect."

"Always expect the unexpected," he said, jokingly.

"I always thought that was a stupid thing to say. It's as bad as saying it'll be in the last place you look for it. Well, duh! As though I'd go on looking after I've found what I'm looking for. But this was beyond the normal realm of what might happen. What I can't quite get over is: where did he go?"

"What do you mean?"

"Well, one minute he was there, in that body, looking back at me. The next, he was gone. Where did he go? What actually happened? What is it that is life anyway? Weird. Really weird."

"Perhaps you're the one who should be studying theology, not me," he said.

Chloe snorted with laughter.

"Can't see it somehow. Anyway, they don't have answers to that sort of question, do they? They're still Mysteries, in the old sense of the world. Gran used to talk about it sometimes, but I never quite caught what she was on about till today. Not even when I saw her in her coffin, her and yet not her at all. Look, I'm going to have a shower and try and get warm. If you want to go to this dance, buy the tickets. It might be fun, but if it isn't we just come back home."

She hauled herself off the rug and headed upstairs, shedding clothes erratically as she did so. Clifford picked up her skirt and looked at the mud and bloodstains. She was probably right; this suit was ruined but maybe a good dry cleaner could save it. As he thought about that, he realised she would never wear it again anyway, not with those memories embedded in the cloth even when the stains were washed away, so he bundled the suit up and shoved it into the bin, feeling some of Chloe's questions seep into his own mind so that when he tried to settle to sleep that night he would still hear her asking, where did he go, what actually happened, what is life anyway?

As big questions go, these were probably enough to be going on with for now.

Chapter 8

The Valentine's Day barn dance was an event Chloe would have trouble forgetting about, even though she would really want to annihilate it from her memory.

The morning brought a huge surprise, something she truly didn't expect. The company who had interviewed her on the day of the accident actually decided on the strength of that interview to offer her the job. She found herself hyperventilating as she read the letter. It turned out that in that crowd of bystanders had been one of the interview panel, who had watched her stay with the dying man till the paramedics trying to revive him said simply it was over. He had been so profoundly impressed with her strength of character that meant she had kept going talking and comforting the dying boy, and only breaking down with very natural shock and emotion when it was all over. They had not thought her a silly, weak woman at all for crying after the interviewer told them afterwards what he had witnessed. Yes, they had given her a tough interview, but she had given the right answers even if she was still in a state of shock, so on the basis of that, they would very much like her to come and join them.

Chloe felt the fizz and pop of joy surge through her, and she punched the air in the classic gesture of triumph.

The day just went downhill from there.

For most of the day she flitted from task to task, slightly dazed by relief that she was no longer unemployed, or wouldn't be for much longer. It was just as well none of the tasks really required much concentration and she was able to rely on her automatic pilot to get her through things, even if she came close to scorching her silk dress when she ironed it. She got ready with unusual care, as if pampering herself as a reward for nabbing that job against the odds, and she knew, really knew, she looked a complete knock-out. Clifford looked at her, as she glowed with health and newly-restored good spirits, and felt the knot of concern loosen that had lurked unrecognised under his heart.

"Let's go," she said, dabbing sandalwood perfume at her wrists and rubbing some through her hair. "I feel like dancing the night away."

Her first surprise was that there were loads of children around, all dressed in their best and wildly over excited, running everywhere squealing and giggling. She'd assumed, quite reasonably, that this was an adult event; she didn't think hordes of under-fives were exactly conducive to romance. Apparently this was not a view shared by the majority of college families. When they found Mike and Jo, she raised the subject but Jo just waved her hands hopelessly around her.

"I know, I know," she said wearily. "I thought it's be a kiddie-free evening too. I mean, Valentine's Day? How weird can this be? I can't imagine anyone getting their leg-over tonight, with their brats keyed up to atomic overload. I am reliably informed that when they did this dance in previous years with the adult only theme, they could never sell enough tickets to make a go of it, because whether people couldn't find babysitters or whether they couldn't bear to be parted from their off-spring for the evening, the whole thing was likely to flop if they didn't throw it open to families. So here we are in Munchkin-land again. Still the buffet looks relatively sophisticated; we're not getting Billy Bear sandwich ham and chicken nuggets. And they've not banned booze; just made sure it's guarded at all times. So just try not to tread on anyone's baby, Chloe, and we'll have as good an evening as we can."

"We've paid for it after all," Clifford said, wincing as a small child nearby began to shriek loudly enough to melt earwax.

The dining room had been rearranged so that the tables, which were normally set in institutional rows, were now set in informal little groups all at an angle to the others so that it looked a bit like a restaurant. Someone had taken the risk of putting neat little candle lamps on the tables with flickering night-lights; the lamps were pink or red so the light should have been delicately tinged with soft colour, but the main lights had been left defiantly on, spoiling the effect. When Chloe went and turned them out, they were turned back on again within a minute; she had a brief tussle with one of the organisers, one turning lights on, the other turning them back off till they finally realised who was doing it, and Chloe was told firmly that the lights had to remain on for safety reasons. There were too many small children around for it to be safe to be stumbling around by candlelight, she was told, and went back to her group swearing under her breath.

"Good job I wasn't looking to pull tonight," she muttered as she sat down again, and glared across as the Principal tried to get the attention of the room enough to say Grace.

"Funny how they can control the kids for the God bit," she whispered to Jo, as they watched children lassoed by maternal arms and made to stand still and (relatively) quiet while the blessing was said.

"I'm starving," she said as they got up to go to the buffet tables. "I've hardly eaten today; I could eat a horse."

The food was good and surprisingly imaginative, with snippets of ethnic-style food, like samosas and satay chicken and onion bhajis as well as the usual sausage rolls and vol-au-vents. There were some cold ribs in a wonderfully rich and spicy barbecue sauce, and a big bowl of couscous filled with seeds and smelling of coriander and lemon. Chloe took her plate back to the table, sure everyone else could hear her stomach growling like an agitated dog. Clifford came back with a can of lager for each of them.

"Apparently we're rationed," he said. "And under penance of death, we're not to leave our drinks unattended at any moment."

Chloe just shrugged and raised her eyebrows expressively.

"Thought-police get some teeth," she said, indistinctly, her mouth full of spring roll. "We're all adults here, why are they counting our cans?"

She shook her head, bemused.

"I mean, if we were supposed to be teetotal, wouldn't Jesus have turned water into carrot juice or Earl Grey tea or something," she said, unaware her voice was carrying over the hubbub to the nearest tables.

"I would have thought so; but I guess it's because this has become a family event they're scared of littlies getting ill finishing cans of beer and glasses of wine," Mike said.

"I suppose so," Chloe said. "But if parents kept a closer eye on where their kids are, perhaps it wouldn't be such a problem, as well as maybe teaching them never to drink something they just find."

She enjoyed her food, though, getting a big jug of fruit squash for them all to share when their allotted beer ran out. She held out her empty can in a wide armed gesture, holding it upside down and letting the last drops trickle out.

"Where's Jesus when you need him?" she asked, and the others laughed.

"This ain't the Wedding at Cana," Jo said.

"They'd never have got as far as a wedding if they'd come here first," Chloe said. "Poor St. Valentine, he'll be turning in his grave, if he had one."

"I know, it's hardly romantic," Jo said, sympathetically. "But then, I guess romance is maybe the last thing the college wants to encourage. I mean, all these couples already together. They wouldn't want to have anyone ending up shuffling the pack."

"Never thought of that," Chloe said. "But what about the single students? This isn't exactly good for them, watching all the smug couples and families."

"I gather the singles are having a party of their own for that reason, later on," Mike said.

"Good; wish we were invited," Chloe said. "But then that'd ruin their party, more smug couples."

Dessert was quickly dispatched. Chloe noticed an increase in the number of children at the buffet table when the kitchen staff brought out the array of cakes and sticky puddings; they had been desultory about the savouries on offer but were making up for earlier lack of appetite. She had a brief image of locusts, then smiled and ate her own portion of Death by Chocolate with as much delight as any three year old.

They were sitting hoping for coffee when Chloe noticed that the woman at the next table was whispering to her little girl and pointing at Chloe. As she noticed that, she suddenly went rather cold as if a draught had played on the back of her neck. The child, an angelic if smeary individual with blonde curls and wide blue eyes, came toddling over, making directly for Chloe, who was suddenly close to panicking.

The little girl was probably about two and a half or three years old, and as well as wearing a lot of chocolate around her mouth had both hands caked with the same gooey mess, and she came up to Chloe with such a big beaming smile, her tiny teeth brown with cake, that Chloe had to grin back at her. Then the child reached for Chloe and put the chocolate covered hands on Chloe's lap and wiped them on the brilliant blue silk of the dress.

Chloe went cold all over, her grin nailed in place, trying to control her emotions. It's not the kid's fault; I saw the mum whispering to her, I bet I know what this is about, Chloe thought frantically. Sod it; it's only a dress.

Her own smile still as radiant as the child's was chocolaty, she took the sticky hands off her dress and held one of them gently in her own and bent down to whisper in the child's ear. Then she got up, leading the child by the hand towards the dining room door. She was barely halfway across the room before the child's mother caught up with her, the alarm on her face very visible.

"Where do you think you're taking Bethany?" she demanded abruptly.

Chloe gazed at her impassively, her smile still shining.

"Down to the loos so we can wash her hands," she said. "That is what you asked her to do, isn't it. See that nice lady in the blue dress, go and ask her if she'll take you to wash this icky chocolate off your hands? That's what you asked, isn't it?"

She met the other woman's eyes, her own quite calm but implacable, daring her to say anything.

"I thought you didn't like children," she said, taking Bethany's hand out of Chloe's.

"Oh, I like children a lot," Chloe said, heading for the door anyway, and then in a lower voice that still carried to Bethany's mum, she said, "I love children; I just couldn't eat a whole one."

She was out of the door before the woman could say anything; but what could she say anyway? It was one of the oldest jokes in the book, so old Chloe felt like a granny basher to have used it, but she hadn't been able to resist. She clattered downstairs to the ladies' loo, and tried to clean the brown smears off the dress. She slipped the whole dress off, and rinsed the marks off under the tap, and then stood in her underwear holding the wet patch by the hot air hand dryer. The problem was that when the door opened for another woman or child to come in, she was fully visible for a few moments to anyone who happened to be walking past, and the sight of her in her undies was not something any of the other wives wanted their men to see. Not that any of them did. It was just the potential that bothered them, and the sight of Chloe, fit and slim and nicely made in knickers and bra that weren't unravelling or the colour of chewing gum from accidental inclusion in a darks wash, black undies that had disturbing connotations, was a sight that made every mother suddenly resent her stretch marks and the rolls of post-baby fat and the meagre allowance they got from their diocese. It made each of the women who saw her standing trying to dry her nearly ruined dress, made them hate her for making them think those things about their lives. So Chloe oblivious and nearly naked was the subject of more resentment than she could have guessed from the startled glances they gave her.

"Nice knickers," Jo said, coming in to see she was all right.

"Aren't they, though," Chloe said. "I like nice underwear; I have to wear very practical outerwear to work; it feels good to know if I get knocked down by a bus, at least the people at the hospital will be able to say, nice knickers as they peel them off me."

"Will that stuff stain?" Jo asked.

"Don't think so. That's why I wanted to rinse it immediately. I think this is about dry," Chloe said, and slipped the dress back on. "God, I'm cold. You wouldn't think I could be, standing next to that dryer thing, but my back's frozen. Are we going to get on with the dancing soon?"

"You'll never dance in those boots," Jo said, pointing at Chloe's red boots.

"I don't intend to," Chloe said. "I shall take them off now if we're going to start soon, and leave them by the coats."

She unzipped the boots and slid them off.

"You've hennaed your feet," Jo said.

Chloe's feet had been painted in swirling designs in that sepia tone that henna makes on skin and her toenails dyed a brownish pink colour by the same substance.

"I had a school friend who taught me to do it; her family used to do it for special occasions. It's much easier to do on someone else, so I'll have to keep my feet moving fast so no-one can see my mistakes and splodges," she said, picking up the boots and padding in her bare but painted feet out of the loos and to the corner of the lobby with the coat racks.

"Don't think anyone will nick them, do you?" she said, and she and Jo went back upstairs where the band was making those vague tuning up noises that usually herald the start of music proper.

The dance itself was being held in the chapel, something Chloe found strange. It wasn't surprising that the chapel had about as much numinous atmosphere as the average bus station, if this sort of event was often held in it. She couldn't imagine that a traditional church building would get used like this, but the chapel was an anonymous barn of a room, without any distinguishing features that would intrude on people's consciousness. Someone had been busy all day, producing banners in red and white card, painted with hearts and cupids and red lips symbolising kisses, and there was a big red heart in crepe paper on every window and door; it reminded Chloe of a school hall decorated for the obligatory Valentine's disco.

"Hmm, sophisticated," she remarked as she walked in, but the irony was very obvious in the tone of her voice, and earned her an acid glare from one woman who was apparently part of the committee who had done the decorating.

"Oops," she whispered to Jo. "Said the wrong thing again. Do you think they'll shoot me at dawn?"

"You should be so lucky; a nice clean easy death? You're joking. I reckon they'll peg you out on the lawn for the ants and the vultures," Jo replied.

"In February? Hardy bloody ants," Chloe said grinning. "And vultures? Here in England?"

"OK, then peg you out for the crows and foxes. Or maybe they'll make you dance in those red boots you left downstairs, like the girl in the Hans Christian Andersen fairy tale, till someone has to chop your feet off," Jo suggested.

"Gruesome. I think I prefer the single gunshot. Should I take up smoking now so I can enjoy a last cigarette?"

"You're daft," Jo said, and they found chairs where they could sit and wait for the dancing to start.

It wasn't long before people started to pour into the chapel, and the caller took the microphone to start them off on the first dance. It was a bit like trying to herd cats, as the first few dances at any Ceillidh or barn dance, where no one quite knows what they're doing and the effort of remembering which way is left and which is right seems beyond even rocket scientists. It was made harder by the effort of avoiding small children who seemed to believe the space in the centre of the chapel floor was their sole territory, and more than one toddler was sent flying by less cautious dancers. The slightly older children got roped into the dance, their hands held firmly and propelled from partner to partner by anxious parents, eager to make sure they were not excluded from the fun by sheer inability to follow instructions or remember anything for more than three seconds.

"This is insane," Chloe said to Jo, in a pause between dances. "I've nearly turned my ankle twice avoiding treading on tiny tots, and one of the little sods stamped on my foot. I'll have some lovely bruises when the henna wears off. How can you have a dance with ballistic babies around?"

"Give it till about nine o'clock; then they'll start to take the smaller ones home," Jo said. "Happens every year; trouble is the mothers seem to think that the dance should be winding down because the kids are going home to bed, so we get this uncomfortable bit where they don't want to go till it looks like things are stopping anyway. If the caller is the same one we had last year, he usually calls a break around nine so the kiddies go home thinking they're not going to be missing anything. If it's not the same caller, we'll get trouble if he just tries to carry on."

Chloe got a drink of water, her throat dry, and stood at the door from the dining room looking in at the chapel. From where she stood she could see a number of children who looked fit to drop but still trying to carry on twirling and whirling in the centre of the room. It was ridiculous and a bit sad. This was the point when any sensible woman who swoop down and abduct her own children; otherwise, as grannies the world over are apt to say, there'll be tears.

There were. By nine, the caller called a break, but the majority of under-fives were beyond reason, had become hyper and unmanageable, and the noise was impressive as one after another, the children were removed by mothers who clearly resented the fact that they were going home and in the main their men folk were staying.

Once the music started again, it was only adults remaining, with a few older children who had been granted a stay of execution. At least no one would fall over children of this age and size, and with many of the women gone home, the man to woman ratio was slightly unequal.

"You'll have to be a man," Nicky said to Chloe as they were trying to sort out partners for the next dance. "You won't find that hard, I'm sure."

Nicky's husband had been the one to fall on his sword, so to speak and take the kids home to bed.

"What is that supposed to mean?" Chloe demanded, but Nicky just looked at her, all innocent eyes, and simply said,

"You're so adaptable, that's all."

"Yeah right," Chloe muttered, but Jo caught her arm and mouthed, "Leave it."

"I can turn my hand to just about anything," she said to Nicky. "Kind of you to have noticed."

The caller started them off but Chloe was still simmering over Nicky's remark and found it less than enjoyable as a result. It would be so much easier if Nicky had insulted her properly, but this sideways sniping was impossible to deal with. If she challenged it as she had done, they just sort of slid away, explaining whatever remark they'd made so that she seemed unreasonable to object to it. She also realised that her bare feet with the exotic henna patterns had become a target for the shod feet of some of the other women; she'd never be able to prove it, but on a number of occasions, it was hard to believe she hadn't been trodden on deliberately.

She concentrated on dancing and avoiding being trodden on, but it was surprisingly hard work; she would have been puzzled about why the men seemed to be able to avoid her feet when the women with smaller feet couldn't. She saw the glances exchanged between Nicky, Felicity and their cronies; she ground her teeth when she saw them grin behind imperfectly placed hands when Nicky's heel came down hard on Chloe's big toe. The pain of the injury was driven away by the rage she felt surging through her; there was no way she could even suggest that it was anything other than accidental, and she knew they were trying to drive her off the dance floor. Despite the growing pain in her feet, she carried on, knowing she was making them more and more angry with her as she danced on apparently without pain; but she knew she'd be hobbling for days afterwards.

"It's so bloody unfair," she hissed to Clifford when she stopped for a drink between dances. "I can't believe they're actually dancing like a herd of drunken elephants just to get my feet; what's the point of that?"

Clifford shook his head.

"They're just jealous," he said, helplessly. "Do you want to bow out and go home?"

She thought about it; the bruises on her feet were beginning to throb insistently.

"No," she said. "If I carry on, I might get worse than bruises, but I'm not giving in to them, not yet."

Another set of dances; another set of bruises. At the end, Clifford headed downstairs to the loos, and after another drink of water, Chloe trotted downstairs too. In the shadowed corner where the coat racks were, she thought she spotted him leaning down by her boots, a coat in his hand.

"Good idea, lover," she said. "Let's nip home for a quickie and then I'll get my trainers on instead of those silly boots. How about it then?"

She knew she'd made a mistake the second she touched his shoulder and she was instantly aware of the alien nature of the flesh. He straightened up and turned round in shock and she saw it wasn't Clifford at all but Felicity's husband, wearing much the same shirt as Clifford. In the dim light, he was similar enough in build, height and colouring to fool her for a second.

"Oh Christ," she breathed. "I thought you were Clifford; I am so sorry."

He was still staring at her, saying nothing when Felicity appeared from the ladies, and saw them standing staring at each other, Robert's jaw visibly dropping.

"What's the matter?" she demanded, her eyes on Chloe's face.

"I'll tell you later," Robert said sharply, and then to Chloe, "You should be ashamed of yourself, speaking to me like that."

"I thought you were Clifford," Chloe said helplessly. "I wouldn't say that to you; I don't even fancy you."

Felicity looked from Chloe to her husband, and then back again.

"You're nothing but a cheap slut," she said, and stalked away, beckoning for Robert to follow her.

Chloe stood in the darkened hall, feeling tears of pain, rage and frustration prickling at the edges of her vision, waves of shame sweeping over her in glorious technicolor.

"Fuck," she whispered as the tears began to fall.

Clifford came out of the gents and saw her standing motionless among the coats.

"What is it?" he asked.

"Nothing, I'll tell you when we get home," she said, picking up her boots and carrying them over to the bench to put them on.

As she straightened the boot to put it on, she noticed a change in the weight of the boot, and delving inside it, found it had been filled with brown gooey matter.

"What the hell...?" she said, holding the boot open to show Clifford.

"Oh, God, someone's filled my boots with shit," she said.

"Are you sure?"

"Hang on a minute," she said and cautiously sniffed at the boot and began to laugh slightly hysterically. "Chocolate cake," she said, breathlessly. "Bloody Robert was filling my boots with chocolate cake; how weird is that? No wonder he was so shocked to see me. Right, that does it."

Chloe got up jerkily and yanked the door open and padded out into the February night, her feet bare and sore, and ran home, ignoring the stones and fragments of glass and twig that stuck in her soles. She stopped at Felicity and Robert's door, and emptying the cake out of her boots, stuffed it through the letterbox, holding the flap open long enough to shout through it,

"Just be glad I'm not as vindictive as Robert."

Clifford caught her up as she unlocked their own front door.

"What the hell's going on?" he asked.

Chloe took a deep breath; her chest was heaving with the effort of not crying.

"Let's get in and I'll tell you," she said, as calmly as she could.

As she put the hall light on and went inside, Clifford saw the blood on the floor as she walked to the kitchen.

"You're bleeding," he said.

"I think I trod on something sharp," she said. "I want to get this stuff out of my boots before it sets."

"Let's get those feet seen to first; the boots can wait," he said firmly, and made her sit down while he fetched a bowl of warm water to wash the dirt off her feet so he could see any cuts properly.

She explained what had happened as he cleaned and dressed the cuts on her feet and rubbed arnica cream onto the bruises. After a second to two, he started laughing.

"And he actually thought you were really hitting on him?" he said.

"Yeah," Chloe said dully.

"Dear God, he must have thought all his birthdays had come at once, and then you had to go and ruin it by saying you thought he was me, and then that you don't even fancy him," Clifford said, still chortling.

"It's not funny," she said sulkily.

"Oh yes it is. It's hilarious, more so since you caught him stuffing goo into your boots. Come on, lighten up; it was a silly mistake, no one will care."

"Want to bet? I bet by this time tomorrow everyone will know I suggested a quickie to Robert," Chloe said.

"Yeah, thinking it was me. I mean we were wearing the same shirt and it was dark and he was apparently getting your boots. No one else should have been touching your boots, so it was most likely to be me anyway."

Chloe began to smile reluctantly, and began to see the funny side.

"If they've got any sense of self preservation, they'll keep quiet about it," she said. "He was putting cake in my boots. I don't think he'd want anyone to know about that bit. I don't think you need worry; they won't tell anyone because it puts them in a bad light themselves."

But Chloe was right; within twenty-four hours nearly everyone knew about the incident, as told by Robert and Felicity and no one seemed to want to hear the other side of the story. It was no satisfaction to be proved right.

Chapter 9

The Valentine's night fiasco rapidly passed into the stuff of myth and legend, after the initial chaos of gossip and speculation had run its frenetic course. Jo, who seemed amphibious as she moved between the world of her work and the world of college, kept Chloe informed of the progress of the rumours and when the overall opinion seemed divided equally between those who thought the whole thing was a silly misunderstanding and those who thought Chloe was the archetypal Scarlet Woman out to seduce every man in sight, she then relayed to Chloe that it was safe to come out of hiding.

"I wasn't in hiding," Chloe protested. "I've just been busy at work. God, it feels good to say that; busy at work. There! I enjoyed that."

"Then it's about time you showed up at chapel or something, or the fallen woman faction will think they've won," Jo said firmly. "Though the day I hear that it was Robert who made a pass at you, that's the day I'm certain the world has gone totally doolally."

Chloe stuck her tongue out.

"What, don't you think I'm worth making a pass at then?" she said.

"Not my type, love," Jo said. "Seriously though, if you don't become visible again the waverers will think the Robert and Felicity version is true."

"Maybe," Chloe said slowly. "But I don't think I'll ever eat chocolate cake again without thinking of that night. I might come to worship this week, but I draw the line at dinner. At least if I just appear and then disappear after Communion, no one is going to nab me and give me the Spanish Inquisition."

"I hope not," Jo said, seriously. "Is the new job going well, then?"

"Fine," Chloe said. "Not very demanding yet, but there's a new project starting fairly soon that might be a bit more challenging."

Chloe had felt an enormous amount of relief to start work again; for a start money had been getting tight. Their diocese was slow to respond to changes in financial circumstances and they had been lucky that the rent from Gran's house covered their own rent here and most of the bills. Chloe had been worried that her spell of unemployment would go on long enough for them to really feel the pinch; all it would take would be a biggish problem with the car and they would be struggling. The new job left her tired in the evenings; even though she hadn't found the actual work demanding, all the new colleagues and routines were difficult to adjust to at first and it was only after a few weeks that she began to sit up and take notice of what was going on around her at home.

Spring had arrived, for a start, without her needing to measure its progress each day. One day, fading snowdrops; the next the proverbial host of golden daffodils. It was a bit of a shock, really. She went out one Saturday morning, to get the milk off the step, and found spring there as well. In her nightie, she knelt at the edge of the concrete slabs that made the garden path, and breathed in the scent of the paper-white narcissi and the smell of damp earth warming in the sunshine, and felt drunk.

Inside, she met Clifford coming downstairs.

"It sneaked up on me again," she said, grinning manically.

"What did?" he asked, still half asleep.

"Spring. Every year, I watch and I watch and the moment I turn away and think it'll be weeks yet, it sneaks up behind me and just happened while I'm not looking. Each year I think I'll catch it as it happens; each year it fools me."

He gazed at her delightedly; her grin seemed to reach from ear to ear and her face was still pink from sleep, her eyes shining.

"You know what a young man's thoughts turn to when spring has sprung," he said.

"Tea," she said.

"No, not unless he's a very strange young man."

"No, I need tea. Otherwise I will go straight back to sleep, and I don't think that's what this mythical young man was thinking about either," Chloe said, heading towards the kitchen. "Call me an addict if you like, but I need my first cuppa or I don't function at all."

"I do," Clifford said, pretending to sulk.

"Then you'll have to wait."

"Can't you just chew the leaves or something?" he asked, as she filled the kettle. "And then drink a glass of water? That'd be quicker."

"Good things come to those that wait," Chloe said.

"Bet that's what your Gran used to say," he said.

She glanced at him.

"Yes, she did," she said. "And yes, it used to annoy me too. Three minutes to make the tea, two to drink it. Five minutes, that's all I'm asking for."

Clifford started laughing, putting aside his pretence of sulking.

"I could murder a cup myself, to tell you the truth," he said. "I was too hot in bed last night; we'll have to put the lighter weight quilt on or it'll be boil-in-the-bag Clifford. My mouth feels like the inside of a postman's sock."

"I won't ask how you know."

He made tea for them both and they went upstairs with it. The bedroom seemed surprisingly stuffy, and Clifford opened the window. The sound of birdsong filled the room as the fresh air flowed in; further away they could hear the sounds of a baby crying.

"Shut the window," Chloe said suddenly.

"Why? It's still stuffy in here."

"Yes, but if I can hear next door's baby, then next door might hear us," she said.

"What, slurping tea?"

"No, you fool. Doing whatever young men think of in springtime."

"Actually I was thinking about Morris dancing."

"Now that is kinky!"

*

"So what are you going to do today?" Clifford asked, later. "I've got essays to finish, so I'm afraid I won't be around to join in."

"I thought I'd weed the front garden; there's a lot of grass springing up round the bulbs and if I catch it now it won't be a problem later. Then I thought I might go to the garden centre and get a few shrubs for the back garden; it's horribly bare and boring. I know we're only here for a few years but I don't think I can stand that weedy patch of grass for that long. At least we can leave this place better than we found it. Though having said that, I am deeply indebted to whoever planted all those bulbs; they were a surprise I wasn't quite expecting."

"That's the point of surprises, silly; you don't expect them," Clifford said. "Shall we have some coffee first? I don't think I can face Crisis Theology without a hefty dose of caffeine first."

Chloe swung her legs out of bed and went to pull on jeans and tee shirt.

"Yeah, coffee would be great," she said. "Do you think you could bring me some out every hour or so? That way I don't have to take my wellies off to come in and make it. You always seem to need a top up at least every two hours when you're essay writing."

"That's because after an hour or so I start dropping off to sleep!"

"Well, each time your nose touches the keyboard, put a brew on and bring it out."

Chloe went out into the garden and began working amid the flowers using a hand-fork. Easing the prongs carefully into the sweet soil, she loosened the earth around the roots of grass and weeds and pulled them out, shaking the roots gently to remove the soil that still clung to them. As she worked steadily from the gate backwards, a pile of weeds grew on the path next to her, and the turned soil writhed with worms, and steamed very slightly in the still cool morning air. Her activity caught the attention of a number of small birds, and she was startled initially by the robin that darted along the border picking out worms and grubs, coming surprisingly close to her as she worked. After a while, she didn't really notice the birds; she became lost in the moment, starting to understand why her Gran had found such solace in apparently mundane and repetitive tasks like weeding. The simple act and focus of her task took up only some of her attention and she found herself dreaming pleasantly amid the flowers, reaching a state of contentment she rarely experienced. As the sun warmed the day, the flowers began emitting bursts of fragrance; the scent of the narcissi was pungent, almost narcotic, the hyacinths overwhelming in their sweetness. By twelve o'clock, Clifford remembered their agreement and came out with both coffee and sandwiches.

They sat on the step together and ate their lunch; the day was warming nicely, though the breeze was still cool.

"Best get on," Clifford said reluctantly, dusting his hands of breadcrumbs. "Let me know when you're off to the garden centre; if I've finished what I'm working on at the moment, I might come with you."

Chloe sat on the step, her plate in her lap, and closed her eyes. She felt the heat of the sun on her face, and the scent of flowers was still strong enough to almost drug her into this semi-trance. There was a small ache in the small of her back, enough so she knew she'd worked hard but not enough to really hurt. The birdsong went on around her as she sat cross-legged, her dirty hands resting on her knees and her eyes lightly closed and her mind elsewhere, flying softly above the clouds.

She was visible from the private road that went past these houses from the main road; she was illuminated by the bright sunshine, her hair making a red-gold halo around her face and body, her pale skin luminous with reflected sunlight. She was unaware of people passing, unaware of anything other than this huge sense of peace and contentment, and the sheer physical glory of being alive. The robin, encouraged by her absolute stillness, hopped closer and began to peck up the crumbs scattered by Clifford, and was joined by several hopeful sparrows. Between them, they made short work of the few fragments of bread, and the robin, true to its famous boldness, fluttered to the plate on her lap and began snatching crumbs from that instead. After a few forays, from plate to path and back again, it decided it was safe enough, and perched directly on her knee, making the short hop to the plate that the sparrows were still too nervous to make.

She was aware of the little claws landing on her knee, and opened one eye a fraction to see the brilliant black eyes of the robin gazing up at her, bold but still cautious, and made herself close the eye and keep totally still, while her heart seemed to stop with delight. Her grandmother had had a rapport with the robins in the old garden, but she'd never seen a robin actually land on the old woman; she suddenly wanted to phone her and tell her about it. She didn't find her heart sink with this thought, as it often did when she remembered the old lady was dead; this time she simply thought, she knows, I know she knows.

A huge smile spread slowly across her face as the little bird bounced around from knee to knee like a pet budgie. She couldn't see that coming along the road at that moment, pushing the finally sleeping baby in a pushchair, was Felicity, who stopped to gaze at the strange, almost unearthly sight of Chloe sitting apparently in the lotus position, seraphic smile on her glowing face, surrounded by a small flock of sparrows and a robin now perched on her arm. She stood and stared, her jaw literally dropped open, until the baby stirred in her sleep and began those snuffling noises that herald waking. She began pushing the buggy abruptly, suddenly very angry for no real reason; the squeak from the wheels alarmed the little birds around Chloe and as they flew off, Chloe opened her eyes in time to see Felicity with a face like thunder glaring at her as she stalked past.

"Hi there," she called to her, but Felicity ignored her, pretending she hadn't heard her and accelerated past Chloe's fence and into her own garden.

"Please yourself, then," Chloe said, shrugging, and then got up to sweep up the weeds and put them in the green recycling bin at the end of the garden path.

The robin had come back and was watching her from the fence; Chloe just grinned at him.

"Worms are all yours, Robin," she said. "Catch them while you can, lad."

*

The first couple of months of the new job were frankly a bit boring; they were completing one project so there was little for Chloe to really get her teeth into. The new project looked much more interesting; a school complex, built for to up-to-the minute specifications, to replace an utterly worn out and virtually derelict secondary school that had gone beyond repairs and periodic patching-up. It was also meant to be a showcase both for government and company, and her first glance at the plans made her heart race.

But the whole project was at risk, something not unusual these days. The land acquired for the school had narrowly missed being designated an SSSI; and when Chloe looked closely at the specifications, she found herself very puzzled about why it had failed to gain the designation that would have saved it from being "developed". To her eyes, it should not have been even considered for such a thing.

Increasingly puzzled by this, she was not surprised to hear rumours that protesters had moved onto the site, making a small community in the trees and even digging in at the borders of the land, constructing tunnels and dug-outs as if preparing for a war. The mood in the office became nasty; there was a lot of swearing about hippies and fluffy-bunny-lovers. Then, after much to-ing and fro-ing on the legal front, Chloe's immediate boss asked her to come with him so they could see the extent of the problems.

"If it's only one or two, we may be able to persuade them to see reason," he said, starting the engine of his company car. "It also depends on the type of protesters we've got."

"You make it sound like aphids," Chloe said.

"Not unlike, actually. If it's just greenfly, we're in with a chance of just brushing them off. If it's scale insect, we're in trouble. But I need to see them for myself to know for sure what we've got. If they're just locals, well, there's ways and means of persuading them to give up. If we've got professional protesters like Swampy, we're stuffed. They don't care about eviction orders or being dragged off to gaol; they don't care about muck and punches, or months of living in tree houses. They don't listen to reason; they're usually immune to bribes and threats and they don't compromise. Still, we'll see. It might still be a mild case of green fly. Let's hope, eh?"

When they pulled up near the site, Chloe could see a group of brightly coloured people, ethnic clothes fluttering in the early summer breeze. Some of them were standing behind the barriers the company had tried to put up, but mostly these were now flat in the mud. Some pieces had been dragged off to augment the tree houses she could see high in the ancient oaks that made up much of the woodland of the area.

"Bugger," said Chloe's boss. "We got scale insect. Crap luck. Well, let's go and have a closer look at them. I'd put your hard hat on if I were you, just to show we mean business. And if they start

123

lobbing rocks at us, it might stop you getting concussion on your first day on this project."

"Does it get violent, then?"

"Are you scared?"

It wasn't a fair question, not really.

"Not really; I just want to have an idea of what's likely to happen, and when it's time to run away," she said carefully.

He laughed, mirthlessly.

"Yeah, sometimes it does get a bit hair-raising, but you look like you can handle yourself," he said, the words "for a girl" remaining unspoken but not unheard.

They got out of the car, the mud thick enough already from the site vehicles to make Chloe glad of her work boots. She walked with her boss, but half a pace behind him, like an Indian wife, until they got to the wrecked barriers. A lot of hostile faces looked back at them, and a few jeers rose from certain individuals, further back and harder to see properly. They certainly were a colourful lot, their clothes making her think of the children's rhyme, "hark hark the dogs do bark"; there were plenty of rags and tags and even velvet clothes, all in brilliant colours. Some had hair dyed in amazing colours, purples and pinks; one woman had hair the exact same colour as Chloe's own, but cropped short so that the curls, very like Chloe's own, curled tightly to the scalp instead of cascading in corkscrew ringlets.

Chloe's boss tried to talk to them but she knew instantly he'd lost any chance of real communication when he used that condescending tone used by headmasters to less than bright classes who had been misbehaving. He got about three sentences into his spiel before they began hooting and cat-calling, and some people started blowing whistles as if at a rave, to drown him out utterly.

"See what I mean? Scale insect; bloody scum the lot of them," he said, flushing with anger and turning away.

Chloe turned too, but the woman with the red curls suddenly yelled at them all to shut up, and stunningly they all did.

"We'll talk to the woman," she called. "But not you, big man. Fuck off while you still can. Come over here, Red."

Chloe looked at her boss.

"Are you up for this?" he said. "If they'll talk to you, you can at least try to reason with them. Keep your mobile on; if there's trouble I'll get the police in to get you out."

Brave of you, Chloe thought but didn't say it out loud.

"They won't hurt me," she said, strangely sure of that if nothing else. "I'll phone if I need help, but give me plenty of time before you try and get me out. It might take a while."

"They'll just give you their whole tree-hugging hippy crap-load of a manifesto, you know, but at least you've got a chance to look at their defences. OK, good luck," he said, and Chloe, her heart pounding hard, walked across to the protesters and stepped over the lowest part of their makeshift barrier and was swallowed from view by the harlequin crowd.

The red-haired woman was waiting for her; she seemed to be in charge.

"Why me and not my boss?" Chloe asked.

"I know his type; you look like a reasonable woman," she said, then bizarrely, "The hair, it's real, right?"

"Yes," Chloe said bemused. "But I don't think you called me over here just to swap hair care tips, did you?"

The woman looked amused.

"No, I didn't," she said. "OK, let's go. I want you to see the place you want to rip up with chainsaws and bulldozers."

The woodland felt much bigger than it had sounded on paper, and Chloe soon vanished from her boss's sight, so he went back to the car and waited there. The leaves were barely opened on the great oaks that towered over them, so the light filtering to the path was bright yellow green and there was a warm green scent of growing things. Amid the ancient oaks were lots of younger trees, oaks mainly, but other species were mingled in amongst them, and there were great tangles of honeysuckle that scrambled up trunks to reach the light high up; the first few flowers had opened and the scent that reached Chloe in waves made her feel slightly dizzy. Around them, birds were singing; she could identify many of them, great tit, robin, even the sound of a woodpecker drumming on a trunk some yards away but lost from view in the density of the foliage.

"You're probably a townie, so this probably doesn't appeal to you," the woman said. "Your sort like neat tamed parks; not true nature in the raw."

"How do you know what I'd like? You don't know me from Adam, so don't make assumptions," Chloe snapped.

126

"Touchy," the woman said. "Fair enough; I don't know you, but I have seen loads of your sort walk through woods like these, and complain that there aren't any benches or litter bins, and that there are too many nettles."

"Stop making assumptions, and just get on with telling me what you want to tell me and then I can tell you what I'm expected to say and then we've both done our job," Chloe said.

Just then, a bubbling burst of birdsong filled the air, more like music than birdsong usually is.

"Nightingale," Chloe said automatically, and the woman looked at her surprised.

"I know quite a few birds by their song," Chloe said. "And I'm not a townie, for your information, so can we get on with this. I'd rather like the chance to enjoy these woods if I can."

"Before you destroy them, you mean."

Chloe shrugged, uncomfortable now.

"I didn't know it's be like this," she said. "How in hell did it miss the SSSI designation?"

The woman looked weary, the fight seeming to go out of her for a moment.

"The usual way," she said. "You know, backhanders and stuff like that. There's a plot of land nearer to the catchment area for this school, but it's a brownfield site, so it requires all sorts of fuss to make sure it's clear of toxic stuff. It *is* clear, at least the historic use suggest it is and we've no reason to doubt it. That all costs more than virgin land like this that's useless as farmland. So they swung this site as a cheaper alternative; the owner is glad to sell it, or has been pressured to sell, I don't know which. So unless we can find something that would prove this site as a Site of Special Scientific Interest, we need to delay your lot as long as possible in the hope that the expense of waiting and trying to evict us will eventually prove greater than the cost of making sure the other site is safe. I've given you our game plan; I'm sure your lot have already figured it out. I shan't be taking you near our defences, as I'm sure that's what your boss wants you to suss out. I just wanted you to see close up what you are going to destroy. Some of the trees here are five or six hundred years old; they have an entire eco-system around them, hundreds of species depend on them for their habitat and livelihood."

"I know," Chloe said. "This is real, true ancient oak woodland, like that which covered this country for thousands of years. I know all this. What can I do? I have a job; I have to do it."

"Or what? You won't be able to afford your big house and your big gas-guzzling car and all those holidays abroad?"

"Stop making those stupid bloody assumptions," Chloe snarled. "That's not fair. I'm not assuming that you live in a commune with a lesbian lover or two and sit and chant OM every morning. So don't assume stuff about me. You know nothing."

"No, you're the one who knows nothing. You know your birdsong, yeah sure, and you know your trees. But it's all in your head. It needs to be in your heart."

"OK, then, so you tell me. Tell me what I need to do to get it into my heart," Chloe said.

"You're one of them, you'll never see what we see, or hear or feel what we feel," the woman said.

"Try me," Chloe said, folding her arms across her chest and looking stubborn.

The woman gazed at her, thoughtful suddenly. Then she reached across and grabbed Chloe by the arm and pulled her rapidly across the path to an absolute monster of an oak tree.

"You gotta really know these trees are alive, like we're alive," she said, and pushed Chloe right up to the trunk, and held her head against the rough bark, pressing it close so that Chloe's ear was in direct contact with the tree.

"What..?" Chloe said.

"Just shut up and keep quiet. You'll know what I want you to know in a few minutes or not at all."

Chloe straightened her spine and leaned closer to the tree. She could smell the woody, damp smell of the bark, even the lichen that grew on it had a scent of its own, and the touch of the bark on her skin was softer than she had imagined, slightly slippery with dew. A small green beetle crawled past her face. Nothing happened. Just as she was about to say, forget it, a great sound like the banging of a wet drum came from the deep interior of the tree, followed by a surge and rush of liquid gurgling inside the trunk. The sun came out from behind some clouds, and the tree sounded like it had a river in it, surging and thundering under her ear.

She hadn't realised she'd closed her eyes till she opened them, to find the woman gazing at her from across the path, a strange smile on her face. The wood seemed very different suddenly.

"You heard," said the woman. "I saw it on your face. Now you'll never look at a tree the same way again."

Chloe stepped back from the tree, her hands pressed palm down on the bark, feeling the strange life in the tree through the skin of her hands. It was like touching a rock and then discovering it was part of something enormous like an elephant, just you couldn't see it before that moment. She tilted her head back to look up at the tree, half expecting some gigantic head to appear and look down at her. She leaned against the tree again, laying her cheek on the bark, feeling herself sag with the knowledge of what she had just experienced.

"Can we go back now?" Chloe said, softly, knowing she was near to tears.

The woman nodded and they began walking back along the path.

"You OK?" the woman asked.

"No," Chloe said. "But that doesn't matter."

"It does," said the woman. "We all matter; oak trees, people, foxes and flowers. We all matter. Even that git you have as a boss; even he matters. We just have to learn how to share."

Chloe just shrugged, and when they got back to the barrier, she left without saying anything and went back to the car where her boss was dozing to Radio Four.

"Any luck?" he asked.

"No," she said, shortly, but he was too tied up in himself to notice she was not exactly chirpy on the way back to the office.

While she drove home that evening, Chloe could still hear the interior noises of the tree, and she thought of her father, whom she'd all but forgotten about. She remembered being very small, snuggling next to him, her head against his chest, listening to the drumbeat of his heart and the more distant gurgling of his digestion. It was a funny thing to think about; but that tree had made her think of her father and she felt very fragile when she got home, almost as though she was still a small child after a day that has been too long and too full to assimilate easily.

When she slipped into sleep that night, she could still hear the tree in her memory, its heartbeat and that of her father mingling until she couldn't distinguish one from the other.

Chapter 10

The day after the incident at the woods, Chloe's sense of unease became acute, when a rumour reached her that it was being suggested that she had been employed solely as a result of pressure from management to conform to equal opportunities directives. The suggestion that this was the case had no direct source; the whisper had reached her via the receptionist who was privy to all gossip that did the rounds of the company, and when Chloe asked her directly where she had heard this, the woman became evasive and uncomfortable, and Chloe realised rapidly that whoever had been making these insinuations was either considerably more senior than herself or else someone the receptionist was more afraid of than her. Either way, she was going to get no more information from her.

The protesters had refused to speak to anyone else, and when the police arrived, they simply took to the trees and just stayed up there, jeering and refusing to come down. So for those who were supposed to be working on this project there was nothing to do till the protesters were cleared from the site. Some people were co-opted onto other projects, but Chloe, as newest recruit, was left at headquarters, twiddling her thumbs and worrying that there was some truth in these rumours, and wondering who had started it.

In the canteen, she drank endless cups of coffee, spinning out her lunch hour for as long as possible, before going back to stare at the paperwork for the school project. She was uncertain what to do; the majority of her mind was with the protesters. She had looked into what the red haired woman had said, and yes, there was another site that had been considered, was in fact already owned by the council, bought before the woodland had been put up for sale. It was all very suspicious; this site was far closer to the community the school was to serve and seemed, even with reclamation costs, much more suitable. Someone was playing games somewhere; games she had always failed to understand, since they seemed to deal with such huge stakes and with lives as well. On a number of occasions, Gran had muttered hotly about politicians regarding life as one big board game; it seemed that there was someone playing such a game now, and this ancient woodland was the life being sacrificed as a stake.

She glanced up as a number of colleagues came into the canteen. There was a certain gung-ho attitude about some of them that irritated her hugely, so she wasn't pleased when they came over to her table, all loud voices and bravado.

"Hello, Red," said Dave, who was the loudest of them all. "Hugged any good trees lately?"

She looked at him evenly, actually feeling her fists bunching with instinctive aggression.

He turned to his companions.

"Red here is turning into a hippy, you know that, lads. She went off into the woods yesterday for hours, communing with nature and having a fumble with that other red haired bitch," he said, and they all sniggered like over-grown schoolboys.

Chloe felt her face flushing.

"Have you not got anything better to do than bother me?" she asked.

"No, we haven't, since all you hippy-dippy sorts have put a hex on this project," he said. "Mind you, what else can we expect, employing a woman when we could have had a man. No point expecting anything from a girl." He said the last word almost as a curse.

Chloe got up very slowly, and faced him. She was actually a little taller than he was but she didn't feel it.

"If you think I shouldn't have this job, just go ahead and say it plainly," she said. "I don't like this sort of insinuation, and I'm not putting up with it."

He glanced at his companions and then began leering at her.

"Red's got PMS, lads, or else she hasn't had her leg over lately," he said.

"Grow up," Chloe said. "You must have some sort of brain or you wouldn't be here at all; try using it for a change."

"It's a scientific fact that men's brains are bigger than women's," he said, still in that jeering tone.

"Yes, well size isn't everything, I'm sure you'll be glad to know," Chloe said. "It's what you do with it that counts."

"I know just what to do with it, love," he said.

"I doubt it."

"Want to try?"

"Drop dead, moron. I'm not here to entertain the troops."

"That isn't what I've heard."

"Then you should get your ears washed out as well as your foul mouth," Chloe said. "If you're the best example of the gene pool, then I'd hate to look in the shallow end."

He went red, then, largely because his friends were listening avidly.

"If you were a man," he started to say. But Chloe cut him off.

"If I were a man, you'd be on the floor begging for mercy by now," she said. "You'd never dare to talk to a man the way you've just talked to me; and believe me, it's not lack of brawn that stops me breaking your nose."

"Yeah? Go on then, try it, Red."

"No," Chloe said. "That isn't exactly fair; after all, you'd not hit a mere woman would you? Even scum like you usually have standards."

Retrospectively, calling him scum was not the brightest thing to have done, because he swung for her then, palm open in token acknowledgement of her gender, and would have knocked her down even so had she not managed to get her own punch in first, burying her fist deep in his paunchy midriff and doubling him over as he gasped for breath. She put out her foot, and with a sharp kick on the bum, toppled him right over.

"Right," she said to the others standing behind him, open-mouthed. "Anyone else care to suggest that I'm not up to my job? No? Good."

Her knees were shaking as she exited the canteen, but they couldn't see that. As she passed the counter where the dinner ladies were still serving up, there was a ripple of applause, and Chloe grinned at them, and went back to her desk to try and think what she could do.

*

She went back to the woods, back to the big oak tree, and sat at its roots, leaning against the trunk to hear the comforting heartbeat of her father. Curling up in the shelter of the roots she stuck her thumb in her mouth, her head resting on the bark, and tried to sleep. The heartbeat was getting louder; she could hear it without pressing her ear to the trunk. The sound was all around her, like the sea on a windy night; the sky was darkening rapidly to navy blue touched with deep pink at the horizon and the first few stars were twinkling fitfully here and there like glitter spilled on a dark carpet.

The ground felt cold, and mist was starting to curl around her; an owl called far off, a harsh sound full of menace. She sat up. The sound had stopped; even when she pressed her ear to the trunk, there was nothing. She felt cold panic rising to choke her with futile tears, and she pounded on the trunk with her fists to make the sound start again. Nothing.

Only the wind in the trees, a faint whispering of leaves and twigs rustling together, and the owl, closer now.

She realised that she would have to dig; her father was under the tree and she had to dig him out before he sank too far to find. She had only her fingertips to scrape away the leaf litter and the soil, but she began burrowing, cautiously at first, then frantically, scooping away handfuls of thick, black woodland earth. She was sweating now despite the chill of nightfall, sweating and desperate. The hole got deeper fast; the tree seemed to move its roots back out of the way like a teenager lifting up their feet so she could hoover under them.

Then she saw a glimpse of colour in the dark soil, and scraped away faster than ever. Toys again, soft toys, their fur unsullied by the soil but damp with the falling dew. Then there were wooden toys, their paint in bright primary colours; board books with single words on each thick page. Finally, still mostly covered with earth, the first tufts of fringe from a blue and pink blanket. Strange that as darkness fell, the colours were still so vivid.

She sat back on her heels, looking into the vast pit that lay before her, the toys barely visible from here but their colours migraine-bright. The sound of the tree's heartbeat was back, pounding away like a drum beaten by a mad drummer, and the sweat poured off her forehead like a shower or a waterfall, filling the pit. She began to topple forward, fighting to keep her balance, but in vain.

She fell endlessly before hitting the water and sinking like a stone, choking and fighting and suffocating with the weight of water and earth above her.

"Wake up, love," Clifford said shaking her firmly and holding her shoulders as she thrashed around. "You've had another nightmare; come on, wake up. It's OK now; you're safe."

He turned the bedside light on, driving away the forest that still filled Chloe's eyes. She sat up, rubbing her eyes to rub away the images still lurking in her vision.

"Christ," she said with feeling. "That was awful."

Her nightie clung to her damply; even her hair was soaked at the roots.

"What was it about?"

She searched for the images, rummaging through her mind to find them but they were evaporating in the light of the electric lamp.

"Something about my father; and about that wood the other day. And… I can't remember any more. Oh God, I can't remember," she said, realising her mind was going blank.

"Shall I make us a drink?" he offered, getting out of bed.

"Please."

While he went downstairs to make a hot drink, she gazed around the room in despair, trying to recall the details of the nightmare but trying in vain. The faintest fragments that remained simply disintegrated as she looked at them. The room was cool; she remembered being cold even though she'd been sweating, but beyond that nothing remained.

The nightie was cooling fast; she hauled it off and threw it across the room to the washing basket, and went to the bathroom and stood in the shower till Clifford returned with mugs of tea.

She sat in bed, wrapped in a towel and sipped at the tea.

"You've been having nightmares a lot lately," Clifford said. "Do you never remember what's in them?"

"Only fragments that don't make sense when I look at them; they don't even seem scary when I wake up. They just seem weird," she said. "But you know when you know something but you just can't quite get at it; you sort of know that you'll remember it if you just leave it alone? It feels like that, a bit anyway."

"Do you ever dream about your Gran?"

"If I do, I don't remember it."

She sighed.

"I can't go on with this job, you know that," she said. "I've been thinking about it a lot since that fight. I'm suddenly not even sure I'm in the right career anyway; every job has been a struggle in some way, even the last one. And this one, well, ever since the rumour reached me about why I'd got the job, I've had even more doubts. The fight was the last straw really. It scared me to know that he would have hit me if I hadn't been that bit faster. Let's face it; it was a lucky punch. Next time I won't be so lucky. He might not try to hit me again but he won't forget what I did. And when it comes right back down to it, I agree with the protesters entirely. It'd be sacrilege to hack down that wood; there's been real dirty tricks going on and I don't like being part of it. So I'm thinking of resigning."

He looked into his tea.

"I think you should," he said. "It scared me, you nearly getting hit by that ape. You seem to have to be twice as good as the blokes to get half as far; it's going to bend you out of shape, working there. Resign and find something else."

"What if there isn't anything else?"

"In that line of work? Well, there's bound to be, sooner or later. And be choosy this time. Find some job or other locally that'll pay the bills and look round for the best job you can find, with a company you can trust. There might even be one that has a real environmental policy that only focuses on stuff like that, you know, solar panels and wind-power and decent insulation. The diocese would be obliged to pay our keep if you were at home with a baby; they should be obliged to look after us if you're out of work. It won't be lavish but we'd be OK."

"I'm not proud," Chloe said. "I think I'd far rather work in a shop or something than have to feel torn apart like I felt when that woman made me listen to that oak tree. OK, I'll talk to my boss later this morning, anyway."

She put the mug down on the bedside table, and slipped out of the bed to get a clean nightie, dropping the towel near the door.

"Chloe?" he said, as she opened a drawer.

She glanced back at him.

"Yes?"

"Don't bother with the nightie!"

*

"Resigning? But you've only just arrived. Why?" demanded Chloe's boss, the following day.

"A number of reasons," she said.

She was quite calm but then she'd rehearsed this all the way to work.

"First reason is I don't like it when I hear that it's assumed I'm here to pacify the equal opportunities people; especially when I have a strong feeling that this is true. Second reason, I don't appreciate working with male chauvinist thugs," she said and from the way his eyes flickered uneasily she could tell he'd heard about the fight though she was sure he'd never admit it. "Third reason, I don't like working for a company that seems so morally corrupt that it threatens and coerces and bribes anyone who gets in its way. I had a look at the website run by the organisation who sent in those protesters; if only half the stories are true, it'd be damning enough. Fourth reason, actually I agree with the protesters. It would be a truly terrible thing to cut down that wood when there's another site closer to the community that school is meant to serve. I also looked that up; it's not an industrial site even, just the remains of an old housing estate demolished some years back. I don't know what's really going on with this; I don't really want to know. But it smells really bad to me and I don't want to be associated with it. So as far as I'm concerned, I want out."

He was staring at her as if she'd gone mad.

"You won't get another job like this," he said.

She grinned at him.

"Funny that," she said. "I don't actually want one. Not like this anyway."

"You know what you're doing?"

"Yes. Getting out while I'm still clean."

"No, you're committing professional suicide. You're good at this job; we've seen that. Leaving now for no good reason, well, that's daft."

"Were you not listening just now? They're good reasons; if you can't see them, then that's another reason for getting out. If you can't understand something like an ethical dilemma, then I can't expect you to understand anything about me. I shall cite inherent sexism as my reason for resigning; and if you dare to claim to know nothing about that then I hope you can sleep easy at night. There's a half dozen witnesses to what happened in the canteen, even if you'll claim to know nothing about it; one of them will be willing to risk the sack to back me up. I should have let him hit me and then you'd have an assault charge in the equation too."

Actually Chloe was uncertain whether any of the canteen staff would really back up her version of events, but she knew he didn't know that either.

He took a deep breath; he was clearly very worried.

"OK," he said. "Let's try this another way. Since this school thing is pretty stuck and probably will be for months what about if I arrange to make you redundant instead. You know, last in first out sort of thing? That way you leave with a clean record, just bad luck that's all it'd look like. I mean, we've got nothing for you to do with these protesters holding everything up. And if I do that, you don't have to give any reason for resigning because you won't be; you'll be made redundant instead. How does that sound?"

It sounded like the compromise it was. Still, it didn't make sense to burn too many bridges, this soon.

"Sounds fair," she said cautiously. "How soon?"

"Soon enough," he said. "And by the way, about the incident I don't actually know anything about?"

"Yes?" Chloe said, raising one eyebrow in query.

"Good punch," he said.

"I have no idea what you're talking about," she said, and then grinned at him.

She'd obviously underestimated him; he understood her dilemma better than she thought. He was just in too deep himself and had too much to lose to rock the boat; but he was willing to help her to jump ship with a life belt at least.

Chapter 11

Summer happened with the same sudden rush as spring had done. The seeds she had sown in the spaces around the bulbs had grown up covered by the foliage from daffodils and tulips and it was only at the point when the bulbs really started to die back that she noticed the first of the marigold flowers peeping through like shy sunbursts in the border. She spent the first Saturday after she'd received her redundancy notice sorting out the garden, tying up the daffodil and narcissi stems and leaves and weeding out the stray blades of grass and the inevitable dandelions.

Jo came up the path shortly before lunch; Chloe squinted up at her, the sun in her eyes.

"Hi," she said. "How's things?"

"Hectic. I hate packing; I know our diocese would pay for the removal firm to pack but I hate the thought of it. It's almost as bad as being burgled," Jo said. "I haven't seen you except in passing since you started this new job. How's it going?"

"I got made redundant again," Chloe said. "No, don't commiserate. I tried to resign, actually, but as they didn't like my reasons, we agreed that it would be better to make me redundant instead."

Jo sat on the doorstep while Chloe told her about the protesters and the fight with Dave.

"So I'm quite glad to leave anyway," Chloe said at the end of her tale. "I'm really not sure any more if this is the career for me; up till now it had never occurred to me. But that business with the wood

144

really got to me. You should have heard this tree; it was amazing. It was almost deafening; I kept thinking it was going to move or something. It was so alive. I don't think it had ever occurred to me before that plants are as alive as we are, just in a different way. Weird. Do you want any help in the packing thing?"

"Thanks for offering, but no. I don't want anyone to see how many pairs of laddered tights I've kept just in case. It's bad enough knowing it myself. Or the number of envelopes I've stuffed behind the clock in the kitchen so I can use them for shopping lists. It's never the packing per se that's the problem; it's the volume of sorting stuff. You never know how much rubbish and junk and actual muck you've stored until you come to move house."

"When I sorted my Gran's house after she died, and do bear in mind she was a very tidy organised person, I found a skeleton of a bird behind the dressing table in my old room. One of the cats must have brought it in and let it go and it must have died there. The room was shut so the smell will have gone unnoticed. And even Gran had odd socks and stuff like that even though she'd been sorting everything out since she'd known she had cancer. By the time we leave here, I'm sure we'll have the same clutter."

Chloe peeled off her gloves.

"Do you fancy a cup of tea? I need a break," she said.

"That'd be great, if you're stopping anyway," Jo said.

They drank tea in the sunshine, sitting on the step.

"Your garden's looking great," Jo remarked. "What are the orange flowers that seem to be everywhere?"

"Pot marigolds," Chloe said. "Nice things to fill in gaps. And useful too. I brought the seeds from my grandmother's garden. She grew a lot of them; but they used to self-seed every year so she never needed to sow them or buy seed. I gathered some seeds last summer so I could grow them here."

"What do you use them for?"

"All sorts, really. You can use them in cooking instead of saffron to colour rice. You can make an infusion of them for sunburn and chapped skin. Gran used to infuse the flowers in oil each year; it's excellent for bruises and sore skin among other things. I was hoping to do the same; last year's oil is used up, pretty much. I've never done it myself. Gran always used to do it so I've never had to," Chloe said.

"You really miss her, don't you?"

"And some. But it's OK. Anyway, I've got her book of recipes so I can at least try some of her stuff out," Chloe said.

"It seems strange her being into that folk remedy thing when she was a doctor," Jo remarked.

"I suppose. But a lot of the places she'd been, none of the usual things like antibiotics and antiseptics were available. She said that most places have a local cure or two worth using. She was a great one for learning that sort of thing; she said some of the local knowledge could save your own life. She also reckoned that people would bother doctors far less if they remembered the old folk remedies and used a bit of common sense to boot. There's a grain of truth somewhere in even the strangest old wives' tale, she reckoned," Chloe said, pensively.

"She's probably right at that. Look at feverfew; relegated to an old wives tale till someone discovers it really can deal with migraines; then it's big business and everyone knows about it," Jo said. "It'll have been the same with tea-tree oil; aborigine grannies have known about it for centuries. All it takes is an open-minded scientist to take an interest, see that it works and want to know more. Manuka honey, that's a big one at the moment."

"I'm not planning anything more than a pint of calendula oil and a few bottles of elderflower cordial at the moment," Chloe said laughing. "Gran used to do lots of things, but I'm the apprentice without the sorcerer, so I'm going to start small and take it from there. I don't have the experience for some of the things she's done."

"I don't want to know; sounds too much like my work," Jo said. "Stitching up episiotomies is a skilled job but not one I talk about at dinner."

Chloe made mock gagging noises.

"I did have one woman ask me if I was embroidering my name down there, I was taking so long," Jo said. "I told her to be grateful; in few months time once everything's healed up nicely, my skills with needle and thread will be subtly appreciated. She didn't know what to make of that, I can tell you. She said, if you've left instructions down there for my husband, you should know he can't put together an IKEA flat pack without mucking it up, so I hope it's just a simple map. Can you imagine, married ten years and he still needs a map to find her clitoris?"

Chloe roared with laughter.

"I bet there's a few like that here," she said. "All those babies and no decent sex."

"I think the point is that the sex isn't decent," Jo said. "Thoroughly indecent I think is the verdict."

"Anyway, had you embroidered your name?"

"Don't be silly," Jo said. "She needed twenty stitches; it was bound to take ages. I had to top up her pethidine; it took so long. I haven't got time to sign my name in strange places."

Chloe put her mug down.

"I'm going to miss you," she said awkwardly. "You've made this year a little less unbearable."

"Good," Jo said. "We'll stay in touch, yeah? I won't miss this place, mind. I shall shake the dust of the place off my feet when we go. You'll be OK, you know. Not everyone here is as mad as some you've fallen foul of. There are some good people; there always are."

"I bet they said that before Nuremberg," Chloe said dourly. "You're probably right. But how do I avoid the fruit-loops?"

"Stick to groups," Jo suggested. "You have a better chance of avoiding the lunatic fringe if you stick to general groups. There's a prayer group meets once a week, might be worth a try. I used to go sometimes; if nothing else I got to snooze in a warm room and got a few brownie points to boot."

Chloe looked dubious.

"It's worth a go," Jo said. "Even once; don't knock it till you've tried it as the actress said to the bishop."

"I'm hoping to get some sort of job to see us through," Chloe said, changing the subject once she'd finished giggling. "I don't know quite what, but there's bound to be something going, at least for while I get my head together and decide what I want out of life."

Chloe had had a row that morning on the phone with their diocesan director of ordinands; he hadn't been exactly pleased that she was out of work again and once more not earning. She'd told the DDO in no uncertain terms that she didn't think he'd be making such a fuss if she were pregnant and therefore unable to work.

"It's a sodding conspiracy, that's what it is," she snarled. "You're quite happy for me to work my socks off just so you don't have to stump up as much maintenance for Clifford. But you'd be happier if I were to conform to the baby-boom stereotypes here and had a baby or two. It's not my fault I've lost my job, is it? So get real. It happens. I'll try and get work as fast as I can, because I sure ain't having a baby."

She'd slammed down the phone, aware she was being unfair and totally unreasonable but was unable to control her anger. She rang back an hour later and apologised.

"I appreciate losing your job isn't your fault," he'd said. "And I certainly have no expectation of you having children instead. We only have a limited budget each year and it's calculated taking probable income of spouses into account. If that changes radically, the figures are out. I'm sure you understand. Try not to worry about it."

Try not to worry? That was a laugh and a half. They would hardly starve but it was the idea of being out of work long term and therefore hanging around here all the time that really bothered her. She might even get so bored she ended by considering having a baby. No way, no how. But the thought still haunted her.

"So you got a moving date yet?" she asked Jo.

"Yep. And there's something else I wanted to tell you," Jo said.

Something in her voice made Chloe sit up a bit straighter.

"Oh yeah?"

"Yeah. I wasn't sure for a while, and then when I was I wasn't going to say anything in case. But I'm past the four month mark now, so I think I can safely say I am pregnant without the thought that tomorrow I won't be."

Chloe stared at her, and then burst into tears.

"That's marvellous," she said, sobbing.

Jo was crying too.

"Isn't it though? And I'll be out of this place for it, too. I promise I won't turn into one of Them," she said.

"Once you're out of here, you can't ever be one of Them," Chloe said. "I'm really pleased for you and Mike. It's great news."

When Jo went, Chloe took the mugs back inside and wept over the kitchen sink. It wasn't that she wasn't pleased, because she was pleased for her friend. It was just that Jo was moving away anyway but this took her into another world, one that Chloe had no interest in at all. It was true that Jo couldn't become like the other college wives once she'd left, but having a baby changed everything. It was like another bereavement for Chloe.

Once she'd cleaned her face of the traces of tears, she went upstairs to where Clifford was working on the computer. He'd given up on his essay for the moment and was playing a game that seemed to involve creeping along corridors and sneaking up on people.

"That looks fun," Chloe said. "I'd do theology if I'd realised it was so interesting. What's it called then, Cosh for Christ?"

He'd jumped when she came in, a slightly guilty jump at being caught doing something other than he was supposed to be doing. She came up behind him and put her arms round him, leaning into him seeking the comfort of his arms.

"What's up?" he asked, sensing her sadness even before he saw her face.

"Oh nothing," she said. "Just with Jo going I'm going to be so lonely. And she's having a baby too, so that changes everything. I was going to pop over to the garden centre; my secateurs have broken so I need a new pair. Do you fancy coming? We can have coffee in the coffee shop there. And don't say you're working, because unless this game is actually a strategy planning programme for mission, I won't believe a word of it."

Clifford saved where he was up to on the game and went to get his jacket. He'd really needed a proper break and while playing computer games was radically different from theology essays, it made it a bit weird going back to the essay afterwards. He kept getting the concepts mixed up. At least a garden centre would get rid of Chloe's insidious suggestion of Cosh for Christ. It was just too much of a tempting thought.

They walked to the garden centre across the fields, holding hands and enjoying the sunshine.

"I hope you don't decide to buy anything big," Clifford said. "We should have brought the car."

"Nope, no plans to buy anything big," Chloe said. "I just need new snippy things. We can't afford to go mad, anyway. But we can enjoy looking thought. And a coffee, too."

Chloe quickly found the secateurs she wanted and then they wandered around the centre, looking at plants and pots and arbours and all manner of garden seats, planning out fantasy gardens filled with all sorts of exotic plants. In the conservatory, Chloe breathed in the sweet scent of gardenia and stephanotis, remembering the jasmine plant that had twined up over the wall at the bottom of her grandmother's garden and had filled the evening air with its fragrance. She sighed.

"Let's get that coffee," she said, firmly. "Best pay for these secateurs first though."

At the till, Chloe saw a notice advertising a temporary job here.

Impulsively, she asked the woman at the till,

"Whom should I speak to about this job?"

"You're interested then?" the woman said. "It's only a temporary thing, filling in while someone goes on maternity leave. Well, I say 'leave'. It's not a formal thing; it's just that she's worked here for years and we want her to come back after the baby. Does that bother you?"

"Not really. I need work now, and it may only be temporary for me," Chloe said. "I'm really an engineer."

"Look, drop off a CV in the next day or so and we'll get back to you," said the woman. "But don't hang around. There'll be plenty after it."

In the coffee shop, Chloe sipped her coffee thoughtfully.

"I'll pop back over with my CV," she said. "I can at least try, even if there's not a lot of chance. It'd be a good place to work; I wouldn't even have to drive to work. We'd save a fortune on petrol, if nothing else. I bet there's a staff discount as well. And it won't bother them that I don't regard it as a permanent job, because they don't either. Nothing ventured, nothing gained. And it'd be a good feeling to ring the DDO back and tell him not to worry about money for six months. And then maybe Greenpeace will be looking for a civil engineer."

"Now you're getting silly," Clifford said. "One thing at a time."

*

Much to her surprise, Chloe was offered the job and accepted with almost comic gratitude. She had three days between ending her old job and starting the new one, which she spent helping Jo and Mike clean out their house as the contents were packed into hundreds of boxes. It looked very bare and forlorn when everything was taken out and loaded onto the removals lorry, but at least it looked clean.

"Now stay in touch," Jo said, hugging first Chloe then Clifford, as the lorry revved up its engine.

"We will," Chloe said, wiping her nose as Jo got into their car. "No lifting at the other end, either. Keep an eye on her, Mike."

"I will," said Mike and eased the car onto the road and began to drive away, the lorry beginning its leviathan lumber after it.

Clifford and Chloe stood out on the road, waving after them till car and lorry were out of sight.

"Well, that's that, then," Clifford said inadequately.

He could feel the tremor in Chloe's arm as he held it; there was nothing he could say that would help, so he said nothing.

"I'm going for a run," Chloe said, and hurried inside to change.

It was too hot really; she preferred to run either early in the morning or at dusk at this time of year. She knew that by the time she got home her throat would be dry and thick with road dust, and her hair would be temporarily grey with the dust and her face red with sun and exertion. But still she ran to chase away the sadness, even though she also knew that when she got home it would be waiting for her, patiently; but by then it wouldn't hurt quite so much.

When she got home, hot, sweaty and thirsty enough to drink pints of water and still crave more, she showered and went out into the garden and sat in the sun, letting her hair dry in the warmth. She'd finally decided to look at the letters that had been in her grandmother's trunk. She hadn't wanted to look. She'd told herself she was too busy, that she wasn't interested anyway; but the truth was that she was afraid of what she would find. She'd carried the trunk out into the thick daisy-studded grass, and sat down next to it, feeling like Pandora, and then feeling silly for even thinking it.

There was a waft of fragrance as she opened the lid, sandalwood and incense and old paper. The contents had become jumbled by all the moving around, so she decided she would empty it out before repacking it. There were a number of silk scarves printed in bright colours and patterns; one was wrapped around a crystal ball. She hastily wrapped it up again, putting it to one side. There were a number of small carvings, of what she took to be Indian deities, packets of herbs she couldn't identify by sight or smell, a couple of silver charms for a charm bracelet, a string of carved wooden beads that must be sandalwood from the sweet woody aroma that rose from them, a lump of amber unpolished except by fingers and a set of Tarot cards, wrapped in another scarf in silk so deep a purple that it was almost black. The other bits and pieces she was less able to identify; there were a number of rocks but she had no idea of what they were or what significance they must have had for Gran. The unique detritus of her Gran's life defied description or understanding. She packed everything but the packets of letters back into the trunk, and began to read.

They were disappointing really, a collection of mundane duty letters, dry and unrevealing it seemed at first:

"Dear Gran, have moved house again."

"Dear Mum, new job! I shall be moving again soon so I'll let you know the new address. Kiss the girls for me; I'll visit soon."

"Gran, can you send me some money? I'll pay it back as soon as I can..."

"Dear Mum, sorry to hear Cathy has been a pain. Teenagers, eh?"

"Dear Gran, have been evicted from the last address. This one is only a temporary one, my mate is letting me stay at hers for now…."

"Dear Mum, Glasgow is great. You must come and visit and bring Chloe to see me."

After she'd read them all, she tied them back up with the bit of velvet ribbon they'd been tied with and put them back in the trunk. The latest one from Cathy was dated nearly ten years ago, the most recent from her father a little after that. Where had they gone? What had happened to them? She made a note of the last known address of either and then shut the trunk. If she'd been hoping for an easy route to her family, she would have been devastated. What made it so strange for her was that she had virtually no memory of either her father or her sister; they had vanished from her life as cleanly as if they'd both died. Apart from that almost kinaesthetic memory of her father's heartbeat, she couldn't even remember what he had looked like; her sister was a dim figure with red hair that seemed about ten feet tall in her memory. But according to these letters they had both kept in touch sporadically, her father had even visited occasionally if the letters were to be believed. They had both sent their love to her; she could not recall at all if her Gran had ever said anything to that effect. She must have done; but Chloe couldn't remember any of it.

She even wondered if they were even alive. Her father must be around sixty now, her sister in her late thirties. Maybe they were both dead, perhaps that was why the letters stopped. She felt her eyes prickle with tears at that thought. How could she ever know? She might as well give up now.

Hefting the trunk onto her hip like an awkward baby, Chloe went back inside and took the trunk back to their bedroom, where Clifford was working on the computer again.

"Anything?" he asked, glancing up as she put the trunk back at the side of the bed where it had been serving as Chloe's bedside table.

"Old letters, the most recent was ten years ago or thereabouts," she said. "Mind you, I did find a few interesting things."

"Such as?"

"A crystal ball, and a set of tarot cards."

Clifford turned round properly.

"Let's have a look," he said.

Chloe opened the trunk and rummaged around to find them both. Clifford unwrapped the ball carefully.

"This is the real thing, you know," he said after gazing at it for a moment.

"What do you mean, real thing? Are you getting Channel Five on it or something?" Chloe demanded.

"No, no, don't be silly. All I mean is that most crystal balls are made of lead crystal, basically very fine very clear glass. This is made of rock crystal; you can see very tiny flaws and inclusions in it. Little rainbows. It's almost perfect. I don't think you could buy one this clear, at least not without spending an awful lot of money."

"You couldn't," Chloe said. "Anyway, Gran was given this one."

"Given it? I sort of expected she'd brought it back from her travels. Who gave it to her?"

"Well, you know she used to help out with the travellers from time to time? Stitched up wounds and dug out shotgun pellets and said nothing? That sort of thing. She used to get me up in the night sometimes when I was little, when someone had come to the door at the dead of night asking for her help. She couldn't leave me at home on my own so she used to pack me up in the car with blankets and sometimes I'd get out of the car and wander around the camps. I loved it, actually, and they were always kind to me. Anyway, this old lady, I think she was a real gypsy, a real Romany, called my Gran out to see her. She wouldn't go to the hospital, obviously, but she needed help. Apparently Gran told her exactly what was wrong with her; which is what she wanted, not someone lying to her with hopeful lies. So she told Gran that she didn't want any of her special things going to the wives of her sons; she didn't like them and they'd gone into brick anyway, that is, they'd left the travelling life. So she gave Gran her crystal ball and her cards and that was that. She died about three days later. Gran said the ball had been in the old lady's family for hundreds of years; she'd been worried about accepting it on that account, but when she met the daughters-in-law she realised the old woman was right. They'd have sold the crystal and binned the cards."

Chloe took the crystal from him and gazed into it. The room was reflected back to her, upside down, but her vision was drawn deep into the rock, following the tiny flaws and rainbows, till she felt almost dizzy as if she'd been gazing down from a great height.

"It is really beautiful," she said. "It does sort of quiet the mind looking into it. Odd."

"Let's have a peep at the cards, then," Clifford said, and Chloe unwrapped them and they looked through them in fascination.

After a while, Chloe sighed.

"I don't know what all the fuss is about," she said. "I can't understand why there was such a terror of this sort of thing when I was hovering on the fringes of the CU. They're just pictures; interesting pictures. I think they're archetypes, like Jung wrote about. There's nothing sinister here at all."

She sounded disappointed, and Clifford laughed at her.

"I don't think it's the cards, really," he said. "I think it's the whole occult thing; people get obsessed with it and that distracts them from God."

"These seem to be pointing at God, not away," Chloe said. "Just look at The Tower, or Judgement, or The Hermit or Justice."

Clifford glanced at them.

"I see what you mean," he said. "I do remember reading somewhere that they were originally used as a Christian teaching aid, but I could be wrong."

Chloe wrapped the cards up again; they felt worn and smooth with use and she felt very strange about them. She wondered now if her Gran had ever used them or whether she had simply accepted them gracefully as the gift of a dying woman and had put them away out of sight and forgotten about them. And how could you use them, anyway? They were only bits of card after all.

Chapter 12

Chloe was haunted by the images on the cards; they seemed to carry such a weight of mystery, seemed to signify so much she couldn't see. She felt like she had woken from sleep hearing a distant melody fading into silence as her eyes opened, and the harder she tried to recall the tune, the more it slipped out of reach, haunting her with those faint trills and phrases until she woke completely with her mind ticklish and alert. The images reminded her of something she couldn't place, like photos of the distant past she felt she ought to somehow remember.

"Get a grip, woman," she said to herself.

She wasn't often given to this sort of introspection, at least she hadn't been till Gran had died, and frankly it annoyed her. Things just *were*; these things were just pictures on bits of worn card, slippery and slightly greasy from long use.

So why did she keep on looking at them with such breathless awe?

She enjoyed her new job, far more than she had expected. Her new colleagues were wary of her initially; they knew she was actually an engineer and that put her as an unknown quality. Once they realised she worked hard, did what she was told and even made coffee without being asked, she found herself accepted; especially when they discovered she was just filling in after being made redundant twice they relaxed. Their absent colleague was popular and no one wanted to think that this new girl was really after her job; she was just keeping it warm for her. It was also so good not to have to fight every inch of ground; Chloe realised with a sense of shock how much harder her original job actually was simply because she was a woman. She'd had to work twice as hard to get half as far. Discrimination was still alive and well in the workplace, but here at least it was kindly meant; help with heavy lifting was always welcome because it was offered out of kindness not out of an aggressive need to put her down by proving she wasn't as good as a man.

The summer sailed by; when the summer term ended at college, Clifford had time on his hands he had never had before, and when Chloe wasn't at work, they spent long hours in the garden, working or simply sitting. They took a week's break in August, a wet week under canvas in Wales, and returned with relief and a lot of dirty laundry. They'd talked till dawn some nights, snuggled into sleeping bags and then slept in till mid-morning, getting up to tour more castles and monuments in the soft Welsh rain. She'd talked extensively about how the cards made her feel, as if they held some sort of clue, though a clue to quite what she was unsure.

"Look at them, then. I don't think there's any harm in it," Clifford had said. "I know there's plenty who'd be horrified about it but you're a sensible woman. If you don't think about this and get it out of your system, it'll go on bothering you till you do. It's to do with your Gran, isn't it?"

"I think so," she'd said, uncertainly. "I don't know whether she ever used them. But I suspect she'll have looked into it at least. She was so without prejudice about things like that. And the weird thing is they sort of feel like, well, like family photos."

"Photos? What on earth do you mean?"

"Well, they sort of remind me of people I know. Right, the Hermit reminds me of your uncle Peter. OK, I know he isn't a monk and he doesn't have a long white beard, but that's whom it makes me think of. He's got that sort of calm kind face as the Hermit, and he does sort of hold up a light for the world," Chloe had said. "And Strength makes me think of Gran. It's a woman holding open or closing the mouth of a lion; it looks like the way she used to give pills to Chainsaw. She had such enormous strength and gentleness. And the Fool, well, the Fool makes me think of you."

Clifford had rolled over and began laughing.

"Thanks a lot!" he's said.

"It was meant as a compliment, actually," she'd said, huffy. "He's got the same innocence and trust in his face as you. He's got no worries about what's going to happen; he knows he's looked after and he's safe from harm and it's all ahead of him. The sun's shining, and his dog's bounding along beside him and it's all full of hope and promise. That's you all over; never any doubts that everything will be OK in the end."

"Well, it will be OK," he's said. "Even this holiday has been fun if wet."

"There you are; you're an incorrigible optimist, like the Fool."

Back at home, at the hot end of summer, Chloe looked at the cards in their room, hearing that distant chiming of a forgotten song at the back of her mind. She sorted them into two piles. One set was rather like a pack of normal playing cards, with a knight and a page as well as a king and queen for each suit, though there were intriguing pictures for each of the cards where there were just symbols on playing cards. The second, smaller set were what really fascinated her; twenty two cards that seemed so familiar and so exotic and far-off at the same time.

She'd written a letter to her father and her sister and sent them off to their last known address with a request on the envelope to forward if no longer at that address, but she got nothing back, which was much as she'd expected. She was considering what to do next, having run both names through Google and a number of other search engines, but it seemed that neither her father nor her sister had their names on anything the Internet would show up. It was also possible her sister had married and changed her name; she'd never find her now without knowing what her new name might be. She also wasn't entirely sure whether she wanted to find them; after all, they'd left her when she was so small she barely remembered anything about them, and they'd had no contact with even Gran for the best part of ten years so they weren't exactly keen to be with her.

The new college year began with the usual introductory weekend, as it had for them the previous year, but Chloe didn't bother to attend though Clifford was obliged to be there and welcome the new students and their families.

"I don't think anyone would exactly appreciate me standing at the door saying: repent, the end of your life as you know it is nigh," Chloe said on the Friday when the first social event was due to take place. "And anyway, after the last barn dance I don't think I'm exactly the belle of the ball. So count me out."

Someone had decided to count her in, however. The woman who was organising wives' events that year had simply gone through the list of wives and had assigned them all to different prayer groups, without asking whether they actually wanted to. She'd also gone to the trouble to assign a host to each meeting, again without once asking if they wanted to host a group; her only criterion was that all the hosts were in at least their second year. On the Monday, Clifford apologetically brought the letter home that had been posted in their pigeon-hole at college, and waited for Chloe to explode.

She bit down on her lip, biting back expletives.

"How dare they? How dare they?" she said after a moment where she had gone very red. "This is ridiculous; no one has bothered asking me if this is all right. Are we all expected to just roll over for the King?"

She sighed; she didn't know quite what to do. Most of her wanted to rip the letter up and post back the fragments; but that would just create a commotion that she couldn't face. When she phoned Jo that evening, Jo was sympathetic.

"Why don't you give it a go, though, seeing as it's been dropped on you and it's more hassle to resist? Be Buddhist about it; take the path of least resistance. You never know, there might be some sane ones among the newbies; after that, if it's no go, then you can go and tell whoever is in charge where they can shove it," she said.

"You might make a friend; and if not, you've lost nothing but an evening that you'd have just spent in front of the telly."

Chloe reluctantly agreed. It would be a lot of bother to refuse, certainly without at least trying it once. Part of her craved the thought of a new friend, however remote that possibility might be. If it was a no-go thing, she could always just write a letter refusing further meetings. And how much hassle could a prayer group really be, anyway?

*

On the Tuesday evening, Chloe was sweating with nerves; she'd cleaned and tidied till the cats had gone into hiding at the sight of a duster. She'd even cleaned behind the cooker, though she'd garrotte anyone who actually looked behind there. She'd lit candles on the mantelpiece, scented night-lights next to the Russian icon of Madonna and child that her Gran had given her as a confirmation present. She'd set out cups and saucers and a plate of ginger biscuits in the kitchen ready for the inevitable social bit with coffee and tea. She was as ready as she could be; or so she thought.

First disaster was the arrival of Nicky, scrubbed and baby-less for the evening, though the bulge of her lower abdomen could be due to either a burgeoning foetus or too many biscuits.

"What an interesting room," she said as Chloe, stunned to near speechlessness, showed her in.

Amazing how the word interesting could hold so many connotations. Chloe bit back asking, well, what's wrong with it then and went to answer the door again. If it's Felicity, I'm out of here, she thought bitterly.

The expected number was ten for each group, including the host, but Chloe hadn't quite realised how many that actually felt like. The room wasn't large and she ended up sitting on the hearth next to the wooden statue of Buddha as every chair and space on the sofa filled up with women.

My bum is going to be so numb, she thought, and was pleased to realise that she'd not said it out loud.

Nicky was nominally in charge, since Chloe had never attended any of the previous year's meetings. But after about half an hour of chit-chat, Chloe began to get impatient; she'd imagined that once everyone was here, they'd get down to prayer, and then they'd have a quick coffee and get out. She also became really jumpy as she saw eyes flickering around the room, taking in the décor and the objects that Gran had collected over the years. She could feel hostility welling up, particularly from Nicky, and wished she'd turned the main light off so all they'd have was candlelight and that'd be too dim to see much of the stuff properly if at all. Too late now. Oh well.

"Do you not use that lovely brass fruit bowl then, Chloe?" one of the newcomers asked.

It took her a second to realise what she meant.

"Oh, this? No, this isn't a fruit bowl. It's a Tibetan singing bowl," she said, picking up the big bowl and balancing it on her open palm. "They use it as an aid to prayer and meditation," she explained and to illustrate, struck the bowl with the wooden beater and a single pure bell-like sound filled the room, vibrating outwards for more than a minute, stunning them all into silence. "You can play it by running the beater round the rim, like this," she said, starting to do so, but the clear silvery sound was cut short by Nicky grabbing at the bowl and stilling the sound so abruptly that Chloe felt violated.

"I hardly think Christians need such an object to help them pray," Nicky said, harshly. "The Tibetans wouldn't need it either if they came to the Lord."

Chloe stared at her, feeling her anger start to rise up, shouting. Then she quelled it, with a massive effort, and simply shrugged, which could mean anything.

"Shall we pray then?" she said coldly.

Nicky looked at her with the dislike plain on her face.

"We usually discuss prayer needs first," she said, speaking as if Chloe were an idiot, enunciating her words very crisply, and then turned away.

Chloe stuck her tongue out at her, and the woman nearest to her giggled and then turned it into a cough when Nicky glanced at her.

The discussion actually shocked Chloe; this was not what she'd expected at all. They shared all sorts of secrets, usually not their own, "for prayer", tales of infidelities, illness both physical and mental, problems with relationships, financial problems, problems with children, problems with infertility; the scope was endless. After ten minutes of this, Chloe couldn't keep her mouth shut any longer.

"Hang on a minute," she said. "I was under the impression that God is omniscient as well as omnipresent; so surely He knows all this. Why do we need to discuss all this? It seems bizarre to say the least. I don't need to know any of this. Can we just get on with praying please?"

There was a stunned, uncomfortable silence while Chloe thought, oh crap I've done it now.

"It probably is about time we did some actual praying," said the woman who had giggled.

Nicky sniffed; she was furious with Chloe.

"The discussion is simply so we can align ourselves with God," she said, virtuously. "If we know what needs praying for, we are better able to offer it to God."

"Yeah?" Chloe said, raising her eyebrows expressively. "OK, I think we all know enough by now."

She settled herself forward into a cross-legged position and placed her hands neatly clasped in her lap, and bowed her head slightly and closed her eyes. In the background, she'd set the stereo to play Gregorian chants very softly, but she could still hear Nicky's intake of outraged breath. Presented with a fait accompli by Chloe, she could do nothing but fall in with it, but Chloe could feel the enmity surging off her like a bad smell. She shut herself off from the room and focussed on her breathing, quieting herself so she could listen for that stillness that she craved.

They prayed much as they had discussed; at length and in depth, and Chloe felt herself slipping from brief stillness to overwhelming sleepiness. The fragrance from the candles and from the sandalwood Buddha was intensely relaxing, and the drone of praying voices was so boring, she felt herself fighting sleep. Fortunately she didn't have to fight for very long. As soon as the list was done, Nicky grabbed the hand of the woman next to her, initiating a flurry of hands to hands, intoned the Grace, and then glared at Chloe.

"Coffee, now, I think," she said pointedly, and Chloe flushed with irritation.

"I'll go and put the kettle on then," she said. "How many for what?"

A quick show of hands told her they all wanted coffee, so she trudged off to the kitchen and got on with that. When she came back, she sensed a change in atmosphere.

"We were just saying, Chloe, we wonder how you can be comfortable living with so many pagan artefacts," Nicky said, gesturing around her.

Chloe looked blank.

"I don't get you," she said.

Patiently, as if to an idiot, Nicky said,

"A lot of these sort of objects come from cultures that hate the Lord," she said. "They often have demonic associations. We just wondered how you live with that."

"Demonic?" Chloe echoed, gazing at the serene wooden face of the Buddha. "I think you've watched too many horror films."

"No, it's true," said another woman, Julie. She'd been the most explicit in her prayers. "We had a deliverance ministry in our home church."

"You were a post-woman?" Chloe said.

"Deliverance. You know, delivering people from the demonic influences. You'd be shocked at how many cases arose as a direct result of artefacts like these being brought into the home," she explained.

"Bollocks," Chloe said, without thinking. "I've never heard such a load of superstitious rubbish in my life. That Buddha, he's from a culture that loves peace. You're surely not saying he's carrying round demons like some sort of spiritual woodworm?"

"Without a shadow of a doubt," Julie said emphatically. "You ought to burn it."

Chloe gazed at them all, barely able to believe what she'd heard.

"I think you should just drink your coffee quickly and go home," she said. "Otherwise you might find you get hitch-hikers coming home with you. This place is probably so infested with demonic influence they could do with spreading out a bit. It must be dead crowded in here; unlike angels I don't think demons can balance on the head of a pin for the sake of compact storage."

She was a bit shocked at the result of that joke. They took her at her word, made their excuses and left. Looking at the half full cups and untouched biscuits on the tray, she sighed and then started laughing.

"I can't believe they took me seriously," she said, when Clifford came through to find out how it had gone. "I'd hate to think what'd happen if they knew I have a pack of Tarot cards on my bedside table and a crystal ball in my jumper drawer!"

Chapter 13

The leaves on the trees surrounding the college were turning buff and bronze and beginning to drift down in ever increasing flurries every time the wind got up, and though the sun in the middle of the day was still warm, the mornings were chilly if not actually frosty. The marigolds in Chloe's garden were still bright but beginning to look a little tatty in places and she stopped gathering them for the big jar of pale olive oil that she had been filling with the flower-heads till the oil took on the orange glow of the petals, wringing them out and adding fresh petals. The warmth of the kitchen windowsill seemed inadequate now for the infusion process so she transferred the jar to the airing cupboard for the last infusion. It should be strong enough by now; her Gran's notebook had been annoyingly vague about the number of batches of flowers needed to make the oil and her own recollections were correspondingly vague.

She had taken to choosing a card at random every day from the Tarot pack, and contemplating its meaning during the day. She had resisted the urge to buy a book about it, even though it might have explained a lot but she had felt that would be going further than she was happy about. Looking at the cards and thinking about the images was somehow acceptable whereas researching it properly wouldn't be, at least not yet. That morning she had turned over the High Priestess, a figure seated on a sort of throne between two pillars, wearing flowing robes and a high headdress. There was a cross at her neck, a crescent moon at her feet and she held a scroll with the word Tora written on it. Her face was calm, implacable and very strong; she had gazed on mysteries and still kept them. Chloe felt that same sense of mystified wonder when she gazed at the figure that she had first felt when looking on the pack. It reminded her of something but she couldn't ever quite place it. She put the card face up next to her lamp and went downstairs to make breakfast. Clifford was on a preaching placement, and had gone out an hour ago and wouldn't be home till lunch.

Munching toast she turned the oven on and put the joint of beef in on low; there was plenty of time to do potatoes and vegetables, but the meat was a cheap, tough cut that would need long slow cooking and plenty of basting to make it tender. She flicked the kettle on so she could make herself some coffee and then cursed when the doorbell rang.

"If it's someone wanting me to go to Church with them, they can just swivel," she said, sprinting to the door still with her toast in her hand.

The first thing she noticed, even before she saw the woman waiting, was a green Transit van beyond their low fence. It was mostly green, but it had been painted with trees and flowers and a big blue ball she realised must be the earth. Then Chloe looked at the woman who was standing their, looking away as if bored. It was the woman from the wood.

Her hair was even shorter, almost as if it had all been shaved off only weeks ago and had only grown back enough to show the deep bright red colour but not the curls. She looked tired, and when she turned to see Chloe standing there, she jumped with as much surprise as Chloe had felt.

"I must have the wrong house," she said, and began to turn away again.

"Hang on a minute, who did you want?" Chloe asked, feeling her stomach turn over suddenly, lurching as though she was on a roller coaster.

"I'm looking for Chloe Williams," the woman said, as if she was certain Chloe couldn't be her.

"That's me; what do you want?" Chloe said, staring at her.

How in hell had this woman got her home address? The company wouldn't surely have given it out.

The woman made a funny noise in her throat as if she were choking on a sweet; then she swallowed, hard.

"I went to the house," she said. "There's an American professor living there; he said I should speak to you."

Chloe said nothing; all she could hear was the thundering of her own blood rushing through her body, deafening her.

"He said that Gran died last year," said the woman. "I should have come back sooner; I was too late."

Chloe felt her knees begin to wobble, horribly. There were ants crawling all over her skin and her hands had gone so cold she couldn't feel them, and it was getting dark so it must be night time, even though she was only eating breakfast. She had dropped the toast, and all she could think was, did it land butter side down?

She found herself on the step, her head being pressed between her knees as she tried to breathe. She was deep under water, the pressure was unbearable and why were there still ants all over her if she was in water?

"It's OK," the woman was saying over and over again. "Just breathe."

She put a paper bag in front of her to breathe into and slowly Chloe began to breathe normally and the ants vanished. Her hands were still icy cold, even when the woman held them.

"Shall we go inside?" said the woman. "You need to have a hot drink and get warm again."

She helped Chloe up and supported her into the house, and placed her in one of the kitchen chairs.

"You must have known I was coming, the kettle has just boiled," she said, holding up the steaming kettle. "Or should I get you some brandy? I have some rescue remedy in the van."

"Coffee will do," Chloe said, half panting. "I draw the line at brandy at ten o'clock on a Sunday morning. Gran used to use rescue remedy; I have some somewhere, but I can't think where."

"Don't worry; I bet I can find it," the woman said. "You've got the kitchen just like Gran would have had it. I bet the first aid kit is in the cupboard near the kettle. Gran never put it in the cupboard under the sink like many people."

"Cathy?" Chloe said.

"I haven't used that name in a long time," the woman said. "But that's what you knew me as, isn't it?"

"What do you call yourself, then?"

"It doesn't matter. Call me Cathy; then we'll neither of us get confused."

Chloe watched her sister rummaging through cupboards, finding the jar of ground coffee, then the cafetière and then mugs.

"I couldn't believe it when I saw it was you," Cathy said, pouring hot water onto the grounds. "I mean, how weird is that? Meeting you in the woods, and then this? How did Gran die? I thought she was immortal."

"Cancer."

Chloe couldn't take this in; it was just too much for her.

"That must have annoyed the hell out of her," Cathy said.

"It did."

Cathy brought the mugs to the table and sat down next to Chloe. Seeing her now, Chloe couldn't understand why she hadn't known straight away who she was.

"I resigned, you know," she said, suddenly, after a sip of coffee. "After the tree, I couldn't do that job any more. I resigned."

"Good," Cathy said briskly. "I could see it had affected you. We won, by the way. They backed off when we found a rare orchid growing in the clearing near that tree. The original survey had missed it; the site is getting its status, and will be made a local nature reserve as well. All we needed was a bit of time to fight off the developers. So what are you doing now?"

"Temporary job at a garden centre, it's fun and it pays the bills," Chloe said. "So you live round here?"

"God, no!" Cathy said. "I live in my van. I do that sort of protest anywhere I'm needed, all over England. The organisation I'm with pays my expenses, sort of, and the rest I just make up myself with whatever I can find. You know, seasonal work, pub jobs that sort of thing. Nothing to tie me down for long. Then when the next protest comes up, I can just go."

"How long have you been doing this?" Chloe asked.

"Years; but about ten years since I've been doing this as a life choice. To begin with I just drifted into it; you know how it is; friends are doing it so you go along just for the fun of it. Then I really got into it; we don't win very often but the buzz when we do! Well, it's better than anything I've tried. If you could bottle that feeling, it'd outsell every drug on the market."

Chloe grinned.

"So what are you doing here? This looks like some sort of college," Cathy said. "And you've changed your name."

"My husband is training here; this is a vicar factory," Chloe explained and laughed as Cathy choked on her coffee.

"You're joking!" she said. "No, you're not joking. Married, and to a trainee vicar! Gran must have gone berserk about that one."

"No."

"Then she must have mellowed with age. I can't imagine it somehow, though," Cathy said. "I can't get my head round the fact that she's dead. Was it bad?"

Chloe bit her lip.

"For her? Or for me?" she said, and heard her sister's intake of breath.

Cathy said nothing for a moment and then answered.

"Both, I suppose," she said.

"Well, for me, it was hell. But that's what you'd expect, my only relative dying. For her? Well, you know how tough she was. She found this melanoma; they treated it and she thought it was dealt with. Didn't tell me about it of course. You know what she was like. Or maybe you've forgotten. It's been a long time. Anyway, the cancer came back, with all its friends. She only told me when I came over unexpectedly and found the Macmillan nurse there. You'd not have realised it to look at her, if you didn't know what she was usually like. She had lost most of her hair with the chemo the first time around, but she wore a wig when I'd visited and I didn't notice because she wore a scarf as well like she often did. But that day, she was different, like the colours were fading in and out. We talked and she told me she was dying. She wasn't willing to have another course of chemo, and I think they may have refused to give her more because of her age. She'd been so fit they tried the first time to treat the melanoma, but with all the secondaries it'd just have been torture for nothing. I don't think she'd have got much longer anyway even with treatment. You're right, though. She was severely pissed off about it; the one thing she had no way of treating, though I think she tried. Then, she died. It was about three days later; the nurse said they had expected her to last much longer because she was so tough and positive. And she was too. I was with her up till the last; she was conscious to the final few moments too. She'd been quoting poetry, T.S. Eliot's Four Quartets, minutes before she started to lose her voice. I went and read it all later, while I was waiting for the doctor to come and certify death. I sat at her side while she went cold and read the whole of the Four Quartets aloud to her, and why weren't you there? Why weren't you there? Why? Why did I have to be on my own then?"

Chloe began to cry, great aching sobs that tore at her and the tears fell like drops of blood onto the table and into her coffee. Cathy stared at her for a moment and then put her arms round her and held her, whispering, "I'm sorry; I'm so sorry."

Chloe rubbed her eyes with her sleeve, and got up and blew her nose on a piece of kitchen roll. Cathy was dry-eyed, but only just.

"Time and the bell have buried the day,

The black cloud carries the sun away.

Will the sunflower turn to us, will the clematis

Stray down, bend to us; tendril and spray

Clutch and cling?

Chill

Fingers of yew be curled

Down on us? After the kingfisher's wing

Has answered light to light, and is silent, the light is still

At the still point of the turning world," Chloe said, her voice cracked and nasal-sounding. "That's what she was quoting. I don't know if you remember how fond she was of poetry or if you ever read any of it, later or if you forgot it all like you forgot me. How could you just leave me?"

Cathy sighed.

"It's all such a long time ago now," she said. "I'm not sure I can explain. I can explain why I didn't come back, that's the easy bit. I thought none of you would want me back. I thought Gran was so disappointed in me, that she'd not want me back. Oh, I'd write from time to time, but I was never certain whether Gran's letters were sincere. She'd say in them that she wanted me to come home; but I was never sure enough."

"That's so stupid. Gran never fibbed about things like that: never. If she said she wanted you to come home, she meant it. You'll have to do better than that, Cathy," Chloe said. "Why did you leave? What did I do wrong?"

Cathy sighed, again.

"You didn't do anything wrong," she said. "You were only little anyway. I don't know if I can explain properly."

"Try," said Chloe, her back to her sister, her teeth gritted.

"Do you remember Mum at all? No? Well, I shouldn't imagine you would. You were only two when she died. I was fourteen. That's a huge difference. I'd had her all those years and you've had Gran. Since you don't remember Mum, you won't understand why it was so hard for me, not just losing Mum, but getting Gran instead," Cathy said. "It's hard to remember that you won't see it the same, because you were so little, but Gran was a horrible shock to me."

"Why?"

"You don't remember Mum, but she was an absolute airhead; sweet and kind and silly. I don't think she was actually lacking in intelligence to be honest, but she was totally, well, fluffy. She and Dad were really only kids themselves when they got married; I think they were both about twenty, not a bean between them. They lived with Gran. After less than a year, it became obvious that things weren't going to work. I don't think Gran disliked Mum, but they couldn't live together, and with me on the way, it was going to get worse. Anyway, Gran did something amazing. She left. She told me about it, when Dad left. She said she thought the best thing to do was for her to get out of the house and let them get on with it without interfering. She thought that she would ruin things if she stayed, so she went off on those amazing travels of hers. I used to love getting cards from her, and the stuff she used to send back. You must have it all here, now. The marriage worked without her around, and that's what she wanted. You see, Gran and Mum were almost total opposites I suppose. Mum was all fluffy and empty-headed and sweet; she didn't know anything about the kind of things Gran was interested in. Gran was, well, she was Gran. You know; an intellect so sharp you could cut with it. Huge general knowledge, could do anything she set her hand to, from gardening to surgery. She had very little patience with lesser mortals though, and Mum always felt she was one of the lesser mortals and it made her even fluffier around Gran. Nerves I suppose. Gran would come and visit every year or so; I loved her visits. She seemed like someone from another world. But she'd only stay a week or so. She'd stay till Mum started dropping cups or doing stupid things because Gran made her nervous, and then Gran would be off again. Anyway, when Mum died and Gran came to live with us, I thought it'd be OK. But it wasn't."

Cathy had begun fiddling with her silver bracelet; she was uncomfortable and awkward.

"I know you loved Gran," she said. "But Chloe, I didn't grow up with her values and attitudes like you did. For me, she was a nightmare come real. Mum hadn't cared whether I was doing well at school, wasn't even interested, and Dad had been too busy to notice much, what with you arriving and everything. Gran cared about stuff like that, and when she saw my school report, she was really upset. She went back and read the earlier ones, just to make sure it wasn't down to Mum's death, and then she set about making me pull my socks up."

Cathy gulped down the last of her tepid coffee.

"Maybe if she'd waited till I was feeling a bit less raw from losing Mum," she said. "Maybe if she'd been gentler about it. I don't know, but it was terrible. All I wanted was my nice fluffy Mum and I got this intellectual dragon, all sines and cosines and poetry and the circulation of the blood and battles and dates and all that crap that doesn't matter. So there we were, she saying it mattered and me saying it didn't. Well, she was sixty odd and I was fourteen; there's no contest about who's going to win, is there? I spent every evening of every week trying to catch up with work I didn't give a stuff about, while all my friends were out having fun. I almost hated her; especially since she was so reasonable about it at first. She'd tell me how it was in my own interest to work hard, do well at school, all that stuff. I bet that's what you did, too. Otherwise, how else would you be an engineer? That's not the point though; the point is that though I tried, I could never do quite well enough for her. Oh God, how I tried! I figured I must be as fluffy as Mum was, candy-floss for brains, but no, she wouldn't listen to that. There was no way a granddaughter of hers could ever be anything less than top of the academic tree. She wouldn't accept I couldn't do it, that I'd never be anything more than average at best, at least in intellectual matters. She drove Dad away; I don't know how she managed that, but she did. They'd have horrid rows, late at night."

"I remember the rows," Chloe said. "The slamming doors and the shouting. I remember that."

"You used to come to my room, and hide under my bed," Cathy said. "So I'd make you get into the bed next to me and I'd tell you stories in whispers so that neither of us could hear the shouting. I hoped Gran would leave; but Dad did instead."

Cathy rubbed her eyes, as if rubbing away tears.

"It got worse after that," she said. "I couldn't do anything right for her. I suppose she was under huge pressure anyway, so she was less and less tolerant. She'd got a job at the local GP practice; they'd been desperate for a woman doctor and she was damn good. But that meant she was working all day, with you at a nursery and me at school, and then she'd be out part of the evening leaving me to baby-sit. Sometimes it was evening surgery proper; other times it'd be because someone had come round asking her to come out, travellers, usually. She should have told them to go to hospital or come to the surgery in the morning, but she never would. She was fascinated by them; the gypsy people especially. Maybe it was her wanderlust that meant she felt attracted by them and their way of life. She broke all sorts of codes of conduct and probably the law as well, when she did some of those visits, and she knew it. I went with her sometimes, and she was quite scary about me never telling anyone what I'd seen. You know how fierce she could be. Not that I ever saw anything incriminating, at least not as far as I can remember. But I knew she was on the very edge of what was proper."

"After you left, I went with her," Chloe said. "In the middle of the night sometimes. It was scary but exciting. And yes, she made me promise I'd never tell anyone anything about it. I remember she went once to dig out shotgun pellets out of one of the men; I think he'd been peppered by a gamekeeper."

"I couldn't take her pressuring me to work hard, do well, not when the best I did was never good enough, so as soon as I could fool her into trusting me, I'd be off and out, staying at friends' houses. Drinking and smoking and doing all the things teenagers get up to. But I was wrong to think I could fool her; I couldn't fool her. She just gave me enough rope to hang myself with and then she'd reel me in and ground me. She always gave me the chance to redeem myself; and then she'd have to ground me again. I must have been a nightmare for her. Anyway, a friend of mine moved away, to Scotland, and as soon as I turned sixteen, I packed a bag and went to stay with her and never came back. Gran was furious with me; then she just accepted it and gave up trying to make me to come back."

Cathy scrubbed at her face; she looked suddenly very much older than she was. Whatever her life had been, it certainly hadn't been easy, and it showed in every line on her face.

"When I saw you at the wood, it shook me up," Cathy said. "Not that I knew who you were. But you look so like Mum. I'd made myself forget about the past; it doesn't do to dwell on things. I'd stopped writing to Gran because I didn't want to tell her I was homeless, and penniless. I got roped into a protest and it became a habit. People share stuff on those protests; so I was sure of being fed, at least. And after a few protests, I got noticed. I discovered I wasn't as stupid as I'd thought, that I had a knack for tactics and organisation and the sheer psychology of protest; and that's what the people who run the organisation noticed too. So they fed me up and looked after me, got me doing more than mindless drone stuff; got me reading ecology books, books on nature and spirituality and I found I had a mind after all. Just not the sort of mind Gran understood. I was looked after, and believe me, I needed to be looked after. And as I got better at the protest thing, I got better at everything. I passed my driving test, finally, after driving illegally for years, and I managed to buy the van and do it up, so at least I have somewhere to sleep that isn't too cold and damp. The weird thing is that when I saw you that day, I'd been thinking about Gran, and how she would understand what I was trying to do. She was always keen on environmental issues even before it became fashionable to be Green; she even had that mystical approach to religion that you find among some Greens. That was why I thought she'd have been appalled that you'd married not only a Christian but a would-be priest too; she always thought the Church was both narrow minded and shallow spirited in the main. Anyway, I saw you there, looking so like Mum, and I thought, how strange, the day I think about Gran I see someone who looks like Mum. That's why I picked you, not your boss; I should have aimed at the top man, but I couldn't. I suddenly felt about five again. I'd managed to forget I had a little sister out there somewhere. But it set me thinking. I thought, maybe if I went to see Gran, and told her what I was doing now, maybe she'd be proud of me, after all. So I went back to the house, and this American answered the door, and told me that Gran was dead, had been dead over a year. I didn't tell him who I was, though. He just said that if I wanted to know more, I should contact the old lady's granddaughter, and he gave me this address."

Chloe looked at her sister and saw she was now crying herself properly.

"I'll make some more coffee," she said. "That last cup went cold on me. Or should we break out the brandy?"

Cathy gave her a painful grin.

"No, coffee will do fine," she said, and watched Chloe making the coffee, and open the oven and baste a joint of beef.

"Sunday lunch, how nostalgic is that," Cathy said as the smell of roasting meat filled the kitchen. "Mum was a hopeless cook, except for Sunday lunch. She was brilliant at that. Best Yorkshire pudding in the world. Gran never got as good at it, even if she could cook anything else. But Mum's roast beef and Yorkshire pudding, well, that's something to remember."

"This probably won't be as good, then," Chloe said. "I sort of assumed you'd be vegetarian."

"I am. Mostly. But once in a while I err. Can I stay for lunch then?"

"Good God, Cathy, what sort of a monster do you think I am? I haven't seen you for years and you have to ask if you can stay for lunch?" Chloe exclaimed.

Cathy gazed at her for a moment. Then she laughed.

"You might look like Mum," she said. "But you sound so like Gran it's scary!"

Chapter 14

Chloe was shaking roast potatoes to turn them without touching them, fluffing up their surfaces so they would crisp up nicely when Clifford came home.

"Interesting van out there," he said. "Do we have a visitor or something?"

"Something," Chloe said. "My sister, actually."

Clifford stared at her.

"She got the letter?"

"No, she went to see Gran and was sent here," Chloe said, shoving the roasting dish back in the oven. "She's gone to have a hot bath, by the way, but she'll be down in a minute because I just heard the water draining away. She lives in the van so she appreciates a chance for a bath when she gets it."

"She's homeless?"

"Well, sort of. She's the one from the wood; she does protesting as a sort of profession. A vocation if you like."

Clifford stood digesting this for a moment.

"I'll be back in five minutes," he said, and went back out to the car and drove off.

When Cathy came downstairs again, she looked very pink from the heat of the bath.

"Did I hear this husband of yours come in?" she asked.

"Yes. He's just popped out for something; he'll be back shortly. Nice bath?"

"Bloody good. I have a washing up bowl in the van and I use that to wash in every day, even if it's with cold water. A lot don't bother; I've always tried to keep up with that sort of thing; it's too easy to lose the last vestiges of self-respect in this life. But a bath, that's such bliss for me. Some of the big stations have showers you can pay to use, so I usually take advantage of the opportunity if I'm there and have the money. Sometimes on cold nights, I dream about hot baths. That dinner smells damn good," Cathy said.

Now she'd shed a number of layers of woollens and velvet, Chloe could see how thin her sister looked, in an underfed feline sort of way.

"Won't be long," she said. "I shall serve up when Clifford gets back. Though I hope he won't be long otherwise we'll be able to use the Yorkshire puddings as Frisbees."

She stirred the gravy, feeling her own mouth begin to water, listening carefully for the sound of their car.

"That's him," she said, and a moment later he came in, hurrying into the kitchen to greet Cathy.

"This is my sister, Cathy," Chloe said as the two faced each other.

Clifford looked at her and then grinned and pulled out from behind him what he had been concealing.

"Champagne?" Cathy said, and burst into tears. "Why?"

"We're just so pleased you've found us," Clifford said, and passed her a clean handkerchief still warm from the radiator.

Cathy blew her nose and became brisk and organised and helped Chloe serve up the dinner while Clifford found glasses and opened the champagne. There was a pause while he poured the wine into the flutes that looked as fragile as soap bubbles, and then he held up his glass.

"To family," he said, and clinked his glass first to Chloe's then to Cathy's.

Cathy looked emotional but said nothing and took a sip from her glass.

"I'm starved," she said. "Can we eat or do we have to say Grace or something first?"

"Let's eat; God already knows we're grateful," Clifford said gently.

When they'd eaten, Chloe said to her sister,

"Well?"

"On a scale of one to ten, I'd put that at eleven. Better than Gran but not quite as good as Mum," Cathy said. "But a million times better than I could do."

"Rubbish," Chloe said. "Besides, no one can do Sunday lunch on a primus stove or a camp fire."

Cathy just laughed at her.

"You do sound like Gran," she said. "On one of her better days, mind, when she was feeling tolerant."

Clifford got up and started filling the sink with hot water.

"You girls go and sit down; I'll do the dishes and bring through some coffee in a few minutes," he said.

In the living room, Cathy sat at the hearth and stroked Sylvester who was drowsing there in the warmth of the fire.

"It's weird," she said. "All this stuff from her house, and yet Gran isn't here. It doesn't seem real that she's gone."

"Not to me either," Chloe said. "And I've had a year to get used to it, not just a morning. She left me everything, you know, but that was only because she hadn't got a clue any more where you or Dad might be. The house is being rented out but properly speaking you have a third share in it, as well as all the effects."

Cathy shrugged.

"I have no use for any of it," she said, ruffling the cat's fur. "You keep it; I don't want any of it."

Chloe glanced at her downcast face.

"It's still yours, whether you take it or not," she said. "I'll keep things safe, in case you ever do want it. You've always got a home with us if you need it. All the hot baths you can eat."

Cathy snorted.

"That's a real incentive," she said. "But you don't mean it."

Chloe grabbed her sister by her birdlike shoulders and shook her firmly but gently.

"Don't be so bloody silly," she said. "This is not about deserving or not deserving anything. This just is. So just nod and smile, it's the easiest way to get me to shut up. Stay with us tonight at least."

She let go, and sat down on the hearthrug next to the cat and her sister.

"You're pretty forceful, aren't you?" Cathy said.

"I've had to be."

"You're Gran's girl all through," Cathy said. "Mum was never into assertiveness; it took me years to learn to stand up for myself after I ran away. Maybe I should have stuck around with Gran. She was right about so many things; I never wanted to admit that to her, but now she's dead, I want to go up to her and say, sorry, Gran, you were right and I was wrong. And I never can now."

Chloe put her arm round Cathy's shoulder.

"I think she'd know," she said. "She knew she'd made mistakes and wished she could make amends. I'd like you to read the last letter she wrote to me; she'd have written to you if she'd known where you were."

Upstairs, Chloe moved her lamp off the trunk and looked at the card she'd picked that morning before opening the trunk and fetching out that letter from Gran. She hesitated before reuniting the High Priestess with the rest of the pack, wrapping it in the purple silk and tucking it under her pillow. The calm face of the image stayed in her mind as she hurried downstairs, back to her sister.

"Here," she said. "Read this. I think it'll help, a bit at least."

Cathy was still reading it when Clifford came through with coffee; she just glanced up at him with reddening eyes, and he put her mug next to her on the floor. Eventually she folded the paper up again and handed it back to Chloe.

"Thanks," she said, somewhat thickly. "Funny to think of Gran admitting mistakes. She seemed cast–iron, arrogant even, in her self-belief. Maybe that was the Grim Reaper prompting her to humility for the first time."

Chloe nodded.

"You see her very differently," she said. "I didn't see her as arrogant, not really. She had plenty to be arrogant about I suppose. Did you know Dad was illegitimate? I don't imagine many did know that."

"No, I didn't know that. I wonder who the father was and why she didn't marry him. Different era I suppose. If her father was against it, well, even Gran was young once. She said she regretted it. I wonder if he's still alive."

"Dad? Or Gran's mystery lover?"

"Both, I suppose. I saw Dad a few times after I ran away; he tried to persuade me to go back. But it's a long time since I saw him, eighteen years maybe. He'd be in his late fifties, I think. Or he may be dead. I don't care, not really. He ran away when he should have stayed."

Chloe just looked at her sister with raised eyebrows.

"That isn't fair," Cathy protested. "I was sixteen, he was thirty seven at least. He could have dealt with Gran if he'd wanted to."

"I don't think so," Chloe said. "Gran could stop a hurricane in its tracks; how much chance would her own son have had? Get real, Cathy, you know he ran away for the same reasons you did."

Cathy raised wet eyes to her; they were full of such pain.

"No, he didn't," she said. "There was so much more for me to run away from. You won't remember any of it, thank God. But if you did remember, you'd not say such stupid things."

Chloe cursed herself; there were things her sister was obviously not going to share with her and she'd push her away if she asked questions that were too close to the bone.

"I'm sorry," she said. "I don't remember anything of what you went through; I'm sorry if I upset you."

"Forget it," Cathy said. "You were just a kiddie; I'm glad you don't remember any of it."

But the way she looked at her made Chloe shiver. As if she were afraid that Chloe might actually remember.

*

Chloe was weeding in the warm autumn garden, her hand fork dipping and rising in the rich soil. The rhythm of her work seemed to lull her like music as she methodically eased stray weeds out of the earth, casting them aside and dipping the fork in again. A corner of fabric protruded from the soil, pink and blue check, soft and damp with the falling dew. She raised the fork and dug in around the fabric, trying to slide it out of the border where it shouldn't be at all, but the material seemed stuck so she had to scrape at the earth that seemed packed hard where it had been loose and friable moments ago. She was annoyed and irritated; what was this fabric doing in her neat garden? How had it become so deeply embedded in a border she'd planted and dug and weeded all the last year? Why had she never noticed it?

The more she dug, the worse it got, so she tried to simply pull the material out. No go; it was stuck. So she began digging harder and faster and while the hole became a huge crater like the impact of a bomb, the material remained stuck fast at the bottom.

She dropped the fork and sat back on her heels and used her fingers to try and loosen the fabric, breaking her nails and bruising her fingertips. Finally, crying with frustration and despair, she caught hold of the material and began tugging at it frantically, feebly, hopelessly.

Suddenly, it gave way, coming free without warning so that she fell over backwards. The hole was empty; she couldn't see the fabric any more, though it should be there, next to the hole. The bottom of the hole was roughed up, uneven; the soil looked like it had just been hoed and raked ready for seeds. As she leaned over to look, she saw eyes in the dirt, peering back up at her. On her knees in the pit, she scraped away the soil, tenderly. Toys again, soft toys, dollies and gollies and rabbits and teddies. She picked them out of the earth, dusting them off and putting them to one side of the hole. There were eyes still, gazing up at her.

She swept the soil away from the dirty face in the hole. It was her sister.

Chloe sat up in the bed, feeling the sweat prickling on her back and her heart thumping so loud she couldn't understand why Clifford could sleep on undisturbed. He slept like a child, his arms flung above his head on the pillow, his breathing even and slow.

She swung herself out of bed and in the darkness felt for her dressing gown. As she crept downstairs, she saw the kitchen light was on.

Cathy sat at the kitchen table, Chainsaw on her lap and a cigarette burning in a saucer on the table next to her.

"I couldn't sleep," she said. "Are you OK?"

"I have nightmares; I had one just now," Chloe explained. "I need to get up and do something else or I can't go back to sleep."

"What did you dream about?" Cathy asked, picking up her cigarette and drawing on it deeply.

Chloe thought about it for a moment. It had been so vivid a minute ago, now it was slipping away.

"I don't know; I always forget once I'm awake," she said finally. "Do you want a hot drink?"

"Go on then," Cathy said. "I could do with something to knock me out."

"I found Gran's recipe book with all those concoctions she used to make," Chloe said, filling the kettle. "She had a good one for insomnia, but I had to find a herbal supplier for the ingredients. They weren't exactly the kind of things you'd find in the supermarket, not even the Indian ones."

She pulled out a jar containing what looked rather like pot-pourri, and shook it to distribute the ingredients evenly.

"This one even tastes nice, especially with honey," she said. "Do you often find it hard to sleep?"

"Not usually; but it's odd sleeping in a bed, and there's been so much going on in my head today that I couldn't just conk out like I usually do," Cathy said. "You're probably the same, yeah?"

"Yeah," said Chloe, warming the teapot. "Too much to take in, I guess. You will keep in touch? I mean it about there being a home here for you if you need it. Even if you just stop by for a bath and a hot meal and a chance to warm up, I want you to know you can come here any time. I didn't realise how much I'd missed having family till you turned up here."

Chloe spooned the herbs into the pot and poured on the boiling water.

"I'll give you my mobile number," Cathy said. "I don't ever leave it on; it's too much hassle for that, I have to charge it from the van. I have it for emergencies. But you can leave a message and I can call you back when I get the message. I hadn't realised how much I'd missed you till I saw you at the woods and I thought you were so like Mum. I've had to freeze out the past, you know. You can't survive if you don't learn that early on; not in the life I've had."

"I'm sorry you've had it so tough," Chloe said inadequately.

"My choice, my fault," Cathy said. "Not yours."

Chloe stirred the tea round and round counting the revolutions and watching the leaves and petals swirl in the steaming liquid.

"It needs a few minutes to brew," she said, fetching mugs and honey.

"What's in it?"

"Chamomile, of course. And passionflower. Skullcap, rose petals, lavender, wild lettuce, spearmint, wood betony and vervain. There was a chant that you're supposed to say over the mix as well, but I wasn't sure whether Gran wrote that down just for completeness. I have no idea where the recipe came from but the chant is Celtic, I think."

She poured the tea through a strainer into the mugs, added a spoonful of honey to each and then handed one to her sister.

"Smells all right," Cathy said grudgingly, and took a tentative sip. "Tastes OK too. I remember this tea, now. She was a strange woman, wasn't she? Gran, I mean. A doctor who played at the things she did; weird, yeah?"

"I suppose she was," Chloe said slowly. " I never questioned it at the time; it just seemed like normal to me. You don't think about your own family until you see other people's families and compare notes. I never wanted anyone else's family, you know; no one else had a Gran like mine. Everyone else's granny seemed colourless by comparison. Oh, I went through a time when I was a teenager of sort of wishing for a normal family life, but it was pretty half-hearted. I'd spend a weekend with a friend's family and it'd be a nice change, but by Sunday night I'd be thinking of my own home and Gran waiting and I'd get this warm safe feeling knowing that she was there. I still sometimes have that feeling, even though I know she's gone."

"You were lucky," Cathy said. "And I bet you did everything right for her, too. Good at school, good at home. Her pride and joy."

"Don't sound so bitter," Chloe pleaded. "She loved you, you do know that don't you?"

"I do now."

Chloe drank her tea, and watched Cathy drink hers slowly and warily.

"I'm on a half day tomorrow, so I don't have to go in to work till lunchtime," she said. "Do you need an early start tomorrow? I can call you if you need it."

"I'll set off when I'm up; there's no hurry," Cathy said. "It's a long drive so I shall take it steady or I'll be too knackered when I get there to be much use."

She set her empty mug down on the table.

"That was OK," she said. "Will it work though?"

"Well, unless you want to sleep at the table, you'd better get back to bed and see," Chloe said, and got up to go back to bed herself. "I usually find it starts to kick in after about ten minutes or so."

"Chloe?"

"Yes?"

"Nothing; just good night, that's all," Cathy said, following her out of the kitchen and up the stairs.

Chloe climbed into bed and snuggled next to Clifford who drowsily reached for her and drew her into his arms to warm her up. Fighting sleep, she thought about that last exchange. She had a strong feeling that Cathy had been about to say more than just good night.

Chapter 15

It was much harder, that next winter, than the last one had been. She began to understand why Jo had kept that calendar, ticking off the days and keeping count of how many were left to get through. The first winter, she had simply been an outsider because she was new. This winter, though, she was an outsider because she was different.

It was also impossible to avoid any contact with the college as she had hoped to do. After that silly prayer meeting, Chloe sent a note to the organiser of the wives group saying simply she didn't wish to participate. It had been a massive effort of will for her to leave it at that and not give any reasons; she'd had a huge struggle with herself over that. She had finally reasoned that it would be more trouble than it was worth to give reasons; that might have opened a dialogue, one she really didn't want. She decided that simply stating that she was opting out would be the cleanest way of avoiding any further involvement.

But it wasn't as simple as that; letters continued to arrive in their pigeon-hole, not just inviting her to things but assuming she would attend as a matter of course. She might have been naïve enough to have believed that there was some sort of official line the college took about wives being involved had Jo not set her straight on that.

"There's no law that says you have to attend anything," Jo had said. "You're technically as free as a bird. The ordinands are obliged to attend certain things, but us wives don't have to do anything we don't want to."

"You could have fooled me," Chloe had said dourly. "The impression I got was that at best I'd be letting the side down by opting out; at worst I'd be committing some sort of minor criminal offence."

"Yeah well, letting whose side down? That's what you have to ask yourself. What side? You make it sound like a football match or a political campaign."

But knowing she didn't have to so much as set foot within the building didn't help. This pervasive assumption that she should somehow be involved even if she didn't actually want to be, was a hard one to fight. She found herself wondering if she was letting Clifford down by her absence and despite his protestations that this wasn't the case, she began to fear that it was true. Every time she found herself avoiding the college, she felt this strange sick sense of shame, that she was not being a good wife. Perhaps she was absorbing some of the anxieties that seemed to float around the campus like unseen swarms of flies, but every encounter with other wives or with the ordinands themselves just seemed to enlarge these fears.

So I stop avoiding the place, then, she told herself. It's just a building; it doesn't hold any power.

One evening after Chapel, Clifford got home and realised he'd left his coat behind.

"I'll pick it up in the morning," he said. "I've got a lot of reading to finish tonight."

"It's OK, I'll go and get it," Chloe offered.

He glanced at her curiously, knowing how little she liked visiting the main buildings.

"It's not urgent, I can get it in the morning," he said.

"I need a bit of fresh air; it'll only take a minute," she said, picking up her jacket.

The night was very clear and therefore frosty; the end of October was approaching fast and all the warmth seemed to have gone out of the world. Chloe walked the few hundred yards from their house to the college and since only a few people seemed to be around she relaxed a little as she tapped the security code into the door lock and trotted inside. The smell of dinner still pervaded the hall and got stronger as she ran up the stairs. Clifford had left his coat on the back of a chair in the chapel and she found it quickly enough, left by the door of the chapel by someone tidying up. The chapel was less unfriendly when empty though it still lacked any real atmosphere and she lingered for a moment, trying to sense any feeling of the presence of God. Nothing, as usual. Once the music stopped, there was nothing left.

She picked up the coat and turned to go, but as she went through the door, the notice board by the door caught her eye. It was intended as a board on which people could write up requests for prayer so that anyone going in to the chapel could read it on their way in and offer up what they had read. She'd not really taken any interest in it before, since her visits here had been fleeting and infrequent. Today though it caught her eye. It might have been the red marker pen ink that stood out, or it might have been her own curiosity that made her look. But in red ink was a prayer request that initially made her blood run cold, then made it virtually boil with fury.

"Please pray for C, who is being lured away from Christ."

After the C, someone had rubbed out the rest of the name, but there was enough residue of the ink for her to realise it was her own name.

After she'd stood there for five minutes, she realised she was shaking. She turned away and ran back down the stairs. Once downstairs, she made herself walk carefully back to her house and after a quick rummage in the toolbox, she returned equally carefully to the notice board. There were still faint noises coming from the kitchens but otherwise the place seemed deserted. She methodically cleaned off every word on the board with the cloth attached to the board by a string, and then very carefully removed the lids of each of the coloured board markers and filled each with super-glue and replaced it on the pen. Then she lined them up on the little shelf below the board as they had been before and went home.

When she got home, she told Clifford what she'd done and why. He started laughing.

"I can't wait to see someone try to get the lid off one of those pens," he said. "Are you sure it was your name on there though?"

"Pretty sure it said Chloe. I suppose it could have been another Chloe, but if that was the case, well, why did they rub out the rest of the name if it was innocent? I think it was me and I think whoever wrote it knew it would be too much to actually have my full name up there so they rubbed it out. But I still think it was me

204

they meant, after that prayer meeting where they thought all Gran's curios had demons attached to them and I didn't seem bothered about it. I am so cross though. I feel almost violated, actually."

"That board is a clearing house for gossip anyway," Clifford said. "Very few people actually use it properly. It'll bring thing to a halt for a day or so, until someone gets some new pens. You'll get spotted eventually if you keep super-glueing the pen lids."

"I wasn't going to do it again," she said. "A waste of glue, doing it more than once. I had to do something though."

Last year, Chloe had noticed that around Hallow E'en a certain vague unease bordering on hysteria had pervaded the college, particularly among the wives, reaching a peak on the night of Hallow E'en itself when a special prayer and praise meeting was held in chapel. This year, she was in the front garden, dead-heading the marigolds and collecting the seeds in a small cardboard box when Nicky came to the gate. She was holding a folded letter.

"Oh, I'm glad I caught you," she said, startling Chloe slightly.

Caught me doing what, Chloe thought? But she said nothing and just looked up enquiringly as Nicky handed her the letter.

"I'm making sure everyone knows they have to be in chapel tomorrow night," Nicky said. "It's very important everyone attends."

"Oh yeah? Why?" Chloe asked, not bothering to look at the piece of paper in her hand.

"Because it's Hallow E'en," Nicky said. "We need as many people as possible praying against all the evil that's being directed against the college."

Chloe did a bit of a double take.

"And why should we all be in chapel?" she asked cautiously.

"Because it's what Jesus told us to do. "Where two or three are gathered in my name, there shall I be also,"" Nicky explained patiently.

"Didn't He also say, "When you pray, go into your room, close the door and pray to your Father who is unseen,"" Chloe said.

Nicky blinked at her, astonishment rapidly giving way to fury.

"We're at war, you know," she said. "The forces of light and darkness are at war and we're part of it. Tonight is a big battle; whose side are you on anyway, Chloe? Maybe you should ask yourself that before you start playing games with things you have no understanding of."

Chloe watched her stalk off, her very back seeming to bristle with righteous indignation. Then she went inside to put the seeds away. She couldn't quite understand what Nicky was getting her knickers in a twist for until Clifford explained.

"There's this myth that goes on being trotted out each year," he said. "That Satanists are praying against the work this place does, you know, training vicars, and at Hallow E'en the whole thing becomes intensified. I don't know when this idea started, but every year, I'm told, this happens. Every time someone's ill or has an accident or something goes wrong, no one says oh well, that's life. They say it's the Devil trying to ruin things, to put a stop to the college and to hurt people. If you ask me I think it shows a remarkably low level of faith and absolutely no understanding of the random nature of life, or for that matter basic human psychology. This time of year, the nights are drawing in, it's getting colder fast, summer seems years away. Everyone is a bit tired and a bit run down after the new term has sort of got a bit stale. Christmas is still too far away to be any help, so this thing about people praying against us gets brought up again and every coincidence is evidence of it. So the hysteria simmers away till November comes and then it's over with for another year."

Chloe snorted.

"So that's why there weren't any kids come round last year Trick or Treating," she said. "I had to eat all those sweeties myself."

"I would imagine any local kids learned years ago that coming round here Trick or Treating earned them a sermon or a tract," Clifford said. "And no kids from college families would be allowed to do it for obvious reasons."

"Bloody killjoys," Chloe said. "At least I didn't buy any sweets yet."

"I take it you aren't intending to go to this meeting," he asked.

"Not a chance."

"Nor me. It just seems a waste of time. And there's a good film on."

"Heathen. Is there not a three line whip then that says you have to be there?"

"Not from the staff there isn't," he said. "As far as I'm concerned a request from the student council and the wives group doesn't count as mandatory."

"It must be a good film, then," she said. "I might even get a bottle of wine and make some popcorn and we can snuggle up by candlelight and enjoy a quiet night in. If our lights are off, anyone going past will assume we must be out at our coven meeting."

He just laughed.

"You'll have to be careful about that sort of joke at this time of year," he said. "There's always a chance someone will take you seriously."

"Nah, no one could be that stupid," she said. "Could they?"

"Don't be too sure of that," he said, and she shivered.

*

It was pretty late when the meeting broke up; Chloe knew this because after their evening in front of the television she was feeding the cats and went to put the empty tin in the recycling box at the front gate. She was obliged to scurry inside, guiltily, as she heard the voices approaching from the main building, so that she wouldn't be seen. It was irrational to feel so guilty; it actually felt just like coming home on the one day she had ever played truant from school and knowing that her Gran would guess what had happened and would look at her with that look that seemed to see right through her.

She headed up to their room and peeping out from under the curtain she could just make out the voices though she was at the wrong angle to see anything.

Clifford crept up behind her, and whispered into her ear,

"Eavesdroppers never hear good of themselves."

"Shut up, I just wanted to see who it is. They're making a lot of noise," Chloe said.

"I think technically it's called singing," he whispered.

"Technically, yeah. In my book that's making an unholy racket at a ridiculous hour. Amazing how they get babysitters for this evening."

Outside, as if right on cue, a small child began crying. Chloe guessed it must be one of Felicity's brood.

"They took the kids? Good grief," Chloe said, shocked. "It's nearly eleven o'clock. That's absurd."

"Nothing like starting young to get kids interested in religion," Clifford said.

"That's not just religion; that's fanaticism."

"Everyone needs a hobby."

"Don't you take anything seriously?"

He slid his arms round her as she crouched next to the window.

"Yes," he said, softly, slipping his hands inside her jumper. "There's one thing I'm always serious about."

Chloe wriggled away from him, but mostly so she could turn round and pull the jumper off over her head.

"If that's so, how come you're grinning like a maniac?" she said.

"Serious doesn't have to mean sombre. But I can be if you like it," he said, pulling a frowning face at her, his dark brows contracting tightly.

"You look like Beethoven on acid," she remarked, and shrieked as he lunged at her playfully.

The window was closed but even so, the sound of her shriek reached the small knot of people at Felicity's gate, who immediately fell silent.

"What was that?" asked Robert.

There was a tense silence; no one could quite place the direction of the sound beyond that it was quite close.

"I didn't like the sound of that," Nicky said, her voice quavering slightly. "It didn't sound quite human."

"No it didn't," Felicity agreed. "It came from Clifford and Chloe's house, too."

They exchanged meaningful glances.

"I think they're out," Robert said, as almost without noticing it the group began moving towards Chloe's house. "He said something today about needing to go to a meeting. Something to do with the church he's on placement at."

This wasn't strictly true; Clifford had simply pleaded a prior engagement, and hadn't mentioned that it was with a pile of popcorn and a film.

Felicity advanced to the door, and rang the doorbell, keeping her finger on the bell. Nothing happened for a minute or so; upstairs, Chloe stuffed a corner of the quilt into her mouth to smother her giggles. It was all she was wearing by now. Felicity put her finger back on the bell and kept it down.

"I'm worried," she said to the others. "That sound definitely wasn't human. If they're home they ought to know there's something else in there with them."

210

Chloe was bright red in the face and almost in agony with suppressed laughter; she could hear what was being said on her doorstep and could hardly believe it. Clifford had stopped tickling her and was lying next to her, holding the pillow he'd been throwing at her and pressing it to his face when the effort of keeping quiet was too much.

"Their car's still here," Nicky said. "They can't have gone far. Where is his placement church anyway?"

Very, very quietly, Chloe and Clifford slid their clothes back on and crept down the stairs. There was no glass in the front door so they couldn't be seen as they slipped down to the kitchen and grabbed jackets from the back of the kitchen door. The door had to be opened very slowly in case it creaked, and then closed equally slowly.

"What the hell are we doing?" Chloe whispered.

"Coming home late," he whispered back.

They left via the rickety back gate and sprinting through various gardens and back onto the main road so that they could come back to their own house from behind their visitors. Felicity was now banging on the door and shouting to the demon she assumed was inside, but she jumped when Chloe and Clifford came down their own path.

"What's going on?" Clifford asked. Chloe was too choked up with amusement to speak.

"We heard something inside; a weird noise," Nicky said.

"Probably one of the cats," Clifford said robustly.

"No cat makes a sound like that," Felicity said.

"Well, maybe we've got burglars," Clifford said "I'd best go and see."

He unlocked the door and went inside to turn the light on, but as he did so, Chainsaw burst out of the doorway, fur on end and spitting with fury. He'd been badly spooked by the constant ringing and banging and wasn't taking any prisoners; in fact he wasn't stopping long enough to see who or what had ruined his nice quiet supper, and shot off into the darkness.

"That's one pissed off pussy," Chloe said, grinning because no one was looking at her. "Probably all the fireworks the last few nights have upset him."

"Animals always know," Robert said ominously.

"Know when it's Guy Fawkes Night? Yeah, hard to miss it these days," Chloe said, being deliberately obtuse.

"They know when there's something demonic around," Felicity said. "You saw the cat; it was terrified."

"Yeah but you lot were ringing the bell and yelling; of course he was terrified," Chloe said. "What on earth did you think was in the house to scare my cat?"

"Something evil and inhuman," Nicky said.

Yeah, right, Chloe thought, and giggled.

"No, I don't think so," she said. "Do try to remember Occam's Razor once in a while, folks. Do any of you know what a fox sounds like, or a barn owl? They can sound pretty eldritch you know."

"It was coming from your house," Robert said, stubbornly.

"Maybe Chainsaw has caught an owl," Chloe said.

"You call your cat Chainsaw? As in the film?" said Nicky's husband Roy.

"No, because he makes a noise like a chainsaw when he purrs; he doesn't seem to draw breath," Clifford explained. "He's quite a strange cat; he does make some unusual sounds. I'm sure that's what you all heard. Now, I've had a long evening, chaps, and I'm sure you'd all like to get home and put the kids to bed."

He gestured to the barely awake figures clustered next to the pushchairs by the gate; someone was going to be too tired for playgroup tomorrow.

This seemed to do the trick, and without any further discussion their unwanted visitors drifted away from their door and off home. Clifford shut the door.

"Well, that was fun," he said. "Amazing none of them noticed we're both wearing slippers; I did wonder about that. Now, where were we?"

Chloe stifled the shriek she felt welling up and bolted back up the stairs.

Chapter 16

Christmas again; strange how it came round again so fast when everything else seemed to take forever. She left a message on Cathy's mobile to say they would be away Christmas Day itself but would be at home otherwise, but had no reply. The weather was bitterly cold and even though she knew it might be milder in Cornwall where Cathy was helping a clean-up operation after a minor oil spill, she still wondered how Cathy could cope with winter living the way she did. They had to make the trip to Clifford's parents in one long day as there was no one whom they would trust to come in and feed the cats, so when they got home early on Boxing Day morning there was a reproachful row of little corpses laid out on the doorstep, stiff with cold and rigor mortis.

"Look at this," Chloe said, holding up a mouse by its rigid tail. "Mice lollies."

Both Chainsaw and Sylvester were enthusiastic assassins of the local rodent population but they preferred most of their food out of a tin or packet and resented being left for almost twenty-four hours without that food being renewed. There was a great deal of grovelling needing to be done before either cat would allow itself to be picked up and cuddled.

"Ungrateful little sods," Chloe said as Chainsaw flicked his tail at her and walked away. "Next time I will put you both in a cattery and that way we can get to see Peter."

Peter was Clifford's uncle, himself a priest, and the one who Chloe jokingly blamed for their current life. He was obviously working on Christmas Day and usually visited his sister on Boxing Day, by which point Clifford and Chloe were back home. They hadn't actually seen him since their wedding; his own lifestyle meant he didn't get away much either. Chloe had liked him enormously, far more than she liked any other member of Clifford's family, and would have liked a chance to get to know him better.

"We can maybe go and see him at Easter," Clifford said. "It depends on this placement."

"No, it depends on my job," Chloe said.

The girl whose job Chloe was doing had had her baby but had yet to return to work; it was starting to look like Chloe might be there on a permanent temporary contract. She didn't like to ask what was happening, in case someone thought she didn't want to carry on working there but she was beginning to feel as though she was becoming part of the fixtures and fittings. The other members of staff even seemed to like her; she had no intention of rocking the boat, as there had been no remotely interesting jobs in her real area of expertise cropping up lately. So as a result of this, Chloe worked when she was asked to, filled in for others off sick or on holiday and generally made herself indispensable, hoping that she would this way avoid having another spell of unemployment.

On New Year's Day, Cathy's van pulled up outside their house, and by the time Chloe had got to the door, Cathy was on the doorstep. She looked pinched and blue with cold, her layers of brightly coloured clothes apparently inadequate. She ate a huge bowl of pasta, drank a pint of orange juice, spent an hour and a half in the bath and then went and slept for eighteen hours without stirring once. Chloe was starting to worry that she'd died in there when she finally emerged the following afternoon looking much better but still grey with tiredness.

"I don't think you're terribly well," Chloe said, when her sister's coughing fit came to an end.

"No, I'm not brilliant. Too much sea air," Cathy said. "And before you ask, I don't really smoke. Too expensive. I just have the occasional cig when I can. It's just been so cold; I haven't managed to shake this last cold off yet."

"I got you a Christmas present," Chloe said.

"Christ, I got you guys presents too," Cathy said. "I totally forgot yesterday. They're in the van. I'll go and get them."

Cathy was coughing again when she came in again.

"I don't believe in wrapping paper," she said, and handed them each a small parcel wrapped in brown paper.

Clifford opened his cautiously; the parcel smelled strongly of seaweed. It was a wooden cross, carved out of driftwood. There was no figure on the cross but there was a beautifully carved crown of thorns where the head of Christ would have been.

"This is beautiful," he said. "Where on earth did you get it?"

Cathy grinned at him.

"The beach," she said, and it dawned on him that she had created this cross herself.

"It's fantastic," he said.

"Not bad for a few evenings with a pocket knife," Cathy grudgingly admitted. "Go on Chloe, open yours."

Chloe unwrapped the paper. Inside was a piece of crystal wound around with silver wire so it could be worn as a pendant. At first she thought the crystal was clear quartz, then she saw that there seemed to be another quartz point inside it. She looked at her sister.

"It's lovely," she said. "What is it inside it?"

"Itself," Cathy said. "It's what they call phantom quartz. The crystal grows; sometimes it stops growing for thousands of years and then starts again. When it starts again, the original point still shows inside the new point. I think tiny specks of dust show where the first point was. I found it in a gift shop; you know, they often have displays of crystals, lots of them in boxes. If you're patient enough to go through them all, you can sometimes find unusual ones. I was lucky that time. So then I did the wire myself, so you can wear it as a necklace."

"It's fantastic," Chloe said. "Wait a minute while I get a chain and then I can put it on."

She ran upstairs to their room and brought down a silver chain and threaded the stone onto that, and fastened the necklace round her throat.

"This is for you," she said, bringing out a big parcel from behind their rather forlorn Christmas tree.

Cathy undid the paper, smoothing it out as she did so. Chloe had gone to the camping supplies shop and bought the best sleeping bag they had, guaranteed to some unimaginably Arctic temperature, and a fleece liner that was easy to wash and quick to dry.

"Cor," breathed Cathy. "I could go to the Antarctic with this. Ta ever so. You've no idea how cold I've been lately."

But Chloe had some idea when she saw Cathy's existing sleeping bag, the following day when Cathy brought it in to put in the washing machine. It had been an excellent bag once, but that was years ago, and it was probably only any use now as a summer bag. She'd been intrigued by Cathy's van, when Cathy agreed to show her it. It was very neat and clean, but very sparse. Cathy kept her belongings in a series of boxes that she admitted were actually old army ammunition boxes, which she could stack and fasten down in the back with a network of bungees. Her bed was a rolled up length of foam rubber, tied up during the day with another bungee. There were a number of old army blankets too, folded up and stored in one of the ammo boxes; that was obviously how Cathy hadn't turned into a human ice lolly one of those freezing nights.

"Brilliant present," Cathy said, stowing it away. "I get scared during the winter, you know, that one morning I won't wake up."

That shook Chloe; she hadn't thought of such things before.

"I'm better off than many," Cathy said, seeing Chloe's look of horror. "I've got the van for starters. I've slept in the odd doorway in the past, but only once at the dead of winter and I was younger then and not on my own. Being homeless stinks in the winter."

"You don't have to be homeless," Chloe said.

"I'm not. The van is my home," Cathy said. "And I took you at your word about coming here when I needed to. And you'd even got me the best Christmas present I think I've had for more years than I can remember, so I know you did really mean it. But you must know I don't want to settle down, not when there's so much I can do. This will make life more comfortable," and she patted the box with the sleeping bag and liner in it. "And I do appreciate your offer, believe me I do. I thought about you two quite a lot recently. That's why I made the presents."

"They're marvellous," Chloe said, touching the crystal at her throat. "That cross you did for Clifford; you know, you're really talented. Was it you who painted the van?"

Cathy nodded, and then shut the van door on her tiny home.

"Do you like it?" she asked.

"It's amazing," Chloe said. "I think it's lovely. You really are good at art, you know."

Cathy flushed with pleasure, and then shook her head.

"It's something I enjoy doing, that's all," she said.

"I think you're brilliant at it," Chloe said.

There was a brief moment of discomfort between them, until Cathy patted the side of the van, fondly.

"Yeah," she said. "With this thing, I can never forget where I've parked."

"It's the first time I've ever considered a Transit van as art," Chloe said. "When we were in Wales in the summer, there was a family turned up at the camp-site we were at in two white Transit vans. We called them the White Van Clan, but not when they could hear us. Imagine White Van Man with a family; that was proof positive that the gene pool has a shallow end."

Cathy threw back her head and laughed hugely, then ended it in a coughing fit. Chloe could see Nicky approaching, her eyes on Cathy and the van; just as Nicky was walking past, Cathy managed to clear her chest of phlegm and spat the resulting gobbet in the grass at the verge. Nicky stopped and stared at her, and then at the van.

"Sorry about that," Cathy said a bit breathlessly. "Bronchitis. Filthy illness, sorry about gobbing like that."

"Perhaps you should see a doctor," Nicky said, beginning to move on. "Other people could catch it from you, you know."

Chloe and Cathy glanced at one another.

"I don't do doctors," Cathy said. "Except maybe witch doctors. But thanks for your concern."

Nicky visibly recoiled at that and moved away.

"Hey, Nicky?" Chloe called, and Nicky stopped moving and called back,

"Yes, what?"

"Happy New Year," Chloe called, but Nicky had moved on without replying.

"Rude thing," Cathy remarked as they went back to the house. "She didn't wish you a Happy New Year. Sour cow."

"That's what she's like all the time, at least to me," Chloe said. "It wasn't anything to do with you. But maybe she was right about a doctor."

"Nah, not yet. If I'm not picking up after a few days in the warm, I'll go. But to be honest, I think I just need a bit of warmth and rest. It's been a hell of a few months," Cathy said. "There's nothing quite as miserable as trying to save sea birds that are just going to go straight back and fill up with oil again the moment they're released."

*

Nicky got home with the pint of milk she'd gone out to get and back at home the impromptu coffee morning could actually have it's coffee. Four other women had come over with their children and the living room seemed awash with a sea of brightly coloured plastic and a swarm of under fives. After she'd put the kettle on, Nicky went through to the living room.

"That van is back outside Chloe's house," she said.

"What van?" asked Susie, one of that year's intake.

"The weird van that's all painted up," Nicky said. "And I'll tell you something else. I saw the person who comes in it too."

They looked at her expectantly.

"Well, go on," said Felicity crossly. "Don't keep us all in suspense. Who was it?"

"How should I know? But she's as weird as the van; she looks like a New Age traveller, you know all those layers of filthy clothes. And her head was virtually shaven. She had all sorts of stuff hanging round her neck, pendants and crystals and things like that," Nicky said, unconsciously touching the small cross around her own neck.

221

"What's she doing here anyway?" Jacquie asked, tucking her youngest under her jumper and fiddling with her bra so she could plug the baby in.

"No idea," Nicky said. "She seemed pretty pally with Chloe though. If you ask me, with that shaven head, she looks like some militant lesbian."

"Maybe Chloe's going to run away with her," Susie suggested and they all sniggered at that.

"We should be so lucky," Felicity said. "That girl worries me, you know. First she didn't come to the prayer and praise meeting even though we'd asked everyone to come; then there were those strange noises coming from her house, and the cat behaving oddly. It's bad enough that she has all those pagan things dotted round the house, without her mixing with people who'd have a van like that. Did you look at it properly this time, Nicky? It's got pentacles painted on it."

This was true. It also had a Celtic cross, a Medicine Wheel, the sign for OM, a Star of David and half a dozen symbols of other faiths; Cathy would add one every time someone pointed out one she'd missed.

There was a sort of collective shudder at the thought of pentacles.

"And the rest of the van is just as bad," Nicky went on. "There's all sorts of vile images on it; I had to distract my oldest when I went past it earlier in case she asked why the lady in the picture was showing her front bottom like that."

The Sheelah-na-gig was perhaps an uncomfortable image for most of them, given both its sexual connotations and its associations with the birthing process.

"Why don't you ask them over for coffee?" asked Annie, who'd so far been quiet and said nothing. "They sound interesting."

There was a brief pause, mostly while Nicky and Felicity tried to let out enough breath to make up for their sharp intake of breath a moment before.

"You haven't met Chloe yet, have you, dear?" Felicity said sweetly. "She's not someone you have over for coffee, not when you've seen her house. It's got a really horrible atmosphere too, malevolent. And she hates children; you wouldn't appreciate that, not in your condition. You're very vulnerable with your first baby; I'm sure you wouldn't want baby to be...influenced by the kind of atmosphere that surrounds Chloe."

Annie was heavily pregnant; but she refused to be completely cowed.

"Are you sure she's that bad?" she said, anxiously. "She looks very pretty; I've seen her out running. You make it sound as if she's some sort of witch or demon worshipper."

The words sort of rippled round the room.

"Well, that's as maybe," Nicky said uncertainly. "That woman with the van isn't far off either, if you ask me. Pentacles indeed!"

*

Chloe put most of Cathy's clothes through the washing machine as well as the sleeping bag; they weren't filthy as Nicky had said, but they did need a good wash to get rid of the smell of tar and oil and rotting seaweed. Cathy wore Chloe's dressing gown, while Chloe went through her own wardrobe for clothes she could borrow while her own were laundered and dried on radiators. When she was dressed, she looked very different from her normal self; the layers of velvet and woolly jumpers seemed already to be so much a part of her persona that she seemed diminished in Chloe's tee shirt and leggings.

"You don't look quite right," Chloe said, as Cathy pulled on the Guernsey sweater Chloe had found her.

"No?" Cathy remarked and glanced in the mirror on the wardrobe door. "No I don't suppose I do. I don't think anyone would recognise me now."

She ran her hand over her cropped hair, leaving no trace.

"It's a bit like looking at a life I never had," she said, pensively. "What I might have been if I hadn't run away."

She shook herself.

"No regrets though. Well, none that matter. And I can't change anything even if I did regret any of it. The past is another country; but we can't go there," she said. "This is a really warm jumper."

"That's why I've lent it to you; you seem so cold still," Chloe said.

"I think I'm permanently cold," Cathy said. "At least nine months of the year I've got icicles on my toes."

No wonder you cough, Chloe thought but didn't say it.

"Come on," she said. "Let's get a hot drink and slob in front of the fire, and I'll tell you about Nicky and the rest of them."

Chloe made hot chocolate for them both, and took a coffee to Clifford who was struggling with an essay that was due to be handed in at the start of term, which was just over a week away. He glanced up at her from the computer, which he'd returned to after Chloe had found spare clothes for Cathy.

"Thanks, love," he said, somewhat absently as she put the coffee mug down near the desk.

"Don't let that one go cold," she said, and went back downstairs to where her sister was curled up on the sofa, wearing the old Pendleton blanket that still smelled of the white sage it had been packed with when their Gran had sent it home from America. She rubbed a corner of the thick wool against her cheek and sighed.

"This takes me back a bit," she said. "Gran sent this home for me when I was about ten, before you were even thought of. She said in her letter that it had been in a real teepee, and she'd been given it as a present for setting someone's leg when they were miles from a hospital. I thought it was the most marvellous thing in the world; it even smelled mysterious and special. It's faded a bit now, but it still smells of that stuff it was packed with."

"You can take it with you if you like," Chloe said.

"No, but thanks for offering. It'd take too long to dry out if it got wet; and I'd rather it were truly safe, here. Now you were going to tell me about this woman who was looking as though we were a bad smell under her nose."

Chloe handed her sister her mug and settled down on the sofa to enjoy her own drink. Foam on her upper lip from the whipped chocolate, she sighed with a mixture of the pleasure of the moment and with her concern for her situation here.

"That was a big sigh," Cathy said.

"I don't know quite where to start, actually," Chloe said. "I don't seem to be able to fit in, even when I try. And when I don't try, I get such a bad response I end up feeling a complete heel for being awkward."

"Square peg, round hole," Cathy said succinctly. "Tell me what happens."

Where do I start, Chloe thought? I've got plenty of places to start.

"Well, it all really started to go pear-shaped at the introductory weekend," she said after a moment of thought. "Though I don't really understand why. I didn't much want to attend, but I thought, what the hell? They can't eat me, after all. But it was vile. All the women just sort of looked me up and down, just for a second, you know the way they do, and then they started talking to me as if I were a complete moron, about where things were, how difficult it can be to find your way around a new place. Well, I just said, this place is hardly big enough to get lost in, you'd have to be pretty thick to get lost, really lost that is rather than just misplaced. Not a good thing to say, as it turned out, because Nicky who's actually in the same year as us, got lost earlier that day and had been going on about how big it was and how confusing it was."

Cathy laughed, sympathetically.

226

"And after dinner, someone asked if we had children and I just laughed and said, with Clifford around I hardly need kids," Chloe said. "It didn't go down very well. I was just joking but some of them have this weird idea about the man being the head of the household and being somehow sacrosanct, at least publicly. Even a jokey criticism was a black mark in my book, especially since I wasn't showing any eagerness to join the pudding club. There are always lots of kids around, and that evening wasn't any different. I'd just avoided being bumped into by one swarm of kiddies and I'd said, I'm not really used to children, and then stepped backwards as another kid came racing my way. Trouble was, I didn't know there was a tot crawling behind me, and I sort of trod on it. I didn't do any harm, not really, because I didn't put any weight on the foot, but I've never heard such a kefuffle. Oh, not just the baby; that I can understand. No, the mother went absolutely ballistic with me for treading on her baby. I don't understand why she was blaming me, when it was up to her to keep the baby where it'd be safe, and I don't think a public room is exactly a safe place for a baby to be crawling around. And then I compounded the mistake by suggesting that she wouldn't have made as much of a fuss if the baby had been a girl, because we all know they're expendable. After that, I thought, floor, swallow me up, please. But I wasn't finished yet; I managed to upset one woman who was truly enormously pregnant by asking someone else, I hasten to add, if she was expecting triplets. I was getting nervous by now, and I wasn't thinking straight, but even so I didn't expect the woman I'd asked to go straight across and tell the pregnant woman what I'd just said. And she burst into tears and ran away. I did try to apologise, but I couldn't deny I'd said what I'd said, so it was a bit of a futile exercise, apologising. Then finally, to cap it all at dinner, someone asked me what sort of ministry did I have? Well, I said, he's the ordinand, not me. And this woman said, no, most of us have a joint ministry with our husbands, what do you intend to do in your supportive ministry? I couldn't think of a diplomatic reply, so I just said, nothing, I don't intend to do anything, it's his calling not mine. You could have heard a pin drop. She didn't know what to say, so I said, well, as far as I'm concerned, the day they start paying a double stipend is the day I might think about a joint ministry. I also said I was horrified that the buy one, get one free mentality had infiltrated even the church. I don't think I could have said anything else that was wrong if I'd set out to annoy them. This was all purely accidental."

"They sound like a bunch of over-sensitive bitches to me," Cathy said. "What's all this about a joint ministry? I didn't think you lot approved of drug use."

Chloe giggled at her sister's joke.

"Not that sort of joint, silly," she said. "The idea, as far as I can make out, is that he wears the collar but both are ministers. I haven't heard of it the other way around, the husbands of the female ordinands waffling on about joint or shared ministry. When it comes down to it, it's rubbish. Let's say Clifford dies while we're in a parish; does the parish or the diocese say to me, oh well Chloe, you've been just as much the vicar as Clifford so stay on and be the vicar now? No, what actually gets said is, our commiserations Mrs.

Williams, you'll need to be out of the house in six weeks so we can get another vicar in."

"You're kidding me?"

"Well, I might get more than six weeks but you get the drift. If it's truly a joint ministry, equal partners, well, there should be a double stipend, that's what they call a clergy salary. I think the reason it gets talked about is simply they can't bear for their husbands to be the total centre of attention. It's not even about playing second fiddle; they aren't even in the orchestra at all."

"That's bloody sad," Cathy said. "Poor cows."

"Poor nothings," Chloe said robustly. "There's nothing to stop them either going for ordination selection in their own right, or getting on with something for themselves, that doesn't involve piggybacking on their husbands. At the bottom of it there's a rotten lot of jealousy and bitchiness."

"It's still sad, " Cathy said. "They can't have much gumption if they can't just get on with stuff for themselves."

"I think it's safe to say that any get up and go they may have had has got up and gone a long time ago. Do you really think it's sad?" Chloe asked.

"Heartbreaking, actually. Talk about dis-empowered, it's criminal. I thought that sort of thing died out in the Middle Ages," Cathy said.

"You think their husbands make them like that?"

"Don't they?"

"No, not at all. This is their choice. Oh, it's not simple at all. My friend Jo talked about it a bit. She said that they had left behind a life where they had been the principal couple in their original church, maybe the only really active leaders, and usually they were what they claim to be, joint or equal partners in ministry. Then they land here, and he goes off to lectures and placements and seminars and Morning Prayer and leading worship and all that stuff. And the wives get stuck at home with the kids and all the college offers is a wives' group and a crèche for Chapel night. And they are told that this is their part of the ministry, for the moment, because the training is really for their husbands. They can do courses if they want to, but actually very few do, because if you want to get a qualification from it, you do have to pay for it, and we're all on a low income here so there isn't money to throw around. So they tell themselves that the academic stuff is just a series of hoops the dioceses make their men jump through that have no real relevance to actual ministry, and that when they get into a parish at the other end it'll all come right again. So they resent a whole load of things and pretend they love it all, so they need never wake up to the fact that they've been conning themselves."

Cathy sipped her chocolate and gazed at her sister with obvious sorrow.

"You should be very careful," she said. "They're about ready to turn on you."

"Don't be daft," Chloe said, uncomfortable. "They're a bunch of sheep."

Cathy laughed, rather bitterly.

"You ought never underestimate sheep," she said. "One of my occasional jobs is helping with the lambing. I know some people with an organic farm, and I go most years to help with the lambing. They like me because I'm good with the sheep and I've got smaller hands than the vet or the farmer. I was in one of the pens, with a couple of ewes that had recently had their lambs and I was supposed to be checking out one lamb that seemed not to be as well as it should have been. One of the ewes started getting twitchy about me being there, and before I could get out of the way, she charged me. I was pretty lucky not to have been seriously injured; they're big beasts, are sheep. If a flock of sheep turned on the shepherd or on a wolf, they'd be damn near unstoppable. I had some horrible bruises from that encounter; it can be enough to rupture you if you're very unlucky. So I've always respected sheep a lot more since then. Don't underestimate these women; if you're shining a spotlight on this life here, they don't want to look. That's what I picked up from that woman earlier. Whistle-blowers are never popular."

"I'm just the square peg," Chloe said, unable to repress a shiver.

"You're also that kid in the Emperor's New Clothes; saying what everyone knows but no one dare say it. You're saying what no one wants to hear."

"I'm not saying anything," Chloe protested.

Cathy gave that bitter smile again.

"You don't need to," she said. "They only have to look at you to hear what you say with every cell in your body."

Chloe gazed into the empty mug, and ran her finger round the rim to collect every last trace of froth.

"I'm not saying stop doing it," Cathy said. "Hell, I've been saying and doing stuff no one wants to hear for years. I think whistle-blowers deserve medals. All I am saying is be careful. Keep an eye on them, don't let them creep up behind you, so to speak."

"What can they do to me; pray at me?" Chloe said sceptically.

"I'm not joking, Chloe. I don't know what they're capable of. But my experience is simply that people are capable of terrible things you'd never have believed of them. Even good people. You only have to read the papers to know that. My experience also tells me that unhappy people are capable of great harm. And from what you've said, and from what I saw on that woman's face, they're pretty damn unhappy here."

Chloe digested this in silence, finding it hard to reconcile her vague contempt for the other women with Cathy's cautions. But when it came down to it, Cathy was twelve years older than she was, and those extra twelve years of experience had not been in the cushioned cared-for world of Gran where the hardest thing you could face was Gran's cutting tongue and the possibility of losing her respect.

"I'll watch my back," she said eventually. "But I can't quite imagine why you're so concerned."

"There's an atmosphere here, of simmering anxiety and borderline hysteria. I saw it in that woman's aura; I bet it's there in all the others to a greater or lesser extent."

Chloe raised her eyebrows.

"What about my aura?"

232

"Toughest damn aura I've ever seen; I didn't know how to see them when I was at home, but I reckon Gran's would have looked like that, full of reds and purples and full-on greens. Not a pastel in sight. You're a survivor, little sister. Just don't let them get where you can't see them."

"What colour was Nicky's aura then?"

"Lots of colours, but all of them a bit off if you know what I mean. Sickly colours, off-centre. That's how I know she'd unhappy; and how I know she's jealous as hell of you."

"Jealous? Of me?"

"Yes. One thing I remember Gran saying was that jealousy was at the root of most unhappiness, that the need to get that greener grass was what drove most people."

"I remember that too. But I can't believe Nicky is jealous of me. I've heard her saying how blessed she is, how she is so happy with her life."

"Then she's lying to herself as well as everyone else. Try to keep out of their way, if you can," Cathy said.

That's a bit difficult when I live in the same campus, Chloe thought. But Cathy seemed so serious about it that she simply nodded in silent acquiescence, and was disturbed by how her sister's face seemed to relax quite visibly with the thought that Chloe would keep out of the way of Nicky and company.

It's not that bad surely, she asked herself, but inside she knew that her sister at least thought it was. It was not a happy thought.

Chapter 17

This year, Chloe didn't need to watch for the arrival of spring as obsessively as in other years; this year it arrived weeks early, in pots and planters, all for a set price and no effort involved. It was delightful though to get into work, to open up one of the greenhouses first thing in the morning and find the air filled with the fragrance of narcissi and hyacinths and primulas. She had begun to feel very settled here; the girl she was filling in for had yet to make up her mind about whether she would indeed return. The word was that she had looked at childcare costs and her wages, and had decided that she wouldn't return to work at all since she was lacking a doting granny locally who might be willing to look after the baby for nothing more than the satisfaction of bringing up a grandchild. But nothing firm had been said to Chloe, and she went on from day to day, simply avoiding thinking about it. They had over a year still to go with Clifford's studies, and she was wondering if she would be better off waiting till they knew roughly where they would end up before making any real decisions about her halted career. But most of the time, she just didn't think about it at all.

Cathy had spent a week with them before heading off to the organic farm, in advance of the lambing, since the farmer had asked her to come early as one of their usual hands was off sick with a broken leg and they needed an extra able bodied worker to fill in for the time being.

"It's nice there," she had said. "I get to sleep in one of the straw barns, which is warmer than the van, and the farmer's wife always provides enough food to fatten an army. And this means I've got money to service the van and things like that. I'll pop back when I can, but it probably won't be before the summer. Keep safe, won't you?"

"I will; you take care and try to keep warm," Chloe had said, and hugged her before she drove off, leaving Chloe feeling strangely bereft. She'd not realised quite how lonely she'd been.

When she wasn't at work, she found she was often alone at home. Clifford's workload had increased that year, with a demanding placement in a local church that was more than delighted to throw at him the jobs that the vicar couldn't face. Chloe actually doubted they should be asking quite so much of him, but there didn't seem to be any way of checking, but he just seemed to accept being asked to help with the youth group during the week and fill in any number of different tasks on a Sunday. There were restrictions to the amount he was allowed to preach, since he was neither ordained nor licensed as a reader to that church, but Chloe felt sure he was being exploited, and got quietly cross about it when he disappeared on a Saturday to prepare his "talk" as they had termed it. That seemed to be the way round it, to call it something other than a sermon, so that should he actually complain they could always say, oh, but you weren't actually preaching.

"Semantics," Chloe said, crossly. "That's all it is; bloody twisting of words to fit what they want."

He shrugged, unconcerned.

"It's all useful experience," he said. "I've had a chance to try out all sorts of things I wouldn't often get a crack at."

"Only cause the vicar's so ploughed under all he can think of is getting himself some breathing space," Chloe pointed out. "That's not exactly fair, is it?"

"No, but it's only for a limited time, and I'm not exactly stretched by it anyway."

Chloe wanted to point out that this was the time when he needed to set his habits for his working life, and she didn't think accepting being exploited was exactly a healthy precedent; but she bit her lip and said nothing. He was finding his studies more enthralling than either of them had expected this year, and was genuinely excited by the chance to try his hand at different roles and different styles of service. It all went over the top of her head, really.

She'd taken to occasionally going to the closest Anglican church, just to attend the very basic Communion service and slip away straight after the Blessing without having to speak to anyone. It was a very ordinary run-of-the-mill sort of place with the standard ageing congregation, and the service was a very ordinary run of the mill hymn-sandwich, but she was astonished how comforted she was by its humdrum style. There was nothing threatening about its straightforward liturgy or unimaginative choice of hymns; she realised that she didn't enjoy ecclesiastical pyrotechnics at all, found them oddly distasteful. The quieter and simpler the better; and the music harked back to school assemblies and those occasions like

Harvest, Easter and Christmas when she and Gran would go to their local church and sing those old favourites without a shred of irony or any hint of those supercilious glances she'd seen exchanged during Chapel night when the old hymns were sometimes sung. The tunes seemed somehow to be a part of her oldest memories and she wondered, not for the first time, whether there was some sort of collective unconscious or racial memory, that such associations should be so strong when her actual attendance at church had been occasional and at the time, sometimes forced.

She also knew that none of the other wives would ever attend this particular church as it was considered notoriously square and behind the times; so she was safe enough from that sort of scrutiny. She knew she was noticed though, but no one made any alarming overtures to her beyond smiling kindly at her, so she relaxed into a routine where if she woke early enough on a Sunday to be able to get to the unfashionably early nine thirty communion, she would go, but never set her alarm clock to wake her. As it turned out, nine times out of ten she was awake anyway because Clifford had unintentionally disturbed her sleep when he got up to go to his placement church, and after a cup of tea and a brief brush with mascara, she would slip out to church, unobserved by any of her neighbours. Effectively it meant that none of the other wives had the faintest idea that Chloe was actually a regular church goer because she simply didn't attend any church they considered worth attending, and no one saw her coming or going. She would have been amused and then horrified by what a complete heathen they considered her to be.

The tarot cards continued to fascinate her in a mild way, once the initial strangeness had evaporated, but she knew this was not something she could share with anyone else, and she pondered their meaning in the secret places of her heart, often waking having dreamed about a particular image. She could seldom remember clearly what she dreamed, which was frustrating, and she was often left with a memory of wonderment and nothing more than a few stray images.

The dream with the hole woke her at least once a week, sweating and panting with almost primeval terror and panic, yet within seconds, she couldn't recall what it had been about, beyond that it was a familiar nightmare. Sometimes she would have to get up, have at least a drink of water before she could ease herself silently back under the duvet into Clifford's warm penumbra and try to sleep again.

One night, she had woken shaking and slippery with panic, and had gone downstairs to the comfort of the kitchen, wrapping herself with the Pendleton blanket. It was four o'clock in the morning and the world felt strange to her, that she should be waking when everyone else was asleep. There was a weird energy about this time of the night, neither quite night nor quite day; it was May and dawn wasn't far away, and the light in the unlit kitchen was navy blue. She made tea without turning lights on and sat at the table to drink it, standing back from herself mentally and watching in a detached way.

Standing at a distance from herself, she could see she was standing still even though she was moving.

"I'm marking time," she said out loud to the light in the kitchen as it brightened slowly towards morning.

It was a strange revelation, and she was sure she wasn't entirely herself at that moment; the light had the kind of luminous quality she sometimes saw during the onset of a migraine, a kind of deepening and brightening of the most basic colours so that it became painful to look at anything properly as it seemed to burn into the retina till it seemed that was all she would ever see. Usually the best thing to do was to close her eyes and try to sleep and hope the moment passed without degenerating into the throbbing pain of the usual headache. This morning was different; she knew that. It was as though a vision was happening to her, even though she could see nothing beyond the luminous brightening of the small world of her kitchen. On the windowsill was vase of lilac blossoms, and each tiny floret seemed to burst with meaning, as the purple seemed to expand into the whole room. On the table in front of her, the tea in its mug steamed and the steam seemed to form patterns that swirled and dispersed and formed again. She felt as if she might somehow understand what the steam was saying to her if she could just concentrate on it for long enough, but the patterns always changed just as she thought she was about to understand.

The fragrance of the lilac filled the whole room, and she felt drowsy but awake as well. Chainsaw bumbled in through the cat-flap, but his arrival didn't startle her; it seemed a part of it all, even the limp rodent in the cat's mouth, which he started to crunch down in front of the boiler. He was just being a cat; after all that was what cats do, eat mice. Flowers bloom, steam swirls; it was all part of the same message.

"What I do is me: for that I came," Chloe said to the cat, to the flowers, to the steam and to the dawn light that had crept into the kitchen without her noticing its arrival.

She grinned as Chainsaw spat out some inedible part of mouse, and started washing nonchalantly, taking no notice of her whatsoever. With a tissue she picked up the rejected bit of prey that looked suspiciously like a gall bladder and put it in the bin so that Clifford wouldn't tread on it when he came down to make tea in the morning, and then scooped up the startled cat and kissed him warmly on his dawn-chilled ears before popping him back on the floor, her heart filled with love for the animal. She ran back upstairs, feeling as if she had figured out the biggest secret of the whole universe, and dived back into the warm bed and held her sleeping husband against her, feeling that surge of affection again, and slid easily back into a deep and peaceful sleep.

When she woke, later that morning, to find both cats asleep at the foot of the bed, and to hear Clifford making tea downstairs and whistling as he did so, she had only the haziest memory of her earlier waking, remembering a feeling of warm bliss and revelation and a few words. Clifford came into the bedroom, carrying two mugs of tea, and as she watched the steam rise and swirl and vanish she remembered the words.

"What I do is me: for that I came," she said, as he passed her a mug.

"Sorry?"

"Just something that came to me about four o'clock this morning," she said, sleepily.

"Who said insomnia doesn't have an up side?" he asked, but she just grinned at him.

"What are you grinning for, like a Cheshire cat?" he asked.

"If I was like a Cheshire cat, I'd be fading away leaving just the smile behind," she pointed out.

"You know what I mean," he said.

"I think I've figured out the answer to the question of life, the universe and everything," she said.

"Well, we all know the answer is forty two," he said.

"Don't be maddening; I really mean it," she said.

"Go on, then, I'm all ears," he said, patiently, because after all it's not often we're faced with deep philosophy before breakfast.

"We've just got to be ourselves, that's all. It's the only way to be happy, just to be only and always ourselves."

She grinned at him, and then her smile faded as it became clear this was not quite the revelation she'd thought it was.

"OK, so you'd already thought of it," she said. "But I thought of it all by myself. No, that's not quite true. I'd known the words for years, but suddenly last night, wham! There it was in me. A real aha! moment. Amazing, truly and utterly amazing. Do you think this is enlightenment, you know, like with the Buddha?"

"If not enlightenment, then a small start towards it, I think. Maybe not the whole hog; maybe just the first candle of enlightenment."

Chloe considered this.

"Hmm," she said. "I like that. Gran used to quote a Chinese proverb: better to light a single candle than curse the darkness."

She stretched, spilling her tea slightly, and then yawned widely.

"Tell you something though," she said. "Lighting candles is exhausting. I feel whacked even before I've started the day."

"Maybe that's why he sat under a tree for so long; maybe he got enlightenment the first day and then had to stay there so long because he was so tired with the effort of it," Clifford suggested.

"Maybe," she agreed. "Now, I'll race you to the shower."

He looked at her for a moment; her face was flushed from sleep and her hair was a wild mass of curls round her face and body.

"Tell you what," he said. "What about we share one?"

Chapter 18

The spring turned to summer and became consistently warm, if sometimes wet, and Chloe spent as much free time in her garden as she could. She spent some time weeding and digging and all the other inevitable garden tasks, but a lot of her time she spent just sitting. That moment in the kitchen repeated for her at irregular intervals, often coming to her when she sat in the sun and a scent from a nearby flower wafted to her, or the song of a wren touched her, or the way the evening light fell onto the leaves of the shrubs and caught her eye. When it happened, she would just lapse into the feeling, sitting so still and so serene that it wasn't unusual for small birds to come quite close to her, but only the robin ever perched on her. She remembered seeing her grandmother sitting with a deep absorbed look on her face, as though listening to complicated but lovely music, and she realised that this must be something similar to what her Gran had felt. She'd once asked what she was thinking about, and it took a few seconds for the old woman to respond.

"Poetry," she'd said, tersely, but not as if she was annoyed.

Now she understood what she had meant; certain lines of poems were a way in to the feeling, as much as birdsong or fragrance or changes in the light could be a doorway into it.

*

A warm June afternoon had drawn out a number of wives into the sunshine of Felicity's garden, and the air rang with the shouts and cries and chatter of small children. Felicity had set out a few folding chairs and a couple of deckchairs at the far end of the garden, where the sun shone down directly on the group of women who sat with tall glasses of juice or water and watched the horde of children play, occasionally getting up to intervene. Annie's baby lay kicking its legs on a rug in the shade of Annie's chair, and a few crawlers had to be retrieved from flowerbeds from time to time.

"What's she doing?" Nicky asked.

Felicity craned her neck so that she could just see Chloe, who sat on the paved area in her own garden, just by her back door.

"Just sitting," she said, disappointed. "Sitting cross legged with her eyes shut, and smiling."

"Smiling?"

"Yes, just smiling. I call that weird. What has she got to smile about?"

"It's a nice day; why shouldn't she smile?" Annie asked, but they ignored her.

"She's weird anyway," said Julie. "Definitely something wrong there; I can tell these things, you know. She behaves unnaturally, anyone can see that."

They kept their voices low, more out of a conditioned need not to be overheard gossiping about someone, rather than any concern for the feelings of the subject of the gossip.

"Did you see that?" Felicity said, sharply. "There was a bird landed on her head; you can't tell me that's normal."

They all subtly shifted their chairs so that they too could see Chloe if they strained their necks a little. The fence was low, more for symbolic division of the gardens than for any attempt at privacy, but from a sitting position they were all a little low to see her easily. As if alerted by their movements, Chloe opened her eyes, and after a second or two trying to focus, she got up from the camp stool she'd been sitting on and turned to go inside, giving her watchers a cheery little wave as she did so. Only Annie waved back.

"What do you think you're doing?" Nicky asked, batting at her arm to stop her waving.

"It's only being polite," Annie protested.

There was an awkward silence, and then they carried on chatting.

"Sometimes she sits there with that Tibetan bowl thing, running the beater round the rim and making that dreadful noise," Felicity said. "And sometimes she has a joss stick smoking away."

"Maybe she's meditating," Annie suggested, but they ignored her again.

"The whole house smelled of incense when we were there," Nicky said. "It's vile, and I'm sure it can't be good for the health either, breathing in the smoke; it must be like passive smoking."

"I quite like joss sticks," Annie said, nervously.

Felicity just looked at her, and Annie dropped her gaze and fell silent.

"It's not so much the smell or the smoke," Julie said. "It's what they mean. They're made for use in temples in the East, where they're offered to these appalling idols. It doesn't matter if they're brought here; what they were made for is still in them, so the association never goes away and they can draw demons into a home. If you've got any at home Annie, I strongly suggest that you bin them straight away. Babies are susceptible to demonic influences, you know."

Annie stared at her, in horror, and then scooped up her baby from the rug and held it closely to her.

"I'd best get home," she said. "She's due for a feed soon, and I haven't brought a bottle with me."

There were glances exchanged and smug looks.

"I really don't think you tried hard enough with the breastfeeding, dear," said Jacquie. "It does give them such a good start in life that can't ever be replaced with the bottle."

Jacquie's three-year-old son was still being breastfed, night and morning, as well as consolation feeds when he'd fallen over or another child had got the toy he'd wanted or when he was tired. Chloe had joked to Clifford when she'd seen the child attached to his mother's nipple in chapel that Jacquie's boobs were more on view than those of a page three model because before very long she'd be able to tuck them into her socks.

Annie gathered her belongings together and left, feeling very churned up and upset. By the time she got home, the baby was fast asleep, so she left the pushchair in the front garden and went to find the packets of joss sticks she kept in her linen cupboard, flinching when she opened the cupboard door as if she half expected some imp to jump out at her. She held the packets in her hand, feeling suddenly very confused, and then came to a decision.

She pushed the pushchair back towards Felicity's house, and then, very nervous, went past it to Chloe's house and rang the doorbell, leaving the pushchair at the gate. When Chloe answered the door with a dazzling smile, Annie held out the joss sticks to her tentatively.

"I thought you might like these," she said, putting them into Chloe's hand, and then retreated rapidly to her sleeping baby and away back home.

Chloe stood looking at the packets in her hand, puzzled. Why on earth would a stranger just give her a gift? There had to be some sort of background to this that she was unlikely to find out in a hurry.

Clifford appeared at the top of the stairs, alerted by the doorbell.

"Who was that?" he called.

Chloe walked up the stairs to join him, still holding the joss sticks.

"Someone just came round to give me these," she said, holding them out to show him. "I'm pretty sure she's a college wife; I vaguely recall seeing her around here, but I don't think I've ever talked to her as such. She just gave me these. I can't quite figure it out. I'm not ungrateful, but it's just such an odd thing to do."

"Maybe she was trying to get to know you," he suggested.

"I got the impression that was not on her mind. She looked a bit scared, to tell you the truth, as if she didn't want to be seen on my doorstep. She rushed off before I had a chance to ask her anything," Chloe said, following him into their bedroom. "Still, these are rather nice joss sticks and I was running low, so I shall burn them and bless my unknown donor for the kindness of her gift."

She lit one and placed it to smoulder in a holder on her dressing table, and the fragrance of sandalwood filled the room.

"Weird, though," she said, thoughtfully.

"I bet Felicity or Nicky are at the bottom of it, though," Clifford said. "The word among the guys is that they've really got it in for you. I hasten to add that none of the blokes can quite see why."

"Comforting," Chloe said dryly. "I suppose I ought to be grateful really that none of the ordinands think I'm whatever their wives think I am; a bad influence or whatever. They should be able to keep control of their wives, at least."

Clifford snorted derisively.

"As if," he said. "All that head of the household and love, honour and obey stuff runs pretty thin when it comes to reality. Those guys have about as much chance of controlling their wives as I have of herding cats."

He went back to what he'd been doing, then, leaving her feeling suddenly a bit upset. It had made her think of what Cathy had said about sheep turning on shepherds, and she shivered. Whatever had prompted that girl to call round with a gift of joss sticks was not really good news for her.

"Sod them all," she said, gazing out of the window at the sunny day, feeling suddenly chilled and soured.

The smoke curled and rose in clouds of filmy blue and made shapes in the air that seemed full of significance and mystery. The scent had been a favourite one of her grandmother and the air at home had always the faintest hint of it, as had her grandmother's clothes. She had stored packets of incense sticks among the bed linen and in drawers where she kept her jumpers and shirts, so as the smoke swirled around the room, she felt slowly comforted as if she were being touched gently by her Gran's unseen shade casting a cloak around her shoulders.

Finally, both the chill and the sourness were driven gently away by sandalwood smoke and Chloe smiled again, and went back outside to sit among the sunflowers at the other end of her garden and enjoy the sun. The flowers bent and swayed with the soft warm breeze; she was very pleased with how they'd grown. Not record breaking in height, but still quite impressive. They reminded her of something, but as soon as she tried to pin it down, the thought slipped away, elusive as a hunting cat.

The sound of children playing lessened and finally stopped, being replaced by the wails of Felicity's youngest child being forced to go inside to have a nap she clearly didn't want to have. Finally, Felicity gave up asking and simply picked the child up and carried her indoors, and the screams grew briefly more urgent then were muffled by the walls of the house.

Not exactly the most restful of sounds but it quickly was replaced by a worse one: the sounds of sobbing from the bedroom the child had been incarcerated in. But even those soon subsided, and all Chloe could hear were the birds, and the sound of traffic on the main road a short distance away. She stretched out on the grass, pillowing her head on her arms, and let herself drift into daydreams and then into sleep.

When she woke, the sky told her it was late afternoon and Clifford was sitting next to her amid the daisies, with two cans of beer.

"You finished for today, then?" she asked, sitting up.

"Done all I can, anyway. Drink?"

"Good thought, that man."

Chloe took a can and tugged on the ring pull to open it. The beer was wonderfully cold but the fizz went up her nose and made her sneeze and choke.

Clifford patted her vigorously on the back; she retaliated by thumping him just as vigorously on the chest.

"You Tarzan, me Jane," she said, beating on his chest like a gorilla, and collapsing into giggles.

"You don't need more than a sip to get you silly," he said, when she had settled down again with her can.

"It's the bubbles," she said. "It's always the bubbles that get me drunk. It's nothing to do with the alcohol. See, now the froth has gone I'm fine."

She took a big swig of the beer and instead of choking, burped, and then began laughing again.

"Any plans for dinner?" he asked presently.

"I thought caviare and champagne, seeing as we're on such a low budget," she said. "Actually I thought we could have pasta, perhaps with a cheesy sauce. I've got a chicken for tomorrow."

They sat out until the grass started to feel cold and the sky was no longer bright with sunshine, and then went in to begin cooking.

She settled for a tuna sauce, instead of cheese, but as she was trying to open the tin with both cats milling around her ankles believing that any tin must naturally be for them, she looked across at Clifford, who was watching a pan coming to the boil. He sensed her watching him and turned to her with a questioning look.

"I'm lonely," she said, sadly. "That girl who came today, I had a feeling she wanted to be a friend and yet she ran away. I'm lonely but there's nothing I can do about it. Jo's taken up with her new baby which is just as it should be, and she's a hundred or so miles away anyway. Cathy I hardly know and she hasn't been since New Year. And you, well, you're working your socks off most of the time. It wouldn't have been a problem when I was sure what I wanted for a career, but now, well, I'm little more than a housewife with a bit of a job. So I'm lonely. I know there's nothing you can do about it, but I thought I should tell you anyway."

"What happened to the secret of life the universe and everything?"

"It's still there. But it only works if you know who and what you are at some level, and it all seems to be changing. I'll be fine in a couple of hours. But stuff has unsettled me and it'll take a while to settle me down again."

"Muddy water, left to stand, come clear," he said with a very bad mock Chinese accent.

"Are you calling me muddy?"

He just laughed and tipped pasta into his pan.

Silently she watched him and heard the words, I'm lonely, echoing in her head.

"I could do with making a friend or two," she said. "But I've had a good look at most of our current neighbours and I wouldn't say any of them are exactly my sort of people.

"Except the joss stick girl."

"Possibly; but I don't think I'm ever going to figure that one out."

"Well, there's people leaving this month, so presumably there'll be new bods arriving in the autumn, so maybe there'll be people we can get on with among them."

Chloe gazed at him, despairingly.

"Yes, but how on earth am I supposed to find them among the usual dreary crew?"

"Sheep and goats, my love, sheep and goats."

"What the hell's that supposed to mean?"

"All I mean is that I think you'll know who's worthwhile and who isn't," he said.

"Yeah? OK, does that mean I should be looking for someone with a beard, because as far as I know that's the most obvious way of telling sheep and goats apart?"

He shook his head.

"I meant metaphorically speaking, not literally," he said.

That night, Chloe dreamed about the hole again and woke to find Clifford was trying to wake her, shaking her shoulder and calling to her.

"You were having a nightmare," he said.

She pushed her hair out of her eyes, and struggled to sit up.

"Yes," she said. "I've been having a lot of them this last year or so."

"Have you? Oh well, I think you'll feel a bit better once we've had our holiday this year," he said.

He thinks I'm stressed, she thought, and lay back down again. Stressed? What have I got to be stressed about? Very funny. I'm only worrying about sheep turning into wolves.

She closed her eyes again and moved into his warm arms. There are plenty of ways to forget your troubles, after all.

Chapter 19

August was hot and dry, and a kind of lethargy pervaded the campus. A lot of people were away on holiday; a fair number had left for pastures new, and most of the new students hadn't arrived yet, so the whole place felt almost deserted by comparison to the usual bustle. The garden centre where Chloe worked, by now a semi-permanent addition to the staff, was busy with people buying stuff like new hoses and fish for ponds. The autumn stock of bulbs and seeds was on order but not yet arrived, and the remaining trays of rather leggy bedding plants were being sold off for a fraction of what they'd originally been priced at. A lot of the potted plants, both perennial shrubs and trees were looking distinctly tired and pot bound and one of Chloe's more enjoyable duties was watering the outdoor pots morning and evening; it was a quietly satisfying task, and she thought sometimes she could hear the plants sigh with relief and pleasure as she turned the hose on them.

Cathy had popped back for a weekend in July, and had stayed to mind the cats for them when they went away on their own holiday. This year they borrowed Clifford's uncle Peter's cottage at the foot of the North York moors; he had bought it as a home for him to retire to, but had this year offered it to Clifford and Chloe as a holiday home. It had been implied that Clifford and his sister were the ones who would inherit from Peter, since Peter had never married, and the money for the cottage had been his half of the money from his parents. The other half had obviously gone to Nadine, Clifford's mother. Nadine had been very scathing about her brother's choice of a retirement cottage, remarking that it was typical of Peter's basic impracticality that he should choose a cottage half a mile from the nearest village at a time in his life when he would not be driving for much longer and would need to be in a place that had easy access to buses and facilities. Peter had been just as robust in his response, saying that he was well aware of his age, and would make other choices when the time came, but for the moment it would be very pleasant to think he had a quiet, peaceful and moreover remote place to retire to.

He had been at the cottage for the first few nights they were there; ostensibly to welcome them and show them where everything was, but really, it was a good excuse to get together with his nephew and his wife without Nadine being around to interfere and criticise. Chloe had enjoyed his company and had been sad when he'd set off back to York, leaving them the cottage to themselves. It was over too quickly though and she and Clifford had got back to a home with two now over-fed and demanding cats and a very tanned Cathy who had been enjoying their garden as well as the chance to clear out and refurbish her van for the coming autumn.

"I've kept the grass cut," she said. "And I've kept the worst of the weeds down. The cats kept crying so I kept feeding them. I think they may have been pining for you."

A pair of very sleek and contented cats gazed innocently at Chloe, and turned away when she went to pet them.

"Typical bloody cats," Chloe said. "Thanks ever so for house and cat sitting. I keep threatening them with a cattery but I don't think they believe me."

"They won't now," Cathy said. "I think they may have put on a little weight."

Cathy had headed off on another environmental campaign, this time to add her voice to protesters aiming to prevent another road being cut across an area of unique woodland, and Chloe missed her more than she would have expected, considering how little she'd actually seen of her.

It was hot and dry and the air seemed to smell of thunder that evening when the doorbell rang. Chloe had been reading in the living room, having retreated from the garden when a number of drops of rain had fallen on her book. She was always a bit worried when the doorbell rang, especially at times of the day when the innocent everyday reasons, like postal deliveries or meter readers, could be ruled out.

On the doorstep was a stranger.

Chloe looked at her; she was unremarkably dressed in tee shirt and jeans, but she was otherwise remarkable. She was about Chloe's age but she had a confidence that Chloe had lost, and her very direct gaze was almost an assault.

"We've just moved in next door but one," said the woman. "I've managed to unpack a couple of tea cups, but we're wanting to celebrate finally getting here, and I have no idea where the corkscrew might be, and I need to open this."

She held up a champagne bottle and again that direct gaze from deep amber eyes was unsettling; there was a hint of a smile in the eyes but none in the mouth, just a smear of very red lipstick.

Chloe felt herself shiver, and for a moment didn't know what to say. There was something very odd about this but she couldn't quite place it.

"Well, unless you've moved from the West Bank, I'm not quite sure why you need to celebrate getting here," she said, and saw the other woman's eyebrows shoot up in surprise. "Second, that's a champagne bottle and it doesn't need a corkscrew at all. Third, I can see what looks like a corkscrew sticking out your pocket. And fourth, you can't seriously think of drinking champagne out of tea cups."

The woman stared at her for a moment, the amber eyes very steady and cat-like, before the mouth broke into a broad grin and she started to laugh, a sound rather like the sound Chloe fancied she heard coming from the plants she watered.

"Yes!" said the woman, punching the air in triumph. "I knew someone would turn up."

"Erm, you're the one who's turned up," Chloe pointed out, quite reasonably.

"Point taken, but I know what I mean," said the woman.

"Would you like to borrow some glasses for the fizzy stuff," Chloe said, and hesitated. "There is a fee though."

"Oh yes?" the woman said, and raised one of those quirky expressive brows.

"Only a small fee; you let us share it," Chloe said, hardly believing she'd said it.

"Yes!" said the woman, and punched the air again. "Double whammy; God loves me. Just a minute."

She pulled out a mobile phone and tapped away for a moment sending a text message.

"I've taken the extreme liberty of texting Mickey to come over here; our house is so full of boxes there isn't anywhere to sit where you can see each other," she said, and after a moment, a man appeared at the gate.

He was very tall and rather thin, dark hair twisted into a ponytail, dressed much the same as his wife in jeans; he had a huge bag of crisps in his hand.

"Party time?" he asked his wife. "I'm Mickey, this is Isobel. She's knocked on a fair few doors the last hour or so, so I'm parched now."

"I should introduce you," said Isobel. "This is Chloe."

Chloe did a bit of a double take at this.

"Relax, I'm not psychic, well not to that extent. It's just I got told at one house not to go to the house at the end, because Chloe was a bit weird and very unfriendly, and I thought, aha, just the sort of person I'm sure to like," said Isobel, grinning madly.

"You'd better come in before they see you," Chloe said, and ushered them in, keen to shut the door on any watching eyes.

"Don't worry, I'm told that Felicity is away, so your nearest neighbour isn't there to spy on us," Isobel said.

"Thank God for that. It had seemed a bit quiet lately," Chloe said, as Clifford came down the stairs.

He looked at the new arrivals in puzzlement.

"This is Mickey and Isobel, they've just moved to college," Chloe said, and they went through the ritual of shaking hands.

"I think Isobel has been out prospecting," Chloe said, giving Isobel a grin.

"I don't believe in letting the grass grow under my feet," Isobel said. "I've unpacked the bed linen and the tea things, and that's all I need for the minute, so I went and found and off-licence and started going door to door here."

"You must be desperate for friends," Chloe said.

"Not exactly," Mickey said. "We thought we ought to get a feel for the place and the people before we get sucked down."

"We've heard stories," Isobel said. "And I rather gather they must be at least in part true."

Chloe led her guests to the living room and went off in search of glasses. When she came back, Isobel was sitting on the hearth stroking the Buddha lovingly.

"What a cool room!" she said. "I don't think I've ever seen such a lovely Buddha. Is he made of sandalwood?"

"I think so," Chloe said. "It's either that or he was soaked in sandalwood oil at some stage because the scent fills the room whenever it gets warm. My Gran sent him back from her travels."

"Shall I do the honours?" Mickey said, holding up the bottle.

"Be my guest, I can never open those things without a blast barrier," Chloe said, setting the glasses down.

Mickey popped the cork with practised ease, and carefully poured the frothing wine into the glasses. He passed the glasses to the others, and held up his own.

"To new beginnings," he said, and clinked glasses with everyone in turn.

"So how come you're so pleased to be here when you've already heard stories?" Chloe asked, as they sat down.

"Complicated, really," Mickey said. "At one stage I didn't think they'd even let me go for an selection conference."

"What was the problem? They aren't usually so funny about sending people to selection conferences," Clifford asked.

"Our director of ordinands had, let's say, a few problems with Isobel," Micky said.

"I'm a second generation lapsed Catholic," Isobel said happily. "He had a problem with that; so I had to jump through assorted hoops to convince him I wasn't going to embarrass anyone later by insisting that any children we may have be brought up Catholic."

"Lapsed Catholic I understand, but not second generation," Clifford said.

"Ah, that's down to my Mum," Isobel said. "She was a thoroughly lapsed Catholic until she discovered that the best school in the area they lived in was Catholic, and then she suddenly rediscovered her roots in time to have me and my brother baptised as Catholics since that was the requirement for the school. I call it hedging her bets, but she calls it keeping her options open. I think my brother was just glad the best school wasn't Jewish. I grew up as a sort of fringe Catholic. Very fringe, actually, as I avoided going at all once we were at the school! I think the DDO was scared I'd turn out to be more Catholic than I thought; he had a bit of a problem with it. So until I was officially Anglican he wouldn't recommend Mickey to the Advisory Board for Ministry for a conference."

"And you nearly ruined it with the mushrooms, too," Mickey said, laughing.

"Mushrooms?" Chloe said.

"Well, after the powers that be had recommended Mickey for training the DDO invited himself over for a meal, not quite sure why. I did braised mushrooms for a starter and just as a throwaway comment I said they were magic mushrooms. It was daft, because they were classic field mushrooms, big ones, you know, and they look nothing like the real thing. But he didn't know that, and got really worried about it, because I only said it as we were finishing the starter. I'm not sure he even believed me when I got the mushroom book out and showed him what the real thing look like because quite obviously no book is going to state which are magic mushrooms. It was another black mark on my record, but hey, many more and it'll all be black anyway."

"Bit like mine. Do they keep records on wives, do you think?" Chloe said.

"Nah, we're just a footnote at the end of the record, often just our names and ages. They aren't really interested enough to care much unless there's any real possibility of scandal," Isobel said. "I think I've scared them though. I say stupid things and they believe me. You see, technically I'm an artist, and we all know what these arty Bohemian types are like, shag anything that moves."

"Only technically an artist?" Clifford said. "Why only technically? You either are or you're not."

"You can tell you're an ordinands," Isobel said. "Black and white and no room for the infinite shades of grey. Don't worry; you'll grow out of it. No offence, I hope. No, all I mean is what I do for a sort of living doesn't count as art for me. To make enough money I have to do stuff like pet portraits and portraits of kiddies and teddies and that sort of thing. I can do them in my sleep and they're hardly taxing; it's one up from painting by numbers, once you've got the hang of it. No soul involved, often I use a photo anyway so I don't even have to talk to the subject at all. My real stuff is very different but we've all got to eat. I suppose as far as prostituting one's talent goes, this probably only counts as manual relief."

Chloe felt herself beginning to relax, and laughed at Isobel's joke.

"I gather from one of your more communicative neighbours that you're a mechanical engineer," Isobel said.

"Not mechanical, civil," Chloe said.

Isobel looked blank.

"What's the difference?" she asked.

"Mechanical engineers build weapons; civil engineers build targets," Chloe said, and they all laughed, and when the laughter ended, Clifford picked up the bottle and topped up their glasses.

"Anyway, at the moment I'm not doing any engineering at all," Chloe said. "I got made redundant twice, once by downsizing and once by an oak tree; it's a long story. I'm working at a local garden centre; it was only supposed to be a temporary post but I'm hoping it'll take me through till next June when we move on from here. And by then I may have decided what I really want to do with my life."

"There's only one thing to do with life," Isobel said. "That's to live. What we do in the gaps is the hard bit."

"Gaps?" Clifford asked.

"Yeah, gaps. You know, the moments between moments; the long Sunday afternoon feeling where there's time to spare but you can't think of anything to do with it. You know the sort of thing, where you just sort of mark time until something catches your attention." Isobel took a sip of her champagne. "I try to have as few gaps in my life as is reasonable. The trick is never to allow yourself to be truly bored. To be bored is to be boring."

"Then I make a new resolution, never to be bored," Chloe said. "My Gran would turn in her grave if she thought I'd got staid and boring."

Chainsaw sauntered in at this point, fortunately without the customary rodent dangling from his jaws, and made straight for Isobel.

"What a magnificent beast," Isobel remarked and stroked his head cautiously. "Somehow I thought you'd have cats, but somehow I'd imagined them to be black."

Chloe gazed at her thoughtfully.

"You shouldn't believe everything you hear around this place, you know," she said coolly.

"I know," Isobel said. "I'm very good at weeding out the inaccuracies; but the end result of the bits and pieces I've picked up since the removals van dumped our stuff and left is that you've managed to unsettle people. And that's something I approve of wholeheartedly."

"Why?" Clifford asked.

"Because I don't like complacency. It's death to the human spirit," Isobel said. "And there's people here that look like sheep that have never heard of lamb chops and Lancashire hotpot. I didn't even have to talk to them to guess that. They look like they believe themselves to be at the top of the tree. And that gets under my skin; don't quite know why," Isobel said. "But it does. I've never been able to cope with smug people."

"You and me both, sister," Chloe said. "Welcome to the Asylum."

Chloe wondered in the next few hours while they drank first the champagne, then several bottles of white wine, quite how someone as apparently anarchic in spirit was going to go down at college, where her own fairly minor eccentricities had been cause of such concern. It was four o'clock in the morning before Mickey and Isobel went back to their own house, and as they left, Chloe felt a strange sense of relief that finally they had made some friends.

She called round at Isobel's house the following day after she had finished at work. The campus was still deserted and felt quite eerie after the usual bustle and busyness. Isobel came to the door, and grinned when she saw who it was.

"Man, I had a hangover this morning," she said. " I hope you had one too. Come in and I'll put the kettle on. Unless you fancy something stronger?"

"Tea would be great," Chloe said. "I'm not much of a drinker, usually."

She followed Isobel into the living room, which was full of boxes and packing material strewn everywhere. There was one large leather sofa and not much else, though a very expensive stereo was set up on a low table and the speakers were equidistant from each end of the sofa. There was also an easel, set up with a canvas on it, a big box next to it, and a stack of canvases propped against it.

Isobel made tea and brought it through.

"We're still in absolute chaos," she said, but she was explaining rather than apologising for it. "I want to get started at once; I've got a few photo commissions to finish and I want them done so there's a chance the people here might ask me to paint their kids. If I've got stuff to show them, they might go for it."

"Might do, I suppose. They are rather devoted to their kids," Chloe said cautiously.

"Good. Nothing like a doting parent for my business," Isobel said.

Chloe had thought about this all day at work, and wasn't quite certain that she should ask this. It might end a friendship before it was truly begun, but better now than later, when she'd got used to having a friend.

"Look, I can't help wondering how on earth you're going to manage here," Chloe said. "You seem to know what this place is like, and yet you seem confident you can even get them to pay you to paint their kids. They hate me, most of them and I haven't really done anything to deserve it. And you said yourself you're one of the arty Bohemian sort that I can't imagine them taking to their hearts. So what's the deal?"

Isobel put her mug down, and Chloe could see the corners of her mouth twitching with suppressed laughter.

"I suppose I'm planning a sort of con trick," she said. "You see, none of them know anything about me yet, and I aim to make sure they only discover what I want them to. When it comes down to it, a jobbing artist like me depends to a certain degree on the goodwill of customers and potential customers. That way I get paid for doing paintings of kiddies and doggies and suchlike, so I can afford to eat and to do the painting I really want to do. So I'm quite prepared to behave myself, at least where people can see me, and keep my mouth shut about what I really think about anything. But I need to know what is most likely to upset people so I can avoid doing it if at all possible."

Chloe looked at her with curiosity.

"Do you really think you can keep it up for three years?"

"Don't know. But I think I can do it for long enough to have them thinking that me painting their families is worth me being a bit arty and weird. You see, I know I'm good at what I do, and I know how to get commissions from people who didn't think they'd ever pay for a portrait. If my plan goes right, I won't have to be good for too long; sooner or later they'll all want a painting so much they'll put up with me as I am."

"I think you're mad," Chloe said.

"Quite possibly," Isobel said calmly. "But I've had to leave behind my home and come here, so maybe I can be excused a little insanity. Look, can you give me the low-down of what sort of thing really winds up the people here?"

Chloe sipped her tea and thought for a moment. Under this bravado, she had a sudden sense of Isobel's very real loneliness and fear.

"OK," she said. "But I'd like to see some of your real work first."

Isobel mulled that for a minute, and then nodded.

"Fair enough," she said. "I've got some of it upstairs. It isn't what I sell, at least not much. Not yet anyway."

Chloe followed her to the smaller of the bedrooms, and Isobel pulled out a number of paintings. They were vibrant and vivid, surrealist images where ordinary things and people had strange twists to them, like a teapot that burst its spout into a camellia flower, or a dog that had fins. They were compelling and a bit disturbing.

"First of all, never let them see this lot," Chloe said. "They'd reckon it was demonic or something."

Isobel leaned on the windowsill and gazed out.

"And?" she said.

"And keep painting them; I think they're brilliant. But they would truly freak out most of the women here," Chloe said. "And never admit any interest in other faiths, even artistically. They wanted me to burn that Buddha, you know, in case he had demons attached to him."

"Fucking hell," breathed Isobel.

"And never use the f-word, or any other swear word for that matter," Chloe said. "And never admit you don't adore all children and want a half dozen yourself, and never admit you deviate an inch from the standard party line. I've never figured out what I'm expected to believe anyway, so that's probably why I keep getting it wrong."

Isobel turned to her from the windowsill, and Chloe had a jolt to see there were tears running down Isobel's face.

"You poor sodding cow," she said to Chloe. "What have they done to you?"

Chloe didn't know what to say.

"It's a long story," she said. "Do you want to hear it?"

Isobel blew her nose, and nodded.

"I'll make some more tea," she said. "And I think it's time for the chocolate biscuits too. Nothing seems quite as bad after a few chocolate Hobnobs."

Downstairs, over enough tea to float a battleship and so many biscuits Chloe began to feel sick, she told Isobel the saga of the last few years. At the end, when Chloe had been to the loo and come back to the big sofa, Isobel was looking a bit grim.

"I'm not going to manage it, am I?" she asked.

"Not for three years, anyway," Chloe said. "You can't hide your real self for too long, or you end up losing yourself altogether."

"I can see that," Isobel said, thoughtfully. "This is a bit tricky. I had hoped to pass as a sheep in wolves clothing for the duration. You see, our DDO was really concerned I wasn't exactly the sort

268

of wife a clergyman should have. You should have seen me before we moved here. I had dreadlocks, even. It was a bit of a wrench to let them go, but I'm not black so I can't even say they were part of my culture. I'm only glad I never had any tattoos. I had my nose pierced, but that's healed over, and my ears have several piercings and I used to wear lots of really Gothic jewellery. I've got that all in a box somewhere. I bought some nice ordinary jeans and stuff, and I pass muster in a crowd now. But it severely pissed me off to do it. Now it turns out you've been victimised for far less. I've got to have a good think about this."

"I'm going to get off home now," Chloe said. "Sorry to have burst the bubble."

Isobel looked at her from a tear-streaked face.

"Stupid bubble anyway, I'll blow another one," she said. "Are you in tomorrow evening? I reckon I'll have thought of something by then."

"I'm in most evenings, and if I'm not I'll only be out running and I ought to be back within the hour," Chloe said.

"I'll see you then," Isobel said, and showed Chloe out.

Chloe felt quite sad that she had so disillusioned Isobel this early in her stay at college; she'd not even got to the introductory weekend yet and her life was in tatters. But she'd reckoned without Isobel's ability to bounce back after disasters. The following evening, shortly after six, Isobel was standing on her doorstep, her amber eyes glowing as though a light had been switched on inside her head, and her smile so wide Chloe thought it must hurt.

"I've got a plan," she said.

Chapter 20

It was a simple plan, really. Isobel had spent hours thinking it up, and in the plain light of evening it looked insane as well.

"I'm going to be a mole," Isobel explained. "No, not the furry underground variety. The spy kind. I'm going to find out from the inside how to even up the odds. And then we're going to bring them all down a peg or two, because I don't think anyone should get away with what they've done to you and what they'd do to me if we don't take action now."

"We?" Chloe asked.

"Well, I sort of assumed you'd want to help. It wouldn't involve direct confrontation, well, not if it goes right. More a sort of guerilla warfare," Isobel said. "I am thinking ahead here, for the greater good of all. Can you imagine the havoc they might wreak on a parish? I can. Because I've seen it once or twice. It's part of the Rector and the Director syndrome; you get my drift."

"You are quite mad, did you know that?" Chloe said.

"But not certifiable, yet," Isobel said. "What do you think?"

"I don't know," Chloe said slowly. "It feels a bit like revenge."

"A dish best served cold. You don't even know what I'm planning yet," Isobel said.

"Tell me then."

Isobel outlined her plan and by the end, Chloe was grinning.

"Well? What do you think now?" Isobel demanded.

"I still think you're mad as a hatter, but yes, let's do it, if you think you can get away with it," Chloe said.

"I won't be breaking any laws and nor will you, so don't worry," Isobel said. "I reckon I can behave myself long enough to be accepted as one of them, though I draw the line at getting pregnant just for that. I think I shall have a," she sniffed theatrically, "I think I shall have a history of miscarriage. And if I look longingly at new babies and bumps and shed a shy tear from time to time, I'm sure I'll get the sympathy I deserve. And we can pool our thoughts on the phone, because after today, I can't be seen talking to you."

"We could meet up for coffee sometimes; I know a place they would never go. There's a sort of alternative centre in town that has therapies and coffee. They boycotted it when they discovered that they had a medium working there; and some of the more extreme people object to stuff like flower remedies and even aromatherapy, so there wasn't much there that someone didn't have a problem with. The coffee's nice too," Chloe said.

"Well, that's great," Isobel said. "I'll have to hide half my medicine cabinet then, and only leave boring stuff in the bathroom. Oh well. If they do catch me out, I can always repent. I'm dead good at that. Or plead ignorance. This could be fun. I can't wait for the introductory weekend now and I was dreading it before."

Chloe couldn't help being infected by Isobel's humour and enthusiasm.

"Of course, we'll need to fine tune the details as we go along and I get the hang of who's who and quite what the best methods are for the plan, but that won't be hard," Isobel went on. "The more information the better, I'd say. Do you know when your next door neighbour, what's her name, Fellatio, is back?"

"It's Felicity, and probably any day now; don't slip and call her that will you? That would ruin it all before you get started," Chloe said.

"This is going to be so funny," Isobel said, rubbing her hands with anticipation. "The biggest practical joke I've ever done."

When Isobel had gone home to get on with her painting, Chloe sat down and felt slightly sick. This was utterly mad, the whole idea. But Isobel's words as she'd left rang in her mind.

"It's payback time," she'd said, and had practically skipped up the path.

Well, OK, vengeance might be the Lord's but He seemed alarmingly slow about this, so maybe it was OK to just help things along a little. No one would get hurt and it might teach a few people they couldn't just trample over other's beliefs and feelings the way they had been. And Isobel was right; it could well be really funny, and she could do with a good laugh at the moment.

"Are you all right?"

Clifford had come into the room without her noticing, and was watching her with concern.

"Fine. I think I'm still a bit hungover, that's all," she said.

"Was that Isobel just now?"

"Yes."

He looked at her curiously again.

"I think she could be a good friend for you," he said, cautiously.

272

"Yes. But I don't think it'll do her much good to be seen with me if she wants to get on with the other wives," Chloe said.

She'd already made up her mind she wasn't going to tell Clifford much about Isobel's plan; he'd not approve and she didn't think a little thing like that would stop Isobel.

The next day the campus began to buzz again as people slowly arrived, either home from holidays or moved into their new homes, and Chloe didn't hear from Isobel at all for some time. About a week later, she phoned Chloe in the evening.

"How's it going?" Chloe asked.

"I've drunk enough horrible coffee to kill the average pot plant," Isobel said. "I've even changed a nappy and held any number of babies, and shed a few crocodile tears. I've got two commissions already, albeit at a discounted rate, because I said the children were just so beautiful I really wanted to paint them anyway, but I still had bills to pay…It's amazing how people will go for a special offer if you lace it with enough charm. I have wanted to punch a number of people especially Fellatio. You aren't the only one they pick on, either. There's this rather sweet quiet girl called Annie, and they all use her for target practise when they think they can get away with it. Christ knows why she puts up with it, but I guess she must be so lonely she'd rather have their company than none at all. The brats are obnoxious in the extreme. Well, they don't get any boundaries to speak of so they just keep pushing them. OK I know that doesn't make sense, but I know what I meant. And the religious intolerance took my breath away. Especially since they don't consider that most Catholics are really Christians at all. I had a job keeping quite about that I can tell you, especially when Nicky said she was sure the Pope was a really nice good man but unless he turned to Christ he'd burn in hell alongside Hitler and the rest of the gang. I feel a great need for expletives but I don't think I dare in case I get into the habit of letting rip whenever I get cross. I'm sick of the word Bother! It doesn't work as well as what I'm substituting it for. How are you?"

"Feeling a bit rough, to tell the truth," Chloe said. "I think I may be sickening for something. Still, nothing to affect The Plan, I'm sure. Best of luck with all the fact-finding missions. I'm sure someone will eventually bring out some decent coffee. I'd bet this Annie would, if they ever let her host one of their coffee mornings."

Chloe went to work the next day feeling distinctly ropey, and just seemed to get worse as the day went on. Clifford had slipped away for a few days to pacify his mother who had begun complaining that she never saw her son, so Chloe didn't even have him to come home to, and she was feeling a fair degree of self-pity by the time she got her afternoon coffee break.

She was just returning to her position in one of the greenhouses when she felt a sharp cramp across her lower abdomen.

Sod it, just the right moment for my period to start. Oh well, better late than never, she thought, but as she walked the pain got worse and worse, till she was doubled over by the time she was halfway back to her greenhouse. She could also feel the flow starting, so she began to hobble back towards the staff loos so she could deal with that. The pain was horrible and she felt rather sick, too. When she got to the loos, she discovered that the blood had already soaked through her knickers and was staining her jeans. She stuffed a sanitary towel between her legs and went to find her boss; she'd need to get home and change at the very least.

When she found her boss, she was feeling very poorly indeed, and it showed on her face.

"Can I have a quick word?" she asked.

"Are you all right? You look terrible," said her boss.

"I need to go home and change; my period had just started and because it's so late, it's really heavy and I'm sure you get the idea," Chloe said, trying not to double over, as the next cramp seemed to squeeze her in half.

Her boss looked at her with concern.

"I think I'll run you home myself," she said. "You don't look well at all; you should be in bed with a hot water bottle at least."

Chloe managed at weak smile.

"That's very kind of you," she said. "And I really appreciate it. I'm not sure I can walk that far now anyway so I was going to get a taxi."

When her boss got her to the house, she was actually quite worried about her; Chloe's face was very pale and a bit grey and sweaty.

"Is there anyone at home to look after you?" she asked.

Chloe just shook her head.

"A friend or a neighbour I can call? How about the people next door to you?"

Chloe shuddered at the idea of Felicity coming to her rescue.

"Next door but one," she said. "There's a girl there who's a sort of friend. See if she's around."

Chloe watched her boss go off to Isobel's house and after a few minutes, she returned with Isobel, who helped Chloe out of the car and up the path.

"Look after her," called Chloe's boss, and then drove away.

"You look dreadful," Isobel said, taking Chloe's keys from her and opening the front door.

"Don't feel so good. I need a shower, I'm in such a mess," Chloe said and Isobel helped her up the stairs.

As Chloe slipped off her stained jeans in the bathroom while Isobel stood by, Isobel suddenly said,

"How late is this period then?"

"Don't remember. I'm always all over the place so I can never be quite sure when I'm due. Very late, I think," Chloe said.

"Put those jeans back on; I'm taking you to the hospital," Isobel said, her voice sounding very firm.

Chloe straightened up with difficulty and looked at her.

"You're having a miscarriage," Isobel said.

"How do you know?" Chloe demanded, suddenly very cold.

"I wasn't inventing that history of miscarriage," Isobel said. "A good liar needs to mix a fair bit of truth with the lies and that was one chunk of truth I'd rather was a lie. Come on, let's get you where you can be looked after properly."

Chloe let herself be dressed again and waited in the hall while Isobel brought her car round to Chloe's house, and helped her into it and then locked Chloe's door behind them.

"I won't mess around; I'll take you straight to Maternity and no farting around at Casualty," she said as they pulled out of the campus. "There's still a chance you haven't lost it."

"I don't want it," Chloe said miserably.

"I know that, silly," Isobel said. "But if it hasn't all gone, they have to do a D and C to get rid of anything left behind or it sort of festers and then you're in real trouble. So the best place to get anything done quickly is Maternity. Do you want me to put a blanket over you head so no one can see who you are?"

Chloe was feeling too feeble to either laugh or protest and didn't see Isobel look at her with worried eyes.

"I want Clifford," Chloe said in a small voice.

"I'll get hold of him once we've got you sorted," Isobel said. "Where is he, then?"

"Away, at his mother's, just to stop her nagging him about us not visiting in the summer. He thought he'd go for a few days before term, while I've got to work. His mother doesn't like me."

"Stupid bitch," Isobel said. "Look just breathe deeply or something, and if you feel sick, there's a plastic bag in the glove compartment. You can give me his mobile number later, when we've got you sorted. OK?"

Chloe nodded, wanting at this moment her own bed and the oblivion of sleep. Isobel drove fast but with the confidence of a rally driver, and by some miracle managed to get parked only a short distance from the hospital entrance. In the lobby in the Maternity wing, Isobel marched up to the reception desk as Chloe trailed behind, clutching her abdomen. The girl behind the desk looked at her expectantly.

"Can we have some help here please?" Isobel said. "My friend is having a miscarriage and she really needs a doctor now."

Chloe staggered up to the desk and saw the girl flinch slightly.

"You maybe should sit down," said the girl. "I'll phone through straight away."

Chloe could feel her knees turning to jelly; maybe that's what all these ants were after, swarming over her skin till all she could feel was their tiny feet running over every inch of her body. The lighting in here was hopeless, dim and dark. At least no one could see her looking such a wreck with such dim lights. She knew she must be swaying, but it felt so like being on a ship she was starting to feel seasick.

"I'll get a chair," said the girl.

"Too late," Isobel said, trying to catch Chloe as her sway became a fall. "She's fainted."

*

When Chloe came round, she found she'd been put on a bed in a side room; distantly she could hear the distinctive cry of a newborn baby. Isobel was sitting by her, and as she tried to sit up, a woman doctor came into the room.

"Back with us, I see," she said, smiling at Chloe. "How are you feeling?"

"I could kill for a cup of tea," Chloe said.

"Not just yet, I'm afraid," said the doctor. "Later, maybe. We need to assess whether you've lost the foetus altogether; and if the miscarriage isn't complete we have to think about what to do, and since that may involve a D and C, which requires an anaesthetic, you can't have a cup of tea just yet. We'll bring the portable ultrasound here shortly so we can have a look inside, but in the mean time, I need to examine you. Your friend can stay if you want her to."

Isobel looked at her expectantly.

"Only if you want to," Chloe said.

"I'll stay as long as I'm needed," Isobel said. "When we've got a minute, I'll get hold of Clifford and get him to come home, shall I? And then I can nip back to yours for your stuff, you know, a nightie and toothbrush and all that sort of thing."

Chloe nodded weakly, glad of her support.

When the doctor had examined her, she seemed serious.

"I can't be sure," she said. "But the ultrasound will confirm what I think. I think the foetus is probably gone. But this isn't uncommon; more than one in five pregnancies end in miscarriage, and most women go on to have healthy normal pregnancies."

"I didn't even know I was pregnant," Chloe said, and to her shame, felt tears spilling over and cascading down her shirt. "I just thought I was late."

The doctor nodded understandingly.

"Not unusual. I take it you have something of an irregular cycle," she said. "So knowing when your last period was, won't be much help anyway in establishing how many weeks pregnant you were."

Were. One small word which changed everything. Well, at least I didn't want it, Chloe thought, but that brought more tears.

"Sorry," she said. "Can I have a tissue? This is silly. I didn't know and I wouldn't have wanted it anyway, and I'm crying like a, like a baby."

"Again, not unusual," said the doctor. "Blame hormones if it helps. They make us do some pretty strange things. It's easy to forget how much we are still animals and how in control of us our hormones are; the need to reproduce is a biological one, and has a greater effect than we ever think it could. Try not to worry, and relax if you can. You'll be fine now you're here."

The ultrasound showed that there was nothing left alive in Chloe's womb.

"There's still quite a lot that hasn't come away yet," said the doctor. "We can either leave it a little while, or we can remove any remaining products of conception with a small procedure called a D and C. I would strongly recommend that, actually. And then you can go home tomorrow, and recover at your leisure."

"I'll take the procedure," Chloe said.

"I'll go and get your over night things," Isobel said. "I've got your door keys. Can you give me Clifford's mobile number and I'll call him on my way home?"

Chloe gave her the number and watched her leave feeling suddenly very small and bereft.

"We should be able to get you sorted in a few hours," said the doctor. "I appreciate you won't want to be here for long; especially so near to the delivery suite and all but it won't take very long, and you can be home tomorrow."

It seemed to take hours before she was taken to theatre, longer because she felt horribly thirsty and wasn't allowed to drink anything. She'd skipped lunch, which was just as well, because they would have made her wait till tomorrow if she'd eaten anything more recently than breakfast. One good thing about the delay was that Isobel got back before she was taken down, and she knew she would at least have someone she knew to wake up to.

"I spoke to Clifford and he'll be on his way by now," she said. "So he'll be here soon. How far away is he?"

"About three hours drive," Chloe said.

"I got you a nightie and dressing gown, and I gathered up all the toiletries I thought I'd want, so blame me if I got it wrong. And a hairbrush and comb and a bobble so you can plait it back or something so it doesn't go everywhere. And I found your slippers as well. I fed those cats too, so that they don't get hungry while you're away," Isobel said, putting the overnight bag next to Chloe. "Oh, and a couple of pairs of clean knickers and a packet of sanitary towels too. I hope you're not one of these people who get really antsy about anyone going through their belongings, but if you are, then it's tough, because how else was I expected to find any of the things you'd need?"

"Just as long as you don't tell anyone what you found," Chloe said, closing her eyes.

"Your secrets are safe with me," Isobel said, soothingly. "Nice Tarot cards, though. Are they antiques?"

Chloe's eyes shot open and she nearly fell off the bed.

"Relax," Isobel said. "I was trying to find your nightie, and I thought, well, I put mine under the pillow, so I looked under what I guessed was your pillow and that's where I found them. I won't tell anyone. I sort of hoped you trust me a bit by now."

Chloe was having trouble speaking.

"Do you use them?" Isobel asked. "A friend of mine has a set and she uses them. She says they're not much use for telling fortunes, but they're good for understanding the past and the present and that goes a long way towards predicting the future."

"No," Chloe said. "I don't use them. Not as such. I look at them though."

She told the story of the old gypsy woman giving them to her Gran.

"What a gift!" Isobel said. "They look old, though; well used. Beautiful too. But I can see why you keep them hidden. I can't imagine Nicky or Felicity or Julie being very happy about you having them, let alone using them. Silly really; they're just tools for the unconscious mind to work with, not actually magical themselves."

"There's a crystal ball as well," Chloe said. "It's in a drawer where I keep my jumpers."

"Didn't come across that, obviously," Isobel said. "It's hot in here; you won't need a jumper for months anyway, not if this warm weather keeps up. Come Hallow E'en you will; or combat and camouflage fatigues, and that funny make-up to black out your face, if you want to go the whole hog. When are they taking you down?"

"Any time now, I gather," Chloe said. "Have you had a D and C?"

"Two; there's nothing to it really. They give you an anaesthetic so you don't even know about it. That can make you a bit sick."

"That's what I was told," Chloe said. "I don't like the thought of it but it's better than hanging round waiting to see if everything comes away."

"Much better," Isobel said, pulling a wry face.

There was a tap at the door and a nurse came in.

"Ready?" she said brightly.

Chloe nodded.

"I'll see you later," she said to Isobel.

"You'll be fine," Isobel replied, and came over and gave her a hug. "See you later, then."

Chloe watched her leave the room as the trolley was brought in. She suddenly felt very alone.

Chapter 21

Chloe pulled the covers up to her face when she heard the doorbell, and hoped Clifford would send whoever it was away. She felt like a depressed sewer rat and probably looked like one. A moment later, Isobel breezed into the room.

"You shouldn't be here," Chloe said.

"I know, but I waited till it got dark and I went on hands and knees past Felicity's house so she couldn't see me go past, and I even crawled up your path just to make sure. How are you feeling?"

"I feel like shit," Chloe said.

"Don't mind me; say what you think," Isobel said. "Really? Is it that bad?"

Chloe struggled upright and scrubbed at her face.

"I can't seem to stop crying," she said. "Which is bloody silly, when I didn't want it anyway so why am I just sort of dissolving?"

"You even get the baby blues when there isn't a baby," Isobel said. "Happened to me every time; even the ones I didn't want had that effect. It's just hormones, really. Do they have any idea how many weeks you were?"

"Roughly twelve, I think. I have such erratic periods anyway, so I didn't even think about pregnancy. I once went eight months without one," Chloe said. "How many miscarriages have you had then?"

"Five for certain," Isobel said. "A few maybes or maybe they were just late periods; it's hard to be sure."

"You must hate all these coffee mornings, then."

"Nah, it isn't a problem. Not really. They're their babies. I don't want them; I'd rather like my own," Isobel said. "Nothing to be done about it; they reckon there's no good reason why I keep having miscarriages, so there's no good reason why I shouldn't carry a baby to full term. The only thing they've said, which is a bit of cold comfort as these things go, is that the body sometimes rejects foetuses that are badly malformed or genetically abnormal."

"Really helpful," Chloe said. "Did Clifford say he was putting the kettle on? Because I'd really like a hot drink and I'm sure you would too."

"I'll go and check," Isobel said, and went and called from the landing.

Clifford's voice drifted up from downstairs,

"On its way."

Isobel came back into the bedroom and sat down on the bed.

"There you go; you've got him well trained," she said. "A good night's sleep should go a long way to getting you feeling better and more yourself. No one sleeps well in hospital, especially after an anaesthetic."

"I don't sleep well, anyway," Chloe said. "I keep waking up with nightmares. Nothing to do with this; it's been going on since Gran died. Sometimes I'm fine for days or even a week or two, and then it begins again."

Isobel scratched her head.

"Any particular theme to these nightmares?" she asked.

"Wish I knew; all that happens is I wake up in a real state and then it all sort of dissolves like mist when I try and recall what happened that was so upsetting," Chloe said. "Sometimes, when it's really bad I don't manage to get back to sleep at all, and I spend the rest of the night in the kitchen or on the sofa. It's vile, though, whatever I dream about. I wake up shaking and sweating and crying like a kid of three."

Isobel looked thoughtful. Clifford came into the room with a tray of drinks, tea for himself and Isobel and a mug of chamomile tea for Chloe.

"Drinks," he said unnecessarily, and put the tray down on the floor next to the bed, and sat on the bed next to Chloe and put his arm round her. "Did you want anything to eat, love?" he asked.

Chloe shook her head.

"Still feel grotty from the anaesthetic," she said. "Maybe in the morning."

Isobel glared at her.

"Make sure you do," she said. "Otherwise I'll come round with half a pound of best steak and I'll make you eat it raw, with an egg on the top."

They drank the tea and Clifford went back downstairs to get on with some of the inevitable housework.

"Are you still game for the Plan?" Isobel asked, after he'd gone.

"More than ever," Chloe said. "I'm hoping no one has noticed the comings and goings here or the fact that our curtains have been shut since I got home this morning; I shouldn't have to live with this kind of anxiety, worrying about whether people are talking about me and my life. I shouldn't even care whether they know what's happened to me; but it makes me seethe to think that anyone here might find out I had a miscarriage. And believe me, I know it's absurd to even care even a tiny bit, but every time they know anything of my life, it makes me sort of go cold inside and full of fear."

"Then we go ahead with the Plan," Isobel said. "We've got weeks anyway to get ready; it's the introductory weekend coming up in a fortnight, so that's a start. I'll have to get on with the pictures I've managed to snaffle commissions for, and that way I'll have loads of free advertisement by then. If I use acrylics instead of oils, they'll be dry that bit faster, and can be on various walls and sideboards in time for the new season of coffee mornings and afternoon tea and play sessions and all the rest of it. Oh, and new prayer groups and bible studies and so on. Look, about these dreams?"

"Yes?"

"I know one or two ways to help remember dreams," Isobel said. "If these dreams are tormenting you to this extent, there's obviously something there. If you can somehow recall what actually happens in them, then that might go a long way to, well, to exorcise them."

"OK," Chloe said, cautiously. "Fire away."

"Well, the first and probably simplest is simply to tell yourself before you go to sleep that you will remember them. The subconscious or whatever responds quite well to suggestions like that. You can also programme yourself to remember, let's say, by telling yourself that when you wake, and touch a certain item that you've chosen, that will trigger the memory of the dream. Some people use a crystal of some sort, that they choose for that purpose only and sleep with it either in their hand or under the pillow, so when they wake and feel it again, it acts as a trigger for the memory. Some people use a cross or a rosary or something like that. Whatever you feel comfortable with."

Isobel looked a bit uncomfortable, then she continued,

"I think dreams are messages from ourselves," she said. "And from the Divine, obviously. Sometimes it's the only way to get through to us, when we're sleeping and our barriers are down. When we don't remember something that is obviously traumatic as these dreams are, it seems to me that we're at some level blocking the message. And if that's the case, then it's vital that we use whatever means we can to remove that block. And if that means using stuff others have told us is New Age or whatever, then so be it. I've had to hide all my crystals since we moved here. No, more accurately I haven't unpacked them. I don't see what the problem is myself, but I know by now that most people here are hopelessly opposed to that sort of thing."

"I do have a crystal," Chloe said, and reached for the small wooden box by the bed, where she put her jewellery at night, and held out the pendant Cathy had made for her.

"Wow, this is amazing," Isobel said. "That's a really clear phantom. You don't see many that clear. This is ideal. Some people reckon phantom quartz is perfect for this as it holds an image of something within itself. Hold this at night before you sleep, and tell yourself you'll remember your dreams. And if that doesn't work, there are other methods."

Chloe felt tears welling up unbidden and unwelcome; she blew her nose loudly and rubbed them away.

"I wish you'd been here two years ago," she said.

"We'd have been thrown out by now if I had," Isobel said. "Now have a good cry; it doesn't do to hold it back. Just make sure you drink plenty and use nice soft tissues or you end up like an out of season Rudolph."

Chloe laughed and let the tears spill over unopposed.

*

The first few nights after Isobel had suggested the method for recalling dreams, Chloe slept too deeply and heavily to dream at all; she was still groggy from hospital and worn out to do more than just slide into the glorious oblivion of sleep. But by a few nights later, she had begun to wake recalling snippets of dreams, something she had rarely been able to do. She was still dubious about the method, ascribing it more to psychology than to the crystal but nonetheless it was a rare night when she didn't slip into sleep without the phantom quartz in her hand or under her pillow.

A week after the miscarriage, she went back to work, and was pleased to discover they'd missed her.

"We were going to pop over and see how you were," said the girl who managed the coffee shop. "Are you better now? We were going to come and see you today, we'd got some chocolates."

"That's very kind," said Chloe. "Tell you what, why don't we share them when it's closing time? I'd like that."

The girl looked at her and then grinned.

"What a great idea!" she said. "I'll tell everyone we're having choccies in the coffee shop when we close tonight to celebrate you getting back. What was the problem anyway?"

"Women's troubles," Chloe said, evasively. "You know how it is."

She was in a good mood when she'd got home that evening, more tired than she normally would be. There'd been an impromptu party in the coffee shop, with the big box of Belgian chocolates being passed round with the coffee, and a lot of jokes and laughter; she'd felt more cared for there than she had ever done here. The staff all seemed to like her and value her, a strange contrast to the women here.

Isobel rang shortly after supper to see how she was getting on.

"I'm fine," she said. "It does seem to be working; I am remembering my dreams but there haven't been any nightmares lately. Maybe there won't be any more."

"Don't bank on it," Isobel said, darkly. "You don't get away from it that easily."

That night, Chloe woke shaking and sweating. And remembering.

*

"A big hole in the ground?"

"Well, that isn't how it started," Chloe said. "It started with just something caught in the soil that I try to get out. I dig and dig, with my fingers, mostly, but you'd need a JCB to get a hole as big as the one I end up in the bottom of. And still I haven't got it out. I've excavated loads of toys and such like, but the thing that caught my attention is still stuck in the soil, just as firmly stuck as when I started. And then I woke up, as I try and try to pull it clear and I fall over as it gives, and I know I can't look at what's under it."

"What is it you are trying to get out?" Isobel asked at the other end of the phone line.

Chloe could feel herself shaking still as she remembered.

"It's silly," she said. "All it is, is this old blanket, pink and blue check, with a fringe at the end. A bit like you'd have on a child's bed or a cot. That sort of thing."

Isobel was so silent Chloe thought she'd gone.

"And you don't look at what's beneath it?" she said finally.

"I can't," Chloe said, feeling the tears begin. "I just can't. I mean, now I'm awake, I think it's silly, but in the dream, it's the worst most frightening thing in the world that is under the blanket, and I can never look."

She heard Isobel sigh.

"I think you may have to," she said, thoughtfully. "Otherwise it'll carry on happening. This is a message from somewhere; it has all the hallmarks of it. Do you think it's the dream you've been having these last two years?"

"Oh yes, no doubt about it. It does vary, a bit, I think, but it's almost like watching a film I've seen many times before," Chloe said.

There was another long pause, then Isobel said,

"I think you'll understand this better when you can finally see what that blanket is concealing. Do you remember a blanket like it from your own childhood?"

"Vaguely, yes, but I can't remember what happened to it," Chloe said. "Do you think it's real then?"

"Yes, both as a memory and as a symbol. As a symbol, blankets stand for a lot of things; comfort, warmth, childhood, you know, comfort blanket. Also, when you're a small child, if you pull the blankets over your head, the monsters go away. Look, why don't we meet for coffee soon, and we can talk properly. I can't think when I can't see someone face to face. Next Saturday morning, shall we say?"

"Yes, fine," Chloe said, feeling the tremors subsiding a little. "And what should I do about the dreams?"

"Keep on holding that crystal, and if you can bring yourself to look, then look. If not, you will do eventually. You've got too much curiosity not to look one day," Isobel said.

Curiosity killed the cat but it won't kill me, Chloe thought. I hope.

*

In the coffee shop, Chloe inhaled the steam from her espresso, and grinned.

"Sometimes the aroma is enough to get me going," she said.

Isobel laughed.

"Good, isn't it," she said. "I can see what you mean that none of the other wives would come here. A place called The Witches Cauldron is certainly not somewhere a God-fearing wife of an ordinand should be seen. You didn't say quite how alternative this place actually was."

"Gran used to come here for herbs sometimes; it wasn't called that then. They changed the name recently, largely as a result of the popularity of various television series; Buffy the Vampire Slayer has a lot to answer for."

"They mentioned it at yesterday's coffee morning," Isobel said. "There was some talk of even picketing it. Anyway, I've got lots of commissions after the first victims, sorry customers, had shown off my works of art. Mostly I just keep schtum when they are talking about things; it's the safest way. I can't trip over my own feet if I don't volunteer information."

"Do they talk about me?"

"Yes, but in a very strange way," Isobel said. "I can't quite figure it out. It's as if they want to be outrageously bitchy but don't dare, so they say all this horrible stuff and then dress it up in concern for your welfare, or I should say the welfare of your soul. They really don't like you, do they?"

"No, they don't," Chloe said. "I don't think I want to know details; it might upset me."

"All you need to know then is they are sure you're at the very least oppressed by the Powers of Evil. They put that down to a number of things. First to you having so many pagan artefacts in your home; second, because you have no fellowship with other Christians and hold views they think are totally unchristian. They think the college should do something about it, but when I asked Mickey if the staff were likely to do anything, he said they wouldn't really be interested unless you were doing something likely to bring the college itself into disrepute."

"Like eating babies?"

"Well, that, obviously. That's another thing they consider desperately against the faith, the fact that you don't have kids and don't want them and don't like theirs either," Isobel said. "That's the cardinal sin, really."

"Stupid bitches," Chloe said, sipping her coffee. "I've never said I don't like kids or that I never want any. Just that I don't want any now. There's plenty of time for that sort of thing in a few years or even a lot of years, if at all. I'm not really a maternal person, not really. I don't have any urges that way, not yet. And I don't see why that has anything to do with anyone else."

"Calm down," Isobel said. "It's not me that's getting at you."

Chloe put her cup down.

"Sorry," she said. "I wasn't meaning to get at you. It just makes me so cross. So you're well and truly dug in then?"

"Any better dug in and I'd have trenches," Isobel said. "They smile at me and make a real effort to include me, and I hear the whispers go round. Poor Isobel, no kid and so many miscarriages; we must be nice to her and ask her to babysit so she can enjoy our children at least. As if that would help. Anyway, I'm becoming part of the gang faster than I'd thought. Annie is really lonely, they sort of exclude her all the time, as if she is barely tolerated, but I don't really know why, because she's really nice. She's a lot more open than them; I guess that's why they marginalize her, because her views are a lot more liberal, but not so liberal that they chuck her out altogether. They're already planning their big Prayer 'n' Praise against the Devil for Hallow E'en; silly, but there you go."

"What do you think we ought to do, then?"

"I've had a lot of ideas," Isobel said. "Do you fancy a sticky bun with the coffee? I'm starving."

"I'll go and see what they've got. Do you want more coffee?"

"Please; nice big latte please. And if they have anything with chocolate on it or in it, go for that," Isobel said.

When Chloe got back to their corner with another tray of coffee and two plates of chocolate éclairs, Isobel had got out a notebook and was jotting down ideas. Chloe glanced at the first few suggestions.

"Hash cookies? You've got to be joking," Chloe said.

"Why?"

"Well, there's plenty of people who live off campus and will have to drive home," Chloe said. "I don't think the idea was to cause fatal accidents, was it?"

"Spoilsport," Isobel said, but crossed it off the list anyway without further protest.

"Pentacles?" Chloe asked, reading from the list. "Where and with what?"

"No idea, but they're scared senseless by pentacles so I thought as many of them as we can manage. In blood, for preference," said Isobel.

"Not sure about that; it never looks like blood when it's had a chance to oxidise a bit," said Chloe. "Some of these artificial bloods look more like the real thing. We could put some on the chapel door."

Isobel looked a bit uncomfortable suddenly.

"No, that's not right," she said. "We have to scare them without doing anything too bad. Doing something to the chapel itself seems sacrilege, really. I was thinking more along the lines of their cars or their windows. I was thinking of doctoring a prayer and praise music tape so that half way through it swapped to Black Sabbath or something, and then swap it back when everyone rushed to see what had gone wrong."

"Do you think you're good enough at sleight of hand to do that with so many people and such bright lights?"

"Probably not," agreed Isobel.

They ran through a whole host of ideas, from Ex-lax in the coffee, itching powder in the vestments and a variety of noises before Chloe finally shook her head sadly.

"We can't do it," she said, firmly. "Anything in chapel you'd be spotted straight away and your cover blown. Outside chapel, well, apart from drawing pentacles on cars, I don't see what I can do and not risk being seen. The thing is, with the position of the chapel as it is, I'd be visible from the bottom of the stairs as well as from the dining room door, as well as the fact that there'll be so many people milling around, even when the prayer time is happening, I'll be seen and caught. Can't be done, any of it. All out warfare is out. We'll have to stick to guerilla tactics. I like the idea of itching powder. Maybe you could put it in the collars of coats when you're at coffee mornings. How about prawns in inaccessible places? They reckon the presence of evil is accompanied by vile smells you can't track down; a couple of prawns down the back of a radiator should be pretty vile after a few days."

Isobel sighed theatrically.

"You're right," she said. "Hallow E'en is out as a major offensive. You could nip round the cars though and do a few pentacles. There's no one in the car park and if you're careful you can easily avoid being seen. Do it in clear lip balm; that way they don't see it until there's either rain or frost on the wind-screen, and it's more mysterious than blood. It's a shame; I was rather looking forward to our Charm Offensive. But maybe it would have been too obvious, after all the blokes would be there and really, apart from their choice of wives, they're none of them unintelligent.

They'd have twigged they were being tricked before too long, and then someone would have realised it was us. I'll buy some prawns on the way home. Down the side of the fridge as well."

"What about itching powder?"

"Already got it," Isobel said. "There's a joke shop in town; I found it the first week we were here. Admittedly, I looked it up in the Yellow Pages. Call me childish, but I've always been amused by practical jokes. Simple ones like itching powder are so effective when no one realises they've been had."

"If you're childish then I must be infantile," Chloe admitted. "I have to admit a certain satisfaction in such jokes."

"Another éclair?" Isobel said suddenly. "I rarely get this sort of thing and I like to make the most of it."

"Go on then," Chloe said. "Spoil me; I think I need it."

Chapter 22

Isobel sat cross-legged on Nicky's saggy sofa, and concentrated on her sketchbook. It was by far the best way to avoid being drawn into conversations where she knew she might give herself away, so she brought her pencils and sketchbook with her every time she went to a coffee morning.

She was sketching a number of the small children playing quietly with a big toy kitchen in bright plastic, complete with plastic frying pans as well as plastic food and plates. Her skill with a pencil had earned her admiration and commissions and a certain contempt that she didn't quite understand. At the moment she was having trouble controlling the urge to draw Nicky's older child with horns and a tail; at almost school age he clearly regarded the swarm of smaller children as an irritation at best, and took the opportunity to pinch, kick or hit any who came too close to him as he played with a toy a little way from the rest. Mentally she'd named him the Antichrist, and was having difficulty in not referring to him as Damien rather than his real name, Daniel.

She was getting used to having to concentrate on drawing and listening at the same time, but she did find it hard to talk as well, and they took her silence for absorption. They'd decided that she was a nice quiet girl with such talent they were only privately contemptuous of her apparent inability to breed successfully; it had become something of a domestic priority to get Isobel to do portraits of their children. No one wanted to offend her just yet, and there was always a chance that she might do stuff for free if they were really welcoming to her.

"No, Daniel, remember you must share," Nicky was saying. "I am a bit cross though. I'd have thought the staff would be behind it, but no, apparently not."

I've missed something, thought Isobel. Damn. Dare I ask? No, let's see what happens next.

"Considering how things have already been this term, I think that's a disgrace," said Julie. "There's a real atmosphere of oppression already and we're only weeks into term."

Felicity nodded vigorously, her long rather horse-like face very serious.

"There's been a strange smell in my house all week," she said. "Decay, but I've searched high and low and scrubbed everywhere but I can't trace the source."

You won't, either, thought Isobel. Not unless you undo the knobbly bits on the ends of your curtain rails.

It had taken more nerve than she'd thought to do it, but it was better than chucking prawns where they might be found by a thorough clean. She'd also tipped small amounts of milk into inaccessible corners of carpet. With the weather turning cooler, heating had gone on in nearly every house and the various things Isobel had secreted in various houses would be breaking down nicely with the increased warmth and releasing their odours.

"That's funny," Nicky said. "There's been a funny smell here too."

"And at mine," Julie said. "Like I say, definite oppression."

Isobel glanced at Annie who said nothing; Isobel hadn't had the heart to drop anything in Annie's house.

"I think the staff are being very short sighted," Felicity said. "If we don't act now and give the devil a good biff on the nose, Heaven only knows what will happen. They have said the wives' group can have a prayer evening in the Common room, though, but not the Chapel. How ridiculous is that?"

"Absurd," Isobel said, looking up from her paper. "How's that, then?"

She held up the book to show them the drawing, and there was a brief respectful silence as they admired the picture.

"I assume you'll be coming along, Isobel?" Felicity asked. "We always hold a special evening of prayer to counteract the influences of Hallow E'en; all the commercial interest and media promotion means that more people than ever are being influenced by evil without always realising it. I had to write a stiff letter of complaint to the Play Group organisers. They were having a fancy dress party, can you believe it, for the Play group, asking us to dress the children as witches or devils for it. I was horrified."

"I'm sure you were," Isobel said, absently, beginning a new drawing. "Yes, I shall be with you, no worries. It should be a good evening; doing something really worthwhile."

Felicity beamed at her with approval.

"It's so nice to have you with us," she said.

Isobel smiled at her.

"Thanks," she said. "Can I use your loo, please, Nicky?"

"Certainly," Nicky said.

"Great," said Isobel. "Too much coffee; must wring out my kidneys."

She locked the door when she got there and looked at the coats hanging from pegs, matching coats to guests and eliminating Annie's immediately. She lifted them down one by one and rubbed the itching powder into the collar of each. She hesitated over Master Damien's fleece; she so wanted to give the little oik a taste of irritation but she stopped herself. Children are the product of their parents; it's not his fault he's such a little shit. Then she used the loo, flushed it and washed her hands with extra care to make sure she didn't have any of the powder on her hands; the little packet she tucked back into her jeans pocket where there was no chance of anyone spotting it, even though she'd taken the label off just to be sure.

Back in the chaos of children that was the living room, she sat back down and focussed half on her drawing and half on the conversation. As usual, the talk came back round to Chloe.

"It's Clifford I feel sorry for," Nicky said. "He seems such a nice man, it's a shame his wife is so…" She tailed off, unable to find a suitable word.

"Unchristian," Julie said, firmly. "In fact she's positively anti-Christian, both in her opinions and her life style."

Isobel bit the end of her pencil. It wasn't easy hearing the only friend she had here being slagged off and not be able to defend her.

"In fact," Julie went on. "I wouldn't be at all surprised if this bad atmosphere was down to her."

Close, but no cigar, thought Isobel.

"I think you're being rather silly and superstitious," Annie said suddenly. "This isn't the Middle Ages and we don't believe in that sort of thing any more."

They all turned to her, even Isobel.

"You don't believe in evil then?" Julie said, her voice cold.

"Of course I believe in evil," Annie said. "But not personalised into a devil or little demons. That's just silly."

"Is it now?" said Felicity.

The temperature in the room seemed to drop dramatically and Isobel had the feeling Annie was already regretting saying anything. Her baby sensed the change and began to grizzle slightly.

"Let me tell you a few things about evil," Julie said. "And then you can tell me it's silly."

The next twenty minutes were filled with a series of harrowing tales from Julie, about possession and oppression and its effects on people, and especially small children. Isobel was shuddering when Julie finished the story about the young mother she'd known from their home church who'd got involved with a Ouija board and had ended up smothering her own children. Annie was crying.

Felicity passed her a handkerchief.

"That's why we're so careful about this time of year," she said. "We all have stories we could tell you of people who have got involved in the occult and have usually lived to regret it. I say usually-" Here she embarked on another tale of dabbling with the occult that ended in a suicide.

Annie was shaking hard by now.

"We're genuinely worried for the welfare of people like Chloe," Julie said. "But she won't accept our offers of help and friendship so we can't get near her to help. But we would if we could."

"I'm going home," Annie said, abruptly. "I need to think about this."

Rounding up her child, she left rather erratically.

Isobel started a new drawing, and sensed the satisfaction of the women around her.

"I think that was food for thought," Nicky said.

While Isobel sketched the remaining children, they swapped more stories, and Isobel longed to ask for dates and names and locations for these events so it might be possible to check up whether they really had happened that way, or at all. Finally, when she'd truly had enough to make her feel quite sick, she tucked her pencils back in their tin and got up.

"Right, I've got to go and get on with some painting," she said. "Time and tide wait for no man, or woman for that matter, and I'm getting behind with my schedule. See you soon."

Outside, in the cooling air, Isobel shuddered again and hugged her sketchbook to her as she walked the short distance home. When she got home, she left her tin and sketchbook by the door and went back out and over to Annie's house.

Annie opened the door; her face was red and blotchy from crying.

"I just wanted to see if you're all right," Isobel said. "I don't think many of those stories are really true, you know. It was a bit like when you're at school camp and everyone tries to scare the others with ghost stories. I bet if you actually asked them all the details, they wouldn't actually know. Urban myths, even."

"Thanks," Annie said, her voice thick and nasal. "It was so horrifying; do you really think things like that can actually happen?"

"No," said Isobel firmly. "But whatever you do, don't tell them I said so. I prefer a quiet life."

"Would you like a coffee?" Annie asked.

It was tempting; she had to admit that, to have another person in on the Plan. But it wouldn't work; Annie was too fragile and had already cracked under pressure.

"Thanks but no; I've got to get some work done today," Isobel said. "Don't have nightmares, will you?"

But Annie's anxious face told her she probably would.

"Look, if it's any help, put a cross in the baby's room," Isobel said. "That'll keep anything nasty away from her, and wear a cross yourself."

And avoid those bitches, she thought but didn't say it. The only way a cross would stop their evil was if you hit them with one.

"Thanks," Annie said again, and Isobel had another pang of anxiety for her.

"Give me a call if you're worried about anything," she said. Tossing a lifeline didn't count as letting her in on the Plan; she obviously needed someone to reassure her that all they'd said was a pile of steaming bullshit.

"I will," Annie said, and Isobel tore herself away and trotted off home again. She felt more tempted than ever to add horns and a tail to the portrait of Master Damien, sorry, Daniel that she was half way through finishing.

When she knew Chloe would be home from work, she picked up the phone and called her.

"Things could be on for Hallow E'en," she said, when Chloe picked up the phone.

"Yeah?"

"Yeah! The staff, by which I assume they mean the principal, have said they don't want to have the usual full-blown meeting that I gather they've always had, but as a concession they've agreed to let the wives have a meeting in the common room."

"That's brilliant," Chloe said. "There's still stuff we can do without getting rumbled. I know where the main fuse box is; I can trip the whole system so you get lights-out for a while. There's nothing like darkness for scaring the life out of people."

"Can you get to the fuse box?"

"Easy; it's in the main building, but in the old bit where the tutor's studies are. I've got a key, and I know the codes. No one in the common room will be able to see me through walls after all. I can do the cars at my leisure; if I'm in my running things anyone who sees me will assume I'm either heading out or coming back. This is great," Chloe said. "How's the guerilla warfare coming along?"

"Smelly but effective," Isobel said. "What with prawns and milk rotting in various corners, none of their houses is exactly a fragrant bower, let's just put it like that. Julie has been spraying air freshener around and that's almost worse. And after today, they're going to be itching like mad. And before you ask, they are all thinking it's the influence of evil not rotting prawns that's causing the smell. They're sort of thinking it might have something to do with you, but nothing definite. More along the lines of they think you're attracting demons or something. Frankly I can't understand it; haven't they got any faith at all? Surely they have faith enough to know they can't be touched by evil, not like that."

"Don't ask me, I'm no theologian," Chloe said. "We'll run through the details on Saturday, but we shouldn't over do it. Too much and even they might twig."

"Fair enough, but the way things are going we don't need to do much. They take an idea and run away with it. It's amazing, it really is. You should have heard the horror stories. And they'd swear blind they were all true, as well."

"Go on, tell me a few," Chloe urged.

Isobel ran through a few of the tall tales she'd heard.

"Funny, but I heard some of those at university," Chloe said. "It's always told as if the teller was there, but it turns out it was they're best friend's sister's boss to whom it happened. I've never heard one where happened to the person telling it."

"I know, I know. But it scared the bejesus out of Annie. I nearly let her in on the Plan, I felt that sorry for her," Isobel said.

"You didn't though? Good. You haven't been the prawn fairy at her house have you?"

"Didn't have the heart for it," Isobel admitted. "Doesn't seem fair to pick on her when she keeps trying to introduce a mite of sanity to the whole thing. Though I think she'd probably go bananas if she had a bad smell appear in her house without obvious cause; she's not immune to their stories. I did tell her to call me if she's worried about anything like that. Poor girl needs some lifelines, after all."

"See if you can't get her to stay home on Hallow E'en," Chloe said. "I don't want to frighten someone like that; she ain't the target after all."

"I'll have a quiet word," Isobel promised. "Are you OK, anyway?"

Chloe hesitated. She was mostly all right, but she definitely had the odd moment of being anything but.

"Yes," she said. "Mostly anyway. I still feel funny sometimes. And I've had the dream a few times and I've bottled out of looking under the blanket. I will look one day, I'm sure. It just sort of paralyses me."

"Well, keep at it," Isobel said. "I think it's important."

So do I, thought Chloe.

"I will," she said out loud. "Anyway, I'm rather looking forward to this little adventure now. See you Saturday."

*

On Hallow E'en night, the turn-out in the common room was not as large as the organisers had hoped; there were plenty of people missing who had been expected to be there. Isobel had prevailed on Annie to stay at home, not hard since her husband was supposed to be at his placement church that evening and baby sitters were in short supply. She had a huge sense of relief when she looked round the room and saw that it was filled with the women she actually most disliked. Having said that, there were more of them than she would have expected, and the common room was packed with them. The night was turning frosty so the room was initially chilled but with that many of them it would surely warm up. The heating was on, juddering away in its usual inefficient manner. Isobel drew the curtains as the women got settled, ostensibly to keep the cold out and the heat in but more so that the lights from outside would not light the room at all when Chloe turned the power off; she also slipped a window open as she did the curtains. There was nothing quite like a cold draught on the back of the neck for making people uneasy.

She was prepared to be bored rigid by the proceedings and wasn't disappointed. Someone had brought along a stereo and a CD of worship music that they all sang along to. Have any of them actually ever thought about the words of what they're singing, Isobel thought? They're banal at best.

She stifled a yawn; she wasn't quite sure when Chloe would be flipping the power off but she hoped it would be soon. After they'd worn themselves into a groove with the choruses, the praying began.

It wasn't what she'd have called prayer. It was more like a sort of harangue, calling on God to protect them from the evil that was being directed at them. She had a brief pang of instinctive guilt at that and let it slip away. The voices were different but the prayers were all the same, really.

Dear God, she thought. They really have no faith, do they? Surely they should know they're safe.

But apparently they didn't.

Felicity was just calling on the Lord to aid them in their fight against the Powers of Darkness, you could hear the capitals in her voice, when the lights went out.

Perfect timing, she thought.

With so many of them there it was inevitable that someone screamed.

"Everyone stay where they are," she said. "It's just a power cut; don't panic."

The thing is, when someone says, don't panic, everyone thinks of all the things they might like to panic about.

A small voice said,

"I don't like this."

"There's nothing to be scared about," Isobel said, aiming to be the ostensible voice of reason.

"It's just a power cut," said Nicky, but her voice seemed to quaver with uncertainty.

"It's just that..." said Jacquie and stopped.

They were all thinking it; Isobel could practically hear them thinking it.

"It's just a coincidence that it happened when we were praying against the Powers of Darkness," she said.

There was a silence that lasted for ten seconds but felt much longer.

"Rubbish," said Julie. "We're being attacked."

The girl next to Isobel had begun to hyperventilate. For God's sake, Chloe, time to put the lights back on before someone has kittens.

"It's OK," she said to the girl in a low voice, and fumbled to hold her hand. "I'm sure the lights will be back on in a minute."

The tension in the room was rising; she could feel it. Someone was crying very quietly.

"Brace up, girls," said Felicity. "We just need to pray, and everything will be fine."

Her voice didn't sound that confident, though.

With the heating off and a surreptitiously opened window, the room was getting colder surprisingly fast, or perhaps the atmosphere was getting to her. Come on Chloe, that's long enough. Any longer and someone will decide to get up and blunder about in the dark looking for candles, and that's when accidents will happen.

There was a collective sigh of relief as the lights flickered back on again, one that Isobel joined in with heartily. There was a fine line between scaring people and scaring them silly; she currently wasn't sure which side of the line they were on.

The faces around her were surprisingly pale and nervous. For goodness sake, it was only two minutes in the dark, she thought. What would have happened if they'd done some of the other things they'd joked about? We'd be up to our necks in fainting, hysterical women; that's what would have happened.

"Just shows the power of prayer," Nicky declared. "We only had to declare our intent to pray and the lights came back on."

"This is serious," said Julie. "I think there's a definite feeling of oppression. There's people praying against us, a coven I think. This happened in our home church a few years ago. They used to meet in the local park, in broad daylight if you'd believe that. They said they were Druids, but that's bad enough. They were evil; I know that. We had such trouble before they moved away finally. They all dressed like that woman who visits Chloe Williams."

"I found a whole load of loose audio tape around the college gate posts this morning," Nicky said. "And we all know what that means."

I don't, Isobel thought. Perhaps someone got fed up of driving to the Best of Queen and chucked the tape out of the window.

"I don't," said the girl next to her. Thanks, sister, Isobel thought.

"Well, what happens is they record a curse on tape and then they wrap or wind the tape around the home of the person they wasn't to curse," Julie explained. "That's pretty conclusive, I think. Someone's trying to curse us. We've had these horrible smells in our houses and most of us have had unexplained rashes and itching appearing, and a whole lot of other things. This is serious."

"What can we do to stop it?" asked the girl. She was sitting close enough to Isobel for her to feel her shaking.

"I think that we might be over reacting," Isobel said. "Perhaps everything will look better in the morning with the light."

Nicky, Julie and Felicity all glared at her.

"We pray and we pray hard," said Julie.

Oh, well. I won't be having an early night tonight then, Isobel thought resignedly.

*

Chloe slipped into the house, out of breath and sweating. She'd gone for her run anyway after turning the power off and then back on again, and she'd done a bit of subtle art work with her lip salve on the way home, so there were a number of cars now sporting barely visible pentacles on their bonnets. She'd decided against the windscreen in case someone only spotted it once they were actually driving, but she reckoned it would be spotted straight away, as the frost would show it up as vividly as if it were paint when they went to scrape the windows in the morning.

Clifford came into the hall.

"Are you all right?" he asked.

"Yes, why shouldn't I be?" she said, feeling suddenly defensive.

"Well, with the miscarriage and everything I wondered if you should be running just yet," he said.

"They didn't say not to," Chloe said. "I'm fine now anyway. Honest."

They stood in the hall, Chloe standing slightly oblique to Clifford.

"You just haven't seemed quite yourself since then, that's all. You've been a bit distant," he said.

Chloe snorted.

"You're a fine one to talk," she said and headed up the stairs. He followed.

"What do you mean?"

She stopped at the top of the stairs.

"I should have thought that was obvious," she said. "You've always got your head in a book or an essay or the computer and I don't mean games. Or you're at the placement church or at some lecture or seminar. If I've been distant, then it's only because you're never close enough to communicate."

He looked stunned.

"That's hardly fair," he protested. "I do have to complete this course, you know. And I did take time off when you were ill."

"When I hadn't the energy to enjoy it," she remarked, and began to strip off her clothes as she padded into the bathroom.

"Look," she said, as she turned the shower on. "If you want the truth, I'm lonely as hell and having that miscarriage has made me realise that if I managed to be totally unaware of being three months pregnant, then what else am I waltzing along oblivious to? It's making me think there's a hell of a lot I don't know about my own self and my own history. It's like discovering you've been living over a great big chasm or cave that could just collapse at any minute and you didn't even know it was there. Once you know it's there, you tiptoe over it and around it regardless of the fact that when you didn't know it was there, you'd just stamp around quite happily. There's a ruddy great hole in my life where my childhood should be and I don't even remember my own mother, and I've only just realised it. Now, can I get clean or do you want me to just stand here and shout?"

She stepped away from him and into the shower. She'd not realised she felt like this. After a minute, she stuck her head round the shower curtain.

"Sorry," she said. "Just ignore me. I know you've been working hard and that's not something you can change. I just get really lonely. I get on with the people at work, but they know and I know I'm not one of them. I'm not exactly one of the crowd here either, and I've only got Isobel as a friend. So, sorry I'm ratty sometimes."

"And Isobel doesn't want to be seen to be your friend in case it ruins her business opportunities so that's pretty limited," he said.

Chloe grinned, thinking of the Plan.

"I can't blame her," she said, rubbing shampoo into her hair. "It'd be nice to think that someone has put one over on them all, after all, even if it's Isobel and not me. I don't mind. At least I see her on Saturdays, and she's at the other end of the phone. And she was there for me when I had the miscarriage. That makes up for a lot."

"I suppose so," he agreed. "Do you want a beer when you've finished in there?"

"Please," she said. "I didn't mean to get at you, you know. It's just that sometimes I think we saw more of each other before we got married. And I know you have to work hard. I can't help being lonely with Gran gone. I don't know if my dad's even alive any more, and meeting Cathy was just a coincidence."

315

"Coincidence is God's way of staying anonymous," he said.

Chloe snorted; he wasn't sure if it was with amusement or scorn.

"Who said that then? Karl Barth? Wittgenstein?" she said.

"No, Albert Einstein, I believe, but it makes you think though," he said thoughtfully. "I mean what are the odds of that happening? Not her just turning up, that might have happened anyway, but you meeting her like that, in the wood. I've never believed in coincidence, myself. Synchronicity, that's a better thought all round. It's more comforting in the pit of the night, to think there might be some sense to it all, that someone is in charge, sort of."

"What would you know about the pit of the night?" Chloe said, suddenly cross with him. "You sleep like a rock."

"I know enough to know how often you get up in the night and go downstairs and sit up for the rest of the night."

She was suddenly furious.

"And you never think to come down and ask if I'm all right?" she demanded. "Or ask in the morning what the matter was? I thought you'd just slept through it, and I didn't want to disturb you. You sod! All I want sometimes is a cuddle and then I might go back to sleep."

She scrubbed at her feet with a pumice stone, hard enough to hurt.

"Sorry," he said in such a small voice that she put her head out again.

He looked as though he was almost crying.

"I didn't want to pry," he said, seeing her wet face. "I know how you keep your feelings to yourself, even about things like your

Gran. I thought you'd shut me out if I'd asked anything. I'd rather think you would tell me anyway than have you tell me to mind my own business."

She could feel the tears in her own eyes spill over with the hot water and the soap.

"I'm sorry, too," she said. "I don't mean to shut you out. I just didn't think you needed any more hassle or worry. You don't need me giving you a hard time at home. I thought I'd better just cope with it on my own, all the nightmares and stuff."

"You silly cow," he said, pulling the shower curtain aside and grabbing her, the water cascading over him and onto the bathroom floor. "What did we get married for, if it wasn't to be able to share everything, even the tough bits? You daft bitch, come here."

He pulled her out of the shower, kissing her and shaking her playfully.

"You're just as stupid," she said, grabbing a towel and wrapping her hair in it. "You could have just asked me what was wrong."

"OK, mea culpa," he said. "Now let's get you dry and we can go and have that beer."

They didn't bother with the beer in the end.

Chapter 23

The coffee shop was a warm haven of cosy corners and tantalising smells on a day when Chloe would have preferred to have stayed at home with a book in front of the fire. The wind roared outside, throwing rain at the windows with enough force for it to sound more like hail. Isobel came into the shop, shaking herself. She was wet through.

"Dear God, it's wet out there," she said, hanging her dripping coat on the back of her chair. "I had to double back; I saw Nicky out shopping and she saw me, so I had to go right round town and come back again when I was sure she was out of sight. Sorry I'm late."

"It's OK," Chloe said. "Did you enjoy all the cloak and dagger stuff, then?"

"Not really," Isobel admitted. "I have to say, it all worked far better the other night than I expected. I had to try and be the voice of reason myself. I reckon that was the longest two minutes I've ever experienced. They were so wound up after that I was horrified. I am so glad that was all we did. I've had a number of people mention finding pentacles on their cars. I think we should just knock it on the head for a while before things get really silly. They were talking yesterday about calling in the diocesan exorcist, so it's time to stop, I think. You should have seen Felicity's face the following morning when she saw her car. She almost had hysterics. I never thought they'd be this bothered."

"Nor me," Chloe said. "All right, we'll not do anything from now on and just let them settle down. I think we've made our point; are we going to admit it at some point? That would be logical."

Isobel snorted.

"And stupid," she said. "The college might chuck us out."

"I don't think so," Chloe said, but she was suddenly not sure. "The joke only means anything once they've realise they've been had. Otherwise, it's just reinforced their fears and prejudices."

"OK, I see what you mean," Isobel said. "But it's best to wait till things have settled a bit, or we might get lynched."

"Give it a few weeks," Chloe said. "And then we can maybe make an announcement at Chapel night dinner. And then run."

"Yeah, OK," Isobel said. "Right, then, let's have some coffee."

Sitting over coffee and cake, they both felt somewhat subdued. Chloe was feeling strangely upset by the success of the Plan, and was apprehensive about letting it be known that it had been an elaborate practical joke. It was possible that the college authorities might well take a very dim view of the whole thing and have both Clifford and Mickey expelled from the college for something they had nothing to do with at all.

It was all going wrong, somehow. She had never imagined the women would have reacted quite so strongly to the things they'd done, because nearly every single thing had a simple normal explanation. The smells could be accounted for by accidentally spilled food, especially in a household with small children where food may have been hidden rather than eaten. The only thing that had no normal explanation was the pentacles, and that was down to her.

"If I admit to the pentacles, and don't mention you, then the college will be angry with me and not you," Chloe said after a while. "Clifford doesn't know anything about it, and I can say it was a spur of the moment thing, a silly joke and nothing more. All the rest can be explained away."

"You are not taking the rap on your own," Isobel said sharply. "This was both of us doing this and for a bloody good reason. No, we share the responsibility for this, because otherwise, what was the point of the whole thing? It wasn't just to wind them up. It was to throw open the sheer stupidity and superstition of them all, and we have to follow through, just not straight away. We need to wait till it calms down a bit."

Chloe shrugged.

"If you're sure of that," she said. "I mean; you'll lose all your business as well. They won't want you to paint their kids after that."

"Sod the business, they've all been trying to rip me off left, right and centre," Isobel said, crossly. "It's ridiculous; they have no conception of the value of time. I've done pictures for half price and they still complain. No, anyway, I've been offered an opportunity to have some of my work included in an exhibition in the city gallery, and if that goes well, they'd never touch my stuff at the college afterwards. I'll include some of my ordinary paintings so that there's always a good chance of commissions for portraits, but I'm putting my real stuff out so that'll change everything anyway.

No, after we come clean about what's been happening, I won't get any work here, but the chances are after Easter and the exhibition I wouldn't anyway. And I'm sick of being someone else. I'd like to be me again."

Chloe nodded.

"I didn't think you'd be able to distort yourself for too long," she said.

"I've not been distorting myself properly yet," Isobel said defensively. "Anyway, I'm fed up with it. It feels like wearing clothes the wrong size."

Chloe stirred her remaining coffee, lost in thought.

"It's something my Gran used to say to me, that we have to be ourselves to have any chance of being happy and fulfilled. There was a poem she used to quote," she said, hesitantly.

"Well, go on then," Isobel said. "Give us the poem then."

Chloe thought for a minute and then in a low voice began.

"As kingfishers catch fire," she said. "Dragonflies draw flame;
As tumbled over rim in roundy wells
Stones ring; like each tucked string tells, each hung bell's
Bow swung finds tongue to fling out broad its name;
Each mortal thing does one thing and the same;
Deals out that being indoors each one dwells;
Selves- goes itself; myself it speaks and spells.
Crying What I do is me: for that I came.
I say more: the just man justices;
Keeps grace: that keeps all his goings graces;
 Acts in God's eyes what in God's eyes he is-

Christ. For Christ plays in ten thousand places,
Lovely in limbs, and lovely in eyes not his
To the Father through the features of men's faces."

There was a long silence, only broken by the sound of the coffee shop around them.

"OK, OK, I agree," Isobel said. "I'll stop winding them up straight-away, but we must leave the big confession for a while. I really think we should let things settle down before we do that. But I will back off from the coffee mornings and the rest of it. I don't think I can stand it any more anyway."

She took a bite of cake.

"I like the poem," she said, after a while. "I shall be a kingfisher catching fire; I like that. I wish I hadn't started this, now. It's just got too deep, much deeper than I'd imagined."

She took a deep breath. But Isobel wasn't one for long introspections, and after a few minutes, she began giggling.

"What's so funny?" Chloe asked.

"It was so funny, though," Isobel said. "I could hardly keep a straight face."

She shook herself, trying to shake off her mirth.

"The following morning, when I got up, I heard this scream, you know a really girlie sort of scream so I went out to the front and there was Felicity standing staring at her car, all gob-smacked. She said to me, have a look at this. So I had a look. I said I reckoned it was just local kids mucking about, and I didn't think there was a coven or anything like that going on. And she just turned on me and told me I was an ignorant fool. Of course we're targets here, for occult forces, she said. I was being naïve and an ostrich to think otherwise. I nearly blurted it all out then; actually, I was so cross she called me a fool. I know I'm a complete idiot for getting this whole thing going, but other than that I'm no more a fool than anyone else. She was wittering on about how it wouldn't come off, even though she'd been washing it and washing it. So I ran my finger over it. I told her it felt like grease of some sort and she should try using washing up liquid neat on it. And then I had to go in before I just burst."

"I used my vanilla lip balm," Chloe said. "So that it wouldn't just wash away with rain or whatever. What did she think it was?"

"I've no idea," Isobel said. "I didn't even want to ask. She'd probably say something truly vile, like baby fat or something equally horrid. They've got pretty sick minds; some of the stuff I've been hearing has turned my stomach. I think some of them have got sort of obsessed with it all. I shan't be sad to get out of it. I might call on Annie; see if we can't rescue her a bit."

"More cake? I know I could do with more coffee before facing that deluge out there," Chloe said.

"Yeah, why not," Isobel agreed. "Do they have any of that chocolate fudge cake they serve hot with cream? I could really do with something disgustingly high in calories."

When they'd ordered more coffee and cake, Isobel said,

"It'll be nice to be able to be friends openly. I've put on three pounds as a direct result of the temptations of this place. How've the dreams been?"

"Not had that dream for a while, but I'd not managed to look under the blanket last time I had it," Chloe said. "I'm hoping it won't crop up again."

Isobel shook her head.

"It will," she said. "It's important, I'm sure of that. Why not talk to your sister about when you were little? She may recall stuff you can't. It could well be to do with something like the death of a pet and you were too little to understand the concept of burial. Something to do with burial, that's what that dream is, I'm sure of it."

"Maybe," Chloe said, uncertain. "There's an awful lot I don't remember, anyway. And Cathy's the only person I can ask now. I'll ask her when she visits next."

"Good. Oh look, here comes the calories. I can feel my jeans protesting already."

Chloe glanced up as the waitress carried a tray of steaming mugs and two plates of hot chocolate fudge cake.

"You can always come running with me," she said.

Isobel glared at her.

"No thanks," she said, and shuddered theatrically. "I think I prefer the extra padding over that."

Chloe laughed, and tucked into her cake.

*

Chloe looked at her filthy hands, caked in blood and mud, nails broken and torn. The hole was huge and she was sitting in the bottom of it, surrounded by discarded toys, heaps and heaps of them.

The blanket was still stuck in the soil, despite her efforts, but it was the sight of her own hands that really struck her.

They were the hands of a small child.

I'm dreaming, she thought. None of this is real, these aren't my hands now; they're too small.

She could hear her heart thudding; her own heart, no one else's. She was quite alone in the pit, and the sky was darkening as if night were falling.

I'm dreaming, she thought again. I can do what I need to. I can do anything I like. I can get up and walk away. I can even wake myself up.

She gazed at her hands again, and watched them as they changed into the familiar strong, but rather square hands that she knew to be her own.

I can do this.

She looked at the blanket again; it looked faded and worn and dirty. She took hold of the corner and flipped it back, holding her breath as she did so. It moved easily, no longer stuck in the soil.

She gazed at what lay in the very bottom of the hole, and then very slowly, got up and walked out of the pit, willing herself to wake as she did so.

The climb out of the wide crater was a long one; she kept slipping on the loose mud. When she finally reached the top, she was beginning to slip out of the dream; she could feel her own sleeping body start to stir. Holding onto the dream for a moment longer, she turned and gazed back down into the depths of the pit. Nothing was visible any more.

But now she knew what had lain at the bottom.

Chapter 24

The November gale was flinging the trees around like twigs, and Chloe wondered how they did not break with the buffeting they were enduring. The encampment was in a clearing away from most of the trees but she still felt uneasy with the wind. She left her car some distance away and made for Cathy's van.

She wasn't there. Someone noticed her and came over, a man in dingy combat trousers and a sheepskin jacket that would have stood up by itself.

"What do you want?" he asked.

His voice was not unfriendly, but the tone of it told her quite plainly, you aren't one of us and you'd better have a good reason for being here.

"I'm looking for Cathy," she said.

"There isn't a Cathy here," he said, and his eyes narrowed suspiciously.

"This is her van," Chloe said, stubbornly. "She knows I'm coming. She told me where she was. So where is she?"

"You mean Red Cat?" he said, uncertainly.

"Red hair, so tall, thin and usually got a cough. This is her van," Chloe repeated, trying to stay calm.

"You do mean Red Cat," he said. "I'll go and find her. You stay here. We don't like people wandering around unsupervised."

He walked off, leaving Chloe feeling very scared suddenly. She was used to feeling an outsider, but this was somehow worse since she agreed with much of what Cathy was trying to accomplish.

This camp was temporary and probably illegal; all Cathy's associates and cronies meeting to discuss the year ahead. She'd told Chloe they used the old Celtic idea of calendar, with Hallow E'en marking the end of summer, and the days after it were used for assessing the past year and discussing the coming one. It wasn't usually as cold as it would be come official New Year so there was hope of having reasonable weather still. Most of Cathy's friends went into a sort of hibernation during the winter, so this was the last time they'd get together officially until the spring.

After a few minutes, the man returned.

"You're her sister," he said.

It sounded more like an accusation.

"Why didn't you say so?" he said. "I'd have been a bit more friendly if I'd known. I didn't know she had a sister. She'll be over in a minute."

He stayed with her till Cathy appeared and then left them, although he was obviously full of curiosity.

Cathy didn't look well, and she didn't look very pleased to see Chloe either.

"I'm pretty busy at the moment," she said after they'd exchanged greetings. "I was coming to see you at Christmas. Could this not wait till then?"

Chloe shook her head.

"Sorry," she said. "It can't. I need to talk to you about stuff that only you can tell me. And it's sort of getting critical, for me at least, that I get some answers before I start going a bit mad worrying."

Cathy glanced across the encampment to where a bonfire was burning.

"OK," she said. "You might as well come over to the fire; at least we'll get a bit warmer."

The ground was damp and soft and Chloe stumbled on the uneven ground a few times before they got to the fire. There were a number of camp stools around the fire, and a kettle hung from a makeshift tripod, steaming gently, over the fire itself.

"What's the problem, then?" Cathy asked, and gestured Chloe to a stool as she sat down herself as close to the fire as she could get without being in danger of catching fire.

"I need to know whether something I've been dreaming is part of a real memory or whether it's something my unconscious has dredged up," Chloe said. "If it's my unconscious playing games, then I have to figure out the symbolism and understand what it's really trying to say to me. And if it's memory, then I need to understand that as well."

"You aren't making a lot of sense," Cathy said. "What do you mean?"

"I started having nightmares after Gran died," Chloe said. "At first I thought it was because of her death, but that should have faded as I came to terms with it. They've got worse, more frequent and more detailed, and I can seldom go back to sleep afterwards. I've kept it mostly to myself till recently, because for a long while I could never remember what happens in the dreams, as if they're too horrible to contemplate even when awake. But when I had the miscarriage, things began to change. I made a new friend, who gave me some advice about learning to remember my dreams."

"You had a miscarriage? When? You never said. Are you all right?" Cathy said, suddenly alarmed.

"I'm fine. It was in September. I'm fine now, but it made me feel very vulnerable because I hadn't even known I was pregnant and that made me wonder how many other things I don't know about myself." Chloe said. "I have very few memories from early childhood; I don't remember Mum at all. I have some shadowy memories of Dad and of you, but it's all very blurry indeed. Anyway, I need to talk to you about this, because I think you may know something that'll help me. My friend Isobel thinks you will remember stuff I can't and it might be enough to let this dream go, get rid of it for good."

Cathy reached across to the kettle and with her hand gloved with the end of her sleeve poured the boiling water into a big brown teapot. There were a number of enamel mugs around the fire that had apparently just been washed up.

"There's no milk," she said, as she poured two mugs full of black tea and handed one to Chloe.

"So go on then," she said. "Tell me about this dream."

"It varies quite a lot, but now I've got the knack of remembering, it goes basically like this: I'm digging in the soil to get this bit of cloth out of the muck. It's a blue and pink check blanket, like a cot blanket. As I dig, I uncover a whole load of toys, soft toys and books and dolls and building blocks. All sorts of toys for very small children, and I keep on uncovering them, but I can't seem to get the blanket out. By this time I've dug half way to Australia practically, and I'm in the bottom of this huge pit, and I still can't get the blanket free of the soil."

Cathy sipped at the hot tea, and gazed into the fire.

"Go on," she said. "That doesn't sound much of a nightmare at all."

"No, it doesn't, I suppose," Chloe said. "It feels quite different though. I feel scared and upset and frustrated and I don't understand why. It feels horrifying to be at the bottom of this pit, and I don't want to be there at all. I know it doesn't sound scary at all. The worst thing is there, underneath the blanket, and I didn't know what was there. I couldn't get the blanket up at all, no matter how I tried. I had a sense that you were involved somehow. I half remember you being at the bottom of the pit, from when I wasn't quite remembering the dreams, but it may just be me mixing up ideas half consciously."

Cathy said nothing; but even so her silence seemed to be very loud nonetheless.

"Anyway, last night I had the dream again," Chloe said. "It was what my friend Isobel calls a lucid dream, where I sort of woke in the dream and knew I was dreaming and I looked down at my hands. It was weird because I'd seen my hands in every dream and never till this time had I realised that they were my hands, but they were my hands from when I was little, about three years old I'd guess. And then I realised I'm an adult, and I have the strength of an adult, and even if I'm dreaming I can take some control. So that was when I finally got to look under that blanket properly."

331

Cathy gazed into the fire.

"I think you know what I saw," Chloe said softly. "If I've been thinking right, then you know what was there."

Cathy said nothing for a minute. Then she got up abruptly.

"Get your car," she said. "I can't do this here. Not with everybody I know here. We'll find a pub or something."

Chloe drove them out to the nearest village and parked near the pub. It was a very picturesque pub, all oak beams and pewter pots hanging above the bar, and the landlady gave Cathy a very stern look as they came in, but obviously thought better of it when she saw Chloe.

"I'd like a brandy," Cathy said, when they'd found themselves a quiet corner. It was early still, and Chloe could hear the kitchen clattering with preparations for lunch.

Chloe ordered herself some coffee and a brandy for her sister and then when they were alone, she turned to Cathy again.

"Do you want to know what I found in the bottom of that hole?" she asked.

Cathy stared into the brandy glass.

"Go on, tell me then," she said after a moment.

"At first I thought it was a doll," Chloe said. "But when I touched it, no doll feels like that. And no one would make a doll that looks like that. So are you going to tell me, what it was?"

Cathy took a sip of the brandy and coughed at the taste.

"I told you I didn't cope well when Mum died and I got Gran instead," she said. "I know you won't remember it. I hoped you wouldn't, too. When Dad left too, I went a bit wild. I was trying to please Gran at first and then I thought, what the hell, let's have some fun. I was unlucky, I suppose. I did all the usual things, you know, condoms and spermicides, but something got through. I was too scared to tell Gran, so I said nothing and hoped it would just go away. I was, what, about 15, I suppose. I was thin, too, so I kept hoping no one would notice I was putting on weight. I couldn't even admit it to myself. Well, I don't know whether it was a late miscarriage or early labour. I wasn't even sure how many weeks I was, but even if I'd been at the hospital with all the special care stuff, this was never going to survive. It didn't even breathe, even though I tried to get it to breathe. Gran was out. I was supposed to be babysitting for you when it happened. It didn't take long, and even though it hurt, I gather it was nowhere near as bad as real full-blown labour. I was panicking, really panicking. I tried to wash it, try to make it look like a real baby, and I was doing that when you came in. You thought it was a doll, a really ugly doll. So I said it was ugly because it was broken. You said you'd put it in the bin for me. I couldn't do that, just couldn't. I know they do that just about with foetuses from abortions, but I felt so strange. However ugly and broken this little thing was, it was still my baby."

Cathy stopped and drank the rest of the brandy in one go.

"So I told you it had been my favourite doll, and I didn't think it was right to put it in the bin," she said. "The cat had died a few weeks before, and that had been upsetting for you, and you'd got burial into your head. So you said, why don't we bury the dolly with other old toys, and then they can go to heaven with Pushkin the cat. I let you wrap her in your old blanket, and then you went out into the garden. Gran had been digging a hole for a new shrub, but she hadn't had time to plant it, so most of the work was done for you. I was in pain and I felt too weak to come out with you. You took out a bag of your oldest toys, and you buried them all with my baby, wrapped up in your comfort blanket."

Chloe shuddered.

"So it was real," she said. "What happened when Gran came home? I don't remember."

"I put you to bed when you came in from the garden. Your hands were covered in mud and stuff," Cathy said. She was very pale, but her eyes were dry and bleak. "When Gran got home, I felt really ill. I'd been bleeding a lot. The bathroom was a terrible mess too. So I told her. I told her everything. She was amazing. I thought she'd be angry; if she was she hardly showed it. She took me straight to the doctor she'd worked with since she got back from India. She was great, never said anything to condemn me, just got me sorted out medically. She said she'd dealt with the foetus herself, told the other doctor it had been too small to be viable anyway. And that was that. It went on my medical record, and was forgotten about. When we got home, she checked you were all right; she'd decided to just leave you asleep. I asked her what we should do about the baby, and she said to leave her where she was, that a burial like that was better than she'd have got from the hospital or anywhere. And the next day, with you to help her, we planted the shrub over that little grave, and you said nothing about it ever again. I wondered if you'd ask for your blanket or the old toys but you never did. I didn't know whether you ever understood what had happened."

"I do now," Chloe said. "And after that, what happened?"

"About six months later, I left, I could stand living there with you and Gran and knowing she knew what I was. I couldn't bear looking at that shrub either. I didn't even know what it was, the shrub. I'm glad I don't know or I might think of that tiny little mite every time I saw the same plant again," Cathy said.

It was a jasmine, Chloe thought, but kept silent. It grew up and over the wall at the end of the garden and flowered and filled the whole garden with scent.

"So what now?" Cathy said. "I bet you hate me now you know what I did."

"No," said Chloe. "You didn't do anything but get in a mess because you lost your mum and dad when you needed them most. Why should that make me hate you?"

"Because I got you to bury the baby," Cathy said.

"I think I offered," Chloe said. "You were too poorly to do it; it's what Gran would have done too, whether that was what you were supposed to do or even allowed to do I don't know what the law was then or is now. But I'd do it again."

"You won't ever have to," Cathy said. "I never wanted kids after that. What about your miscarriage?"

Chloe shook her head.

"After it started my friend Isobel took me to hospital and they did an ultrasound and said it was dead, so they did a D and C, and I never saw anything of the foetus, just this tiny dead blur on the ultrasound screen," she said. "At least yours got a decent burial. What was left of mine got washed down a drain in a sluice room, I reckon."

She reached across the table to her sister and held her thin arm.

"It's over now, and done with, and at least I know now what this dream is about," she said. "And we can be proper sisters now, without these secrets between us. Let me buy you a bit of lunch, and then I'll have to go home. I took a sick day today, but I need to be home again tonight."

Cathy smiled, rather weakly.

"I could do with something to eat," she said. "I feel like I've been put through the spin cycle of your washing machine."

As they ate, Cathy glanced up at Chloe.

"Is everything else all right though?" she asked.

Chloe thought briefly of the mess at college and of the growing uneasiness around her.

"Everything is fine," she said. "Couldn't be better."

"Sure?"

"Absolutely sure."

Chapter 25

Chloe sat curled up on the sofa, listening to the wind howling outside and rattling around in the chimney and the soft hiss of the gas fire. December had arrived with frost and fog and the promise of worse; most mornings brought a layer of ice on car windscreens and on puddles, but the snow she craved had not yet appeared. Clifford had left about half an hour ago for a meeting at his current placement, so apart from the cats she had the house to herself.

It had been a strange few weeks, after seeing Cathy. She found it hard to take in, that the dream was actually a distorted memory, twisted up and confused, but a real memory. It explained so clearly why Cathy had left and had not been able to return to the old house or to see Gran or her little sister again. What a thing to have had to carry all those years, what pain to have endured. She'd sat long hours trying to imagine what her sister must have been through, because of it and because of her subsequent choices.

She'd told Clifford about it and he had been quiet for a long time when she'd finished. Finally, he said simply,

"Poor Cathy."

She'd told Isobel that she had found the source of the dream but she hadn't told her what it was; Isobel's miscarriages would surely mean that the story would devastate her, however breezily she denied her maternal instincts. In the end, it wasn't her story to share, and it seemed that Isobel was too distracted to pursue the truth. Isobel had backed off from her college associates, pleading pressure of work, she'd said. She'd been trying to finish all the

337

paintings she'd promised to complete for Christmas, and was working so hard she'd been so tired when Chloe had last seen her that Chloe had felt sorry for her.

"Don't feel sorry for me," Isobel had said, buoyantly, fighting off yawns. "It's sheer self-interest that's driving me. The sooner I can finish these and collect my money, the sooner I can get myself completely free of them all. I've annoyed a lot of people by refusing more commissions, and by avoiding all the gatherings I'd been expected to attend. They don't let go easily. I've had to start ignoring the doorbell. I'd never get anything done if I trotted down to answer it every time someone called round for a coffee or a chat."

"So what's the mood like now?" Chloe had asked.

"I've no idea," Isobel said, her tone off-hand. "Probably much the same as before; borderline hysteria. But I've not been around to gauge it lately. They'll go off the boil before very long, I'm sure."

Chloe had felt disappointed at first that Isobel had ceased to be a mole. There had been something wickedly satisfying about knowing what was going on without having to be a part of it. But there was also a sense of relief, of a resumption of interrupted integrity that felt better than the childish satisfaction of spying. Isobel had said she was going to come round this evening but had rung her to say she was going out with the much-neglected Mickey for the evening.

"He's not been whinging exactly," Isobel had said on the phone. "He doesn't whinge, not really. But he is starting to look a touch forlorn so I thought an evening out, have a meal somewhere nice and then home for an early night, know what I mean, will keep us both much happier. You don't mind too much, do you?"

"No, I'm pretty tired, actually," Chloe had said. "Clifford's going out too, so I might just catch up on some slobbing. There's a book I've been promising myself I'll finally finish and I can have a few of the beers I got in for us. It'd be good to get together soon, though."

"Tell you what, let's see how the next week goes, and then maybe we can come clean at dinner the week after. That way, everyone will be in a better mood because of Christmas holidays about to start and we can get away with it better than if we did it now. Then I want to get totally blotto," Isobel said. "It's been a huge strain being someone I'm not."

"Remember the kingfisher," Chloe had said and then rang off.

She thought about the kingfisher for a while, thinking of what it meant to her to be herself. It had been fun for a while, all the plotting; but she hadn't felt good about it, not inside. It had actually undermined her sense of personal integrity in a way she would never have predicted.

What I should have done, she thought, is simply speak about it at chapel or at dinner or at Morning Prayer. Simply stand up and say what I thought about the way the women were with me, about the prejudice and superstition and stupidity. Not all this sneaking around and the spying and silly jokes. That wasn't me at all. It wasn't just Isobel who was distorting herself. I was too. Well, no more of that. What I do is me: for that I came. I certainly didn't come to be a malicious joker.

339

She sighed, and then snuggled down closer to the sleeping cat next to her and stroked the silky fur.

Chainsaw stirred and opened a wary eye. His ears flickered. Chloe tried to be very still, to hear what he heard. Yes, footsteps on the path. The cat sat up, his posture that of cautious alarm, ears pricked and twitching.

A moment later, the doorbell rang, loud and insistent.

"Shit, who's that going to be?" she asked herself out loud and rolled off the sofa, the Pendleton blanket still wrapped tightly round her shoulders.

She reached the door as another ringing commenced, urgent and somehow threatening, someone's finger pressed hard against the button and pushing it many times in rapid succession. When she opened the door, she felt the door lurch open, crashing against her shoulder and sending her reeling backwards trying to stay on her feet.

To her astonishment, Felicity pushed past her into the hall before she had a chance to stop her, her feet noisy on the hall floor as she strode inside the house. Chloe recoiled, unbelieving, trying to understand what was happening. Felicity moved closer to her without speaking, coming to a standstill almost touching Chloe. Her body had that cheesy scent of old milk, hidden but not eliminated by the deodorant that Chloe's sensitive nose recoiled at.

"What the hell do you think you're doing?" Chloe shouted, as Nicky, Julie and a half dozen others poured into her hall. The tiny hallway was tightly filled with bulky bodies, and the brightened eyes of the intruders shone in the light of the street-lamps that spilled through the front door.

Chloe tried to pull away as Felicity and Nicky seized her arms with hands that seemed as icy cold and as strong as steel and to her surprise, Chloe found herself thinking she'd never have believed they could exert such a grip that she could feel her arms bruising. Ignoring her shouts of distress and outrage, they half lifted her off her feet and dragged her into the living room. Chainsaw rose up off the sofa snarling and hissing at them, the image of feline fury with his tail fluffed out like a bottle-brush and his ears flat against his head. One of the women nearest to him lashed out at him with a foot, and Chainsaw swiped at her legs with his claws before he saw a second women kick at him. This time he leapt back, spun, and then bolted for the cat flap in the kitchen door. The sound of the flap snapping shut after his escape was a tiny crumb of relief as Chloe felt herself pushed back onto the sofa, and she stared at them in horror and bewilderment.

"What do you want?" she said, as they all filed in, standing in a rough semi-circle around the sofa, all of them silent, their eyes gleaming with the excitement. She tried to get up, but was pushed back immediately by Julie who stood nearest her.

She could feel her heart pounding as if she'd been running hard, yet thumping as if it would burst out of her chest. She drew in her breath trying to steady herself, hoping that both cats would stay away. Each of the intruders watched her, familiar people she'd despised and discounted but now they looked very different from the mums whose greatest concern had seemed to be whose baby breastfed the longest. She'd seen faces like that before, but on the television, in films and in the history books. The faces of fanatics, cold and blind to all reason staring back at her.

Oh crap, she thought. This is not good.

"I think you should all leave right now before I ring the police," Chloe said, but even as she said it she knew she would never get to the phone. "You've got no right to barge in here like this. Get out."

Her words sounded hollow, her voice thin and wavering and not at all like her usual tone. They were still staring at her, their bodies blocking her exit from the room. She'd never felt so scared, not ever, as she did now.

"What do you want?" she asked again. This time her voice sounded like a little girl's.

"We want to help you," Nicky said but her tone didn't sound promising. There was a threatening sneer in the words that Chloe could not ignore.

"I don't need your help," Chloe replied, folding her arms across her chest, her fists clenched and nails biting into her palms.

"We thought you'd say that," Julie said. Unlike Nicky, her voice very calm and reasonable. "We thought we should wait till you asked for help, but that isn't going to happen and the evil you've called down is getting too much to ignore. So we have to help you whether you want it or not."

"I don't know what you're talking about, you mad bitch," Chloe said, her anger flaring without warning. "How can you just walk in here and accuse me of God only knows what? You're barking mad.

I have no idea what you're on about. Now just fuck off out of my home and leave me alone."

She tried to get up again, but Felicity and Julie grabbed her arms again and she saw Nicky bringing out a roll of duct tape that she'd had hidden in a pocket.

"You're not responsible for this yourself, Chloe. You asked in evil and it's taken over. We're here to help you be free of it. It'll be much easier if you co-operate with us, and help us fight the evil that has entered your body and taken over your life. There is still some Chloe alive in there, I'm sure of it, and it's up to us to free her, and free the college of the evil that has been attacking us all," Julie said.

"You are completely mad," Chloe said, and felt the hands on her arms tighten alarmingly, long nails digging into muscle. "You're here to exorcise me? Mad as hatters, all of you."

Nicky came closer, unrolling the duct tape with the end tucked between her front teeth that caught the light like fangs, and Felicity and Julie started to pull Chloe's arms behind her back.

"No," said Chloe and then shouted it and really began to fight back. "You can't all of you think I'm demon possessed, can you? You brainless bunch of sheep, this is mad."

Her sister's words about sheep turning on people came back to her, unbidden, as she scuffled to get out of the grip of her attackers, feeling their solid if soft bodies pressing in on her, but for all their single-minded determination to subdue her, Chloe was fit and strong and after a short struggle she wrenched her arms free of the women holding her.

She jumped through the semi-circle of her guards, spinning so she could face them and see what they would do next. If all of them grabbed her at once she could not hold them all off; she had now raised her balled fists in defence, ready to land serious punches if they came closer.

"She has the strength of many," Julie said. "It's another indication of demonic influence."

"It's an indication of the fact that I exercise," Chloe said, backing away from them. "Nothing else, except perhaps that you're a bunch of flabby weaklings with baby food where your brains should be. Get out of my house."

She'd backed into the hall, hoping to get to the front door, but there were two of them blocking the way, though they were keeping their distance now she was in a fighting stance. She doubted whether they had the stomach for broken noses and cracked heads, so while keeping an eye on them as well as the others, she moved towards the kitchen. If she could get out through the back door, she could get out and round and onto the main road.

Felicity roared,

"Don't let her get out; grab her."

Her voice was harsh with hysteria but it held no small measure of command in its tone and Chloe felt rather than saw the attack coming. Pre-empting it, she bolted for the kitchen, cannoning into the woman in her way and knocking her aside and sending her sprawling onto the floor in an untidy heap that would slow the others. Her hands shaking so much she could barely turn the key in the lock, she flung open the door and ran out into the garden. Behind her in the house she could hear them yelling and screaming but out here the air was cold and her ragged breath rose in wreaths around her as she bounded over the garden and out of the back gate and into the access road at the side of the house. She ran round to the front and found they'd been far quicker than she'd expected from the chaos inside and had blocked her route to the main road. She could risk charging them them and hoping they wouldn't manage to get hold of her, but she felt sick at the thought of the duct tape and those restraining hands, cruel and grasping as they gripped her flesh. There was a gap between her pursuers standing poised at her garden gate and those standing at the exit to the main road, but it meant she'd have to sprint to get enough distance to be able to use the college itself as a cut through to the main car park and thence to the road.

Well, that's why you go running, isn't it, she asked herself, so that you'd be fast and fit if you ever needed it.

She moved, then, from standing still to running full tilt, heading straight for the college buildings. It was only a few hundred yards away, but she was sure she'd not have run faster even if she'd been chased by a tiger. In the still evening air, the sound of her feet on the path echoed, drowning for her the sound of her pursuers. Ornamental flowerbeds, filled with winter pansies and wallflowers empty of blossom waiting for spring were in her way, so she hurdled them, landing in the concrete corridor roofed with a sort of sloping cloister roof that led to the chapel complex. The impact of her landing made her stagger, but she halted her fall and glanced

345

around her for her next route. There was a door in the wall that led down to the main car park; she rattled the latch frantically but it was locked. A few steps further and she'd reached the door to the main building that housed chapel and dining room upstairs and common room, library and lecture rooms downstairs. If she went in there, she could leave via the fire exit at the end of the library. She tapped in the security code and pushed at the door. It was locked for the night, needing an actual key rather than simply the password. She groaned inwardly; her keys were still in her own front door.

"Crap," she said, and turned to see where her pursuers were. Her few seconds head start were about gone and they were catching her up.

Their persistence in chasing her was possibly more frightening than the original mention of exorcism. It suggested that they had in mind something more extreme and probably outlawed in the modern church, and her escape was only making her more culpably in need of the rite than they'd first decided. Images of medieval exorcisms and scenarios from famous horror films reinforced her determination to get well away.

She jumped back across the flowerbed and with some difficulty managed to scramble onto the sloping cloister-style roof using the drain-pipe as her step-ladder. Even though the slope was steep, the tiles seemed secure and she was pretty sure none of them would be able to climb up here after her. She moved cautiously along towards where the roof came close to the kitchens, but when she got there, she could see the only window even vaguely in range was shut. But there was a drainpipe.

"Get down from there," she heard Felicity calling. "We only want to help you, free you."

"Fuck off," she yelled back, and started to climb the drainpipe.

It was an old one, solidly made and securely fixed to the brickwork. If she'd seen this in daylight she would not have thought she could have managed to climb this at all. Amazing what you can do when you're scared witless, she thought, almost detached from it all. If I can get across to the other side, I can either see if there's away down or I can stay up there and yell for help. It might take a few hours, but surely someone will come before too long.

She tried to think what the layout of the building might be, and then realised there was a fire escape on the far end of the chapel part of the building. She could get down onto that and away. She scrambled across the main roof, her hands clinging to the edges of the tiles until she reached the end and looked down. Yes, there was the spidery metal gantry of the fire escape opening from the library.

Just as hope had risen, it died away as she saw that at the bottom of the fire escape a group of them waited, faces upturned to watch out for her appearance. Someone had a key with them and had used the cut-through to get through the building while she was messing about up here.

She doubled back, and made her way across the roof of the older building, the original house the college had started from. If she could get to the ground from the far end of this building she might have a chance to sprint across the grounds and away. She could feel her chest hurting with the exertion and maybe the fear too; she'd never had a problem with heights before. Yet adrenaline blocked out all the terror, all the pain, and left her only the need to run till she dropped to her knees with exhaustion.

It's not the fear of falling that bothers me, she thought. It's the fear of landing.

They couldn't see her properly from the ground; they'd have to back up quite a way to be able to see her and gauge where she was going and no one seemed to have caught on to that idea. She could hear them calling to her, but not loudly and she found she was unable to understand anything they were saying. Someone seemed to have twigged to the fact that this was not something they wanted anyone to see.

She reached the end of the building, having slipped a few times and righted herself, feeling more and more like an escaped spider monkey, scrambling around using both hands and feet to hold on to surfaces slick with forming frost. There was a down-pipe here, thank God, another nice heavy metal one, with solid-looking attachments fixing it to the wall. She swung her body lightly over the edge, gripping the pipe firmly with her hands and feet, and began her descent.

She tried to focus only on inching down, her hands cold and sore and yet slippery with fear, her whole body shaking now. When she heard voices coming nearer she glanced away from the wall she had been staring at and then glanced down.

Oh shit, she thought. I am not going to freeze; I'm not.

The momentary paralysis borne of fright held her tightly, fingers welded to the drainpipe. After a moment she began moving again, but not how she wanted to. The fixings were good and solid, but she could see that some of the brickwork needed repointing; with the comic slowness of disaster the drain-pipe began to come away from the wall, and as it sheared away, it tore the fixings completely free and then bent and crumpled the pipe she was clinging to, pitching her out into space. She felt a fraction of a second's worth of stomach lurching before she hit the ground and after a moment of exploding stars and the bright colours of pain in her head, felt nothing else.

*

Isobel drove past the entrance to the main car park and saw the flashing lights of an ambulance.

"Wonder what's happened?" Mickey said, but without much interest. He'd had a good meal, a few glasses of wine and was now looking forward to the early night part of the evening.

"No idea," said Isobel. "But you know me, second cousin to the mongoose. I'll go and find out. Can't think who's due to drop a sprog this month."

"Don't be long," he said, and she grinned at him.

When she got to their house, she'd seen Chloe's front door left wide open and both cats sitting very close together on the step, and she felt herself shiver at the sight.

"There's something wrong," she said to Mickey as she got out. "I'm going round to where the ambulance was. Can you go and get Chloe's keys and meet me round there? She wouldn't like anyone to just walk into the house just because she's got distracted by whatever's been going on."

Isobel half ran across to the building; the door in the wall had been unlocked; within half a minute she saw the crowd of onlookers. The ambulance was backing up as close as it could get to the building and one of the paramedics was kneeling by a very still figure lying on the grass by the corner of the building.

The group was mainly wives, but Isobel saw the college principal there too, and as she got closer, everyone moved aside to let her through. Then she saw who was lying on the grass.

She felt faint; for a moment she could say nothing.

Felicity moved forwards to her, her face pale but composed.

"It's Chloe," she said. "There was a kitten stuck on the roof. We told her not to but she insisted on going up to rescue it, but she slipped."

Isobel stepped back from her; the fear was coming off Felicity was almost like a kind of rank steam.

"What have you done?" she asked, in a very quiet voice. "What have you done?"

Louder now.

"WHAT HAVE YOU DONE?"

She was shouting now.

Felicity backed away from her, her feet slipping in the frosty grass and making her stumble.

350

"I told you," she insisted. "There was a kitten stuck on the roof."

"Yeah? Well, where is it now? Tell me that. Tell me where that mythical kitten is now. You can't, can you? Because you're lying through your foul teeth," Isobel said, drawing back her arm, ready to hit her.

Then she dropped her arm, shoved her out of the way, and ran to Chloe.

"Is she breathing?" she asked the paramedic, and tried not to look at her friend.

"Yes," he said. "Heart rate seems good too. She's broken a leg badly, and possibly a collarbone. I'm most concerned about her spine and the head injury doesn't look good. Are you a relative?"

"I'm her best friend," Isobel said. "I can call her husband, though."

Trying not to look at the crumpled form, face so white the freckles stood out like plague marks, Isobel pulled out her mobile and with shaking hands rang Clifford's number.

"Voice mail," she said.

Mickey appeared at her shoulder.

"What the hell has happened?" he asked.

Isobel shook her head.

"I don't know," she said. "All you'll get from this lot are lies and more lies. Look, I'll go with her to the hospital. Will you keep ringing Clifford and then bring him when he gets back."

The paramedics were easing Chloe onto a spinal board. Isobel glanced at her and then back to the small muttering crowd.

"I hope you're pleased with yourselves," she yelled and turned away and followed the paramedics as they carried the unconscious figure to the ambulance.

One of them glanced at Isobel's face, tear streaked and white, and set with fury.

"Why do you say that?" he asked.

"There was no kitten," she said quietly. "This was down to them; no question of that."

She looked at his puzzled face.

"It's a very long story," she said. "And I don't think it's one with a happy ending either."

"She'll be all right, I'm sure," he said, hoping to reassure and soothe her.

"Yeah, right," Isobel said. "I know what happens in all the films when they say that."

Chapter 26

Isobel had been pacing up and down the corridor, unable to sit for more than a moment at a time when Mickey finally brought Clifford in. He'd not checked his mobile all evening and it was half past ten before he'd got back to the house to find Mickey sitting on the sofa.

When he saw Isobel, he nearly ran.

"How is she?" he demanded.

"Not brilliant, but she'll live," Isobel said. "One leg's badly broken and they'll have to operate on it and put pins in. She's badly concussed. Apparently falling onto frozen grass isn't much better than falling onto concrete. She's got a broken collarbone and a lot of bruises as well."

"Where is she?"

"Through there. The doctor is with her at the moment; she's sort of come round but she's very muzzy," Isobel said, indicating the direction. "They said she's going to be all right."

Clifford started to move towards the ward, and then stopped.

"What happened?" he said. "Mickey said she fell off the roof. What was she doing up there in the first place?"

"I don't know," Isobel said, truthfully. "I have no idea."

Clifford was horrified when he saw Chloe; not just because of the bruises across her face. She looked so small and helpless; she'd been crying too. He reached her and took her hand, and tried not to look at the mess that was her leg. The doctor looked up at him.

"She's heavily sedated," he said. "And in a lot of pain. We shall get that leg sorted in the morning, when she's stable. I didn't want her under anaesthesia after the knock she had to the head. Don't tire her."

Chloe's eyes were barely able to focus, but she managed a weak smile when she realised it was him.

"Hi," he said. "How do you feel?"

"Vile," she whispered. "I feel sore everywhere, even places I didn't know I had. Sorry."

"Sorry? What for?"

"All this; silly. Sorry," she said, and muttered something incoherent.

"She's very tired and the morphine will be making her confused," said the doctor. "I suggest you let her sleep now."

Reluctantly, Clifford went back to where Mickey and Isobel were waiting.

"Let's get some coffee," he said. "Then you can tell me what you know."

Mickey glanced at Isobel.

"We don't know any more than you do yet," he said.

"I'm not sure about that," Clifford said.

The hospital café was shut but the coffee machine provided a hot drink that roughly resembled coffee and they sat down in the waiting area.

Mickey had told Clifford about the story of the kitten and Isobel's reaction to it on the drive to the hospital and Clifford had been thinking about it.

He turned to Isobel, and put his plastic cup down on the floor.

"What happened?" he asked quietly.

"I've told you, I don't know," she said. "We got back and the ambulance was there. That's all I know."

"Mickey said Felicity and Nicky and the others were there. What would they be doing with Chloe?" Clifford asked.

Isobel sighed.

"I don't know," she said. "I can guess, but I don't know. Has Chloe said anything yet?"

"She hardly knows which way is up at the moment," Clifford said. "OK, then what is your guess? I can't imagine any good reason why Chloe would be hanging around with people I know dislike her. Can you? Or why our front door was left wide open when Mickey got to it? I have this horrible feeling there's been things happening that I knew nothing about."

Isobel rubbed her eyes; she was feeling rough now, and close to tears.

"It's my fault this happened," she said after a minute's silence. "Entirely my fault. And I don't know what I can ever do to make it up to you both."

Clifford looked at her, mute with astonishment.

"What on earth do you mean? It isn't as if you threw her off the building," he said.

"I might as well have done," Isobel said, and felt the burning behind her eyes become critical as the tears began to fall.

Mickey was just as puzzled.

"What on earth are you on about?" he asked, putting an arm around her. "You're not making any sense."

"You are both going to hate me when I tell you what's been happening," Isobel said in a low voice that was almost a whimper, and scrubbed at her face with her sleeve.

"Just tell us what happened," Clifford said.

"I don't know what happened tonight," Isobel said. "Chloe will tell us when she's better. But I think I know roughly what must have happened. They must have tried to tackle her and it went dreadfully wrong."

"You still aren't making any sense. Tackle her, what do you mean? And why would they want to tackle her? I don't understand," Clifford said.

"Like I said, it's my fault," Isobel said. "I wanted to punish them for being so horrible."

Mickey and Clifford just looked at her, worried.

"Are you sure you haven't had a bang on the head too?" Clifford said.

Isobel blew her nose on a pathetic scrap of tissue.

"I wish I had. I wish it was me in there with my leg all mangled," she said. "OK, I'll try and explain. But don't shout at me, please."

Isobel took a deep breath and told them about the Plan and what they'd done and the effects it had had, and how they'd called it a day after Hallow E'en. When she'd finished, there was a long silence. Finally, Clifford got up jerkily and took several paces around the room, his hands almost fluttering with pent up emotion.

356

"You stupid, stupid woman," he said at last. "How could you have been so stupid, the pair of you? Did you not think what it might be doing or what people might do?"

Isobel stared at the floor; her shoulders slumped.

"No," she said. "Of course we didn't think. We didn't think we were on the set of a horror movie. We didn't think we'd get the reaction we did. Yes, I know it was bloody stupid. I know that now. But have you any idea how lonely and isolated we were? No, I bet you didn't, either of you. You charge off on this new life of yours and we have to follow. And while you get on with all your enthralling studies and everything, and the whole world ahead of you bowing down and worshipping the baby priests for immolating themselves on the altar of service, what the fuck is there for us? Tell me that. What is there for us? We leave behind our homes and our friends and our lives, and for what? Fucking coffee mornings and a society so narrow it'd be marked absent if it turned sideways."

She was on her feet now, facing Clifford.

"So don't tell me how stupid we've been," she said. "Because I know how stupid it was. I know now. But you should know that it was that sort of light relief that kept me from walking out on this place and I expect Chloe felt pretty much the same. We're people too, God damn it. Mickey, you asked me whether I was happy for you to become a priest. How the fuck could I not agree? What sort of question is it anyway? Don't you see what the question is really asking is do I love you enough to throw away my own needs and wants and everything? How could I say no to that? Because saying no means the end, I could see that. So what if we played a huge con trick on the other wives? It was the only way I had any chance of getting through this, I had to step away from it in some way. And it should be me lying there with a mangled leg; I know that. But it isn't. And I can't change the past, so don't tell me how fucking stupid I've been. Maybe you should be asking yourselves how stupid you've both been."

Isobel kicked her empty cup across the room and ran away.

"Oh dear," said Mickey, inadequately. "That wasn't what I was expecting at all. I'd better go and calm her down."

Clifford said nothing, but put his head in his hands and listened to Mickey's footsteps echoing as he went in search of Isobel.

This is a nightmare, he thought, hopelessly.

Maybe I'll wake up in a minute.

*

When Chloe woke up after the orthopaedic surgeon had finished putting her leg back together, she was relieved to find Clifford waiting for her.

"How do you feel?" he asked.

"As if I've been chewing moths," she said. "It feels better now the leg is immobilised. I had a horrid night. Every time I twitched it hurt like crazy. I feel a bit sick though. Did Isobel go home?"

"I sent them both home some time after midnight," he said. "Isobel told me about what you'd been getting up to."

"Oh," said Chloe. "So you know. OK."

He'd wanted to ask her all sorts of things after that wretched conversation with Isobel. Mickey had found her and brought her back and they'd talked about it till Clifford was sick of it.

"It was silly, but I do sort of understand why you did it," he said, finally. "What actually happened last night? There was some sort of strange story from Felicity about a kitten stuck on the roof."

Chloe managed a laugh.

"No, no kittens, I'm afraid," she said. "It's all very blurry now. I think it's the anaesthetic making me woozy. Do you think I can have some water? My mouth feels vile."

"I'll ask," he said and went to find a nurse.

"She really needs to rest," said the nurse. "You can't have anything to drink just yet, Mrs. Williams, in case you're sick. But we can give you some mouthwash to freshen your mouth. And then I think you need to rest, not talk."

While the nurse went to find the mouthwash, Chloe said,

"They burst in. They decided I needed exorcism. I disagreed, they disagreed with that and I ended up trying to get away over the college roof. Unfortunately I'm not a superhero and I couldn't fly when the drainpipe gave way. End of story."

"Christ," said Clifford, appalled.

The nurse came back in.

"Time you got some rest," she said.

Clifford leaned over Chloe and kissed her.

"I'll be back this afternoon," he said.

"Clifford?"

"Yes?"

"Don't be angry with Isobel. It wasn't her fault. We bit off more than we could chew. We didn't even imagine it would go that far," Chloe said.

"I'm not angry with her. Nor with you," he said. "I'll come in later. Sleep well, love."

*

Isobel came in that evening, after Clifford had gone home. She kept telling herself she wasn't avoiding him; but she knew she couldn't quite manage to look him in the eye just yet. Give me a few days and it'll all be in the past, she thought. But today is the present and I can't quite live with that yet.

Chloe looked drowsy and pale; they'd got her leg slung up in some sort of contraption that might have come out of the Inquisition, and one arm was in a sling. She looked utterly miserable.

Isobel took that moment to decide whether she could actually face her friend or not.

"Hi there," she said, brightly and came over and sat next to Chloe on the bed. "I didn't bring grapes and I didn't bring flowers, but I did bring a few trashy novels. You won't be able to concentrate very well just yet. Let me know when you're ready for War and Peace."

"I think I've got it in my head already," Chloe said. "I've got a dreadful headache that nothing seems to touch. And they've been giving me lots of things to take for the pain."

Isobel slumped, feeling that awful surge of guilt.

"This is all my fault," she wailed.

"Sod off if you're going to whine," Chloe said. "No, this isn't your fault at all. Or if it is, it's mine as well. I had no idea they were going to decide I was the conduit for evil. I still can't believe they actually thought I was possessed. God knows what they might have done if I hadn't legged it. Having me fall off the college roof was probably not on their list of things to do, either. But I'm bloody glad I ran for it, actually. I heard some pretty hair-raising stories about exorcisms by fanatics when we were at university. Things can get out of hand horribly easily. Anyway, how are you?"

"Miserable," Isobel said. "I keep blaming myself. If I'd kept being the mole, I would have had some warning. They must have been winding themselves up to it, once I stopped trying to be the voice of reason. I should have kept an eye on it."

"Well, you didn't," Chloe said. "And I wouldn't have done either. You'd just expect they'd go off the boil without extra fuel. I had no idea they thought me, well, whatever they thought me to be. A witch or something I guess. That'd have made Gran laugh her socks off, given the various things she'd done over the years. It's amazing what you get away with if people know you're a doctor too, she used to say. She used to use all sorts of home remedies and no one thought anything of it. I wish she were here now. She'd know something to stop this sodding cast itching quite so much; it's going to drive me mad. It's worse than the pain in some ways."

"Can you get something down to the itch, like a knitting needle?" Isobel asked.

"Probably not, at least not till the muscle starts to waste away a bit. And I don't knit, either, if you hadn't noticed," Chloe said.

"Will you tell me what actually happened?" Isobel said, taking the plunge. She was actually unsure she really could face knowing what had happened. But then, she was totally certain she couldn't face not knowing. It's the mongoose in my genes, she thought, and then giggled.

"What's so funny?" Chloe asked.

"Just one of those random thoughts," Isobel said. "I was just thinking about mongooses."

"Shouldn't that be mongeese?"

"Not a clue. Now, are you going to tell me what happened last night?"

Chloe shrugged, and then winced.

"That wasn't a good move," she said. "Go and get me a cup of tea, first. My mouth still tastes of moths."

"I don't want to know how you know that," Isobel said. "Was it from your failed impersonation of a bat?"

"Tea, first. Or I won't tell you anything."

When Chloe had finished her narrative, she felt wrung out. Isobel had been silent through the whole story, an unusual occurrence at the best of times. She was obviously thinking of some of the stories she had herself heard.

"I think, on balance, you were better off running away than risking staying," she said finally. "Though a safer descent might have been a better choice. I still can't believe they actually barged into your house. They have broken so many rules."

"There are rules about these things?"

"Oh, yes, lots of them. I asked around today from various acquaintances. The ministry of deliverance has rules and regulations, same as any other. Good. At least I know you didn't ask them in."

"What have you got in mind? I can tell you're plotting again," Chloe said.

"Not plotting as such," Isobel said, thoughtfully. "Damage limitation. I'll tell you about it when you're not dropping off to sleep every few minutes. Get some rest, if you can. Is there anything I can get you that'll make this easier to bear? Chocolate, sweets, books, moths?"

"Get lost," Chloe said, leaning back on her pillows and wishing for her next lot of drugs. "Some sort of nice fresh cologne would help. I'd kill for a nice hot bath but I think the best I'll get is a shower in a few days time when I really start to smell horrible."

"I'll go to the shops first thing and get you something nice," Isobel promised. She hesitated. "I am really sorry about all this, you know. I didn't mean for anyone to get hurt, least of all you."

Chloe looked at her and smiled, rather weakly.

"No sweat," she said. "These things happen. Well, they do to me, anyhow. Consider it collateral damage. It was fun while it lasted. Let's enjoy that. I'll never look at another prawn again without thinking about it."

"Good job it isn't me in that bed," Isobel said. "I'd be plotting revenge, I would."

"For what? For what they did, or what you did? Either way, I think what's going on in your head is enough punishment and more for you. And for them? Well, I don't know. If they knew what had really been happening, maybe what happened to me might actually mean something, in the end."

Isobel nodded, as if she'd been thinking about that too.

"I'll see you tomorrow," she said. "And if you think of anything else you might need, just give me a call, Batwoman."

"Don't call me that."

Isobel leaned over and kissed her forehead.

"I'll call you whatever I like," she said. "You're nearly a superhero after all and can take whatever the world throws at you."

Some superhero, thought Chloe as the door closed. I bet they never have to pee into a bottle because they can't get out of bed.

Chapter 27

Chloe didn't enjoy the prospect of Christmas in hospital, particularly when she heard quite what was likely to happen.

"Jollity and sing-songs are not exactly my idea of a good Christmas," she said to Isobel when she came in that day. "I'm tempted to say I'm Jewish just to escape being visited by Santa."

"Wouldn't work," Isobel said. "People who have other people's happiness at heart are not swayed by anything, let alone religious convictions. No, I suggest you just give up and give in and be happy and jolly the whole day long in the secure knowledge that when you get out of here and off this huge long list of medication, your best friend will take you out and get you totally ratted at her own expense, I might add."

"Very nice. Are you feeling guilty by any chance, again? I haven't seen you for days," Chloe said.

"Spot on, missus. Any sharper and you'd be cutting yourself, not to mention the sheets. No, I've been in hiding," Isobel said.

"From whom? I thought you and Clifford were talking again."

"Ah, but I'm not talking to me at the moment," Isobel said. "I have to relay messages to myself by any useful intermediary."

"What are you going on about, you daft baggage?"

Isobel laughed.

"Nothing," she said. "I've just had a really tough week or two, and I needed to lay low for a few days to recover. I did the confession thing the other night at dinner, like I said I would, before all this happened. It is not a memory I cherish."

Actually, it was. Isobel had not enjoyed the prospect or the experience as it happened, but once it was over, she had had trouble not being smug about it. She'd done her best to minimise damage, and her plans had worked better than she could have expected.

"Tell me about it; I could do with a laugh," Chloe said.

"It doesn't exactly show me in a good light, you know. A true light, but not a good one," Isobel said. "Fine, you can condemn me later. Well, it's been a bit subdued recently since your Batwoman act off the roof, well, except for the doorbell ringing the whole time not to mention the phone. I've managed to sneak in and out to the car to come here, and avoid everyone. But I went to chapel night dinner and when they were all pushing the last bit of apple pie round their plates, that's when I got up on a chair and asked for a few minutes of their time. I'd sort of written it all down, but I didn't follow my own script too well. I cut out all the swearing. Most of it, anyway. I wasn't sure where to start; I'd written this tirade about how stupid they all were but when I looked at all these faces looking back at me, I knew it wasn't right.

"So I said I knew they all had heard about the strange accident that had happened to you, and how I knew people were wondering how it came to happen, so I thought it was only fair to let them know. Then I said that I knew there had been a lot of concern and stuff about occult forces being aimed against them, and I had to tell them that it wasn't true. So I explained about all our tricks and jokes, and then I told them why we'd done it. All

366

about the exclusion and the narrow mindedness and superstition and bitchiness and sheer bloody stupidity.

"I said I knew I didn't have a leg to stand on when it came to intellectual superiority, when we'd done something so childish it beggared belief."

"Tell me about it," Chloe said ruefully.

"Then I said, I had been horrified at the response, particularly to the Hallow E'en jape. I couldn't understand how sensible intelligent Christians could have behaved like that, I said. Or how they had come to focus on you as the source of the evil. Or how they could have been so arrogant and inhuman and unchristian to have tried to perform an exorcism. Well, the staff were having kittens by this point. No one has asked the right questions, you see, or really any questions for that matter. The Principal had accepted the tale about the kitten on the roof and had left it at that. He was practically hyperventilating at this point, with the horror of it. So I just said it was time we all had a good look at our consciences and ask ourselves quite what we could all learn from this episode. Episode of what I didn't say, but I was tempted to say Blair Witch IV, but hey, why spoil a great speech with a cheap joke."

"Then what? Did you get mobbed?"

"No, summoned to the Principal's office. 'Well,' he said, 'a word please, Isobel.' It never is, though, just one word. Unless of course that word is bollocking, and that's what he had in mind. Good job it wasn't in mine," Isobel said. "He waited till the door to his office was closed before he started shouting; I didn't know he had it in him to shout like that. Bet he didn't know I had it in me to out shout him. Trouble is, I'd second-guessed what he'd do and I was right. He immediately threatened to contact our director of ordinands and have Mickey chucked out of college. You try that, I said, and see where it gets you. All over the national newspapers, that's where. How'd you like them potatoes, Mr. Principal? I dropped a few names; someone I was at school with works for the Daily Mail and I meet her for a drink about once every two years so I know all the names. And I knew that'd be enough for him to stop and listen to me for a minute."

"Would you have told the press?"

"Course I would. Not that they'd have been terribly interested, but it might have made page five if the world was a bit quiet. No adultery, see. Not nearly as interesting without a bit of illicit nookie. Anyway, he shut up then, and tried to start back pedalling. I told him there were other people who should be chucked out if they could be chucked out for what their wives had done. After all, there are codes of conduct and rules for deliverance and a posse of hysterical women who've taken matters into their own hands hardly fit the requirements for a real exorcist. I'd asked around and really, that was so far from Anglican it was practically Pentecostal. I told him that too and said, I've been stupid and a bit malicious but I haven't actually broken any laws, whether civil, criminal or ecclesiastical. I'm not entirely sure of that, mind you, and I reckon a good solicitor would make a meal of that; prawns left to rot and itching powder are probably almost vandalism or some offence or other. Anyway we stood there glaring at each other for a few moments, and then the weight of the Daily Mail was too much for him, and he told me if I would give him the names of the women who'd actually been at your house that night, he would speak to them all and make sure they never thought to behave in that way again. And that would be the end of the matter, he said."

"And will it, I wonder?" Chloe said. "I'd quite like an apology, actually, but I think I'm wishing for the moon."

"'Fraid so," Isobel said. "When I got out of his office, I was sweating like the proverbial piggy. I felt like crap, I can tell you, fit for nothing at all. So I've been holed up, ignoring the door and the phone. I had Felicity yelling at Mickey for half an hour this morning after Morning Prayer; she'd waited for him so she could tell him what she thought of me. I doubt she'll be saying much once the Principal has seen her; I suspect he'll do the thing with the threat. If Robert is being threatened, she'll just roll over. She so loves the martyrdom thing, after all."

"I should just be glad we were weeks past Guy Fawkes night," Chloe said. "I might have ended up as the most lifelike guy for miles around."

"Don't!" said Isobel, and shuddered theatrically. "When we brought you in, they told me you were very lucky to get away with the injuries you got. You could have been killed or paralysed for life."

Chloe looked at her plastered and elevated leg.

"I know," she said. "Don't think that hadn't occurred to me. Usually at three o'clock in the morning when everything hurts and I can't sleep. I tell myself, count your blessings, Chloe girl. You could be dead, I tell myself. It's very comforting, I can tell you."

"Do I detect a note of sarcasm not to mention a distinct whiff of self pity?"

"What do you think?" Chloe said. "I'm stuck here, unable to get up and go anywhere and this thing itches like mad and the more I try to ignore it the worse it gets. And Christmas just makes things worse. The nurses are all wearing Santa hats. Even my consultant was wearing one when he came round yesterday."

"Bah, humbug, is it? Oh well, I understand that. Tell you what, I was going to ask you something. A favour if you like."

"You're asking favours from me? That takes some cheek. Go on, what is it then?"

"I want to paint you. Well, draw you at least. I want to do some drawings, take a few photos and then do the picture at home. I can't see any of the staff here appreciating the smell of my paints or me hanging round for hours on end staring at an easel, and in any case, the picture won't be a standard portrait. I have something in mind," Isobel said.

Chloe stared at her friend and then shrugged in amazement.

"You really are the limit," she said. "All right then, you can paint me. But why?"

"Couple of reasons, actually," Isobel said. "First reason is there's something in your face just now that I need to capture; I can't define it but I can see it. Second reason, you're bored and I can't sit still and talk to you for hours and hours. I can't sit still anyway. Third reason." She hesitated.

"Go on."

370

"Third reason," Isobel plunged on. "Third reason, if this goes how I want it to, it could be my best picture ever. It's certainly one of my best ideas at any rate."

"A picture of me? Don't talk daft," Chloe said robustly.

"You don't understand," Isobel said. "There's something in here–" she tapped her forehead between her eyes, "that I can see in my head and I need to get it down in a way other people can see it too. I don't expect you to understand just yet, anyway. I hope you will, though."

"Fine, go ahead. When were you planning to start?"

"Now, actually," Isobel said, and rummaged in her bag and pulled out sketchbook and camera and her tin of pencils.

"You knew I'd say yes?"

"Not exactly. I brought these along just in case you did. And if you'd said no, well, I'd have just used that time-honoured technique for persuasion: incessant nagging. Always works for me."

She selected a pencil, opened her book and began to make her preliminary marks.

"Hey wait a minute, can't I put on some make up or brush my hair," Chloe protested.

"If it makes you happy. Won't make any different to me; I've already seen you as you are. I suggest you just relax and try and stay still when I tell you to; I'm just going to do a few lightning sketches to get a feel for your face before starting properly."

It was quite disconcerting to have someone looking at her in the way Isobel was now staring at her; her eyes had become at once dreamy and unfocussed and at the same time somehow very sharp, as if she was seeing more than what was in front of her. She also went unusually quiet, a state for Isobel as unnatural as any she could imagine.

"I've never seen you like this before," Chloe said after a while.

"Well, you hardly know me yet anyway," Isobel said distractedly. "Only since August, isn't it? There's a lot about me you have yet to discover."

"Hmm," said Chloe pointedly.

Isobel drew until Clifford came that evening and after greeting him with rather manic cheerfulness, left them together.

"She seemed happy," he remarked after she'd gone.

"She's a different animal when she's working; did she say to you she wanted to paint me?" Chloe asked.

"She did mention it, but I said she should ask you," Clifford replied. "What way is she different?"

"She doesn't talk the whole time, for a start and she's suddenly so focussed," Chloe said. "Anyway, how's your day been?"

He'd been coming in for most of the day recently until Chloe told him they'd both be better off if he just came in morning and evening; otherwise they'd both be sitting around bored and trying to think of something to talk about. It had been easier, in the end, that way. Chloe was still stuck in bed, and hated it, and was not easy company and had been irritable, because the only thing that made time pass was to go to sleep. She'd been awake off and on most nights, running through things in her mind, as a result of napping during the day.

"I was thinking," he said after a while. "Perhaps when they let you out of here, you might not want to go home, not just yet anyway. I wondered if you'd like me to ask Peter if you can go and stay with him?"

He must be psychic, she thought. How did he guess I couldn't face the thought of going home?

"If he'd have me," she said.

"Er, I have asked him in a purely hypothetical way if he would and he said yes. It would be easier, since his house has a downstairs loo and ours doesn't. You'd only have to cope with stairs twice a day if you were there; if you came home, you'd have to live upstairs, or face dragging that cast up and down ten times a day."

"I had thought of that, actually," she said. "What about you? What would you do? You'd have to stay at the house though, once term starts again."

"I know, I know. I did feel like telling them where they could shove it, but it seemed stupid when we're almost at the end now anyway. I've had a letter about a possible curacy that I can go and see in the New Year, too," he said.

"Oh yeah? I hope they aren't expecting me to go along too," she said.

"Under the circumstances, no. But would you have done anyway?"

"Well, yes. At least so I could have a look at the house," Chloe said. "The rest is up to you anyway, nothing to do with me. Yes, I'd like to go and stay with Peter. I know it may be complicated changing hospitals what with physiotherapy and all the rest. They think I may need further operations anyway. But if we're moving that way anyway in June, it makes some sort of sense, even if we aren't in the exact same area. I can't face going back to our house, you know."

She said it as if it was some great secret that he could never have guessed, but he just nodded, and said,

"Yes, I thought it might be a problem."

He is bloody psychic, she thought.

"Oh, someone called round the other day to ask how you were. Annie, I think the name was; shy girl with a toddler," he said. "I said you were fine given the circumstances. Would you mind her visiting? I said I'd ask you first and get back to her. I didn't think she was quite one of them. None of them have so much as dropped a card round or asked how you are."

"No, I wouldn't have thought they'd have the nerve," Chloe said. "I don't think I could ever look at them again without seeing the ground rising up to meet me again."

Clifford looked at her with pity; it wasn't just her body that would carry scars after this.

"It'll pass," he said. "Look, as soon as they say you can go home, I'll ring Peter and arrange it. I think you need some very quiet time."

"It's pretty quiet here, you know."

"Not that sort of quiet. Oh and the people from your work said hi."

"Yeah, a number of them came in a few days ago, big bunch of flower and a lot of chocolate," Chloe said. "Did you go over then?"

"I was trying to find a Christmas present for my Mum," he said. "I though a trowel set might be a good idea; I can post it and she does garden after all. Not my most imaginative offering, but hey, I have had other things on my mind."

You aren't the only one, Chloe thought ruefully.

"Anyway, I was going to come in for the whole day on Christmas day," he said. "The nurse said they're hoping to get you into a better mood for then so I though I should come and share the task. After all, you need to shout at someone, and better it be me than some poor hard working nurse who drew the short straw of trying to jolly you along for Santa's visit."

"I'm trying to see if they might take me down to the hospital chapel for Communion," Chloe said. "And then I might just try and stay there. I don't mind carols but if the hospital radio plays bloody "Mistletoe and wine" or any of the other awful seasonal crap from thirty years of pop, I shall go mad."

"Do you know?" he said, "All it needs are the crutches and you'd be a cross between Tiny Tim with his gammy leg and Ebenezer Scrooge."

"Go on in that vein and you'll be the ghost of Christmas past pretty damn quick," she said. "It isn't you that has to put up with it all. And I could do with some proper fresh air soon. And a bath."

"There's a pond in the grounds; we could manage both of those with one trip," he said, and she managed a smile.

"I know you're fed up being here," he said. "But it won't be for long. And as an excuse for getting out of visiting my possible curacy, no one can fault it."

"I suppose so," she said, and sighed. "Give Peter my love and tell him that I really appreciate the offer. If he can put up with me, that is."

"He will," Clifford said confidently. "He said he was looking forward to it."

She glanced at him curiously.

"Strange man," she said.

"It runs in the family," he said.

Unlike me, she thought. I won't be running anywhere for a long time yet.

Chapter 28

Chloe lay on the sofa and tried to ease the ache in the small of her back; every time she managed to get up or down the stairs, she ended up with an aching back. The sheer weight of the cast on her leg made her surprisingly tired anyway, so she avoided moving if she could.

Peter came into the room. He looked at her for a moment and then said,

"Would you like some tea?"

"That would be appreciated," she said.

Even things like getting up and putting the kettle on were problematic; she could make the tea all right, but she would have to drink it leaning against a cupboard since there was no way of carrying a mug while she walked with the crutches. That sort of thing had never occurred to her before.

He came back through a few minutes later with a tray of tea and put it on the table in front of her and looked at her expectantly.

"Well? What?" she said.

"I thought you might like to pour," he said.

She considered this; it showed he understood how helpless she was feeling and was offering a task she was able to do without falling over, but she was irritated.

"No, I'll let you," she said, as if conceding an honour, and he smiled at her.

He was in his sixties, but she had no idea of his exact age; Clifford had said he had always seemed the same, his hair simply getting increasingly silver with years but his eyes remaining the same shade of clear grey. He'd never married; Chloe had often wondered why and had never enough nerve to ask. The busy suburban parish he served had contained numerous women who had tried to make themselves agreeable, but Peter had remained indifferent. The vicarage was large and the doorbell and the phone seemed to ring continuously, echoing in the bare hall, and making Chloe jump. Clifford had brought her here a few days ago, and had gone back to their house yesterday, and Chloe felt very lost suddenly. She'd been scared she would be expected to socialise with the frequent visitors, but Peter must have sensed this and brought visitors through to his study, rather than to the living room that had become her daytime lair.

It was that late afternoon sleepy feeling that seemed to fill the whole house, like an extended Sunday afternoon with nothing to do, and Chloe was starting to feel drowsy. She didn't want to doze off; last night she had been unable to sleep till four in the morning, or thereabouts. The small hours can be very lonely when you can't even sneak downstairs for a cup of tea; with the cast she couldn't sneak anywhere. She wanted to be so tired by bedtime that she would drop off straight away and not notice the empty side of the bed where Clifford should be.

"How are you feeling?" Peter asked, filling her mug and passing it to her.

"Oh, well, you know," Chloe said vaguely. "Bit achey most of the time. But I can get by without taking painkillers, if I try."

"That wasn't quite what I meant," he said. "I didn't mean physically. Clifford told me what happened, you know."

She gazed at her leg, entombed in plaster, and said nothing. She'd known he'd ask her about it; she'd expected it really, but now he'd asked, she didn't know what to tell him.

"I'd like you to tell me what went so badly wrong," he said. "But if you don't want to talk about it, I'd understand that."

"I'd like to talk but I don't know where to start," she said. "I don't know what to tell you, beyond I've made the biggest hash you can imagine and I am honestly not sure how I did it."

"Clifford said he thought the trouble started at the introductory weekend," Peter suggested.

"Initially I thought that too," she said. "But I've had some long nights in hospital when I couldn't sleep even with sleeping tablets, and when you can't get up, you end up thinking about things, and really, the trouble started even before that."

"But what makes you think that?"

"Well, we moved in that summer, straight after our honeymoon. It seemed silly paying rent on anywhere else, when Clifford's job had finished anyway and my new job was in commuting distance of the college. So we were there much of the summer. Well, Clifford was; I was working. The second or third weekend we were there, we got asked to a college picnic. There were all sorts of activities going on in the summer for students and their families, and since we were there early, so to speak, we got invites. This was the first invite and I thought, well, what the hell, we might as well. I'd had a long week and I wanted to do something completely different. So we went. They had the picnic in the college grounds; there's a big area almost of parkland and it was a lovely day, all sunshine and flowers. But by the time we got home again, I felt really depressed."

"Why was that?"

"I'm not sure," Chloe said slowly. "I thought about it a lot and there were several reasons. The wives were so competitive; I can't put it any better than that. They were full of stories of what they'd done, groups they'd run, stuff like that. They were also full of what they were going to do. Most of these were final year students' wives; they were on the home strait, if you like."

"Why should that make you depressed?"

"Because I didn't fit anywhere," she said. "I have no interest in any of the things they do; I don't even see the point of them, in the main. I started to wonder if there was something wrong with me, something that meant I was an inadequate Christian. I've only got the most tenuous of faiths anyway. And it got up my nose how full of themselves they all were, all self-congratulatory and smug. As if they were absolutely God's gift to the church; and me, I was no one, hardly even a Christian at that. It put my hackles up; I'm not used to feeling second-rate."

"No one in their right mind would ever call you second rate," Peter said, firmly.

"They didn't have to; they just had to look at me and that's what I felt like," she said. "And they had this awful way of looking at me. They'd look me up and down, pausing at the abdomen to see if I were pregnant. And I didn't have any anecdotes about our sending parish or a year as a missionary to wherever or anything they wanted to hear about. Gran came over to visit just after that; I told her I didn't want to be involved at all."

"I can't imagine her accepting that," he said.

"She didn't. She told me I was involved whether I wanted it or not; simply by marrying Clifford I'd effectively said yes to a certain basic level of involvement. We didn't argue, but I was cross with her. I wanted to ignore all the women who made me feel so hopelessly inadequate, I wanted the college to be no more than where we lived and where Clifford studied. No more than that. But it's insidious and it starts creeping in. So by the introductory weekend, I was in a state about it, and I don't think I could have upset and annoyed more people if I'd gone out of my way to try. As it was, I just effortlessly offended so many people without even knowing how. I said the wrong thing every time. I've never had that happen; I made friends at school and university within days or even hours of arrival. This time I had enemies. I couldn't believe it. And then Gran had to go and die on me just when I needed her the most. I began to feel even more helpless and at sea than I do now with a leg in a ruddy great plaster cast."

She drank her cooling tea in three gulps and looked at him.

"So it's not surprising I wasn't happy," she said. "Clifford got really immersed in his studies; I mean really immersed. He'd read twice what he needed to for essays; he'd research things almost to death. That was all right while I was working, because we'd have Saturdays and some evenings to be together, but his focus was always slightly elsewhere."

"That must have been hard for you to accept," he said carefully.

"I didn't even think about it, actually," Chloe said. "You don't, do you? You just tend to accept things as they are without questioning whether they're right or if they could be better. Then I lost my job, not long after Gran died. That was so annoying. I'd been getting on well; enjoyed the job, liked my colleagues, that sort of thing. When I finished, I couldn't quite get to grips with being around during the day. I brooded, I think. I'd see the other wives going about their daily business and I'd been so miserable. And all this time I'd been having disturbed nights. After Gran died, I started having this recurring nightmare. It used to so freak me out, no matter how many times it came it was still as bad. I thought it was to do with Gran; after the burial I felt so terrible that she'd gone, the image of her grave stayed with me. It seemed so final. I suppose it isn't. That's what I mean about having a very tenuous faith; I could never be certain about the things everyone else seems rock solid about. I don't have those sort of certainties; just a whole load more questions and doubts."

She stretched her good leg and subsided onto the sofa cushions.

"That seems more healthy to me," Peter said. "The thing about faith is it's often more about questions than certainties. For me, the only certainty is God's love for us."

"I sometimes wonder even about that!" Chloe said. "Anyway, we had some friends that first year that made it sort of bearable. I had someone to ask questions of, to have a moan to, who seemed to understand. They left at the end of that year; things have drifted, since then, though. We get Christmas cards; but they've moved on and things have changed. The next year was so lonely. I resigned my next job for reasons of conscience, and I was out of work again. I got a temporary job at a garden centre, just to pay the bills; and I enjoyed it far more than I had enjoyed the job I'm trained to do. I think I've made a big mistake in my choice of career; and I need to change it. But I have no idea what to do. I'm so confused about so many things. Then just before this academic year started, Isobel arrived."

"This is the girl who was the mole?"

"That's right. If I'm a square peg, then she's a triangular peg. I liked her straight away. She's funny and so full of life that she'd cheer anyone up. She's also something of a natural anarchist, I think. But she was so determined that she'd cope with the college; she'd radically altered her appearance, she told me, so that she'd not stick out too much. When I told her about what life had been like for me at the college, she got really angry. That's when she came up with the Plan."

Chloe sighed.

"It was so stupid, really, but it seemed harmless," she said. "A way of making them sort of sit up and look at what was happening to them, at what they were doing to others."

"Can you tell me more about it?"

"It was very silly, very childish," Chloe said, rather sadly. "We shouldn't have done it, however much fun it seemed."

She explained what they had done, running through the various jokes and plotting, and was relieved that he began smiling.

"You think it's funny?" she asked.

"Excruciatingly so," he agreed. "But you are right. You shouldn't have done it. Not with people like that. There was obviously a vein of hysteria running along under the surface at all times, ready to emerge with the right conditions. Did you think it would have such a profound effect?"

"No. I could kick myself, really. My sister said I should be careful, that they might be dangerous and I virtually laughed out loud. I said they were just sheep. Cathy said that if sheep ever turn, the shepherd is in trouble. She was right. After we'd done our last tricks for Hallow E'en, we decided to quit. It had worked too well. So Isobel backed off from all the coffee mornings and prayer meetings. She'd had enough of pretending to be something she isn't, and she wanted out. If she'd stayed around, maybe she'd have got wind of the fact that things didn't settle down and fade away. One of the women, a girl called Annie, came to see me in hospital. I didn't know her as such, but she'd been trying to moderate things and getting in their bad books for it. She said that after Hallow E'en, things seemed to get far worse. Every little mishap, every illness or injury, or bad feeling or argument, was down to some sort of evil influence. And they fixed on me as the source; I wasn't quite sure why until Annie told me. She said they thought there was something strange about me; the way my garden grew so well, how the birds didn't seem scared of me when I sat out meditating, how I seemed to be serene and happy all the time, and Gran's collection of curios from exotic cultures was the clincher. The statues and things all had demonic connotations for them. I was apparently unaffected by it; I obviously had good health and

384

happiness and luck, so I must be in some way evil. They used the word witch, even. Gradually over the weeks after Hallow E'en, they came to fix on me as being the source, the conduit for the evil they thought was being directed against them. It makes me laugh that they saw me as being happy and serene and lucky. That wasn't what I felt like, I can tell you. I felt so alone sometimes it was scary. Anyway, Annie said they worked themselves up over some days, until they decided the only way forward was to perform an exorcism. They argued about it; some didn't think it was right to do so without authorisation, and some had such contempt for the church processes that deal with this sort of thing, they reckoned they could do it better themselves. That was when Annie decided she couldn't be a part of it any more, and pulled away completely. She said she would have warned me if she had known exactly when they were going to come for me; she was crying and asking me to forgive her for not stopping them."

Chloe could feel tears in the corners of her eyes, prickling and tickling, until she scrubbed at her eyes firmly.

"Poor girl," she said. "I told her it wasn't her fault. She felt so guilty that she hadn't stood up to them properly; she said she'd never have forgiven herself if I'd been killed or paralysed. It'll be months before this leg is sorted, but I think I got off lightly."

"What did the college do after the accident?" Peter asked.

"Nothing," Chloe said. "The Principal accepted Felicity's story about me trying to rescue a kitten off the roof. But Isobel blew all that sky-high when she got up at chapel night dinner and told the whole story."

"She told the whole story? That was brave."

"It was, wasn't it," Chloe admitted. "But you haven't met Isobel yet. You'd like her, I think. She never takes the easy option. She's also pretty cunning. The danger of letting the truth out was that the Principal would decide that he wanted neither Clifford nor Mickey, (that's Isobel's other half) at the college. He might complain to our sending dioceses and that might well be that. Anyway, Isobel got called into his office and yelled at. It did look like that was what was coming too, only Isobel told him that she had friends in the national press and wouldn't it be a good story for a dull weekday? And did he not think that if anyone should be censured for their wives' conduct, it should really be the husbands of the women who caused the accident. He agreed, though whether it was him changing his mind about the apportioning of blame or perhaps the thought of the Daily Mail headlines had some part to play; I don't know. He told Isobel he would speak to the women concerned in the strongest possible terms."

"And has he?"

"I have no idea," Chloe admitted. "I don't have any moles to give me any feedback. But the Principal never visited me in hospital; there's been nothing from the college by way of friendly concern. So if he has spoken to them, I don't know it'll have made much impact. I have an idea he's a bit of a fundamentalist himself, so he might even have agreed with their conclusions, even if he wouldn't have liked them taking the matter into their own hands. So that's that, really."

"So there'll be no inquiry?"

386

"Nope, the whole thing is being buried. Even though the incident could have got me killed, it's going to be forgotten about as soon as possible. Most of those involved are like us in their final year; the main instigators all leave in June same as us. It hasn't made any difference, what we did. Not that it ever does. Maybe we should have written letters, or made speeches or pressure groups or something. Oh, I can see it more clearly now, of course. I can honestly say I have the same spiritual and emotional maturity as the average turnip."

She shifted uncomfortably on the sofa; it was hard to be so still, so inactive.

"And I've got things to think about still," she said, presently. "Difficult things."

He stood up, and bent to pick up the tea tray.

"Such as?"

She just shook her head rather vaguely.

"I need to think," she said.

"Well, you can have a quiet evening to do it. I have a meeting this evening, so I'll try and make sure you've got everything to hand before I go out," he said.

At the door, he paused.

"Chloe?" he said.

"Yes?"

"It will be all right, you know," he said. "The worst is over, you know."

Is it, though? she thought

*

It was after ten when Peter got back, and found Chloe trying to wash the dishes with one hand, leaning on one crutch and swaying.

He didn't say anything, just handed her the other crutch.

"I got bored, and then I got guilty," she said and began to hobble back through to the living room. "I'm a lot of extra work for you, and I thought I should at least make an effort."

"And if you'd fallen over, doing that little balancing act, and broken something else, an arm or a wrist, what would you have done then?" he asked, rather severely.

She swung her cast onto the sofa with some difficulty.

"Point taken," she said. "I just feel so useless. I even found myself wishing I'd been able to go along when Clifford saw that parish a few days ago; just for the diversion from myself."

"You aren't finding this very easy, are you?"

"That has to be the understatement of the century!"

He sat down on the armchair opposite her.

"What is troubling you to this extent?" he asked. "I know that you regret what happened, and that is understandable. But I can sense something else niggling away."

"The old spider sense still working, eh?" Chloe said. "I'm not sure I can tell you what's been on my mind lately."

"Why not?"

He sounded as reasonable as ever, as calm and as gentle as he normally was; nothing seemed to faze him for long.

"Because you're Clifford's uncle," she said.

"Oh," he said, and she got the sudden feeling he had more than an inkling of what she was brooding about.

"I'm going to get us both a drink," he said, after the long silence had stretched out far enough. "Would you like wine, or would you prefer tea?"

"I daren't have wine," she said. "I'm not sure what the combination of wine with my medication would do. Do you have camomile tea?"

"I bought some specially," he said, and gave her his rather special, gentle smile. "I won't be long."

As he left the room, Chloe felt her heart sink.

How can I tell him I think I should leave his nephew?

Chapter 29

Peter came back into the room with a china mug that steamed fragrantly and a glass of red wine for himself. He put them both on the table next to her and went to light the gas fire. Chloe watched him silently.

"So," he said, sitting down in his usual armchair. "What's been on your mind?"

How do I do this? She had no idea.

"I've made such a mess of everything," she said finally.

"Everything? That seems something of a sweeping statement," he said.

"I meant everything for us," Chloe said. "I might have got Clifford thrown out of the college for what Isobel and I did. And even though that didn't happen, I think I've been so far from the ideal wife for him. I won't even go to church with him. There's no way you can tell me that's being a good wife."

"And yet you did go with him before you were married?" Peter said. "I seem to recall that you did."

"Yes, when I stayed with him, we'd go to his parish church. When he stayed with me, we'd go wherever we fancied, pretty much," Chloe said. "High Anglo-catholic, Nigerian Pentecostal, Methodist, whatever seemed interesting."

"Why do you feel you should have gone with him once you were at college?"

Now there's a stumper, she thought.

"I don't really know. Because all the other wives either went with their husbands or they got involved in one of the local happy-clappy places. I stopped going anywhere for a while. Then I found the most staid local church I could walk to and just sort of lurked there, not being involved. I don't think anyone even knew my name," she said.

Peter picked up her mug and passed it to her, and took a sip of his wine, gazing at her reflectively.

"Did Clifford ever ask you to go with him?" he asked. "Or express any wish that you might sometimes accompany him?"

"No," she said thoughtfully. "No, he never did, now you come to mention it. In fact, he's always seemed slightly relieved that I don't. I have no idea why."

"Ah, but I do," Peter said. "I've kept out of Clifford's way while he's been training; not because I don't love you both, but because I do. You know, Clifford is very much a perfectionist. Maybe that isn't the right word, but he likes to do things well. I remember when he was about six, and he'd got a new bike for Christmas or birthday. He wouldn't let his dad help him learn to ride it; he wouldn't let anyone watch him try and get the hang of it. But a few days later, he rode it for us, perfectly, scarcely a wobble. Mind you, he had more sticking plasters visible than actual skin from all the falls he'd had. He wouldn't want you there while he's learning to ride the metaphorical bicycle; that's how he is."

Chloe put her head in her hands, feeling the whole weight of her anxiety. Camomile tea splashed down her skirt.

"Damn," she said, and put the mug down on the floor.

"That makes it so much worse," she said. "I don't think I can go on any more. I can't face the thought of what our life is going to be like once he is ordained."

Peter said nothing, and then passed her a box of tissues so she could dab at her eyes as the tears began to fall.

"What do you think it will be like, then?" he asked presently.

"Like college only worse."

Chloe could feel the sob beginning to build in the centre of her chest, a real heavy physical pain.

"I can't bear it," she said. "I'm going to have to leave him for his sake and mine. I'll be a disaster as a clergy wife, just as I've been a disaster as an ordinand's wife."

"Rubbish," said Peter suddenly. "Absolute unmitigated rubbish. And I speak not as my nephew's uncle, I assure you. You're a clever girl, but you've got this so very wrong."

"Wrong?" Chloe said wonderingly. "Wrong? How? How can you say that? Everything I've done has gone wrong. I've been utterly wrong in every way. I've upset and offended nearly everyone, I've done nothing useful or supportive or even vaguely spiritual. I can't imagine anyone wanting me around them. I don't even know if Clifford will get a curacy because of how I've been. I should just leave, but even the thought of it hurts so much."

He moved across and sat next to her on the sofa, and took both her hands in his.

"My poor dear girl," he said. "I hate to say it, but you've been brainwashed."

She stared at him.

"You've absorbed all the lies without knowing it," he went on. "The thing is, none of that is true. Clifford has been happier than I've ever known him since he married you; you give him his space, which he needs more than you can imagine. My sister is apt to eat her young, so to speak. Clifford doesn't need someone who shadows his every move or hangs onto his every word; he needs someone like you who challenges him, who thinks and feels and tries everything. And as for a parish, why do you imagine that anyone minds what you do or don't do?"

"I don't know," Chloe said. "I sort of assumed they all would."

"Some might, I grant you that. But most are just content that they have a vicar at all; anything his wife might offer is an unexpected bonus," Peter said. "It'll *never* be like college. How on earth could it be? There will only be you in a parish, usually. Certainly never a horde of other clergy wives all competing with one another for second prize."

"Second prize?"

"That's right. First prize always belongs to their husbands. They can never win. But you, that's different. You have chosen not to play that particular unwinnable game."

"I don't understand," she said.

"The thing about wives like that is they compete against one another simply because they know deep down they can never compete against their husbands. And it's that tension that powers the whole thing at that college. They know they've already lost; so they try to win a different game. Chloe, listen to me: it will never be the same once you've left college," he said, emphatically. "It will never be bad in that way again; it can't be. Do you understand me?"

Chloe nodded hesitantly.

"When you move to Clifford's curacy parish, there will be curiosity about you and even criticism," he went on. "But it means nothing. There is nothing that says you ever have to do what the last curate's wife did. You have only got to be yourself. That is all that is asked of you, at the end of it. Because that's the only thing that counts, the only should or ought in the matter that ever has any weight, is that you should be your own true self. Do you believe me?"

"Yes," she said, without hesitation this time. "Because that's what Gran used to say, and because I know you'd never ever lie to me."

He smiled and patted her hands before letting them go.

"I wish I'd had a better chance to get to know your grandmother," he said. "She had such an instinctive grasp of reality, I rarely come across such clarity of thought. And she was such a warrior for the truth, too. I understand your sister has followed in her footsteps, in her own way."

"I miss my Gran," Chloe said. "Maybe I'd not have got into such a tangle if she were still alive."

"Perhaps," Peter said. "But then, I think she knew it was time to go; that's what she said to me at your wedding, that she knew it would be time to go soon. I think that it was time for you to let her go, too, and begin to really live your beliefs for yourself and not just for her. No one can grow up entirely when a parent is always there to muck out the messes; one day you have to do it yourself. And as these things go, it was a pretty stylish mess, and you're doing a good job of clearing it all up. So don't go making any silly decisions about Clifford until you've had a chance to tell him what you've just been telling me. I think he'd not have you any different; and any parishes he may hold in the future will not change that, either. He needs you; and you need him. The world is changing; the church changes more slowly but it is still changing. The day of the vicar's wife who ran the Mothers' Union and all the rest of it is almost over. The days where you can all be only and utterly yourselves are beginning; there may be teething troubles, but there always are. But something good is starting."

Chloe drank her cold camomile tea and looked at her leg.

"I've been very silly, haven't I?" she said finally.

"A bit. But under the circumstances, it's not surprising really," he said. "You were under a lot of pressure, and that can affect even the most robust psyche. Now, I suggest you get upstairs to bed. You look wiped out."

"Another understatement," Chloe said, retrieving her crutches and struggling to her feet. "Peter?"

"Yes?"

"Thanks."

He smiled.

"Any time," he said. "Now, go and get a good night's sleep. I thought I might take you for a drive tomorrow, so you can have a look at the parish that may well be offering Clifford a curacy. This way you can be incognito."

Me, incognito, with this hair? I don't think so, she thought. But she smiled at him anyway.

"I'll look forward to it," she said.

*

The day before Clifford's ordination, Chloe's new house seemed ridiculously full, even though Clifford himself was away on his pre-ordination retreat.

Isobel was such a huge personality that she could practically fill a house by herself; she was on good form, full of jokes and big laughter. Cathy had slipped away into the garden to escape, and Mickey had gone out to join her with a beer.

"I'm so glad my mother-in-law has elected to meet us at the Minster," Chloe said, tipping beer into a glass for Isobel. "I can't imagine her enjoying this sort of house party at all."

"I'd have her loosened up in no time," Isobel said, and somehow Chloe thought she might even manage it.

"Oh, I finished the picture," Isobel said casually.

"I'd forgotten about that," Chloe admitted.

Isobel had done a lot of drawing while she'd still been in hospital, and had taken a number of photos, and then one day had simply stopped bringing her sketchbook with her and had said nothing. Chloe had wondered if the picture had not gone the way Isobel obviously wanted it to, and had chosen not to ask about it in case whatever snag it might be turned out to be one Isobel was sensitive about. And then, because she had other things on her mind, she'd forgotten about it totally.

"I brought it with me, actually," Isobel said, just as casually. "I want you to have it, but not this weekend. It'll have to go back with me as I want it in the exhibition."

"Can I see it then?"

Isobel put down her beer.

"I'll go and get it," she said. "If you don't like it I won't be offended, so don't fib. It's not exactly a portrait, you see."

"Fine," Chloe said.

Isobel ran upstairs with all the energy and bounce that Chloe remembered, and back down again bearing a large shrouded picture. It was wrapped in what appeared to be an old curtain.

"Ta dah!" Isobel said and pulled away the wrapping with a flourish.

Chloe stared at the picture in astonishment. Her face was there in the centre, turned slightly away as if she were looking at something off to the right of her, but even on the days when the eye make-up had gone astray, she had never had blue serpentine coils painted on her face, swirls and spirals and Celtic knots. Her hair had begun its usual mad coiling and curling in a cloud around her face and down her shoulders, but where the curls would have begun to drop with gravity and cascade down her back, each curl became a single tiny kingfisher, an effortless seamless metamorphosis. Each kingfisher in all its brilliance and flashing colour then transformed into bright flames that grew brighter and more vivid as they spread out to the edge of the canvas where they became almost white-hot in a kind of halo around her.

Holding the picture, Isobel grinned at her.

"I call it "Kingfishers catching Fire"," she said. "What do you think?"

"It's stunning!" Chloe said. "Is that what you see, then?"

"Not exactly, no," Isobel said. "Not see. It's more of a sort of vision thing, if you get my drift. That stuff you were saying about the poem and being oneself, it sort of got me thinking and dreaming and wondering. This was what I came up with. Do you like it?"

Behind the bounce and the Tigger-like approach to life, the insecurity showed suddenly.

"I love it," Chloe said. "Come on, let's show Cathy."

Out in the garden, Mickey was chatting with Cathy; Cathy seemed to wilt when she saw Isobel coming out.

"Is there any more beer?" she asked when Chloe and Isobel reached them.

"Loads," Chloe said. "I wanted to show you the picture Isobel has done of me."

She held up the painting for Cathy to inspect; saw Cathy's jaw drop in astonishment and smiled.

Cathy looked at Isobel with changed eyes.

"I'll get the beer," she said.

Isobel watched her across the garden, her own eyes moody.

"I don't think she likes me very much," she said.

"Not till she saw the picture, anyway," Chloe said. "You have to admit you can be a bit full-on for some people."

"But surely she's used to that!"

Chloe said nothing and waited till Cathy came back with another six-pack; she was grinning even through the tears.

"You can see it," she said, handing Isobel the first can. "You can see what she is, can't you, and that's what you painted."

"I don't see it as such, not with my eyes," Isobel said. "But in my mind, yes, I see it. And the stuff with the poem, kingfishers catching fire, that's all a part of it too."

"I don't even pretend to understand," Chloe said happily. "Now would someone get me two chairs? One for me and one for my leg. And another apple juice would be nice too. And the menu for the Chinese is in the knife drawer."

Cathy hurried back inside, followed by Isobel.

"How long will you have that cast for?" Mickey asked.

"Not much longer, I hope," Chloe said. "It's the third one; I've had a new one every time they've operated. So much for the NHS cutting back; imagine! A new cast each time: luxury! It'll be nice to have a leg again instead of a dead weight; though I am told my leg will look like something that crawled out from under a rock when the cast finally comes off. But they are confident that with a fair bit of physiotherapy it'll eventually get back to normal, give or take a few scars."

Cathy returned with two dining room chairs.

"You'll need some sort of garden furniture," she said, glancing round the overgrown garden. "Gran had a lovely bench. I assume that stayed at the old house."

"Yes, it didn't seem right to move it," Chloe said, sitting down awkwardly but gratefully and managing to lift her plaster bound leg onto the other chair.

"Here's your juice and here's the menu," Isobel said, handing her both. "I don't suppose your chinky does that traditional Chinese dish, lame duck in plum sauce?"

Cathy stared at her for a moment and then began laughing; she'd finally got the measure of Isobel and had made up her mind not to resent her. The whole story had been told shortly after Christmas and Cathy had previously been too furious with Isobel to even begin to understand her. She'd barely even spoken to her when they'd met at Chloe's bedside. Chloe had rather been dreading having them both under the same roof, even for a day or two; but it looked like they understood each other rather better than either had imagined.

"I'm starving," Chloe said. "Let's decide quickly and order before my stomach thinks my throat has been cut."

"Jumping juniper, Batwoman," Isobel said. "Give us a chance!"

"It's a well known fact that anyone ordering a Chinese takeaway will read the menu for five minutes and then choose exactly what they had last time," Chloe said. "I'm living proof. I'm going to have sweet and sour Chinese vegetables with fried rice same as last time. But as this is a special occasion I am also going to have sesame prawn toast."

As the light faded in the garden and moths started to appear round the candle Isobel had lit on the small patio, the laughter and bickering filled the air. Chloe sat back on her chairs and enjoyed the evening, with only the smallest of anxious pangs in the pit of her stomach about tomorrow.

Chapter 30

Early the next morning, Isobel came into Chloe's bedroom holding two mugs of tea, and put one on the trunk next to Chloe. She sat on the edge of the bed, slightly dislodging Chainsaw. Chloe's eyes flickered and then opened.

"Tea? Great," she said muzzily. "What time is it?"

"Just gone half six," Isobel said. "That's what you said, wasn't it?"

"Yes; but somehow it feels much too early to be awake."

"You're telling me! You didn't have any beer last night either," Isobel said ruefully. "It's a good job I don't get hangovers from beer."

"Then why do you look like an elephant has sat on your face?"

"Shut up and drink your tea!"

Isobel stroked Chainsaw tentatively, until he put out a paw, claws still sheathed, to warn her that all he wanted was sleep. Sylvester snored gently at the end of the bed. Both cats had been first offended, then confused and finally ecstatic about the move; the new house was in a housing estate at the very edge of the market town they'd moved to and the garden bordered directly on meadow land, that gave way first to forest and then finally to open moorland. Chloe had been impressed and then irritated by the number of very dead rabbits both cats had dragged in through the cat flap left on the hearthrug or under the kitchen table. They'd moved their belongings in as soon as the house had become available, in the March, when the previous curate had moved out

402

having obtained a new position earlier than predicted. Chloe had lived with Peter until then, and when the opportunity had arisen to move into a house with a downstairs loo, she had jumped at it. Clifford had then moved into the spare room in Mickey and Isobel's house to finish his course. It had meant a massive saving in rent, which meant that they could afford the petrol for Clifford to visit Chloe as often as he could.

The vicar for his new parish had been told the real story of how Chloe came to have a leg that looked like a jigsaw puzzle when viewed on X-ray, and had been robustly indignant and had promised all the support for her they could give her while she lived alone in the new house. So as a result, she'd been taken shopping twice weekly, had been offered (and had accepted) help with housework and gardening, and had been ferried to the hospital for her out-patient appointments. Someone had checked she was all right every day; she was by now feeling rather crowded and overwhelmed by unaccustomed kindness that she couldn't help feeling she didn't deserve. Most people had been told the version of the fall that Felicity had invented; it was simpler, in the end to let people believe she had done something mildly heroic but essentially rather daft, because it wasn't far from the real truth and the real story was far too complicated to explain.

Chloe struggled to sit up, the cast a dead weight as she lay in bed, and fumbled for her mug.

"I reckoned that with three extra in the house I'd be better off getting up early so I can take my time in the shower," she said after the first blissful sip. "And my hair has a chance to dry properly without having to use the dryer on it."

"Fine with me," Isobel said. "Just don't expect me to do much smiling till I've had a lot more tea and probably some coffee and a shower myself. I like your sister, by the way. She's amazing."

"Isn't she, though?" Chloe said. "I'm glad she showed you some of her art work; she's got real talent I think. I might be biased though."

"Well, obviously," Isobel said. "But you're right. Some of those sculptures from driftwood are spectacular. I said I'd see if I could have some included in my exhibition, you know, sort of sub-letting. I reckon she'd get a lot more for them in a real art market type thing than she does at the moment; they're original enough to tickle the punters."

Chloe drank her tea and then struggled out of the bed, reaching for her crutches.

"Right, I'm off for a shower," she said. "I may be some time."

Later, when all the slightly hung-over guests had surfaced, Chloe sat at the kitchen table in her dressing gown and listened to the coffee machine burbling away to itself as the fragrance filled the air and lured the others from the garden.

"It could be a lovely garden," Cathy said as she came in. "Especially with the view of the forest just over the fence. But it's a bit boring at the moment, not a lot but grass. I know you could have trouble with rabbits coming in and eating your plants, but a bit of care and a lot of chicken wire would take care of that. Not to

404

mention those furry assassins you call cats. Is that coffee ready, do you think?"

"About ready," Isobel said. "Shall I pour?"

They ate toast and fruit and drank coffee, and all the time, Chloe could hear her own heart racing. Somehow everything had been leading to this day, and she felt more nervous than she had for her wedding day. It's not as if it's even me that's being ordained, she thought, crossly. What must Clifford be feeling like if I'm this scared?

"OK, I'm going to drag myself up to get ready," she said finally. "Will someone else deal with the dishes?"

"Yep, I'll put them in the sink," Isobel said. "I think they can wait. Do you need any help getting dressed?"

"I'll yell if I do," Chloe said, hobbling out of the kitchen, and beginning her ascent of K2, otherwise known as the stairs.

She managed to dress unaided, her new skirt nearly tangling her up as she tried to get into it without falling over. The swirls of black velvet didn't quite hide the cast entirely but it at least didn't emphasise it. Which was something of a relief, because when she'd gone home to supervise the removals men she'd visited the garden centre where she'd worked and all her old colleagues had insisted on signed the cast and while most of it had faded there were one or two rather ribald messages that she didn't think would be appreciated in the Peter-tide Minster. She tried and failed to tame her hair, in the end simply tying a broad piece of ribbon in blue shot silk around it to hold it off her face, and then started her make-up.

"It's going to be hot," Cathy said, coming in without knocking. "You look nice; like a happy Goth or a reformed vampire. All you need is a load of silver occult jewellery and you'd pass muster at a pagan Moot."

Chloe snorted, amused.

"Are you OK with all this?" Cathy asked, suddenly.

"I wasn't, no, but I am now," Chloe said. "I'm just nervous now. I don't want to trip over my crutches or drop them at a crucial moment during the service. And Clifford's mum and dad will be there and I'm not sure I can stand any crap from his mum this time. I think I've got a shorter temper than before; you know, light the blue touch paper and stand well back."

"It'll be OK; we'll be there and that nice uncle of his. We can keep Nadine off your back," Cathy said. "Can I borrow your eyeliner?"

"Help yourself to anything," Chloe said, and watched with amusement as her sister rummaged through Chloe's make up box and painted her own face carefully.

Cathy had let her hair grow out a bit, so her head was covered in tight red curls, shot through with a fair sprinkling of silver that Chloe had never noticed while her hair had been cropped. She was wearing deep maroon velvet and she had only a single pendant on, a small equal armed cross slung on a leather thong. When she came and sat next to Chloe on the bed, Chloe could smell the comforting scent of wood smoke and patchouli she had begun to associate with her sister.

Isobel put her head round the door.

"Oh, you're ready," she said. "Mickey is still in the shower, and I need someone to do me zip up?"

She sidled into the room, holding her dress to her. Chloe grinned.

"Knock 'em dead," she said. "Will you do the honours for Madame de Pompadour, Cathy?"

Cathy grinned and stood up, and helped Isobel adjust her dress and then zipped it up, accompanied by a squeak of pain as a snippet of skin got caught. The dress wasn't exactly low cut but it was a lot more daring than was probably appropriate for the event, showing Isobel's generous curves to perfection.

"It'll give Mickey something to think about during the service," Isobel said defensively. "It is supposed to be a celebration isn't it?"

"You look great," Cathy said. "I'd show off my curves if I had any."

"Did we get together and agree to all wear velvet or something?" Chloe said. "I mean, me in black, you in maroon, and you in bottle green? I'm sure I'd remember agreeing something like that if we had."

"Pure coincidence," Cathy said, grinning.

"There's no such thing," Isobel said. "What is it Einstein said about coincidence being God's way of staying anonymous?"

"That IS what Einstein said," Chloe said, watching Isobel leaning over her dressing table mirror to apply her usual brilliant red lipstick.

Mickey tapped nervously at the door.

"Er, Isobel," he called tentatively without coming in. "Do you think you can sort my tie out for me?"

Isobel shrugged elaborately.

"Men!" she said. "They can do anything but their ties."

"That's not fair," came Mickey's voice. "I haven't worn a tie in years; it's easy to forget something like that."

Isobel got up and stretched.

"Coming," she said. "We're about ready for the off then, once we've got Mickey's tie sorted. I'll meet you downstairs."

"I don't want anyone watching me come downstairs in this skirt," Chloe said as Isobel left the room. "It's not too bad in a normal skirt because I can just tuck it under my bum as I slide down; this one will ride up and reveal everything. Not to mention generating enough static to make my hair stand on end."

"No one will watch," Cathy said, reassuringly. "Are you ready, now?"

"As I'll ever be," Chloe said, and heaved herself off the bed and onto her crutches.

*

The air inside the Minster was cool after the searing sticky city heat from the crowded narrow streets; Mickey had dropped them as close as he could get and had then circled off to try and park.

The air was filled with suppressed whispers and a thousand scents as they filed forward, heels clicking on stone and the rubber tips of Chloe's crutches making a dull stony sound as she swung herself along towards their seats near the front. She concentrated on moving steadily and left Isobel and Cathy to do the navigating.

"Just over there," Cathy said. "We can get you into an aisle seat so you don't have to try and squeeze past any chairs."

Peter was there, smiling, sitting next to his sister and brother-in-law, and Chloe sank into a chair next to him at the end of the aisle.

"I've seen Clifford," he whispered to her. "He looks fine, a bit nervous but fine."

Nadine leaned across.

"You could have ironed his surplice a bit better though," she said.

Chloe felt as if she'd been slapped. I shouldn't have to take this, she thought dazedly.

"It's perfectly possible to iron while sitting down," Nadine went on.

Whatever I do or don't say now is crucial, Chloe thought. I just want to slap her, though.

"This isn't the time, Nadine," Chloe said. "Whatever gripes you may have about me, this isn't the time to bring them out. Now just be quiet and think about your son for once."

Nadine gave a shocked gasp and then drew breath to retort, but Peter simply took her hand in one of his, smiled at her and put his finger up to his lips in the childhood gesture of bidding silence.

Cathy had watched the exchange in silence, feeling Isobel's rage surging up behind her, and now she gently steered Isobel into the chairs behind Peter and Chloe and sat down herself, putting her hand on her sister's shoulder and giving it a squeeze. Next to her, Isobel sank forward onto a kneeler, crossed herself and closed her eyes, an expression of profound annoyance on her face. She closed her own eyes, feeling for the core of silence that the building held and sinking into it. Some habits never entirely vanished.

Chloe couldn't kneel, and usually didn't anyway, but she used the opportunity to distance herself from the seething emotions she could feel emanating from her mother-in-law in the next seat but one. Peter sat like a cool rock on a hot day, giving shade and shelter from the blaze of the sun. She closed her eyes and folded her hands in her lap, and tried to stretch out her legs as best she could; the crutches lay on the stone flags next to her, ready to hand but with any luck not in anyone's way.

The air space above her was huge and even the whispers echoed up into the ceiling many yards above; the slightest sound seemed to reverberate around so the noise of a dropped book seemed like the voice of doom, endowed with the significance of amplification. Gradually she managed to still her mind so that she no longer felt Nadine's anger, nor even Peter's calm, but could only feel her own fear, that curled and writhed like a frightened snake in the pit of her soul.

This will change everything, she thought, and I can't do anything but just accept it. Some changes are to be resisted to the death, but

I know where that would lead and I will not follow that way. This is a good thing, a hard thing maybe but a good one.

As she sat in the quiet space inside herself, the snake ceased its terrified writhing and settled itself into a spiral of smooth coils, and slept.

There was something happening; she opened her eyes. Music had begun filling the building, and everyone was rising to their feet. Chloe watched the service starting as if from a great distance, and then struggled to her feet in time to see the procession of ordinands, Clifford looking outwardly calm among the flowing whiteness of brand new surplices, but she knew that look of old; he was as terrified of this change as she was. Somehow that made it so much easier. The snake stirred and slept again.

*

The new parish had arranged a bun-fight for their newly ordained curate; after the service they'd all travelled back to the parish and down to the church hall. Nadine was refusing to speak to Chloe at all which was actually a blessed relief. On the drive back, Chloe had gone back with Clifford in their car, leaving Mickey to drive back Isobel and Cathy, and she'd told him what the row was about.

"Silly woman," Clifford had said. "I'd ironed it perfectly, but a day in a suitcase creases anything, and it wasn't exactly the most

411

pressing thing on my mind this morning. Oh well, she'll just have to get over it."

"How do you feel?" Chloe asked him when they pulled up by the church hall.

"Odd. I don't feel any different, yet, not really but I think I will do when I've got my head straight again," he said, coming round to help her out of the rear passenger door. "I am so glad we have a five door car," he remarked as she struggled to get herself out.

"I shall be bloody glad to have normal leg again," Chloe said, as he steadied her as she got the crutches into position.

"Are you ready for this?" he asked. "I'll take you home as soon as you want me too."

"I'm fine," she said. "Park me by the food and forget me."

She followed him into the hall, and as he appeared a huge cheer went up from the crowd that thronged the building, followed by a round of very British applause; she felt her eyes grow suddenly unaccountably wet and he drew her awkwardly to his side and another cheer went up, and Chloe felt her face grow hot as well as wet.

Later, much later, when she'd eaten tiny scraps of food in between being hugged and kissed by almost complete strangers, and had felt herself grow dizzy with the sheer enthusiasm of the welcome, she sank into a chair at the side of the room and wished for home and bed. She had seldom felt so exhausted even after running long distances.

Clifford came over to her, holding a chicken leg and a glass of wine; the same glass he'd been carrying all afternoon.

"You look like you need to get home," he said.

"I'm fine," she said. "But yes, I'd like to go home soon, if we can."

"I'll just say goodbye to my mother and father, and then I'll round up the others and we can go," he said. "Unless you want to help with the clearing up?"

"I offered," she said. "I feel so useless with this cast so I offered, and I was told very firmly, no. Oh, you were joking? Oh, well."

He went off to find his parents, and Peter came over to her.

"That was a very pleasant service and an lovely reception," he said. "Can I get you anything to eat or drink?"

"No, thanks," Chloe said. "Do you think Nadine will ever get over what I said?"

"No," he said. "But she will forget it eventually. She'll have to; I can't imagine that with you living within a decent visiting range she'll want to ignore you forever. She knows that'll only annoy Clifford, and she doesn't want to do that now he has a direct line to God."

Chloe snorted with laughter.

"Is that how she sees it?" she asked.

"Only for a while," he said. "When I was ordained, she treated me differently for years, until I came back into parish work again and then she saw I was the same brother I'd always been and started treating me the way she had always done. It was only because she didn't see a lot of me that she ever got the idea that I was somehow holier for being ordained."

He looked down at her.

"You look tired," he said.

"I am," she said. "I didn't realise how exhausting people being kind and pleasant can be. And the cast must weigh a stone, so that's tiring too."

"I think you can go home very soon," he said. "I must be off too, so stay well and come and see me again soon. I did enjoy your stay, you know."

He kissed her forehead and headed off to say goodbye to Clifford and to Clifford's parents.

Cathy drifted over, Isobel following.

"I feel an unaccountable urge for a big gin and tonic," said Isobel. "I've had some wine but it just hasn't hit the spot. I think I must be becoming middle class, with this strange craving for a G and T."

"God forbid," Chloe said. "I think we have some gin at home, I think I was going to make some sloe gin and never got round to it. If you pick up some tonic on the way back, you can have your wish."

Finally, after the endless farewells and good wishes, Chloe managed to get home and after a hilarious and slightly drunken post mortem of the day sitting at the end of the garden where the resident horse came over to join them, leaning over for the handfuls of dandelions and grass Cathy kept tearing up for him, Chloe dragged herself up the stairs once more, shed her clothes like a new butterfly shedding its chrysalis, and fell into bed.

*

Chloe looked down at her hands and at the crystal that glowed in them and knew she was dreaming. The garden around her seemed familiar in the way that dreamscapes always do, and she knew it to be her grandmother's garden even though so much was so very different from how she remembered it; it was far smaller for a start.

She walked through the long grass, and watched as the hem of her long black velvet skirt brushed and bent the daisies as she passed them; they were curled up tight against the falling dew and the advancing dusk. I thought I'd taken my skirt off, she thought, and then let the idea go as she reached the bench at the end of the garden.

It seemed newer than she remembered; the last time she'd seen it, a respectable crust of lichens had formed on many on its less accessible surfaces. Now it gleamed, and she could even smell the warm aroma of cedar wood as it gave back the sun's heat to the cooling air. Folded at the end of the bench was a little blanket, worn and faded, the blue and pink check pattern barely visible. She picked it up and rubbed it against her cheek, fondly, and as she put it down, it faded away entirely.

There was a blackbird singing somewhere amid the trees and shrubs that overlooked the walled garden, and the grass felt damp under her bare feet; the hem of the skirt was beaded now with fine drops of dew. The jasmine twined and climbed up and over the wall, the trellis that had supported it completely hidden now by the mass of foliage and flowers that filled the evening air with their perfume, the pink tinged buds opening into the starry white blooms as she watched them.

The whole garden seemed to be waiting with held breath as she approached the jasmine and knelt down on the damp grass beside it. She leaned forward and pressed her face into the mass of flowers, inhaling deeply and feeling the scent fill her. She placed her hands palm down on the soil and willed her blessing to what lay below and to her own fleeting child who had no resting place.

She sat back on her heels and gazed at the plant and saw how as the flowers fell softly from the bush, they did not reach the ground at all, but in the same seamless way Isobel had painted the kingfishers becoming flames, as the tiny flowers fell they became white doves that rose up and flew away.

Now this is the kind of dream I like, she thought.

Acknowledgements

Writing can be lonely work but though a book is written by one person, there are others involved who seldom get the thanks they deserve. Square Peg owes a lot to my dear friend and editor Kate Price. She's very good at working with me to tidy up a manuscript after it's technically finished and also can take a more objective approach to scenes I've found hard to write. While Square Peg is entirely fictional, some of the deeper aspects of it have their roots in real memories and those made some of it tough to write.

My thanks also go to Linda Griffiths for her help and encouragement; it's greatly appreciated.

Finally, thanks must go to my wonderful family for their constant support and belief in me, not to mention cups of tea and the occasional sandwich at my desk.

If you have enjoyed this book, please consider writing a review and telling friends about it. Independent authors rely on word-of-mouth recommendations; we don't get to have posters on stations or or books piled high at the front of bookshops. You can keep in touch with my work by following my blog at http//:zenandtheartoftightropewalking.wordpress.com or by liking my Facebook author page.

Other books by Vivienne Tuffnell
are available from all Amazon stores.

Away With The Fairies

Irrepressible artist Isobel has survived most things. She's coped with everything from a sequence of miscarriages, her husband's ordination, the birth of two small and demanding children, and finally the recent death of both her parents in a bizarre suicide pact. She's managed to bounce back from everything so far. A sequence of domestic disasters finally signals to Isobel that perhaps things aren't quite as rosy as she'd like. With her half of the inheritance, Isobel buys an isolated holiday cottage where she hopes to be able to catch up with some painting, as well as have the occasional holiday.

The cottage is idyllic, beautiful and inspiring, but odd things keep happening. Doors won't stay shut, objects go missing and reappear in the wrong places and footsteps are heard when there's no one there. One of Isobel's new neighbours suggests that it is the fairies who are responsible, but Isobel is more than a tad sceptical: there's not a hint of glitter or tinselly wings or magic wands.

Isobel's inner turmoil begins to spill over into her daily life when she hits a deer while driving back from the cottage. Her family hold crisis talks, deciding that she needs to have time alone in the cottage to get over long repressed grief and to paint it out of her system. As she works at a frenetic pace, the odd happenings begin to increase until even Isobel's rational, sceptical mind has to sit up and take notice. And that's when she gets really scared. Up until now, her motto has been that there's nothing in life that can't be made better by a cup of tea and some Hob Nobs. This time it's beginning to look like it'll take more than even chocolate biscuits to make things better.

The Bet

Jenny likes a challenge and Antony is the biggest challenge of her life…

"Boys like you get preyed upon," Antony's father tells him in a rare moment of honesty and openness, but Richard can have no idea just how vulnerable his eighteen-year-old son truly is. From a family where nothing is quite as it seems and where secrecy is the norm, Antony seems fair game to the predatory Jenny. Her relentless pursuit of him originates in a mean-spirited bet made with her colleague Judy, Antony's former history teacher, who has challenged Jenny to track him down and seduce him.

Jenny is totally unprepared for Antony's refusal to sleep with her or to have any sort of relationship other than friendship. She's never met anyone quite like him before and her obsession deepens the more he rejects her. She's no idea what he's already been through and as far as she's concerned it's irrelevant.

Pretty soon, for both of them it becomes a much more serious matter than a mere bet and the consequences are unimaginable for either of them.

Strangers and Pilgrims

"My heart is broken and I am dying inside."

Six unconnected strangers type these words into an internet search engine and start the journey of a lifetime. Directed to The House of the Wellspring website, each begins a conversation with the mysterious warden, to discover whether the waters of the Wellspring, a source of powerful healing, can heal their unbearable hurts.

A journey of self discovery and healing awaits them, but will the Warden grant them their wish? Invited to spend some days at the House of the Wellspring each of the strangers comes with the hope of coming away whole again.

But where is the Warden they all longed to meet and where is the Wellspring they all came to find?

The Moth's Kiss

A collection of ten short stories to unsettle, disturb, chill or terrify. From the creeping unease of The Moth's Kiss of the title to the eeriness of A Fragrance of Roses, the stories seep into the consciousness of the reader. Shivers down the spine and a need to check doors and windows are a probable outcome of reading this collection alone at night. You'll never look at willows or mosquitoes the same. Or moths.

The Wild Hunt and Other Tales

The Old Ones are still with us... Six short stories of encounters with forgotten deities, demi-gods and otherworldly beings.

The Piper at the Back Gate ~ a woman discovers a primeval forest beyond her night time garden and waiting there is someone from her childhood days.

The Wild Hunt ~ a wakeful woman joins the hunt first as prey, then as hunter, in a frozen land millennia ago.

Snag ~ a man meets a strange girl who seems to know all about everyone, to great effect.

Snuggle ~ as a premature baby lies hovering between life and death, a girl sits spinning wool in the hospital foyer.

Snip ~ an arrogant young man fights a battle with post-operative infection and his conscience.

The Faery Trees ~ an angry child discovers why you should never fall asleep beneath the elder trees.

Printed in Great Britain
by Amazon